Laena's Elite

Eidolon Survivors – Book 1

By Quinn Fisher

Published by Scarlet Lantern Publishing

Copyright © 2021 by
Quinn Fisher & Scarlet Lantern Publishing

All rights reserved.

This is a work of fiction. Names, characters, businesses, places, events and incidents are either the products of the author's imagination or used in a fictitious manner. Any resemblance to actual persons, living or dead, or actual events is purely coincidental.

This book contains sexually explicit scenes and adult language.

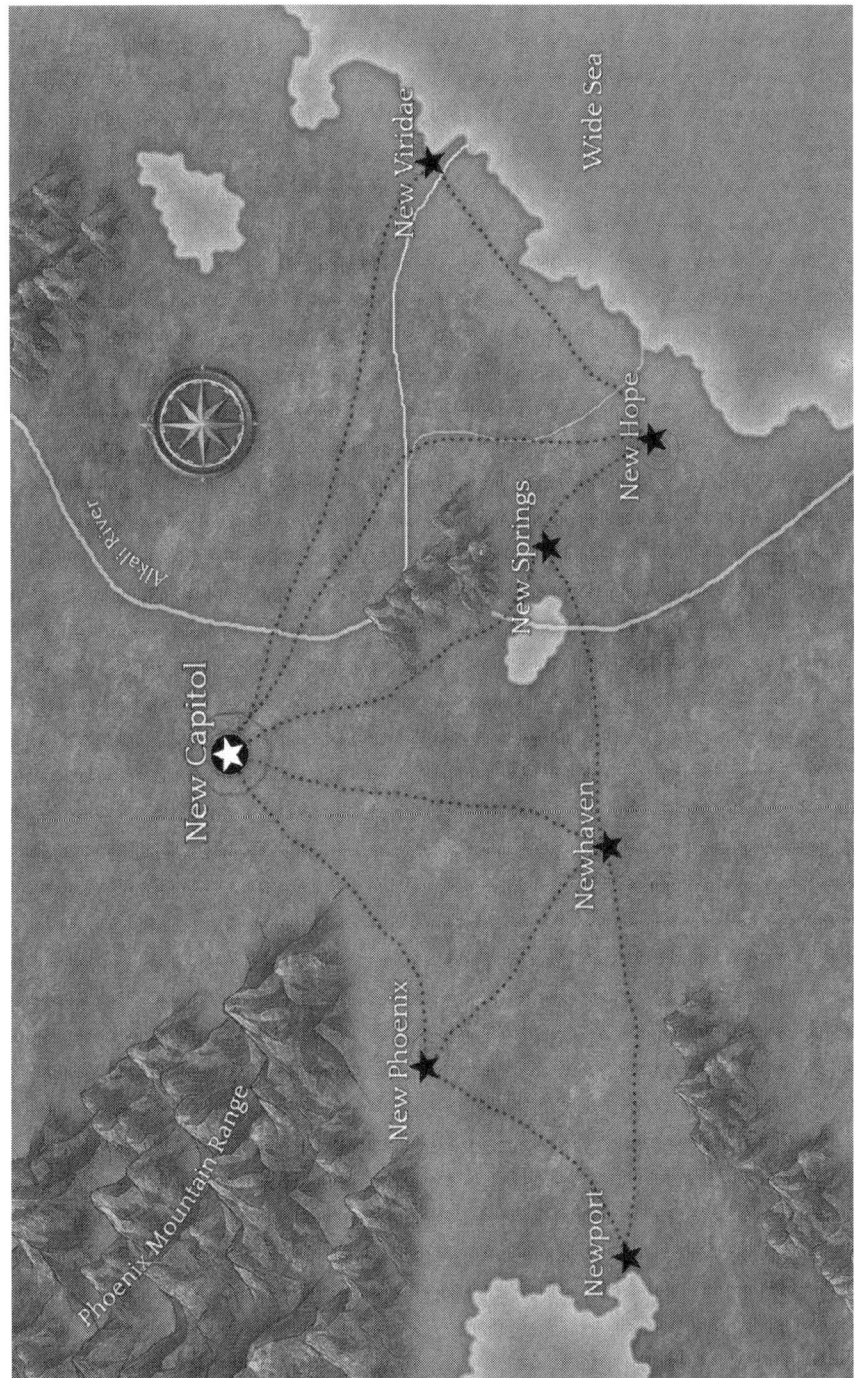

PROLOGUE

VANCE
FIVE YEARS EARLIER

We had just finished a round of patrol on a rainy afternoon just outside our home city of New Phoenix, and we were ready to kick back and relax. With no Eidolon monsters around and the ones we did encounter dealt with by us personally, my friends and I were ready for some fun. Although for Rennick, Reese, and me, that usually means that we're ready to let our guard down and play a rather violent version of a three-on-three soccer game, skins versus shirts. With the next set of guards up for patrol setting up a wide perimeter, we were assured of playing our game in relative safety.

Soon into the game, the wind picked up and the rain pelted down upon us harder. But still we played on. Our previously grassy playing field became a field of muck and kicked-up turf, and my skins team which included Rennick and Reese, played all out like our lives depended on it. Bare-chested and barefoot, our sweat soon mingled with mud, and maybe a little bit of blood. It looked like a few of us sported a few bloody noses, but it was all part of the fun. Deep down, the six of us were just beasts who loved the fight, the ruthlessness, and the aggression. And the good-natured trash talk that was thrown around was just our brotherly way of showing our affection. Completely harmless.

The only thing that we were missing was some good alcohol to round out the afternoon, but we weren't allowed alcohol on our missions. We could always grab a drink once we get back into town.

In the middle of my water break, I stood at the side, watching the game rove on. I wiped a dirty hand over the back of my neck after a long swig from my canteen, getting the feeling that I was being watched. It didn't make any sense; it was just us patrols out here. I irritably gazed around the area, looking for the person with the staring problem.

Both Rennick and Reese jogged off the field, coming up close to join me and take swigs out of their own canteens. The game was still in play, and the two had tagged in two other soldiers to take their positions in the game.

"Taking too long of a break, old man," Reese ribbed me. "Can't let these youngbloods think we tire too easy." The recruits were eighteen to our twenty-five.

Instead of reacting to his comment, I shook my head. "Naw, I get this weird feeling like someone's watching us." Rennick and Reese scanned the area carefully, taking in the tree line on one side, the wide expanse of our makeshift soccer pitch, and the high walls of the Outer Ring of New Phoenix. The rain blurred out some of the landscape, and it wasn't easy to distinguish what could be hiding in the underbrush below the tall trees.

"There," Rennick points at a small gap in the trees. Out of the three of us, Rennick had eyes like a hawk, and it still stymied me how he could spot the most minute things from a great distance.

The three of us followed the invisible line from his finger towards the trees. Through the rain, I spied a slight figure who had a bow nocked and readied, aiming at what? Us? Narrowing my focus more on the figure, I noticed it was a female, her clothes dirty and drenched, but she held motionless and poised for a shot. The three of us froze, but we weren't given much room to react to where the business end of that arrow was pointing because she let the arrow fly. She didn't blink, and I held my breath as her arrow flew then whistled past us, dangerously close between Rennick and me.

All of us swiveled our heads to follow the arrow's trajectory as it shot past the both of us and beyond. The arrow accurately found its target in a sizable rabbit that wasn't there just a moment ago. It was a fantastic, well-done shot, and I doubt any of us could do better. Archery wasn't a sport we were versed in as soldiers, since guns were our weapons of choice.

"That's my kill," the female announced, stepping out of the shadows, with a fresh arrow nocked in her bow aimed at the three of us. The other players stopped the game to watch as this lone female, a girl, really, emerged from the tree line, their faces mirroring the shock the three of us had on ours. We signaled to the other soldiers to stay back; as their superior in rank, I was responsible for these men and their safety, just as we were bound by law to secure the safety of any female.

I took in the sight of her, noting that the girl looked young, but not scared. Cautious was a better description for how she observed all of us, and she looked pretty handy with that bow. Her tank top, which must have been white once upon a time, was stained with dirt and drenched through. Her short khaki hiking shorts served only to highlight how shapely her legs were. And as she turned this way and that with her bow, I could see that those shorts did nothing to hide how beautifully her ass was curved. Her wet mane of black hair lay flat against her head, but a lock curved against one cheek, making me ache to reach out and place it behind her ear.

Her eyes flashed, her pink lips in a pout as she neared her felled prey. The stony expression on her pretty face warned *back off*, and we held our hands up to show her we meant her no harm. Curiosity sparked, and I had to find out what a lone girl was doing out here with no one around to protect her. It was unheard of to have a woman traipsing outside any of the Seven Cities like this without an escort or protection of some kind. Most of the women we knew were relatively helpless when it came to danger. This one seemed to be used to being out here where danger could be found just about behind every tree or bush.

As she retrieved the good-sized rabbit where it lay just behind Rennick and me, I asked, "Are you lost? What are you doing out here?"

"No and it's pretty obvious, I'd say," she replied tersely. "This is tonight's supper." She held up the rabbit which still had an arrow pierced through its neck.

"Sweetheart, do you live out here?" Reese asked kindly.

"If I did, I admit nothing."

"Okay, well, are you with someone? I can't imagine that you'd be out here all by yourself. Aren't you worried about the Eidolon creatures roaming around here?"

She said nothing and stared back at us coldly. In the several beats of silence, I took the chance to closely study her, but all I could dredge up was this insane arousal the more I perused what was underneath the dirt, and wait, was that dried blood? She was exquisite; her body lithe and toned, her eyes penetrating me to the bone with that unwavering gaze. I couldn't for the life of me take my eyes off of her. No one I knew looked like she did, nor were they brave enough to face the expanse between cities alone.

Rennick put out a hand as if to assure her we were no danger to her and said, "Okay, we'll stop prying into your business if you tell us if you need help."

"Don't need it. I'm fine." She continued her own study of us, but I couldn't tell if that was recognition in her eyes that suddenly flared into a measure of shock. Judging by where her eyes were looking, I'd say she abruptly caught sight of the bulge in my pants caused by her. I saw her dart her eyes to both Rennick and Reese then the three others with us, and I took her shock to mean that they all had the same reaction to her, too. It had been a while since any of us were in close contact with a female, and she was definitely a sight for sore eyes.

She slowly backed away, clearly feeling like this was a dangerous place to be: one lone female and six men in one place. But I didn't want her to leave so soon. I merely wanted to know who this beauty was and if she was attached. I don't know what I'd do if she was meant for someone else when my innermost being screamed *she's mine*. Whatever it was about her, I was inexplicably drawn to her, and the need to protect and squirrel this little woman away was sudden and urgent.

Maybe I'd better find out first if she's unattached. "Do you have a husband or fiancé waiting for you here?"

"I have neither." The narrowing of her eyes told of confusion, like she didn't know what I was talking about.

"Fathers or mother maybe? But I find it hard to believe that they'd leave you by yourself," Rennick mused. The three of us stepped in closer to hear her answer when it looked like she going to give us one.

Instead, she sighed like this whole interrogation was boring and it was beneath her. But I caught a small shivering of her form as she looked almost longingly at the three of us standing there up close, shirtless, and muddy. I stole a peek at her chest and noticed the pebbling of her nipples there, and I'm sure if I had a canine's olfactory senses maybe I'd smell her arousal.

"I gotta go," she said, and she turned and ran, leaving us gaping after her. Rennick, Reese, and I shared a look, and we sped after her. Reese yelled at the other three to stay put and keep watch as the we crashed through the trees.

She was a nimble thing, and we still hadn't gotten a name out of her. She already had a good head start, but we were slowly closing the distance. Watching her maneuver through the trees and uneven terrain, I was amazed she didn't fall on her face. The rain made the ground slick and a few times one of us almost took a header into the squishy mud.

I had less than a few feet to reach her, but she broke through the end of the forest and hopped aboard an old ATV. It started with a belch of the motor, and then she sped off and away, without even looking back at us once.

Through his heavy panting, Reese managed to speak. "Did you see what I saw? A woman who could fend for herself out here and we're letting her go?"

Rennick shook his head. "She's nothing like anyone we know back home. Makes you wonder how she's able to survive out here."

I wiped the rain and sweat out of my eyes. "But did you see how she looked at us? She was just as curious about us as we were of her. I think we scared her off."

"Yeah, by that monster in your pants, buddy," Reese cackled.

"Same could be said of both of you," I returned. "But can you blame us? She was fucking hot. And she could shoot."

Rennick sighed. "I guess we're just that unlucky. Plus, we just put in an application for another girl, remember?"

"Yeah, yeah. Pickings are slim, I know," I replied. "I know we're duty bound by our families to set up the next generation, but I don't just wanna settle, you know?"

The other two nod, but I continue, "Besides, if we're going to go through with this marriage application, we still have a fifty-fifty chance of being rejected."

"God, now you sound too damned hopeful we'd be rejected, you ass," Reese grumbled. "Don't we all want a woman who would be happy with all three of us?"

"Of course we do," Rennick replied, stepping between us before I could smack Reese. "Come on, guys, let's think with our heads and not with our dicks, shall we?"

"Rennick, you saw her, didn't you?" I wasn't going to let the subject of the mystery girl go so soon.

"Yeah, but she didn't seem to want to let us get any closer. So, why force that issue?"

I shook my head again. This world did not make dating easy. With so few women left to us, it was hard to find one that would suit the three of us and round out our family of four. Like so many other marriage applicants out there. Women had it easy compared to us when it came to finding significant others. But then again, they were slowly becoming a dying breed now that birth rates have gotten so low.

"Let's head back. Those asswipes are probably thinking we got eaten by a horde or something."

"Like we'd let that happen." Reese chuckled.

"Yeah, aren't we supposed to be heroes or something?"

I smiled and teased back, "Or something."

2ND PROLOGUE

LAENA

  I shouldn't have let my curiosity get the better of me, but it had been a while since Dad and I had been around anyone. Anyone that could think and speak anyway. Eidolon creatures abounded out here, and they weren't inclined to stay in one place and behave like a normal person just so I could have someone to talk to. They were more the type to bite my head off to satisfy their hungry bellies rather than keep anyone company.

  Speeding away on the ATV, it was more likely to draw out more of them because of the noisy engine, but it was just fast enough to keep me out of their clutches. Our camp was further north and much further away from the city of New Phoenix that its patrols wouldn't find us out in the thick brush of the forest. The city was more concerned about the creatures getting in than the ones that milled around, wandering aimlessly.

  Dad and I had travelled the three days it took to get here; the last city we had been in being New Hope. He never explained why we kept hopping from city to city; sometimes living just in the Outer Ring of each of them or camping out just outside of them. For as long as I can remember, this nomadic way of life had always been our way.

  Now that I'm eighteen, I was curious about the people who live in these cities, and why we're not among them. Every time I asked Dad, I got shut down hard and given a long-ass lecture about the old Boogeyman story he used to feed me as a kid. That the moment our true identities become known, I ran the risk of the Boogeyman separating the both of us. And that explanation didn't fly anymore, because I knew that the Boogeymen I've recently had to deal with were mostly Eidolon creatures out here in the boonies. On occasion, we've encountered them within city walls.

Because of what tech we do carry around with us, I've been able to research a little about what life was like within those city walls. Mainly through news reports and trending articles, I'd been able to find tidbits of what other people see and experience.

And I distinctly remembered seeing an article that had a video file on those shirtless men. I knew who they were the moment I spotted them: Colonel Vance and Captains Reese and Rennick. Lauded for their heroic efforts, they were the most nauseatingly celebrated people among the Seven Cities. And though they made New Phoenix their home base, they've made many a fan base among said cities because they are our heroes in winning the battle against Eidolon horde invasions. Not to mention how strikingly good looking they were.

Having travelled between all seven cities and having seen and observed countless others from a distance, no other males had drawn my attention as much as those three had earlier today. Spotting them unawares as I was chasing down tonight's meal, I felt my heart leap at the sight of them, thinking I'd never seen so much male beauty in one place. Heat crept up the back of my neck, between my breasts, and lower down; it was the first time my body reacted so strongly just at the sight of these men. And I had thought that I had complete control of my body's reactions until then.

Being only eighteen, I have no prior experience with people in general, never having any opportunity to form friendships or relationships because of our constant being on the move. While I envied girls my age of their seemingly carefree lifestyle, I knew that I'd much rather be on this side of the wall than inside of it. God knew I didn't want to be subjected to being treated like another numbered, registered female who was only good for perpetuating the human race. And to top it off, polyandry was the law. I couldn't understand how it would work with two or more men, let alone one.

However fleeting that meeting today had been, I couldn't afford to indulge in any kind of hope of meeting them again. Dad had made it a rule that I was never to be found by anyone; if I were discovered and captured, he had explained that I might never see the light of day again. As a child, the prospect of being locked away in the dark scared the hell out of me, and back then, the dark was more than just the absence of light. To me, the dark was a monster that could eat me alive, worse than a whole horde of Eidolon. To this day, I still have nightmares of being trapped in a dark, cold space with no one to answer my cries of help.

But now that I've been seen, I wasn't going to let them catch up and get me. The fear of that dark place rode my ass so hard that it sparked extra strength into my legs and arms as I ran away. I was glad I had taken the ATV with me, even though that meant Dad was stuck back at our camp, but it had offered me a way to lose those men.

Vance. Rennick. Reese.

Once Dad went to sleep tonight, I'll most likely be up all night doing as much online searching as I can about those men. If I could find a few pictures, even better. Little did I know, that these men would become an obsession of sorts for me.

1

LAENA
The Outer Ring of New Phoenix, Year 125 AEc (After Eidolon Crisis)

Under the late morning sun, I was sweating profusely, and I bitterly muttered curses in complaint under my breath as I hid in the brush. I'd been out hunting like I was told to do but had to hide the moment strangers had shown up. And I still hadn't caught anything at this point. Waiting for the strangers to leave looked like it was going to take a while; they didn't seem to be in any hurry.

Strange as it was, my life up till now had always been this way. Hiding from being detected. Never staying in one place for too long, moving from one city to the next among the Seven Cities. Training every day. Only, I still never found out why we lived like this.

I was in disguise like Dad had instructed. After my last run-in with people, aka Vance, Rennick, and Reese, five years ago, Dad had insisted that I dress like a boy to keep a low profile. A female alone anywhere in the Seven Cities was a red flag to anyone, depending on who discovered said lone female. If it was Elite soldiers, who acted as police as well as military, they'd be demanding identification to search for their families and return them promptly. If it was a male civilian, it could mean a possible engagement could come out of it, especially if the male had a buddy or two to apply as potential grooms for the marriage.

But I knew the drill; discovery would lead to unwelcome consequences. I couldn't risk the Elite finding out about me or Dad. After a blistering lecture of being seen that one time, Dad had told me what would really happen if I were to be found. Because I'm an unregistered female not in any records, I would be locked away, treated as a criminal. But I had gotten the feeling that Dad was withholding a bit more of the truth and he wasn't at all willing to share.

A patrolling band of soldiers had come across my usual hunting grounds, but they hadn't been initially looking for me. The only reason I could think of for them to be out here is to be on the lookout for the Eidolon monsters that somehow trickle through and past our walls. There had been a small breach in the outer wall close to my location where the creatures must have wandered in, and the soldiers had only been following protocol by moving in on them.

In the small band of six men, I gasped when I recognized three of them. Having done obsessive research for anything to do with them over the past five years, it was hard not to stare overlong. Their pictures were plastered everywhere within our city—not only did they come from upstanding families of the Elite class; they were heroes in their own right—confident and alpha to a tee. Colonel Robert Vance, Captain Adrian Rennick, and Captain Ansel Reese had been instrumental in scouting missions for supplies, in addition to ensuring the safety of the city from the outside. With the might of the Elite Army behind them, they had led many a mission to keep the city safe from hordes of the living dead from infiltrating our walls. Dad never failed to roll his eyes in mild disgust whenever I had brought up these men in casual conversation, but then he'd shut me up by dragging me into a sparring match that had us both panting for breath.

Finally, as luck would have it, I got the chance to see them again, even after I had doubted I'd get a second encounter. Safe as I was in my hiding spot from these men or their companions, I happily took score of the changes in the objects of my five-year-long obsession. All three looked bigger and more toned than I had last seen them. A few new scars on bare forearms and upper arms were more noticeable now that I was semi close-up. If anything, their gorgeous looks only served to heighten their status as celebrities, and I was sure that it brought them into the realm of sex symbols.

Each of them couldn't be more different in looks, but the way they interacted and teased each other told me how close as brothers the media made them out to be. Their faces were so familiar to me just from the countless hours I pored over their photos. Reese with his slanted brown eyes and olive skin like mine, always ready with a quick grin. Rennick with his tanned skin in contrast to his auburn locks and bright green eyes, and his expressions usually deep and mysterious. And Vance with the intense tiger-gold eyes and smooth, mocha-colored skin was known for his sharp intelligence and quick thinking in the field. They'd certainly grown up together, but it was evident that their bond extended into a makeshift brotherhood of their own making.

Unfortunately, as I had been too engrossed with making these observations, one of the infected had gotten too close to where I crouched in my hiding spot. I sensed the approach of one of the creatures just behind me, and my defensive reflexes born from hours and hours of training swiftly came out to play. I blame my being too damned distracted by three pretty faces that I wasn't cautious enough to notice one of the infected closing in behind me.

"Look out behind you!" I heard one of the men cried out in warning, almost seconds too late. I had already freeze-framed, but I was also a little jarred that one of the men had caught sight of me after all. Dammit! I had been stupidly confident that no one could spot me.

In the same moment that a putrefying hand had clamped down on my shoulder, I shot out my own hand to grasp it. Looking behind me at last, I counted four of the hungry creatures flanking my rear. Thank God for Dad's insistence that I train every day; it came in handy as my body instinctively reacted to the threat. From there, I became a flurry of throws, kicks, and punches as I fought off four of the infected all at once. Armed with just my bow and hunting knife, I took down two of them, efficiently dispatching them with my knife embedded straight through to their brains.

As for the other two creatures, the soldiers threw themselves into the fight after they shook off their shock at the sight of either me or the creatures. They managed to cleanly dispatch them with a single shot to the head from their high-powered assault rifles. With the immediate threat gone, I could do no more than warily stare at the soldiers who stared back at me in disbelief.

My disguise had been shucked off during the fight, but one of the infected's claws must have shredded at my shirt and cut through the bindings at my chest. I no longer looked like a dirty male urchin; instead, I looked very much like a *female*, with my breasts poking through my threadbare t-shirt.

Females were rare after the Eidolon virus had ravaged three-quarters of the population. A mutated version of the measles virus had arisen, one that was more virulent than its predecessor and just as deadly. In a last-ditch effort, a vaccine had been created to combat its spread, but it had been released too soon to the public before its effects could be further studied. As a result, the vaccine had caused the virus to evolve further to become the Eidolon virus, causing its host to become a flesh-eating living corpse in as little as three days.

Large city centers with enough wealth had been able to build tall walls to keep out the infected, and the city of New Phoenix was no exception. Only the wealthier citizens of New Phoenix had thought it important to also build walls around their own smaller community to keep out the rest of the unwashed masses. New Phoenix had been constructed as one large circle, with two other concentric circles within. The Outer Ring contained the entire city from the infected outside; the Inner Ring contained the working and middle classes; and the Inner Circle was where the wealthy Elite citizens and the Elite Army Headquarters resided.

Dad and I were currently camped out in the Outer Ring, having been there only a week. This nomadic life had been our existence for all of my twenty-three years. As isolated as we had been, I hadn't been allowed the luxury of friends my own age, and I had never gone to school. But Dad had taught me himself: history, the classics, and science aside from reading and writing. He must have been trained as a soldier himself for him to have trained me in hand-to-hand combat, marksmanship, and tracking. Our existence was supposed to be a secret, and I think I've just busted that wide open.

Then, Captain Reese held up a hand in my direction, but I turned and fled. I wasn't supposed to be seen. How many times did Dad warn me? "Wait!" he cried after me, trying to catch up. The rest of his friends followed behind, but I kept running. I didn't know where I was running to, but I just had to get away. *Don't get caught*, Dad had warned me many times over.

As fast as I thought myself to be, one of them managed to catch up with me and tackle me down to the ground.

"Oof," I grunted as a large body crashed on top of me from behind. Before I could catch my breath and try to wrestle my way out from underneath him, I was hauled up bodily from the ground quicker than I could blink.

"We're not going to hurt you," said the man who now banded his arms around me, despite my struggles. "After seeing you fight the way you did, we've only got questions." Then, the man who I now could see up close was Captain Ansel Reese flared his eyes in recognition once he got a good look at me.

My struggles strengthened anew, but I didn't want to hurt him. I was sure I wasn't going to like those questions. Females in this day and age weren't supposed to be hidden away like I was; they were supposed to be registered the day they came of age to be part of the repopulation effort. It had been mandated over a century ago that each female was to have more than one husband since there weren't enough females to go around.

I only knew I wasn't meant for such a future, according to Dad.

I didn't want to be breeding stock, and Dad had always said that I had a higher purpose. Only I still had no idea what that was, and he still hadn't gotten around to telling me.

The others caught up behind us, and still I continued to try and fight him off. "Get the fuck off of me!" I gritted through my teeth at the man still on top of me. Up this close, I could see his dark hair falling over brown eyes that held pleasure and mirth at realizing who I was.

"Reese, you know the rules," the one known as Colonel Vance said. I knew it was him by his strange, glowing tiger-gold eyes contrasting with his mocha skin. "We have to bring her in."

"Look who it is," Reese pronounced to the rest of his companions. "It's the archer girl from before. Remember her?"

Vance seemed pleased at Reese's claim because he smiled, probably from the memory of our last encounter. "Yeah, what are you doing here in the Outer Ring? I thought you were living out in the wilds of the Expanse."

I kept quiet. I didn't need to tell them anything even while they waited for an answer.

When I didn't volunteer one, the one named Adrian Rennick shrugged, "It's no skin off our backs if she doesn't want to say. We'll just have to bring her in and report her." Rennick looked just as devilishly handsome as his online pictures: a dimple in one cheek, auburn hair, and bright green eyes.

"No! I did nothing wrong!" I protested, ready to run away again when the chance came along. But I heard the sound of the safety being clicked off of several guns behind me, and I froze.

"Of course, you didn't, sweetheart," Captain Rennick cajoled. He came around to inspect me upon a closer look, his gun raised and trained on me. And his look of pleasant surprise lit up his entire face. "While you have amazed all of us with your, er, skill, we thought you were a young boy at first. Now we know better."

Just glad that they didn't mistake me for a young girl, I shouted, "I'm twenty-three, dammit!" I shouldn't have told them even that much, remembering too late I wasn't in a position to flee. But something about them made me uncharacteristically want them to know me, to know who I was. Like suddenly, I needed someone, these three men in particular, to know something about me after being in isolation for so long.

I had promised Dad I would be careful not to let anyone see me, but this was an accident. I should have run off at the first sight of them, but I let my curiosity get the better of me. These three men could quite possibly be my downfall.

Colonel Vance also came around to stand beside Captain Rennick, and remarked, "She has to be brought to the court. Look, she has no ID stamp on her wrist, no status marking on her finger." Citizens were stamped with barcodes on their wrists as means of identification, and status markings were for women only. Different status markings on a woman's ring finger signified marital status, station, and how many husbands you had. Since I had none of those things, I was an anomaly.

Captain Reese had me cuffed with my wrists behind me; they kept their guns aimed my way. I wasn't going anywhere without these men. Turning me to face him, Captain Reese asked, "What's your name?"

I hesitated. Looking from him, then to each of the men with identical inquiring looks on their faces, I sighed. "Laena," I barely breathed out. I had no idea what was going to happen from here now that I've been discovered. Then in a much stronger voice, I said, "My name is Laena."

"What are you doing out here, Laena?" Captain Reese asked. "It's strange to see a girl out here on her own, with no protection."

Stubbornly, I stated, "I don't need protecting. I can do that fine on my own."

"I'm sure you can," chuckled Captain Rennick. I could tell he was the most charming of the three. "But don't you have a father around? A brother or husbands, perhaps?"

I kept silent. Dad had also warned me not to give away any information about him or our life together. Instead, he had given me instructions to give different answers to deflect such questions. The less people knew about us together, the safer I'd be. Or so, he told me. I was quickly discovering that I had been blindly following Dad's instructions without truly knowing the reasons behind them.

"Ok, then, don't tell us what we want to know," Captain Rennick said, jovially. "But before we move along, we have to do a simple screening test. It's standard procedure to make sure you're not infected or on the verge of turning."

Before I could protest, my head had been pushed to one side and a scanner pressed to the side of my neck. The object beeped once, twice, then a third time with an elongated note.

"She's clear," Colonel Vance pronounced loudly. "Let's get a move on and have the wall breach reported before more find their way inside. We'll need it repaired ASAP."

Everyone murmured their 'yessirs' before they escorted me along with them.

I had never pressed Dad for answers about anything that had to do with our lives or about how we lived in isolation from everyone. But I should have; instead, I had believed him when he said everything he has done has been for my safety.

But now, I have my doubts. Now, I have a million questions.

When most women my age are setting up house for their three husbands, I'd been living like a hermit with Dad. For as long as I can remember, he had been training me to fight to protect myself, to survive, and to prepare for the future.

I just wish I knew why. Why all the training and all the secrecy? What was Dad trying to protect me from? Now, I may never get those answers from him. These men were taking me further and further away from Dad and our impromptu shelter. And there is no way to let Dad know I've been taken.

For years, Dad himself trained me to fight in the styles of Krav Maga, jujitsu, and Muay Thai to name a few. I was taught to shoot both guns and arrows, on targets both moving and still. Using old burner laptops, Dad had also taught me how to hack into simple systems, and when those proved a piece of cake, I moved on to more complex encrypted systems.

With my unconventional upbringing, I had no chance at a normal life. My definition of normal would have included a friend or two who wasn't Dad. Roaming city streets without the need for a disguise. Living in a house with four walls instead of canvas ones.

I was pretty sure most girls my age wouldn't have learned how to fight like I do or be as isolated as I was. While I have no doubts that Dad loved me and cared about my safety, I now had to wonder if Dad suffered delusions of paranoia that had no basis.

I remembered asking Dad when I was eight, "Why don't we live in a house like other people?"

The answer I had received was, "Because we aren't like other people. If we were, we wouldn't have to hide who we really are from the people who would keep us from being together."

In my eight-year-old mind, I only knew I didn't want to be separated from my only parent. Even then, Dad had me dress as a boy on our rare forays into the city marketplaces for supplies.

I never knew any other way to live except for the brief glimpses I had seen around the city. I secretly longed to know what the other half lived like, even when I knew it was dangerous for Dad and me to live out in the open.

Why it was so dangerous to come out of hiding, I would never know from Dad himself. While I can agree with Dad that we didn't have the best life, I was about to find out if his efforts to keep me safe were indeed in my best interests.

These three heroes of the Seven Cities just might be my chance to find out what secrets surround my existence.

2

VANCE

Until I had seen that Eidolon monster reach down, I didn't even know she was there.

Laena. The girl we hadn't stopped thinking about since we first met her on an impromptu soccer pitch outside New Phoenix. The girl who had inspired lustful thoughts and desires ever since. The girl the three of us had worried over and wondered about for five long years.

When I had shouted to her in warning, I thought it had been warning a young boy who was in danger of being eaten by one of those things. I'm sure I speak for the guys when I say it was a thing of beauty to see a girl of her miniature stature move like she did. As warriors ourselves, we appreciate a good fight, and this little lady definitely delivered.

But at the time, I was still under the impression it was a young man who demonstrated a superb amount of skill, fighting off four of the infected. Other than the damage that was done to her clothes, there wasn't a scratch on her. And if it weren't for the damage done to her shirt, we would have still gone on believing that she was a boy.

With a chest like hers, there was no mistaking her for a boy. The dirt and the boy's clothes may have all been part of her disguise, but none of us could unsee what that torn shirt was clearly displaying: a set of nice, plump breasts.

If her fighting ability wasn't highly suspicious enough, her attempt to run away was even more so. A girl like herself would have been hidden away, protected, and pampered. No woman her age would have been without a protector, be it a father, a brother, or husbands. Neither would a woman have learned to fight like she did unless she had signed up for a military life, but not many women did.

The fact that she had no ID stamp or status marker was highly unusual. Everyone should have been stamped with an ID barcode at birth, and all women were required to carry a mark that tells of their marital status. That Laena had neither only raised more questions. The lack of both had us all surprised, and I had caught the same look of incredulity on Rennick and Reese.

I knew we were thinking the same thing: *who the fuck is this girl?*

We piled into the old converted van we used for transport, on our way back to HQ. But something about the girl tipped off my protective instincts. From the driver's seat, I quickly glanced at Rennick and Reese to find them sneaking glances at Laena. She gave off vulnerability in spades as she sat unmoving in her seat, her head bowed, and her eyes closed. She could have been pretending to nap for all I knew, but we knew better to say anything around someone we had just met. Twenty minutes later, she produced soft snores that told us she had finally drifted off.

The other three privates who were assigned to us weren't part of our unit, but I watched their reactions to our newest addition in the rearview mirror. I should have thought to give her my jacket to cover herself; her shredded clothes left little to the imagination. The three privates were leering and gesturing at her crudely, and I wanted to smash in their faces for thinking of her that way.

Reese sternly barked, "Eyes forward, soldiers! She's not yours to ogle." The three privates snapped to attention and sat straighter in their seats, their faces impassive.

Thank you, Reese, I thought gratefully. She wasn't mine either, but I felt this strong pull vibrating from her to me. I couldn't put my finger on why, but I was irrevocably drawn to her. The moment I spotted her today, a small female fighting for her life, I felt like I had woken up, suddenly alive and revived once she stepped in. Like Laena's unexpected appearance was necessary for me to see the deficit that I had occupying my life.

Rennick, Reese, and I had grown up together, groomed to be proper representatives of our respective families among the Elite. The three of us had an understanding that we would one day have a wife to share, one who would uphold our families' ideals. With a short list of women to choose from, none of them held the same appeal to the three of us as much as Laena fascinated me right then. Every instinct in me screamed, *she's yours!*

I wouldn't know until I got a chance to talk to Rennick and Reese in private about how they felt, but it was clear that there was much we had to discuss about her. We still didn't know her origins; why she was left alone in the Outer Ring; and where she learned to fight the way she did. Because women were a precious resource, not many were allowed into the military. Those that did were exceptional at what they did and held positions of higher rank.

Next to me, Rennick turned on his phone, presumably to let HQ know we were returning with one extra person on board. I stopped him with a signal from me to leave Laena out of it. Rennick look surprised, but he didn't miss a beat like I expected him to.

"All right, HQ, we'll file our report later tonight. We have to head to medical first," Rennick explained, then hung up. With a puzzled look, he asked me, "What the hell, Vance? We should bring her in and maybe someone who's smarter than us can find out who she is."

"I know," I said mildly. "I think she could use a better change of clothes and have a doctor look at her first before we interrogate her."

Reese agreed, "Yes, and maybe get some food in her. She looks like she could use some extra calories."

Rennick said, "Let's drop off the boy band in back first, and then we can head out from there."

I nodded my agreement and changed direction to head towards the barracks. We passed through the south gate that separated the Outer and Inner Rings of New Phoenix; the sentry guards stationed there waving us through. With the Inner Ring having a smaller radius to the epicenter of the city, it didn't take us more than fifteen minutes to reach the barracks where the privates resided. Dropping them off with the order to report to HQ in the morning, we left them to make our way out to my quarters in the Inner Circle.

Reese remarked, "Why are we heading to your place?"

"Because knowing you two, your fridge wouldn't have more than a case of beer and something that may have once been food three weeks ago. We're going to feed Laena, and maybe get some answers from her once her belly is full."

"Good thinking. And maybe she'll look a little more human once she jumps into a shower," Rennick said. "I know Drayna swears she feels like a new person fresh out of the shower when she's had a long day." Drayna was Rennick's younger sister who had joined with the Elite Army as a cadet five years ago at the age of eighteen. Her career choice wasn't making fans out of her family members, but an agreement had been reached where she can continue on her career path as long as she quit by the date mandated by the law and her family. Women at the age of twenty-five must register for potential marriage matches to help populate the world with more tiny humans. The world was running low on babies.

"I have a lot of questions for her, but most of all, I have one to put to the two of you. But not until we get to my place," I declared gravely, as I stole a glance at Laena, still sleeping, in the rearview mirror.

The guys, my brothers from other mothers, only nodded. I knew I could count on them without my saying in so many words why I wanted a private word with them.

With a long history of thirty years between the three of us, we shared everything together. Being born in the same year; sharing the same classes in school; our chosen career paths; and…women. It was rare for any of us not to share most things, especially when it came to women. With what few single women were out there, we managed to forge only one serious relationship in the past, Carisse. It had amounted to nothing when she had chosen three other men to marry; men who were much higher in status and much wealthier than us.

Rennick, Reese, and I must not have had our feelings too engaged with Carisse, since neither of us were terribly hurt by her abandoning us. We had wished her well, in fact, when she had told us she wanted to break up and marry a different trio. Last I heard, she was expecting her third child any day now, and her husbands couldn't be more thrilled. Our government lauded her for birthing that many children and her family was highly esteemed by them for it.

"But can we grab a bite to eat first? I can whip up a decent meal for all of us before we get all serious and shit," Reese drawled. I rolled my eyes with a heavy sigh; Reese was known to be ruled by his stomach. He was one of the main reasons I kept my fridge and cupboards properly stocked. If I didn't, Reese just might take to chewing on the furniture.

"Ok. Eat first then talk," I allowed, with a hint of impatience. I'd never admit it to either of them, but I secretly enjoyed Reese's cooking. Any time he offered to cook, I couldn't pass up the chance to sample anything he whipped up, he's that good a cook.

"That sounds amazing," piped up a groggy-sounding female voice. Laena was finally awake and joining in the conversation. She hadn't slept long, but she looked wide awake and refreshed from her catnap. "Thing is, I haven't eaten since yesterday." Her stomach chose that moment to complain how empty it was.

I could hear the smile in Rennick's voice when he told her, "We'll get you fed as soon as we get to Vance's. While we scrounge up some food, you can get cleaned up and change into something that's not so, um, revealing."

In the rearview mirror, I watched as she looked down at herself and slightly shrugged, like she didn't care that she was showing more than she should. She stared back at Rennick with a lack of shame for her appearance, surprising me with her brazen attitude about it. Most women I knew possessed modesty around men who weren't their lovers or spouses. And that thought alone—of her feeling comfortable enough in front of us—sparked a jolt of anticipation inside me.

"I can lend you some clean clothes until we can get you something more your size," I offered. Just imagining the visual of her in my clothes sent a possessive thrill through me. Obviously, it didn't take much to set me off when it came to this tiny spitfire of a woman. And I couldn't be more excited to explore more of her unplumbed depths. In more ways than one.

She may be the first woman who got me hot and bothered in a while, but I couldn't forget that Laena herself remained a tightly wrapped mystery. One I was all about solving ASAP.

We pulled up in front of my house soon enough, and I got out to help Laena out of the backseat. If I hadn't told her, "We've arrived" when I opened the door on her side, I think she wouldn't have known to get out of the vehicle. But she wasn't sheepish about her hesitation and swung herself easily out of the backseat with her hands still cuffed behind her. I stayed close behind in case she decided to bolt, but she made no move to even try.

Rennick and Reese led the way ahead of us and called for Laena to follow them inside, with me trailing behind. The guys knew the lay of the land when it came to my place, and they both headed into the kitchen to start a late lunch.

That left Laena and me in my entryway. I stared down at her, studying her slightly Asian features beneath the dirt smudged on her face, and I could finally see what the color of her eyes were, a startlingly clear, golden brown. Her cheekbones stood out starkly, reminding me she was underfed, but not to the point of malnourishment. She looked up at me expectantly, not saying a word, until I realized neither of us had spoken for some time.

"Sorry," I mumbled. "Follow me, and I'll get you a clean change of clothes. Then I'll show you where the bathroom is."

Laena nodded and I steered us upstairs. First stop was my room, where I meant to grab a long-sleeved shirt and a pair of sweats. Laena followed me in as I rummaged through various drawers in my lone dresser. When I came up with the items I thought she would need, I held them up against her to see how they might fit on her much smaller body. Seeing her hands still behind her back, I whipped out the cuff key to uncuff her, mumbling a small apology.

While she massaged her wrists, I lamely added, "I know the clothes aren't anywhere close to your size, but they'll have to do in the meantime. If you'd tell me your size, one of us can go out and buy you what you need."

"Size?" she asked, looking very perplexed. "I don't know what you mean."

Incredulous at her confusion about something so basic for most females I knew, I blurted, "You don't know your size? Then, I can have Reese take a look at you. He'd know off the bat what would fit you best."

I took a more careful look at what she was wearing, and I should have clued in that she wasn't like most women I've known. She wore an oversized men's work shirt that now lay in ribbons around her torso. Whatever bindings she wore to bind her lovely breasts were in the same ragged condition as her shirt. Her legs were encased in dark, baggy tie-waisted pants that hung low on her hips. The bronzed skin of her belly peeked out between the rips of her shirt, revealing a toned torso and a tiny waist.

I had to look away before I stepped closer to examine her further, and I brushed past her to exit my room. "Bathroom's this way," I gruffed out, waving her in its direction. I entered the bathroom first, laying the clothes on the counter next to the sink. As a courtesy, I placed a new bar of soap next to my own, then started the shower for her, explaining, "The water takes some time to warm up."

And I turned around to get the shock of my life. I watched, rooted to the floor, unable to move a muscle, as Laena stripped down to nothing, straightforward as she pleased. She undressed with swift and abrupt movements; her intent to do nothing more than strip was more than obvious. My eyes flared as I surveyed and appreciated her naked form: svelte, toned, and curves for days!

Still frozen, I watched as she nonchalantly stepped past me and into the shower. She acted as if I wasn't in the room with her, ignoring me as she liberally doused herself under the warm water's spray. When she reached for that bar of soap and began lathering up all of that bronzed skin, I almost jumped in there to join her, clothes and all. I growled under my breath, barely restraining myself from following through on that impulse.

Before I made an idiot of myself, I fled from the bathroom, away from the sight of Laena's wet, soapy body. I raced down the stairs, my blood thrumming in my ears as I couldn't completely wipe away the memory of Laena in my shower.

In the kitchen, I found Reese at the stove, frying up slices of smoked meat in a griddle pan. Rennick stood at the island counter, slicing bread and cheese. A plate of mixed veggies had already been prepped by one of them and sat, ready-to-eat, on my kitchen table. At my entry, they both looked at me, their brows raised almost to their hairlines.

Rennick narrowed his eyes at me as he asked, "What did you do?"

I flipped him the bird and gave him a look of disgust as I said, "It's what I *didn't* do that should have you both proud of me. I'm not the impulsive little shit I used to be."

Reese widened his eyes at that, turned off the stove, and quickly removed the meat from the pan to place onto Rennick's slices of bread. While he worked, Reese asked, "Why do I get the feeling you wanted to revert back to the dumb little shit you used to be? What's happened?"

I sat heavily into one of the chairs at the table, and sighed, "Laena's what's happened. Have you seen her? I mean, have you really looked at her?"

Rennick traded a look with Reese, their expressions, resigned. Rennick said slowly, "Okay. We've all seen her, and even saw her in action. But we don't know a thing about her. Who she is, where she came from, nothing!"

Reese only grinned, bringing his tray of smoked meat sandwiches to sit next to the plate of veggies. "I think Vance wants to ask us something and that it has to do with Laena. And I think I know what he wants."

Rennick was fighting a smile, and I knew I had them both. Maybe we were on the same page when it came to this tiny woman after all. We had been fixating over the girl for the past five years, wondering if we'd ever get to see her again.

"Here's the deal," I began, ready to lay it all out there. "This might just be the lust talking, but I really want this girl. In every way possible."

Rennick's smile faltered a little. "But she's unregistered. If you want to marry this girl, and I think you do, there are a lot of hoops to jump through first."

"And even if she was registered, it's her right to choose who she marries. The law is on her side, remember?"

"If we play this right, she'll pick us," I said. I don't know why I was so confident, but something about Laena spoke to me on so many levels. Something about her just clicked with me. "But what I want to know is, are you guys in? Do we want Laena with us, forever?"

The guys looked at each other, and when they looked back at me, they smiled broadly. "We're in!"

3

RENNICK

Crazy as I think Vance is, I found that I'm on the same fucking page as him. Same bloody word.

And I may not be the first to admit to my OCD ways as much as the guys ride my ass about them, but Laena was everything that I—that *we*—wanted. She was badass, gorgeous, and the complete opposite of every woman we knew.

Once we figured out that *he* was a *she*, I took one solid look at her and thought, *thank God we found you* and *where've you been all this time?* Watching her fight with such precise skill without even losing her breath? I was captivated the moment she executed that clean jab-left hook combo that had the Eidolon creature flying several feet back. The little lady wormed her way into my heart after she delivered a beautiful spin back kick to the creature that crept up too close from behind.

She was obviously trained by someone, but it was highly unusual for most females to undergo such training in these troubled times. Which was why my family wasn't too happy about my sister Drayna signing up as an Elite Cadet. Society couldn't afford to lose what few females we had left. But I loved everything about the way Laena moved, knew how to counter and parry. It was a true thing of feminine beauty that had nothing to do with sex or desire. And yet, she managed to betray an innate carnality in her fluid maneuvers, movements that started the blood pounding in my chest, not to mention, my groin.

One glimpse at both Vance and Reese's faces spoke volumes; they were just as admiring of Laena as I was. But who's to say that this girl is no danger to us? We don't know her from Joe Blow on the street, and we can't afford to let our dicks do our thinking for us in this case.

If we can figure out who she is and dispel the mystery surrounding her, maybe we can keep her. The three of us have talked it over once before: we were ready to settle down now that we've reached the age of thirty. We would like to start a family and maybe have a kid or two, but to do that we need to find a mother for those babies first. But it's slim pickings out there for men like us. And birth rates haven't improved much as of late. The only girls we knew growing up came from a good number of Elite families, but they were coddled, sheltered little bitches who thought they were the shit. There was no way the three of us would choose a wife among that rotten crop.

The three of us were from Elite families ourselves; we grew up in the Inner Circle, the city center of New Phoenix where most of the Elite lived. When it came to choosing a career, we shunned the thought of taking on a job in politics, and instead we chose to join the military. It was a mutual decision for the three of us. We knew we wanted to break away from the influence of our respective families just as much as we wanted to see what else was outside beyond the walls of New Phoenix.

We moved up in the ranks quickly as we took on mission after mission: fighting off hordes of Eidolon-infected that blocked our major routes to other cities like ours. Trade was still active between our city and other ones nearby; but it was dangerous to make such trips without the help of the military as protection. For me, the beauty of our job was visiting these other cities and sampling what the girls were like there.

Thanks to our experiences there, the three of us found that we liked sharing a woman between us. We were already compatible in so many ways, it only made sense that we had a good dynamic in the bedroom. Now, I love these men like brothers, but it never went beyond that. We just knew that we liked the thrill of bringing a woman to pleasure with our combined efforts; we got off on it.

It's just ironic that the one woman I think that all three of us want just happens to be a complete unknown. We can't be sure she's innocent enough until she starts talking. Looking from Vance to Reese, I knew we were in for a world of trouble with those smiles on both of their faces. Unlike me, they didn't look worried about what we could possibly find out about Laena.

Before I could say something about it, Vance stated, "She'll need a doctor to take a look at her, but I didn't want the ones at the infirmary to do it. You know how by-the-book they are." Translation: he didn't want any anomalies about Laena being blabbed to the higher-ups. Turning to Reese, he asked, "Think you can call your brother over here real quick? Tell him he owes us one for the Newport fiasco and to bring his ABI analyzer with him."

Reese rolled his eyes and replied in a voice dripping in sarcasm, "I'm sure he'll appreciate the subtlety." He plucked his phone out of his pocket and scrolled through his contacts as he commented, "He may be doctoring the rich and famous, but he'll make time for his baby brother and our crew." Reese must have connected since he stepped out of the kitchen to dispatch Vance's orders.

I could hear Reese speaking in low tones in the next room. I seated myself across from Vance before I blasted out, "Do we know what we're doing here? What's your plan?"

Vance calmly stared back at me, looking the least bit unruffled. Which was a one-hundred-eighty-degree turnaround from what he looked like when he first walked into the kitchen. When he first walked in, he looked shellshocked, and I guessed it had something to do with the girl upstairs in his bathroom.

Leaning forward, Vance looked me in the eye, and said, "I got this. Now that I have the two of you on board, the first thing we do is find out as much as we can about her before we make her public knowledge."

"If she didn't tell us much earlier, what makes you think she'll spill everything now?"

"Simple. Don't you remember our training? Interrogation was something we all trained in unless you skipped school that day."

"Hm," I muttered tersely. Crossing my arms, I continued, "Ok. Let's say she does tell us everything about herself. What if it's something we won't like hearing? What then?"

"We'll cross that bridge when we come to it."

I shook my head. "I don't like that we're going into this blind."

"Come on, Rennick! Haven't we gone on missions where that was the case? Don't tell me you wanted to turn chicken then. 'Cause I know for a fact that you were right there with us in the thick of it!"

"Those were missions! Our duty! This is--we're talking about someone we're tying ourselves to for—forever!"

"Keep it together, man!" Vance blew out a sigh and continued in a lower voice, "Look, I'm just as nervous as you about this. But I took one look at Laena and thought that—she was it for me."

I let a few beats of silence go by before admitting, "Yeah, it was the same for me, too."

Vance smiled and said, "I knew I didn't read you wrong. Or Reese. We all reacted to her the same."

Reese chose that moment to walk back into the kitchen just as he signed off with his brother. "Good news, guys. Trey'll be here in twenty, and he's bringing his full kit," he said cheerfully.

I've known Reese forever and knew all of his tells. I waited for the other shoe to drop as Reese popped his butt into a chair and dug into the sandwich closest to him. With his mouth semi-full, he continued, "The bad news is that he's bringing Dylan with him." Dylan Thompson was our CO and Trey's husband.

Vance groaned along with me as we both shared looks of disbelief. I threw a cucumber slice at Reese as I said, "You couldn't shut up about Laena could you?"

Reese picked off the slice that him in the chest and threw it back in my direction. I dodged it as he defended himself, "I couldn't explain why we needed a full DNA sequencer brought here without giving him some details.

Dylan was listening in and wanted to know what we were up to and that's why he's coming!"

Vance shook his head at Reese. In resignation, he said, "All right then. Plans can change at a drop of a hat, we all know that. Let's just roll with the punches here. Trey can do a full examination of Laena, ID any close relatives with a DNA test, and we already know she's Eidolon-free. With Dylan here, maybe he can help us get to the top of the list in applying to be Laena's suitors."

That was another downside to finding a wife. We had to apply to even be in the running for the woman we wanted. What sucked was that she could "date" everyone who applied, and then she had a time limit to choose who she would shackle herself with. We've been through it before and came up empty-handed for our efforts. With Laena not being in the system, the odds were in our favor to have a mate we wanted who would choose us first.

The caveat being that she had to be convinced she needed us. We had our work cut out for us with this one.

Dylan's coming here may put a damper on those plans; he could easily rat us out for not bringing her straight to the Courts to have her registered. Now, I doubted that the future we wanted was even attainable. With a sigh, I got up from the table, and stated, "I'm going to check up on her. She hasn't come down yet."

I didn't hold a lot of hope for something finally working in our favor when it came to our love lives. We've been burnt before, and I dreaded the thought of being disappointed once again. Heading up the stairs towards the woman who had the guys' hopes up, I steeled my face into an indifferent expression. If I held my emotions close without giving anything away, maybe I wouldn't be too hurt when Laena's taken away from us.

Knocking on the bathroom door, I called out, "Can I come in?"

She answered loud enough to be heard through the door, "Yes!"

Since the door was ajar just a crack, I pushed the door wide open to let myself inside. What I didn't anticipate was a naked Laena stepping out of the glass shower, still dripping wet, her black hair slicked back like the fur of a wet seal. Without the dirt and mannish clothes camouflaging her, she was beautiful and clearly not shy about who saw her naked. I knew I was ogling every inch of her, but she didn't seem to care. Not the reaction I was used to seeing in females of my acquaintance.

Unless I was about to sleep with one.

I stammered, "Th-there's a towel right there." When she didn't make a move and only stared at me expectantly, I moved forward quickly to grab the towel off the stand and wrapped it around her. Briskly, I rubbed the sections of the towel that covered her, feeling hard, lean muscle beneath my hands. I was surprised not to feel softness where I was used to feeling it on a woman.

She wasn't eating enough. It was obvious by how small her frame was, but I couldn't ignore how well-built she was for someone her size. She had the body of a lithe warrior, and it alarmed me that someone had trained her for one of two reasons: for her own protection or for a more nefarious reason.

Assassin came to mind first, and I looked down at this freshly showered woman, assessing the possibility from my perusal. She looked up at me with wide, clear brown eyes, her expression reminding me of a child's hopeful look. How do I know it's not all an act?

Neither of us spoke as we locked gazes for some time; I couldn't say how much time had passed. Then, she surprised me out of my daze by saying, "I'll get dressed now."

She stepped away, the towel dropping from her body as she moved away from me. And again I was struck by how gorgeous she was—curves in all the right places that called out for my hands to explore. I don't know what this says about me, but I didn't move as I watched her dress swiftly into Vance's old high school sweatshirt and sweatpants. No underwear, I noted, and stopped myself from trying to stare through the fabric to where a bra and panties would have been.

When she was done, I said, "Let's get some food in you. There's lunch waiting downstairs." I took her by the hand, but found it encased by the long sleeves. Looking down her body, the sweatpants were also bagging around her feet.

"Here, let me," I said as I bent my head to roll up the sleeves. Getting down on one knee, I rolled up the pant legs for her. This close, I could smell her freshly clean scent with an undertone of something womanly to go with it, and my olfactory senses reveled in it.

Straightening to my full height, I took her hand once again and led her downstairs. She meekly followed after me, and I felt her tentatively grip my hand before she clung to it with a firmer hold. Like she trusted me.

In the kitchen, I led her to the seat next to Vance, and pulled a plate with a sandwich closer to her. I seated myself across from her just as she dug into her food with gusto. Clearly, she had been starving; I had never seen a female make food disappear so fast. The three of us sat frozen as we watched her ferociously polish off that sandwich, and Reese pushed his half-finished sandwich in front of her. She dug into that, too.

Looked like Vance wouldn't get the chance to carry out his interrogation while plying her with food and drink. There wasn't anything left on the table for her to dig into.

I looked at him, waiting on him to start his "interrogation". Arranging his chair so he was facing Laena, he leaned forward and began, "Laena, can you tell us anything about yourself? About your family?"

Laena had been downing the glass of water Reese had offered her when Vance started talking, and I saw her give him a sidelong glance. She set the now-empty glass down and angled her body to face him.

"My name is Laena Kanata. My father's name is Atsushi Kanata. We both live in the Inner Ring in Area 5. Our house address is Sector 12, Block C." That was a poverty-stricken district, where people practically lived on top of each other in those crowded apartment buildings.

My brows raised at her answers. Reese did the same and looked at me. Everything she said sounded too planned and rehearsed to be true, but Reese, who had a laptop in front of him, announced, "I'm on it."

As Reese clicked away on the keyboard, Vance continued, "Laena, my name is Robert Vance. This guy here typing away is Ansel Reese, and that's Adrian Rennick. But we prefer being called by our last names." I offered her a small wave. "We have questions for you I hope you won't mind answering. But first, I want you to know that you're safe here. We just want to help you."

Laena gave a quick nod of her head in acknowledgement. Reese exclaimed at that moment, "Her address checks out. Atsushi Kanata has a lease there until the end of the year."

Vance asked, "What were you doing in the Outer Ring by yourself?"

I watched as Laena visibly swallowed, before answering, "I was hunting for food."

4

LAENA

Here we go.

Dad's training was supposed to come in handy here, and I'm glad we practiced over and over what I would say when asked. What I didn't count on were these three virile alphas to be my interrogators, and this situation was wreaking havoc on my hormones.

Especially moments before in the bathroom upstairs. I knew both Vance and Rennick were watching, and it was part of the act to pretend I didn't have an ounce of modesty.

"I was hunting for food," I said calmly, since it was the truth. I was grateful that my hacking skills were holding up since Dad and I had never set foot in Area 5. But if asked, I could point it out on a map.

Rennick said, "You've said as much. But where is your father now?"

"I don't know." I really didn't. Dad left without saying where he was going that morning. But we had planned for this day far in advance. If we were ever separated, if one of us were taken into custody, we were to follow a protocol of sorts. In this case, since I was the one taken, I knew Dad would find me missing. He was supposed to go to one of our safe houses, load up on supplies, and he would look for me.

If the opposite was the case, under no circumstance was I allowed to risk being found. I had promised.

"Did he say anything that might give you an idea where he went?" Vance asked.

"He woke me up to say I needed to go find us something to eat for tonight's dinner. Then he left, but he didn't say where. He's done it so often, I never thought to ask where he was going." Appearing helpful while still telling the truth would hopefully keep these guys from discovering what I was hiding. Even though I don't know what it is I'm hiding and why.

Reese frowned at whatever he saw on his screen and piped up, "Guys, there's no other records for either Atsushi or

Laena Kanata. No birth records, no transactions, no financials, nothing."

The three intimidating-looking men all looked at me with a pointing stare. Just like Dad and I rehearsed, I cried, "That can't be right. I was born in Area 5 in that very apartment. Maybe the midwife forgot to register my birth."

"What about your mom?" Reese asked.

"She died when I was born." Truth. Dad said she died having me.

"What was her name?" Vance asked.

"Dad named me after her."

Reese clicked away again at his laptop. "Nope. No death records for Laena Kanata either."

I knew all of that was on purpose. Dad had said he hacked into the system and deleted anything to do with us.

Vance had an inscrutable look on his face as he turned to me once again. "Okay, this is too strange to be just a coincidence. Laena, are you and your Dad in trouble? Is this why there are no records of you two? Why you're not registered?"

Feigning confusion, I stuttered, "I-I have no idea why we're not in the system. Dad's not mixed up in anything bad; we just like living privately. I'm not registered be-because Dad wasn't ready to be anyone's father-in-law. It's just been him and me for so long. He didn't like that the government has to tell us when a girl has to leave her family."

I could tell these men weren't buying what I was telling them because they were sharing dubious looks between them.

Rennick sighed and asked, "What about school? Which ones did you go to?"

Again, like we had practiced, I rattled off, "PS Number Five for elementary. CKJS for middle school and NDCK for high school." I had never attended either of those schools; everything I learned, I learned from Dad. I had soaked up everything he had ever taught me.

"Do you work, Laena?"

"No. No one would ever hire me."

"Why is that?" Vance asked.

"I've always been passed over by people more skillful and qualified than me."

"What do you do, then, if you're not working?"

"Scrounging up enough to live. I hunt not just to feed us, but to sell off what I can catch." I knew I looked the part before I got cleaned up. Besides being on the thin side, the days-old dirt I had worn gave more credibility to my story.

"Okay, why the disguise as a boy?" Reese asked pointedly. "As a woman, a registered one, you wouldn't have to work as long as you had someone looking after you."

Now that's just it right there! If there's anything I hate most about the way this world works today, it's that cavalier attitude towards us women! In a sullen tone, I gritted, "Maybe I don't want to have to fucking answer to anyone else but myself. I don't need anyone looking after me. As a boy, I had more freedom than a lot of other women out there who sure as fuck don't know any better."

Instead of being taken aback by the venom behind my words, the trio smiled at me. Which was unnerving.

"What? Do I have something stuck on my face?" I asked, unsettled by why they're still grinning at me.

Rennick shook his head and answered, "It's just refreshing to hear you talk like that. I--we like that you're fiercely independent."

It's not a usual thing for me to hear a compliment about myself, and I think I blushed for the first time. Someone other than Dad just paid me a compliment, and it was over something I'm deeply proud of.

But as far as this interrogation went, I still wasn't out of the woods. I'm sure that nothing I've said was able to satisfy their need for answers, and I wasn't going to give them any.

Vance opened his mouth to say something, but a ringing sounded throughout the house, interrupting him.

Reese bounced up, "That'll be Trey and Dylan." He rushed towards the front entrance, to let them in, I guessed. I didn't know who the newcomers were, but their being here made me feel uneasy.

Vance lifted a hand and placed it gently overtop mine. "It's all right. They're here to help." He stood when the two new arrivals entered the kitchen, and greeted, "Trey, thank you for coming. I trust Reese explained to you about your new patient."

The other newcomer growled from behind the man Vance called Trey, "You three should know better than to bring Trey into—whatever this is. If the higher-ups get wind of this, they'll—"

"Dylan, calm down," Trey urged. Kneeling at my side, Trey introduced himself, "Hi, there. I'm Dr. Treyvan Reese. Don't mind Dylan; he's a regular Mama bear when it comes to protecting me."

I looked back and forth between these men, trying to understand how such a huge, gruff man had been paired with this gentle, soft-spoken doctor.

I got a little nervous as Trey took me by the hand to lift me from my seat. But Vance assured me, "It's ok. Go with Trey. He's going to make sure you check out health-wise." All the more reason for me to be nervous. I've never had a doctor look me over before, and I had no idea what to expect.

Trey smiled at me warmly, in a manner I was sure he meant to make me feel at ease. I was anything but. "Let's park ourselves in the bedroom and away from the nosy old ladies in the kitchen, shall we?" he asked, my hand still in his. I nodded once, and he led me into a guest room on this floor.

We entered the room, and he motioned for me to lay out on the bed as he closed the door. He had with him a large metal case, and he plunked it down beside me. When he opened it, I could see all sorts of gadgets I couldn't name, and my anxiety ratcheted up a notch. Some of those things were pointy and scary-looking, and I hoped he wouldn't be using those particular instruments on me.

Trey assured me, "I won't hurt you. I promise you." He grabbed a gadget that looked similar to the scanner Rennick had used on me earlier, only it was larger and looked to have more features on it. "This is to check your vitals," he explained.

"My vitals?" I asked, confused.

"Blood pressure, heart rate, things like that." He waved the scanner down my body slowly. "Looks good," he concluded after the scanner had done its work.

"Now for a blood sample," he declared. My eyes widened at his pronouncement, and I shot straight up, plastering myself against the headboard. A memory flashed: Dad telling me to never let anyone take a sample of my blood if captured.

Trey tried to soothe me by saying, "Easy, easy. I won't take more than a drop. From your fingertip."

"No!" I yelled, and I sprung from my crouching position to dive into Trey, tackling him to the ground. Not expecting me to pounce on him on all fours, Trey fell backwards with me on top of him. I took advantage of his prone, surprised state to use his body as a launching pad to spring back up and escape through the door.

Before I could reach the front door, I was grabbed tightly from behind and lifted off my feet. "No, let go!" I yelled. With my feet off the ground and my arms held immobile, I wasn't helpless yet. Dad taught me this move himself: cranking my head as far forward as possible while bringing my knees close to my chest, I snapped my head backwards into the unsuspecting nose behind me. At the same time, I swung my legs back to hook around his hips, then somersaulted forwards the exact moment I felt him loosen his grip. I let go with my legs and dove between his open ones to end up behind him when I came out of my somersault. With a swift quick to his behind, I had him sprawling forwards onto his face.

I sprung into a low crouch and quickly scanned the room, ready for any more impending threats. The guys had come running from the kitchen to stand next to Trey who had recovered enough to chase after me. They stood in a semi-circle some distance away. And instead of menacing looks like I expected, I was surprised to see them all sporting amused glances.

"She got you good, didn't she, Dylan?" I think that came from Reese, since I recognized his unique laugh. From the groan that came from the man on the floor, the man I had just bested, I could safely say that was an affirmative.

The others laughed at his response, and Trey came forward to help Dylan to his feet. I didn't move from my low stance as Dylan turned to face me, and I prepared to spring up again in case he decided to try and finish me off. I was shocked yet again when Dylan looked at me with a huge grin.

Still grinning, he approached closer with arms outstretched and exclaimed, "Little darlin', why am I only meeting you now?! I've never seen anyone as small as you fight like that!" *Who is this guy?* Looking at him warily, I backed away from those wide-open arms, careful not to let him trap me into a bear hug again.

Trey sidled alongside Dylan and pushed at his arms. "Don't mind him, Laena. He loves the fight as much as he loves watching someone else doing the fighting." To Dylan, "You're scaring her, Dylan. Can't you see she still hasn't let her guard down?"

That's right because I won't until I'm assured that I'm safe.

Vance stepped between Dylan and me, facing in my direction. "Laena, you can kick his ass as many times as you want for our benefit. Later. But first, why didn't you let Trey finish examining you?"

"He wanted a blood sample," I said simply, not wanting to explain why. Even *I* didn't know why Dad made this a Do-Not rule in the first place.

Rennick tsked from the kitchen doorway. Moving closer, he took my hand gently and said, "Are you afraid of a little poke, is that it?"

Now they were making me sound like a little wuss. But I kept silent. Better they think I'm afraid of a needle prick than for them to ask questions I didn't have solid answers for.

Trey said, "So far, she checks out as a healthy human being. No illnesses or disease. I just need blood for her hematocrit and tissue to analyze her DNA."

"Can't you get a sample that doesn't require bloodletting, you vampire?" Reese said, mockingly. "Like a swab or something?"

Trey sighed. "I suppose I can get away with a cheek cell swab. But it wouldn't be a thorough examination if we forgo the blood sample."

Vance turned to me once again, and asked, "Laena, if I promise that nothing will harm you as long as I'm around, will you let Trey take some blood from you? It won't be more than a drop, I swear. We just want to make sure you're as healthy as you can be."

I hesitated; the look in Vance's eyes as he looked into mine almost made me lose my resolve. They were kind eyes, eyes that made me want to drown in them the way he was looking at me. I couldn't explain how he was looking at me; I just knew that it made me more conscious of taking in air more deliberately. I felt like I couldn't breathe when he looked at me like that.

"O-okay," I said, too easily convinced by his pretty face. "As long as you swear that whatever comes from this blood sample will not put me in danger."

"That's an odd request, but okay, I'll honor it," Vance said, his smile dropping in warmth a few degrees. But he grabbed my hand, caressing my palm with his thumb in assurance. His gentle touch warmed me even further.

Because he was being so nice, I stopped myself from uttering, *it wasn't a request*. But I had his word. That's all that mattered.

Trey stepped in between us again, this time brandishing a lancet device. Vance, who still held my hand, gripped it, and turned it palm-up in Trey's direction. Before I could ask what he was about to do, Trey pressed the pointy side to the tip of my middle finger and triggered the device. I felt a sharp poke then it was done. The lancet retracted into itself as Trey said, "Got it! I'll be a moment." And Trey retreated back into the guest room.

Holding my pricked finger captive between two of his fingers, Vance brought it to his lips and lightly kissed it, his tongue flickering out to lick at the micro wound. My eyes flared at the action, my heart speeding up to a rapid tattoo. "There. I've kissed it all better," he said, as he looked at me from under his lashes.

Oh. My. God.

Aside from it being the most unsanitary thing to do to a wound, I was floored. Why would he do such a thing? And why was I feeling so unlike myself when he looked at me like—like he wanted to eat me!

But underneath my astonishment at what Vance just did, I felt a tiny bit of regret for breaking one of Dad's big rules. I let someone take my blood.

I felt nervous at the thought of them finding out something cataclysmic about my blood. For a long time, I had believed that whatever was in my blood would be enough to turn the world on its axis.

Now that microliters of my blood were up for analysis, it was too late for any do-overs. I guessed it remained to be seen what my blood would reveal.

5

REESE

Ask and ye shall receive. I was never much of a believer in those words, but the one time I prayed for a miracle, there she was standing before me. Laena.

We finally have a name for our mystery girl, and she's finally here in front of us.

The guys, who knew almost too much about me, never knew that I suffered from an aching loneliness. I knew I came off as a pretty carefree guy, but to me it's a poor disguise for what I've really been dealing with. Out of the three of us, I desperately longed to be part of something bigger than myself. And I believed having a wife whom the three of us could share would go a long way towards that goal.

Maybe that's why I risked life and limb everyday outside the walls of each of the Seven Cities—the expanse. At the least, I could admit to myself that my acts of heroism were just a front. It's just lucky that I happen to be good at what I do.

Excellence was also something very stressed in my house growing up. Unfortunately, it was at the cost of a safe, loving home. My parents just weren't the love and nurturing type, as embroiled in politics as they were.

I've considered and always will consider Trey my only family, despite the fact that our parents are still alive. Trey had been my protector from our own sperm-and-egg donors from day one, and it's because of him that I'm the man I am today. No matter how much my parents attributed my successes to their solid parenting, I will only ever acknowledge Trey's part in my upbringing.

Other than my issues with dear old Mom and Dad, I'd been left with this cloying need to belong, to be loved. One-night stands with registered females in other walled cities left me feeling empty, although temporarily satiated, and I ached even more to have someone I could call *mine*.

Now, here in Vance's house, I've been unsettled by my own reaction to this beautiful woman. I knew I fell hard the first time I saw her, recognizing her for a woman right away. No longer looking grubby, she was more than I could ever hope for. Small as she was, she was fit, agile, and whip smart enough to make Dylan look like an idiot. And Dylan was one of our generals.

    But most of all, she captured all of my attention and my heart along with it. I don't think I could dredge up the name of any other woman of my acquaintance with Laena right in front of me; she was all that mattered to me. And more to the point—she mattered to us. Hard to believe that all of the feelings have already welled up, and no more than a day had passed.

    A softie at heart, I may be; and watching her lovely face turn doubtful, I wanted to take her into my arms and shelter her from her own perceived hurts. She had been so scared of giving blood, she had knocked the wind out of Trey and had taken Dylan down just to avoid it. Now that the deed had been done, she looked so helpless. I wanted to whisk her away where we could be alone, where I could assure her that she was safe. With me. With us.

    Reaching out for her, I was compelled to just touch her, for my own assurance that she was real. I took her other hand, the one that Vance wasn't holding, and said, "Laena, are you all right?" With my other hand I felt her forehead for a rise in temperature then slid my hand down to cup one cheek.

    She closed her eyes and sighed into my touch. "I'm fine. I think I'm just overwhelmed." She looked a lot like a contented kitten rubbing her cheek against my hand.

    Frowning, I looked at Vance, and said, "Let's get her seated." The both of us led her to the sofa nearby, and we seated ourselves on either side of her. Dylan and Rennick joined our circle in the sofa chairs across from us.

    Dylan piped up, "While we wait for the results, I'd like to ask you boys a few questions." Looking at Laena, he said, "Don't worry, I have plenty for you, too, but these boys have some explaining to do."

I rolled my eyes, thinking, *I was wondering when he was going to get around to his own version of the Spanish Inquisition.*

"Where did you find her?"

"In the Outer Ring, close to where the newest breach was found. The East Wall," Vance said. With Vance higher in rank than us, maybe it's better he gave all the answers.

"I see that she has no marks of identification. Have you found out who she is?"

"Family name is Kanata, and one remaining family member, the father. Atsushi Kanata of Area 5."

"Why haven't you followed protocol and brought her straight to the Courts?"

"Because she had been involved in an altercation with those things, sir. We had to make sure she was unhurt."

"So, why not bring her to Medical?"

Vance stayed silent at that question, so I answered for him, "Because we promised her protection." Laena looked at Vance, askance. We hadn't yet discussed that part with her.

"Protection from what?"

"From *whom*," I stressed. "The law requires her registration, and that would put her beyond what protection we can provide."

"And why have you three taken it upon yourselves to assume such a duty? What has she done to earn your loyalty?"

Laena's head snapped up, and I watched as her eyes lit up in interest, anticipating the answer.

Vance cut in. "Because we want her."

Laena straightened, that frightened rabbit look leaving her eyes to be replaced with a look of interest that later changed to fury. She looked ready to bolt. Reaching across, I gently laid a hand on her knee, feeling a lot like I was trying to reassure a wild, spirited animal from dashing off.

Dylan shook his head in disbelief, then continued, "Okay, let's say we have her checked out and she's clear. Then what?"

"That's why we called Trey. He'd know through her DNA whose family she might belong to," I said. Everyone had their DNA registered in some database somewhere, a listing by which our identities were confirmed. With the Eidolon virus still sweeping across the globe, we had to ensure we preserved the best traits in our families. It was how our class system was created; it was all DNA-based.

Then Trey came rushing into the room, his eyes wild, for all intents and purposes, looking floored by whatever he had discovered. "Guys! You're not going to believe this! I just cross-checked Laena's DNA against the database, and it looks like she's an exact match with someone who could be her family. But that's virtually impossible! Even fraternal twins don't have identical sets of DNA."

Thoroughly confused, I raised a hand. "Uh, Trey? What the hell are you talking about?" I asked uncertainly. Although the guy was super smart, sometimes he forgot we weren't on par with his level of intelligence and went on ahead babbling in science speak.

Rennick stated firmly, "Trey, please, for the benefit of those who don't understand every other word in that sentence, could you say that again in dumb-dumb speak? You know because we clearly don't get what you're saying." Vance grabbed the tablet from Trey's hands that had a read-out of Laena's results, and he scrutinized it until he looked back up and sighed. Clearly, Vance had no idea how to interpret what was on there.

Taking in a breath to ramp down his own excitement-slash-bewilderment, Trey tried again. "Laena is an exact match for someone we all know. She's about the same age as him, so she could really be his twin. But the results don't lie! I ran it three more times to make sure. There's just no way that she could be his identical twin down to the molecular level!"

"*Who* could be her twin?!" I exploded, impatient to hear the rest.

"Kane Ardarien," he answered with finality.

Silence descended as we all took a moment to digest that information. As far as I knew, Kane Ardarien was the son of one of our Elite's councilmen, the Ardariens. Kane was an arrogant little prick, having just graduated from university. Theirs was a family that were powerful influencers in how our city was governed. New Phoenix, after all, was not too far from being one of those city-states from the olden days, and the Ardariens ruled the roost here, being the founders of our Elite Army. However, there were no known daughters listed in their family registry.

Laena broke the silence, "I have a brother? A twin brother?"

We all turned to her; even more questions than there had been earlier arose about her existence.

We couldn't give her a definite answer, not when we ourselves had trouble believing the results of her DNA test.

Vance rounded on her, "You said your father's name is Atsushi Kanata, but according to this report, your biological parents are Barclay and Marguerite Ardarien."

Her small face hardened in expression, looking meaner than a snake about to strike. "I told you the truth," she insisted forcefully. "Atsushi *is* my father. I don't even know who this Barkley or Mar-gah-reen even are."

I'm sure my eyebrows disappeared straight up into my hairline as I looked down at Laena. She was telling the truth, yet we couldn't dispute the more relevant truth that lay in her DNA.

"Who are you, Laena Kanata? The more we uncover about you, the more confused we get," I whispered down at her, musing more to myself than to her.

Fiercely, she jumped out of her seat and rounded on me. She hissed, "I haven't a clue! None of this makes any sense!" She gestured wildly, her frustration escalating to greater heights. "And another thing. What is this about you three wanting me? Well, I don't consent at all! I was fine by myself, just me and Dad. You didn't have to bring me here, but you did. Why?"

Dylan smirked at all three of us, while Trey looked entirely confused. Trey said, "You guys want her? Just what did I miss?"

"Isn't it obvious, Trey?" Dylan chuckled. "These knuckleheads want the whole enchilada with this little spitfire here. God knows they'll have their hands full if they rope her into marrying them."

"MARRY?!" Laena screeched. My ears rung at her otherworldly high pitch. "You guys are fucking insane! I'm not up for grabs just because you spotted me first!"

I clenched my jaw at her words. Little did the guys know, I had been deadset on this female since the moment I laid eyes on her. There was no way she was going anywhere without me dogging her.

Vance and I stood to our full height, attempting to stare her down. Laena was both fire and ice, both burning and frosty all at once as she stared back at us. Rennick stood up behind her, and gently said, "We're not cavemen, and we're not going to club you over the head to drag you back to our cave against your will."

Rennick raised both hands in the air with palms facing her, to show her he had no intention of harming her. For a very long minute, she looked at each of us, as if she was trying to weigh us at our word. I could tell she was softening, her expression morphing into one of reluctant resignation. Dylan shot a triumphant grin at her; I had no idea why he was so happy at the thought of her joining our fold—he was already married to my brother.

I stepped towards her just as she turned from Rennick to face me. I assured her, "Baby girl, we are the last people on this Earth to bring you harm. But because we found you first, in our collective minds, I think we have a case of finder's keepers here."

She frowned deeply at my words, and was about to continue shouting, when Rennick zapped her in the neck with the mini-taser he wore, disguised as a pendant. As she crumpled to the ground, I shot an angry look at him as Vance bent to check on her.

"She's breathing, but she'll be asleep for a while," Vance said, then swore. "Give us some warning, hey?" he growled at Rennick, picking Laena up and placing her on the sofa.

I grabbed Rennick by the collar and brought him in close to hiss, "Why'd you do that? And after I told her we wouldn't harm her! You think she'd trust us after that stunt you just pulled?"

Rennick pushed me off of him; not an easy feat for the average guy, but he was just as strong as me, if not more. We did wear the same shirt size, after all. "If we're going to do this—keep her, I mean—then I do my thinking better when I'm not scared she'll turn tail and run. Couldn't you see that she was ready to take off?"

Dylan chortled from where he still sat. "You guys are hilarious! Already whipped by a tiny little thing that could wipe the floor with all your asses! And you go and do *that* to her? Priceless!"

I grumbled at him, "Well, Kettle, meet Pot! And don't forget, Laena had just done that with you!"

"But I don't want her!" Dylan defended. "I'm already spoken for."

Trey butted in, "As glad as that makes me, I'm even gladder that I don't have to deal with the bullshit you three boys would have to go through just to find a woman." With sympathy, he added, "And here you found the woman all of you want, but we still don't know too much about her. With this obvious connection to the Ardariens, why would she have been raised as someone else's child?"

Vance, Rennick, and I could only look at each other; none of us knew the answer. We could speculate all we want, but Laena wasn't exactly as forthcoming as we had hoped.

Rennick said, "You'd think the Ardariens would be happy to have a daughter to help carry on their legacy. Anyone who married her would take on the Ardarien name and all of the power to go with it."

Vance nodded, "Let's take a look at the registration records, say about twenty or twenty-five years ago? Maybe there's something there that would tell us more."

Trey helpfully added, "Well, Kane is now twenty-three, so that'll narrow the search. You might also want to check out the sealed records. The ones I know you three don't have clearance for."

I rolled my eyes at him, "Then why suggest it if you know we can't get into them?"

"Because, as your superior who does have clearance, I think my husband is trying to get me to help you guys out," Dylan groused. Looking at Trey, he complained, "This stunt could get me into trouble. You know how guarded the Ardariens are."

"But this is my baby brother's happiness we're discussing. Don't you want him to be just as happy as we are?" Trey teased lightly. "But seriously, I don't get why all of this secrecy surrounds poor Sleeping Beauty over there. Something this juicy and mysterious is just too good to keep a secret forever."

I agreed with a noise of affirmation for the last part and saluted Trey with my middle finger for the first. I'll let him figure out which action was meant for what part of what he said.

The more I thought about it, the more circuitous my thoughts took a turn. Laena wasn't immaculately conceived, and there's no way the Ardariens would have willingly given up a daughter. Or would they? And if they did, what was the motive?

Because she had been raised differently, Laena hadn't a clue how most females in our society behaved. She was entirely capable of caring for herself when other women lived to be spoiled and pampered by the men in their lives. Laena could fend off attackers as well as any of us standing in this room, and she proved that so many times all in the better part of the day.

But why would she be hidden away in isolation from the rest of the world? And at her father's instigation? Didn't he want what was best for her? There were so many secrets, and not enough time to uncover them before she lost our protection.

Once the Elite Council found about her, least of all the Ardariens, she would no longer be ours to protect.

She would belong to New Phoenix.

6

LAENA

I stood at the bottom of the old canyon Dad had used to take me for my training sessions. But always only at night. But Dad wasn't there to guide me into his routine instructions like we've done so many times before. Looking around, against the backdrop of the full moon, long, distended shadows stretched across the canyon floor. Three of the shadows in the outline of three familiar figures.

Looking up, I found the possessors of said shadows staring back at me. Vance, Rennick, and Reese. All three maintained wide-set shoulders, V-shaped torsos, and roughly hewn muscles encasing their forms. Their imposing forms spoke of power and fluid grace in the way they moved as they slowly moved towards me.

A closer look at them told of readiness for what was to come next; muscles gliding underneath smooth skin were held taut as they awaited me to make the next move. Dad had taught me that in a situation like this to never look as if I was battle-ready; it was more important to catch my opponents off guard by being less predictable with my movements. And so, I relaxed my stance, loosening my muscles as I rotated my body from the shoulders down towards each of them, one after the other. All while keeping my head stable as I used my eyes to track and lock on each man.

The sound of a booted foot slid across the sandy canyon floor, which was my queue to jump into the fray that they didn't know about yet. I smiled as I leaped at the closest man, readying a full body punch as I twisted in the air. This was what I did best, according to Dad: surprising my opponents with the timing of my first move. Then at the same time, I land my punch into someone's jaw (Reese, maybe?), just as I deliver a swift, sweeping back kick to whoever I had sensed coming up from behind me.

From there, it was a delicious, familiar back and forth of offensive strikes and defensive blocks and evasions. But like most of my dreams, my movements progressively became jerky and slow, to the point I felt like I was moving in a bog of thick, sticky mud. Maybe my mind was teaching me a lesson in what to do when your body suddenly becomes useless to you in a fight kind of scenario.

Sluggish as my strikes and kicks were, Vance, Rennick, and Reese soon closed in on me in a circle, entrapping me within. With my heavy limbs and shortened striking distance, I was rendered completely defenseless.

However, I was still aware that this was just a dream. None of what was happening was real. And so, I shut my heavy-lidded dream eyes in one long, slow blink, then slowly opened them with great effort.

Upon opening them, I was startled to find myself no longer upright but lying face up and no longer standing at the bottom of that canyon. Instead of night sky, I was now staring at a mirrored ceiling that reflected myself in a wide, oversized bed. Complete with fluffy pillows behind and around me and a luxuriously soft duvet covering me. I had never before owned such an extravagant bed, having always slept on the ground under the stars on a pallet of blankets.

But what I originally thought were pillows surrounding me had suddenly morphed into my earlier opponents. No longer alone in the bed, Vance, Rennick, and Reese were underneath the duvet with me, moving around me, surrounding me. With slow, writhing movements, they moved their bodies against mine in a manner I never knew existed or was even allowed.

For most of my life, I had been taught to move my body purposefully in many ways to either fight or defend. But never in my limited experience have I ever known or seen how sinuously a body can move against another. Until now. And not until I saw for myself how sinfully delicious these three stirred against me.

They slid their hands, their bodies in slow, skimming caresses up and down, back and forth, so lazily against me. Touching me oh-so-slightly with enough pressure to leave a fleeting but slow-burning memory of their touch. The heat of their hands skimming along my sensitized skin absorbed deep, heating me from within. As I looked up into the mirror, I could see their bodies slowly writhing against me like winding snakes in a mating ball.

Suddenly, I ached in a way I have never ached before. Never before have I had occasion to, not since my life had only ever been about training my body to its optimum performance, from sunup to sundown. Never before have I experienced achiness in a place that I had never given much thought unless it was to clean myself or it was the start of my monthly cycle.

Every slow slide of their fingers against my highly sensitized skin generated electric shivers that reverberated throughout my whole body. And with each touch, I wanted something—wasn't sure what—to help ease that ache.

The guys didn't let up and were downright merciless. Their combined touches spawned unfamiliar feelings from deep within, ones that radiated towards that place between my legs. Copious amounts of heat pooled down there, but I couldn't do anything to stave it off. I didn't know how. I just wanted the ache and the heat to lessen in their intensity, so I didn't feel like I was struggling for air.

I wished they would do something—anything!—to alleviate the ache they created within me, but they continued to take their time, continuing the slow pace of their caresses at the same leisurely speed. It was both agonizing and delicious all at once, and I felt an urgency I had never felt before. Like there was something imminent at the end of this state that I had to get to, but I didn't know how to get there.

The feelings inside me, foreign but welcome, were building and building, and I thought I was soon going to ignite into flames then burn down to ash. Every touch, every lick, every moan was spurring me on towards this inevitable fiery fate.

Then I woke up, eyes blinking open rapidly as the phantom feelings in my body followed me from my dream and into the waking world. Even while I still ached deep inside, I stayed immobile as I fell into my usual habit of mentally scanning my body for other aches and pains.

Everything seemed normal. Except, I remembered being hit with the prongs of a military-issue taser before feeling so much voltage painfully coursing throughout my body. The last thing I had seen was the hardwood floor rushing up to meet me as I fell.

Those fuckers tased me! What the ever-lovin' hell were they thinking? And they claimed that they want me? It was just like a male to force their way into my life, by abducting me in such a cowardly manner. Assholes! Now, what the fuck am I going to do?

Surprisingly, I should have felt a bruised temple or forehead when I reached up a hand to touch my face, but there was nothing out of the ordinary. Other than my wrists being encircled with handcuffs and shackled to the rails of the bed I lay in. Feeling frantic, trapped, and betrayed, I sat up panting heavily, my mind spinning.

In my mind, I screamed, *how do I get out of here? I'm not safe here! I'm not safe!*

Looking around the tiny room, any hope of escape was futile. The room was sparse with one point of entry—the door, which was closed and most likely locked from the outside. The frosted glass on the door was backlit from the hallway's lighting, and I could see the shadowed outline of a man, most likely a soldier, standing just outside. And even if I could wriggle out of these cuffs with my wrists intact, I wouldn't be able to reach the one lone window in the room. It was too high and too narrow.

Dad's training kicked in; in times like these, slowing down my breath and thinking more rationally was more likely to keep me alive than giving in to panic. If an opportunity presented itself, I was going to get out of here and hop a transport to get back to Dad. He'd know what I'm supposed to do now that I've been exposed. They most likely know more about me than I ever did, and Dad said that would be too dangerous. For him and for me.

Closing my eyes, I breathed inward slowly on a five-second count and let out my breath just as slowly. Continuing this pattern for several breaths, my heart rate eventually slowed but my mind plugged away at different scenarios to escape.

Just then, the door rattled open and the trio walked right in, along with Dr. Trey, his husband, Dylan, and a stern, official-looking man in uniform who brought up the rear. The new guy was much older, and I watched him curiously just as he couldn't take his eyes off of me. I couldn't guess why there were so many of them crammed into this tiny room, but the looks on all of their faces told me that things might not work in my favor. Plus I didn't want to look Vance, Rennick, or Reese in the eye; I was still embarrassed about the dream I had of them together.

I guess if I were any other woman, I'd be shaking underneath this paper-thin hospital gown, what with these intimidating men lined up around the bed. But these men didn't scare me; it's what I think they're going to tell me that scares me.

My fears were confirmed when the older man leaned down and spoke. "This girl is supposed to be mine?" he said dubiously. "And she's genetically identical to my Kane? I think I'd remember if my wife had birthed a girl. I was there when Kane was born!"

I looked away from the man's gaze; he held too much scorn for me in that one angry look as he spat those words down at me. Before Dr. Trey had forcibly taken my blood, I had firmly believed that I solely belonged to Dad. Then the results were read, and I almost couldn't deal with what that meant. As tough as Dad was on me, I knew deep down that he loved me. He used to tell me so when I was younger, but I hadn't heard it much as of late. With this Ardarien person speaking like I had no blood claim to him, I was glad; I didn't want to belong to anyone other than Dad.

"Good," I said with mock cheer. "He confirmed it; I'm not his daughter. Can we let me out now?" I held up my shackled wrists in a mini shrug. I didn't want to be here any longer than I had to be. It was imperative that I find Dad; get answers from him that these guys weren't giving me; and make plans to get the hell out of Dodge.

Dylan frowned. "Nuh-uh, sweetheart. Not until it's been decided who you belong to."

Fury bloomed hot underneath my skin. "I belong to no one," I hissed, my tone quiet in a deadly way. I really hated that these overbearing men completely bought into this women-are-helpless-and-need-men mindset.

Trey held out a hand as if to placate me. "At the moment, that is exactly the case. But we've run further tests, and we found some surprising things."

Shit! They must have taken more blood from me when I was out. What more could they have possibly found out about me? Curious, I stayed silent, waiting for them to dish out all the details.

Dr. Trey turned the tablet he was holding so I could see its display. Then he asked, "Have you ever been bitten by one of the Eidolon-infected?"

What? "No. I wouldn't be sitting here talking to you if I was."

His mouth formed a slight grimace as he pointed to the picture on the right. "This picture is a scanning EM of what's in your blood. There's a huge difference to what's in there versus what the rest of us have."

"And what's that?"

"You carry antibodies that somehow completely weaken the Eidolon virus. We're not sure exactly what the mechanism is behind it, but you are completely immune."

Barclay Ardarien roared at first Trey, then me, "How is that possible?! Our scientists have been searching for a cure for years, and this girl with my stolen DNA is our answer to the cure?" The man looked positively livid; his eyes bulged, and his skin was turning a mottled red, retracting a little from his relatively good looks for an old guy.

Dylan stepped in to get Barclay to back up a little. "Hold on, we don't know that someone stole your DNA, as you say, to create this girl, but I assure you we're looking into it." Looking round at the trio on the other side of the bed, they all nodded to acknowledge their part.

Barclay refused to be cowed. "Well, what other possibility is there? I'm devoted to my wife just as she is to me and her other husbands. Don't tell *me* that I've been unfaithful!"

Trey argued back, "You're not truly listening to what I'm trying to tell you! Your DNA couldn't have been stolen to produce Laena. For her to be identical to Kane in every way other than lacking a Y chromosome, she must have been cloned straight from *his* DNA."

"Then I want you to find the culprits! This is completely unethical and unheard of!" Barclay thundered. "And why has she only been discovered now?" Everything about him

My heart pounded heavily with all of this new information, and I still didn't know why Dad thought it was so important that I was kept hidden away.

I exhaled a slow, staggering breath, then answered Barclay directly, "Because it was an accident. No one is supposed to know I exist."

All heads turned to me, and I felt the weight of their gazes rest heavily on me. Rennick asked quietly, "And why is that, Laena?"

I shrugged lightly, raising my hands in the universal gesture for I-don't-know. "Dad never told me. Maybe he thought it was better that I didn't know. All I know is that hiding the way we did, our survival depended on it."

Out of everyone in the room, I chose Barclay to observe and gauge his reaction. For a split-second, a heavy look of menace and fury aimed my way colored his face before a mask of cold indifference replaced it.

Huh. Interesting. You'd think that a loving father would welcome a long-lost daughter into his fold, but it looks like he already hated me on sight.

Then Vance asked, "And who is your dad? We did a more thorough search, and Atsushi Kanata has no other records on file other than the address you've given us. Meaning there are no birth records, transport records, nothing. Same story on your end, too. It isn't possible to be completely off the grid as you two are. Just who are you two?"

Tersely, I said, "I'll tell you who I'm not. I'm not one of your coddled females looking only to further the human race. I'm not some fragile flower who will wilt at the slightest sign of trouble. Living as we did, we lived by our own rules and no one else's."

Reese cut in, "But why? Wouldn't a father who loves his daughter want to give her the best life? From the sounds of it, you two lived like gutter people."

Defensively, I shot back, "And maybe I'm okay with how we lived! I'll tell you right now, that everything Dad taught me was to make sure I could take care of myself. Can other women say the same?"

Wryly, Rennick asked, "I don't know about these other women, but you can ask my sister Drayna when you meet her. She sure as hell wouldn't let any of us in the family coddle her."

The one word that caught my attention in his statement: *when*. These people weren't going to let me go. "What do you mean, when I get to meet her?"

Dylan smiled at me. "Sweetheart, you are a big mystery not just to us, but to a lot of people out there. The lab techs who've seen your blood results; the archivists who helped us research your bloodline; and the higher ups who caught wind that you are immune." At that last bit he looked directly at Barclay.

Trey interpreted, "What he's trying to say is that you are very much a person of interest. You can't resume your old life."

That sounded suspiciously like I was going to be held here against my will. Raising a scornful brow, I asked, "Then what options am I left with? That is, assuming I have any."

Reese aimed a sheepish smile my way. "There are two actually. One being that you marry the three of us, me, Vance, and Rennick. That way, we three are the devil you know as opposed to the devil you don't." I frowned heavily at that option. I still didn't know them at all. Then, he continued, "And the other is to become a ward of the state, bypassing the Women's Registration Act altogether."

That last bit sounded intriguing. "What does that mean, being a ward of the state?"

Dylan said matter-of-factly, "It means that you would be declared a civil servant to do the will of our city's leadership. You could choose which sector, at least; that narrows your options a little bit."

"Which are?"

Barclay sneered, "Would you prefer to be our laboratories' guinea pig in the research sector? Or would you like to join our cadet forces in our military division? Either way, you will be under strict surveillance until we find evidence that you are trustworthy."

Without hesitation, I declared, "Sign me up as a cadet!" Beside me, the three let out small sounds of disappointment, as I flashed them a triumphant grin.

I continued, "If you think offering me a marriage to you three is the more attractive part of the deal," I swallowed, suddenly remembering that outrageous dream, "well, it just isn't. Not for me."

Barclay narrowed his eyes at me like he was trying to see past my skin and discover my secrets. He said, "You are nothing like a daughter of mine would be. Any daughter of mine would have been raised to accept her place in this life and to uphold the Ardarien family name." He was looking at me like I was an animal he had never seen before and didn't know what to do with it.

I sneered, "Then it's a good thing that I'm not your daughter, hm?"

For all that this world championed women as crucial to humanity's survival and that all family lines were now matriarchal, I just couldn't stomach the thought of being raised to know my place according to this creepy man's dictates. I knew what he meant by his words: that females were only good for being a dutiful partner to more than one male and to bear children.

Dad had raised me to know my own worth and value, and I knew with certainty that it had nothing to do with what these guys were trying to enforce on me. Now that I was no longer anonymous, I had no choice but to play by their rules.

Soon enough, I was tattooed with a barcode on the back of my neck and with another on my ring finger. Dylan made sure I was signed up for the Cadet corps as Vance, Rennick, and Reese looked on disapprovingly.

What had Reese said earlier? Better the devil you do than the devil you don't? In this case, the devil I didn't know seemed like the safer option.

7

LAENA

Thank God and Dr. Trey that the bickering about my fate moved outside the room and spilled out into the hallway. It was Dr. Trey's quick, sharp whistle over the cacophony of voices that caught everyone off guard, and he had shooed everyone out so that his patient could rest.

With the space alone to think, I was resolved to remain as free as I possibly could be under my new circumstances, and that meant no marrying anyone just yet. I was willing to be a cadet or whatever, as long as I didn't have to be tied down. And I still couldn't get over the fact that I'd been tased by the people who allegedly want to have me as their shared wife, and I wasn't ready to forgive that. No matter how tempting they may be, I wasn't going to easily give in to the temptation those three presented.

I would bolt the minute I could, but I'm barcoded and registered now. Any scanner at any of the gates would track my every movement, and it won't be easy to leave the city without alerting someone. If I could somehow leave undetected, then I could make it out into the Expanse where it'd be easier to hide and I'd be harder to track.

As worried as I was, surely Dad would be when I didn't show up at our makeshift camp in the Outer Ring, I wasn't too worried about making sure I could get word to him. We had planned for an event like this and had gone over and over on what to do if we ever got separated. If one of us got taken in, then for safety's sake, the one who was still free had to lay low and wait for word. No sense in both of us being caught by the Elite.

But neither of us could make use of high tech means of communication, unless we wanted it traced. Thankfully, there were other ways to get my message across that would be meaningless to anyone who found it. I just had to find a way to get to our designated "mailbox". And I needed access to our server to plant the message. If I could just find a public computer terminal or a tablet with a good connection, it wouldn't take much to apprise Dad of my new situation.

My hospital room door opened suddenly, and Dylan and Trey walked in. I was happy to note that Vance, Rennick, and Reese didn't follow them in, and I could no longer hear their voices out in the hall.

"You're clear to leave," Dr. Trey announced and looked at his husband expectantly.

Dylan took that as his cue to explain. "Like he said, darlin'. You're being discharged and you'll be immediately moved into the Cadet barracks with Trey and me to escort you there. I'm seeing personally to your conscription as per Barclay Ardarien's orders."

I frowned. A personal escort meant that they didn't trust me on my own. "Ah, I take it you think I'm a flight risk."

Dylan shrugged in apology. "Yeah, Barclay Ardarien thinks it's a good idea to keep a close eye on you. In turn, we are not advertising the fact about your immunity."

"Oh, yeah? Why's that?"

Trey lowered his voice to an almost whisper. "Because the moment anyone gets wind of what's in your blood, you're more likely to end up as an experimental test subject instead of a free woman."

That sounded almost preferable to being a shared wife or an indentured Cadet to the Elite army. But Trey warned, "Laena, before you back out of signing up as a Cadet, know this: those who've been suspected of immunity or—um, other things, have never been seen again. I've heard rumors that 'volunteers' don't make it out alive."

Dylan shushed him. "Say that any louder and both of us could be under suspicion for harboring Eidolon sympathies." Another thing about this world? There have been rumors that the Eidolon virus did more than just create undead creatures that roamed the expanse, hungry for living flesh. Dad mentioned that it was suspected that there might be a new evolutionary step that the virus' presence had driven and may be presenting in certain individuals. But the Elite have quashed any talk about it, making it unpopular by jailing anyone who spread these lies.

I assured Dr. Trey, "I'm not backing out of my decision to go the Cadet route. I just wondered what being an experiment would involve."

"Nothing you should ever experience." Trey shivered, possibly envisioning whatever horror stories he'd heard about such things.

Dylan cut in. "Okay, Laena, get dressed, and I'll drive you down to the barracks. How old are you by the way?"

"Twenty-three."

"Really? I thought you were much younger. Doesn't matter; looks like you can only serve two more years until you're obligated to marry."

Huh? "What do you mean by 'obligated'?"

"By signing up with our Cadet Corps, you're only delaying the inevitable. All registered women are required to marry at the age of twenty-five."

"And you failed to mention this earlier?" My temper sparked. If I had known this earlier, I would have ran. My registration and tracer be damned.

"Sorry, I thought you knew." Dylan had the decency to look contrite. "If it makes you feel any better, just think of your time training as a Cadet as a reprieve from the presence of the shitheads who got you here in the first place."

Trey nudged his husband hard. "You left the conversation when those shitheads you're talking about came up with a new plan."

"What new plan?"

"The one that Barclay Ardarien insisted on. It was the only guarantee they could give him that Laena would be under careful watch."

"Still not following."

Trey sighed. "I mean, those three had just signed up as the Cadet Corps newest instructors. You know that the new hires always end up with the newbies."

I groaned right along with Dylan. So, I was going to be stuck with those three dogging my every move and step? Give me a fucking break! Now, my likelihood of getting a message to Dad was going to be further reduced. Dylan shook in his head at disgust at the new pronouncement, as he unshackled me from the cuffs.

Freed from the restraints, I jumped out of bed as Trey handed me a wrapped package. "You can change into what's in there, and Dylan and I will take you to your new temporary home." Then a phone trilled somewhere on Trey's body. He pulled it out of a back pocket, glanced at it briefly, then groaned. "Sorry, looks like it'll just be Dylan going with you. I'm needed in surgery so I gotta get back to work." To Dylan, he said, "I'll see you when I get home. See you, Laena."

Both men left the room and I quickly dressed into a long-sleeved shirt and sweats that reminded me of the ones that Vance had let me borrow. Joining Dylan outside my hospital room, he grasped my elbow and escorted me off the premises. Nothing looked familiar, and I had no idea where I was relative to where Dad and I had made camp.

"What part of the city are we?"

Handing me into his truck, Dylan chuckled. "Sorry, I keep forgetting you know nothing of the area. We're in the Inner Ring, Area 7. We're on the opposite side of the city from where the guys found you in the Outer Ring."

Ah, so nowhere near our camp that I could get to within walking distance. Shit!

Driving along the Inner Ring main roads in the waning daylight, I watched for signs to better orient myself. We also passed through three other checkpoints for Areas 6, then 5, and finally 4 where we stopped at an impressive-looking base.

Dylan led me towards a small building where only a few people were busy typing away at their terminals. Those who were in uniform saluted when Dylan entered, and they relaxed only when Dylan told them to 'at ease'. With Dylan beside me, my Cadet registration didn't take too long, and I was soon given a brief tour of the base; outfitted with a new uniform; and assigned a bunk with orders to report to my new instructors. If there were any questions as to why an Elite army general was overseeing my registration, none of the workers batted an eyelash at its strangeness.

I growled low at the thought of my now former idols and thought better of dragging my feet to meet them at the base's training field. The sooner I report in, the sooner I can get this shitty day over with. Lo and behold, the three of them were already there ahead of me with no one else in sight, deep in conversation, but I couldn't hear what they were conversing about. Floodlights lit up the rectangular training field and illuminated the three men standing imperiously waiting for me.

They looked up the moment I appeared. Vance greeted, "You're here. Don't worry, this is just an informal meet. Your real training starts tomorrow. We just wanted to talk with you."

I raised one brow in answer as if to say, *so, talk*.

The three of them look at each other with a look I couldn't identify, then Rennick began. "Okay, we know we fucked up. The taser thing—shouldn't have even happened. And we're sorry."

"Nuh-uh. Not forgiven. Because of the three of you, I'm stuck here."

Vance sighed. "We thought you might feel that way. But we couldn't risk someone else who's not me or the guys here finding you and not giving you the nice treatment as we would have."

"So, you think that your noble intentions should make me forgive you? Sorry, but your actions matter way more here than that."

Reese rubbed a hand to the back of his neck and blew out a heavy exhale of breath. "We discussed that. And you have every reason to be mad. But the only way we could see this going is if Barclay Ardarien gets to have us personally keep an eye on you while keeping you out of some mad scientist's clutches."

"Yeah, Dr. Trey said something about that. And?" I wasn't going to let up this fierce wall of indignation, not when they were to blame for my having been caught and registered.

"And we also know that there are some scientists in the Elite's payroll who aren't above doing illegal, unethical things to get the answers they want." Vance looked damned fierce as he confessed this, and he looked damned hot doing it, too.

"And we don't want that being your fate, not if we can help it." Rennick said, sincerity in his eyes and voice.

"And it's our choice to keep you safe. Barclay may have ordered us to be your watchdogs, but we want to do this."

"You're doing all this for a stranger? Someone you don't even know?" I found it hard to believe that they were willing to do all this at all. And for what?

Vance answered simply, "You're not a stranger. For five years, we tried to find out who you were, based on your description alone. It baffled us that there was nothing on record about you."

"We think it's lucky we found you today. We've been wanting to meet you again for so long." Reese looked at me with pleading eyes.

"And now you have," I said darkly. "But at the cost of my freedom. We were never supposed to meet. Ever."

"And that's too bad. Now that you're here and are officially in the Cadet Corps of the New Phoenix Elite army, we've decided that we can keep you safe from other prying, inquiring minds." Rennick's handsome face was set hard with determination.

"Safe from what? From who?" They keep saying that, but I didn't fully understand.

Reese put it to me straight. "If we weren't first on the scene, you would be subjected to a not so nice interrogation, tortured until they know you fully inside and out, and then treated like a criminal. The Elite Council wouldn't believe a lone, unregistered female wandering around is some kind of innocent. They'd believe you were a spy or some kind of assassin."

"No! I just wanted to be left alone, minding my own business," I protested loudly. I guessed it wouldn't help my case if I were to mention my training and upbringing. Even if I just mention that my training is meant for self-defense, it might not hold up well as a good reason.

"No one would believe that if they've seen you fight the way you have." Rennick made a good point.

"Then why do you think I'm not a spy or an assassin?"

"Sweetheart, we still don't know that for a fact. Which is another one of the reasons we're keeping an eye on you. Despite all that, we still find you insanely attractive," Reese said, flashing me a flirty grin.

That had me blushing. I hoped they couldn't tell what I really thought about them, deep down. "So, you can't trust me, you can't let me go, and you're all keeping my immunity a secret. Still haven't heard the real reason you're doing this."

"Because if we don't do anything, we lose you. Do you know how extensively we searched for you these past five years? We're not going to risk losing you again."

I let out a small screech. "Do you hear yourselves? You arrogant sons of bitches are telling me—not asking—the way my future is going to play out. Is this how other women suffer under you bossy shits? I was happy not knowing that this is the way of things."

"Sorry, but we're your caregivers now, with Barclay Ardariens' blessing. For now, you're a ward of the state unless you either get married or adopted."

With a snort, I replied, "Well, thank God for two years of freedom then. I don't see anyone willing to adopt an adult anyway."

They shrugged noncommittally in agreement with what I said.

Vance took two long strides to reach me so that we were up close, and I had to crane my neck upwards to look him in the eye. "Laena, we promise you that we'll give you time to adjust to this new way of life. But we also promise you, that we aim to make you ours. Be it soon or we wait the two years for you, that choice is entirely yours."

"Can't fault you for your determination. But you might be waiting a while." I narrowed my eyes at them.

"Okay, as long as you know what we're about." Reese smiled.

Vance proclaimed, "In the meantime, you'll have your training to occupy your time. If you do well, you have the chance to move up in the ranks, and there'll be chance for field work."

"I'm no stranger to hard work," I stated.

"Good, we look forward to watching your progress," Rennick said. "Oh, and you'll be in the same platoon as my sister, Drayna. But she's been a cadet since eighteen. She can definitely show a noob like you around."

"Noob?"

"New recruit. We'll see you in the morning, Laena. Have a good night," Vance said, dismissing me into the direction of my bunkhouse.

I didn't answer; instead I did an about face and walked away. I wearily wondered how I was going to get myself out of this mess, and how I would be able to fight this mounting attraction to these men on a daily basis. Maybe if I got a good night's sleep, I'd see this all in a different light.

At least, that was the hope.

8

LAENA
ONE WEEK LATER

One week in, and Cadet training didn't feel much different than my usual daily routine that Dad had set up for me. Actually, in a lot of ways, the routines seemed eerily similar. Warm-up exercises, drills, marches, combat training—everything reminded me of how Dad had put me through his disciplined physical regimen of training. Just minus the hours of reading and studying.

One week of being put through my paces at the instigation of Vance, Rennick, and Reese, and I was determined to show them my choice to be here was one I was excited about. I was willing to do the work, and I wanted to show them that being a Cadet was indeed preferable to a sudden, forced marriage to them. As my instructors, they had to have seen the way I pushed ahead of everyone else; my ruthless need to excel and perform drove me to work harder and run faster. I wasn't going to fail in this new calling.

I'd say I was adjusting well to this Cadet way of life. Having Drayna Rennick as a companion and fellow bunkmate was a welcome change as well as a surprise. I'd never had any kind of interactions with another female before and certainly not as close and personal as this new friendship between us. I was even more grateful to have Drayna be my guide and mentor in the ways of New Phoenix society since I'd run into several incidents that showed my complete lack of proper upbringing. Like proper greetings, table manners, and the like. In exchange for her generosity, I helped her with navigating the fine points of physicality in our daily training. Like the proper way to shoot, approach an opponent, or swing one over one's head.

While my days were kept busy with the sounds of barked orders, running drills, and the like, I still needed to get word to Dad. He isn't a patient man, and I'd need to get a move on before he did something stupid like look for me here. He had mentioned that if he got caught, it'd be the same as signing his death certificate. I assumed that he was a wanted man for reasons he didn't or couldn't explain and that we were on the run because of something he did.

Cadets were usually given weekends off, and Drayna had asked if I'd like to do some shopping with her on a Saturday. Her mother was giving some kind of party and that, as a Rennick, Drayna needed a new dress to properly represent the family in. From what I know about Drayna, the more skin and leg a dress showed, the better, so I imagined her mother would not be happy with her usual party attire.

I agreed to go, and together we took transport to the neighboring area which just so happened to be the place I needed to be. My three watchdogs consented to the outing with General Dylan insisting I go and have fun, seeing as I'd be with Drayna the entire time. Driving to Area 5 reminded me that it was mainly a poor district, with the mix of residential apartments and struggling industrial factories comprising most of the area. Drayna parked our vehicle just outside of this rundown apartment building where she swears the best designer resided and worked from his tiny 400-square-foot walkup.

"Why does he live here?" I asked, not understanding why the best in his field would want to live in such squalid conditions.

"He's a little eccentric," she explained. "He likes to keep to himself, and only those who truly appreciate his work are willing to come here for one-of-a-kind finds."

If she said so. I'm no proper student of fashion, but I'd take her word for it. The girl had a better eye for what was trendy and looked good on her.

The four-flight trek up the stairs to this designer's apartment made me wonder what I was actually going to expect once we met him. The stairwells were littered with trash and things that might have been crawling under all of it, and it made me wonder if the man's apartment would be any better.

I breathed a huge sigh of relief when a clean cut, nice-smelling man flew open his door to receive us, and the apartment he waved us into was also clean and tidy in a minimalist style. I didn't bother offering my name since I wasn't exactly invited to this party, so I let Drayna and the designer, Kiev, gush over what he had on a nearby rack.

Their conversation was pretty much gibberish to me, so I tuned the two chatty people out. I had formed a plan earlier to get my message to Dad that depended on Drayna being distracted. So when she ducked into one of the rooms with Kiev to try things on, I called out, "I'm going to head out for some air. If you'll be much longer, I can wait in the car."

Drayna poked her head back out of the room, and asked, "You sure you don't wanna see which one I'm going to pick?"

"You can surprise me."

Her eyes narrowed thoughtfully. "Hm, well, don't wander off too far. My brother would have my head if something happens to you."

"I promise I'm not going anywhere."

"Okay. When I'm done here, we can go grab something to eat."

"Sounds good." I left the apartment, my heart pounding at the thought of my next step. Sector 12 wasn't more than three city blocks from here, and as soon as I hit the ground floor, I took off running. The address I'd given to Vance, Rennick, and Reese as Dad's and my last known address was an actual place, one that was truthfully owned by Dad. We just never lived in it.

While I was sure that there would be cameras inside the apartment's lobby area, I just needed to steer clear of the building's main entrance and away from their range. My goal was to get to the top of the building without being seen. An easy enough feat for me since I shimmied up the drain pipe; jumped from off the side and onto the fire escape stairs; and then used the top floor's window ledges to haul myself up onto the roof.

On the roof were cages meant for individual tenants to use for storage of all kinds of things. Some of them were even used as greenhouses or herbariums. I was looking for the cage that said Block C on its door, and I squealed when I found it.

The cage door was unlocked and well-oiled; it didn't even squeak or groan as I opened it. A small safe lay inside, one that was bolted well into the building's concrete roof. Dad said that this was our 'mailbox' in the event things get hairy, and that even if it were discovered, the messages inside would make no sense to anyone else.

Entering the combination of keys that spelled out a string of letters and numerals, I cracked the safe open and reached inside. A note from Dad, written on fresh, unwrinkled paper, was waiting for me. I placed my own coded message inside, detailing what has happened, where I currently am, and where he can next find me.

Dad's letter looked like a shopping list for food items and household items, complete with prices for each item. He had circled certain words and digits on the list; having written up this code between the two of us, each number and letter signified a certain word in our made-up database of coded words. Scanning through it quickly, the gist of Dad's message was clear:

Keep your eyes and ears open—don't trust anyone. Follow orders from them but keep a low profile. Stay away from the Ardariens. They are dangerous.

God, Dad. Easier said than done. They already know I exist, and Barclay Ardarien was suspicious enough of me to warrant having three babysitters under his employ to watch over me.

What I needed badly was a way to get an email out to Dad, but not until I could set up my program on a safe terminal for multiple firewalls and major encryption to keep the message untraceable and hidden.

The scuff of heavy boots on the concrete behind me sounded, and I ducked as an arm reached out for where my neck used to be. Sweeping my leg out in a low circle in my crouched position, I thankfully connected with an ankle, causing the heavier person to fall flat on their back.

"Laena, it's me," Dad groaned from his spot on the ground.

"Oh, my God! Dad!" I rushed to him on my knees, not caring that I scuffed my uniform.

"Nice kick, baby girl. How 'bout you help me up, and we can talk."

"Not enough time. I have to head back before Drayna notices I'm gone."

He grabbed me roughly into his warm embrace, holding me tightly against him. I savored the feel of him surrounding me; his strong, wiry arms enfolding me safely to him.

Then, just as quickly, he released me. "Laena, you've listened to my instructions except for the one concerning your blood." Sheepishly, I nodded. Dad had an uncanny knack for knowing things before I could even tell him.

"Okay, what do they know about it?"

"That I'm immune to the Eidolon virus. Did you know that about me?" He nodded, and I asked, "Then why keep that from me?"

The skin around his mouth tightened, and I thought he wasn't going to reply when he didn't move a muscle. "I did know about it. It was one of the reasons I had to hide you. I went to great lengths to hide you, and a lot of sacrifices were made. And now I need you to search for sealed records that tell the story of your past."

"But why did you have to hide me? What is it about me that no one can know?"

"It's a long, complicated story that needs more time than I can use to tell it. But now they know about you, too. Just follow my instructions, and I'll come to you as soon as you uncover the truth."

I turned worried eyes up at him. The truth? He caught my glance and his eyes softened. He grabbed my hand and squeezed; I squeezed back, a small sign of our affection for each other.

He continued, "I can't stay long. I came looking for you as soon as I could. Now that they know you exist, there will be hell to pay and they'll come looking for me. And I'm sure you have a million questions, but there's no time. I won't be able to see you for a while. They'll be watching you too closely. Once you unseal those records about your past, I'll find you, and I'll tell you everything you want to know.

"But right now, you need to do some investigating of your own. They will already know you have no records online, but I've taught you enough to find backdoors that will reveal who you are. Only when you unseal those records, and not a moment before, I will come and explain everything."

Stepping further away, he looked back at me with a sad, longing look, then he jumped off the roof. I scurried to the roof's edge to see him already making his way down the fire escape stairs, and once he hit the ground, he took off running.

There was no time to waste; I'd already been gone for fifteen minutes. And I was sure Drayna would have already chosen her dress and was probably out front wondering where the hell I was. Leaping from the roof, I twisted in mid-air to grab hold of a fire escape landing two platforms down. I proceeded to make my way down to the alley below by letting go then grabbing the next set of iron bars until my feet found solid ground. From there, I rushed back down the way I'd come until I spotted Drayna's car, still parked next to the building.

But no Drayna, in sight. Breathless, I slumped in relief, realizing she must still be inside. But I didn't have to wait much longer as she appeared with a large box in her arms, sauntering smugly towards me.

"Found yourself a dress?" I asked, thankful that my breath had slowed down enough for me to speak coherently.

"Laena." She said my name like she was chastising me for not knowing anything. "It's not just a dress. When it comes to Kiev's work, I'm happy to say I always find THE dress. So, yes, I'm happy that this dress will stun, stupefy, and amaze."

I raised a brow at her. "Will your mother approve?"

"You know, I almost forgot that's why I was here in the first place."

I grinned. Drayna was as sassy as her brother had claimed.

She wryly smiled back. "But I think she had called ahead and made sure that Kiev only showed me the ones she personally okayed."

"Good. Shall we go?"

"Wait, Laena? Are those scuff marks on your knees?"

"Yeah, I got tired of standing still and did some pushups and mountain climbers." The lie came out easily, but it wouldn't matter if she believed me or not.

She shot me a look with both of her brows cocked and eyes wide as if to say she accepted what I said but didn't believe it. "You're fucking weird, you know?" I shrugged at her obviously rhetorical question, and she just smiled. "But you know I like that about you."

I said nothing as I helped her load her boxed dress into the car. We sped off, ready to find lunch. As we approached the gates back into Area 4, I just happened to glance up at the tall building of Area 5. I could have sworn I saw Dad's silhouette up there on the roof, but I thought maybe I was just imagining things. Maybe I only wished to see him there, seeing me off before I completed his objectives.

After all, I had no idea how long it would take me or how long it would be before we saw each other again.

9

VANCE

A week later, and we were still being treated with hostile glares and sharp tones from a certain little lady who won't acknowledge us outside of her training schedule. I told the guys Laena wouldn't forgive the incident with the taser, but they argued that she would've ran and be lost to us again for God knows how long. It said something about her stubborn resolve when she saved her civil tone just for training but was snappish.

The beautiful girl was driving us demented with her unwillingness to give an inch. Because of her, all this pent-up frustration inside had us all tempted to either shake sense into her or shove her up against a wall and kiss the daylights out of her. But she made it almost impossible to get close to her.

We had no problems gaining the adoring attention of the other female cadets under our care, with Drayna being the exception, of course. She knew way too much about us to give us the fangirl treatment. But most of the time, our fans, including the female ones, only ever wanted from us the gory, juicy details about how horrific our Eidolon kills were. The problem with that was that we preferred to keep those details far from our minds. Killing Eidolon gave us no satisfaction; it was just what we did to protect our people from extinction.

And of course, there was the other subset of females who would love to further their acquaintance with us, in all aspects, including physically. But since Laena stepped back into our lives, she'd proved herself the only one Rennick, Reese, and I could think about. She was frustrating, beautiful, and challenging. All we wanted was someone like her to round out our family circle.

But we couldn't convince her she was perfect for us if she was nowhere for us to find.

After training, she was the first to leave the grounds, usually with Drayna as a human shield she used against us. There was no time we could find her alone, and it didn't take long for us to figure out she was avoiding us on purpose.

We never offered her special treatment during training, careful not to play favorites. After all, we were there officially to keep an eye on her, silently watching and observing her, and waiting for a chance to state our case. We opened up our homes to her, offering her home-cooked meals, but she only accepted if Drayna was also invited. If that was the only way we could get her through our front doors, then we happily took it.

Then, the day came when a sliver of opportunity presented itself, and the three of us jumped on it.

Training was over for the week, and Friday night signaled a night of relaxation, fun, and a few drinks mixed in for most of the Cadets. All of them were excited over plans that didn't include having to wake up early the next day. Rennick, Reese, and I were the last ones on the training field; everyone else had left to get ready to revel in their fun plans for a Friday night out. Through our good natured banter, we didn't hear the sound of sniffling behind the pile of mats as we worked to put away pylons and practice rifles in the equipment shed.

Rennick was the first to notice. "Hear that, guys?" he whispered, then shushed us.

I strained my ears, and I heard the distinct sound of a sniffle. "Someone here?" I called out.

"Idiot, isn't that obvious?" Reese punched me in the arm. Rounding the pile of mats, he approached slowly to check who it was crouched and hiding there. I watched as his eyes widened in recognition, and he whisper-shouted at us, "It's Laena," before beckoning us over.

Concern rose in my chest, wondering why she was here alone and crying. I traded a glance with Rennick who looked just as worried

"Sweetheart, what's the matter?" Reese crooned, while stroking a finger down a tear-streaked cheek.

On the floor with her arms hugging her knees to her chest, she sat there with tears streaming down to pool at her chin, which rested atop her folded arms. She shook her head, closed her eyes against another flood of tears, and replied, "Homesick? For my dad?" I had almost forgotten about her absentee father and realized only now that she must be missing him terribly.

That was another thing that I didn't understand. What kind of father would willingly leave his daughter alone like he did Laena? And for so long with no word? Since the day we found her, he hadn't shown his face once, and it was very telling of how much more he was concerned over his own hide than his daughter's.

I growled, "That bastard has no right to you. Not when he's abandoned you like this."

She scowled back at the three of us. "You don't know him," she said simply in his defense. We've already learned how fiercely loyal she was to him, and there was no use trying to sway her thinking. "And why are you still here anyway? Aren't you supposed to be gone by now?"

"We thought you'd be out having fun with Drayna tonight." I remembered hearing somewhere of Drayna's plans for a night out after an obligatory appearance at one of her mother's parties and we had thought that Laena was included.

Rennick donned a sour look. "Ah, shit. I think I know what my sister is up to tonight." Given that look on his face from previous occasions, it meant that Drayna was planning to stay out all night, usually with male company included. She didn't think we all knew; Rennick had discussed it with us once, expressing his disgust over it. Drayna had a friends-with-benefits situation going on and thought it a secret from us.

Laena's scowl hadn't wavered. "You leave her alone. She's entitled to a good time."

"And you're not?" Reese gently asked. Sitting on the floor next to her, Reese made himself comfortable. "We're not your jailers either, Laena. You're allowed to go out and have fun."

"Yeah, but only if one of you is around, right? Can't have me going anywhere unsupervised because I just might turn on one of you." Something got into her head and made her distinctly more prickly today.

"Did something happen? Did your Dad get a hold of you?" Rennick guessed. When her face fell once again, Rennick's guess seemed to be spot on. I wondered how that would have happened; we've stuck close to her all this time, except for that Saturday when the girls made a quick shopping trip. When we had asked, Drayna had said Laena was out of sight for the ten or fifteen minutes it took for her to try on clothes. To me, that was time enough for any kind of message to get to Laena. But maybe not long enough for Laena to leave, meet her father, then come back before Drayna noticed anything amiss.

"Baby girl, you wanna talk about it?" I offered.

She turned her scowl on me. "Just because I'm a sobbing mess right now, doesn't mean that I'm ready to open up and share everything with you. You had me tased, remember?"

Shamed, the three of us knew she'd throw that it in our faces. However, I didn't fail to notice that she deftly avoided the topic of her father. Looking contrite, I sighed. "I know, and we're very sorry we did that to you. If you'd let us, we would love to make it up to you."

Narrowing her eyes suspiciously, she asked, "How? Can you turn back time and undo what you did?"

"Of course not. But we can be better for you. Do better." Rennick reached out to stroke a loose strand of her hair.

She sighed. With her eyes closed like that, it almost looked as if she could feel Rennick's touch through her hair, like a cat being petted. At the moment, she was nothing like the stony-faced, impassable woman of the past week. She looked vulnerable, scared, and small as she huddled there.

"I'm still mad at you for tasing me. If it weren't for that, I wouldn't be stuck here with you three. My choice to live a life free of your rules was taken from me because of it."

"We know. And you can be mad as long as you want, if it means that you'd stick around." Reese chuckled.

"Why is it so important to you that I do? Stick around, I mean."

Million-credit question. So, I spat out the answer I had ready for her this whole time. "If you could understand what it means not to share your most precious possession with the rest of the world because you're scared someone might break it, then maybe you might have a tiny window into what's behind our wanting to keep you."

She drawled out, "I guess so."

"In a world where men have to share one woman through a contest of marriage applications, it doesn't hold a lot of hope to have the woman we do want," Rennick explained.

"Believe us. We tried once and lost." Reese shook his head in disgust at the admission.

"Really?" she asked curiously, her tears forgotten. "I find that hard to believe with the three of you as well-known war-heroes."

"Even we're not immune to rejection," Rennick replied.

"When we saw you that day five years ago, you were like something pure and undiscovered, no one knowing you've ever existed except us. Can you understand that we, me especially, wanted something in our lives that we didn't have to share the knowledge of with anyone else? To me, denying you your freedom out there in the expanse meant keeping you safe from discovery by someone else." I sighed heavily, not meaning to pour out my heart into that answer, but there it was.

"Yeah, if it had been someone else who had found you out there, they wouldn't have been as kind or friendly." Reese said, point-blank.

"Then, why do you insist on butting into my life?" she almost screeched.

"Because we want you in ours. Are you that afraid of us?"

She shook her head no.

"That's good. There's no reason to be. If you trust us, we swear a taser will never come near you again."

A ghost of a smile appeared on her full lips, and I wanted nothing more than to lick them to discover their taste. She asked, "But if I have the taser, what then?"

"Then, to prove our point about making it up to you, you have my permission to use it on us." Reese said with an over-the-top sweeping gesture.

"Speak for yourself," Rennick retorted. "I can make it up to her in other ways more enjoyable than that." And he gave her his hand to help her up.

Laena had the innocence enough to look curious about that bit as she let Rennick bring her to a full stand. What Rennick said gave me ideas of ways I'd like to show her I was sorry, in ways that would make her feel good, and in turn, myself, as well.

Observing her closely, she no longer looked sad as she did earlier, and I guessed that the subject of the tasing had something to do with keeping her mind off of her father. I met her eye, and she gave me a strange look. I must have been staring too long because she taunted, "Finally, at a loss for words, Colonel Vance?"

I stepped up to her, and she plunked her hands on her hips as her gaze never left mine. "Ooo, you using your size to intimidate me? For what? You don't scare me."

Like I said, she was one frustrating, difficult woman to understand. I was eyeing her suddenly like I wanted to eat her up. My pulse jumped as she passed me a look that I took as sultry temptation.

"That's fine. I don't want you scared. If I'm going to make you scream, it's because you're being pleasured by me," I growled just before I tugged her into me and brought my lips down to cover hers. *Finally,* my head screamed as I pulled her even more tightly against me, and I demanded a response from her with my tongue. I ravaged her mouth, plundering the heat and wetness of her there, suddenly wanting all she was willing to give. God, did she give as good as she got! Her response was an equal match to what I took and gave.

Then, suddenly she was pulled away, and still affected by Laena's allure, I was dazed to find Rennick responsible for the loss of her from my arms.

"My turn," he explained when my expression turned thunderous. I softened a little watching with some satisfaction as Laena's mouth was taken skillfully by Rennick's eager lips. Watching one of my closest friends and a brother by choice ravage her mouth as hungrily as I did, I was proud that he was able to scatter Laena's thoughts from all else except what he was doing to her mouth. I surmised that it would take our combined skill—mine, Rennick's, and Reese's—to make sure there was no room for no one else in her mind except us. She was ours, and we were going to work as hard as needed to keep her.

"Wha--? Stop, I need to breathe!" Laena panted heavily to the point of gasping, as she pulled abruptly away from Rennick.

"Don't leave me out," Reese wailed. And he didn't give Laena room to back away, wrapping his arms around her and swooping in to match his lips to hers. She moaned in his mouth, as he delved into hers, tasting her deeply.

Kissing her affected all three of us; a glance at our crotches made it that much more obvious. Finally, kissing the woman who alluded us for so long made up for the lonely years without her. Now, we've discovered the secret to getting her to shut up, and I was sure it would be one of our favorite ways to get her to remain quiet.

Laena herself was just as affected by our kisses if the number of moans and gasps she uttered were any indication. Reese pulled away long enough to ask her, "How was that?"

She looked dazed and tried unsuccessfully to regain her customary calm and composure. "What was that?" she asked instead. She looked like what I assumed what butter would look like left out in the sun, completely soft and pliable.

I grinned. "That's what you would regularly receive if you'd give us a chance. Now we know you're not immune to us after all."

She protested, "Still not sure if this means that you're forgiven! I—it's just—I've never experienced anything like that before."

"And you're not likely to try that with anyone else," Rennick warned.

"What would happen if—" she started.

"We kill the other guy," Reese said, deadpan.

"No, I mean, what if I think we're not suitable? All of you are so convinced about me, but I still don't know about the three of you for me. I'm just a little bit confused by all of this."

"Just know, we won't rush you. But please don't make us wait too long," I urged.

"Yeah, as for you being suitable? Let us be the judge of that. We already know we like everything about you."

"Okay," she started slowly, "but if you are going all in, then you can't pursue any others."

"That's fair, as long as you promise the same," I answer easily. "Just so you know, there is no one else we're interested in, but you."

She didn't look convinced, but at least she made long strides in accepting us in a half-roundabout way. And the three of us were eager to take what we could get, ready to exercise what patience we had left to wait for her to come around.

10

VANCE

Over the coming weeks, little did we know how hard it was going to be to keep up with our Laena. It was like she was determined to be rid of us, but little did *she* know how much more determined we were to keep an eye on her and keep her safe.

She was going to be ours one day. The three of us just had to be patient enough to wait around until she realized that she belonged with us. If anything, she did us a favor by signing up as a cadet, keeping her out of the line of sight of others who would be higher on the list as her potential husbands. Reese, Rennick, and I had discussed everything; she was it for us. There wasn't going to be anyone else but her for us.

The day she had been cleared from Medical, we had not foreseen how well she'd do being thrown into getting settled as a cadet in the Elite's Cadet Corps. As her self-proclaimed protectors, the three of us had signed up immediately as instructors, specifically assigned to her unit. The staff sergeant had been taken aback by our sudden decision, but he had been immensely grateful to have experienced, blooded soldiers to be instructing the new recruits. It hadn't been too long until he realized our reason for being there and had even taken us aside to mention it.

"Look, I know you're trying your damnedest to not play favorites among the recruits, but it's more than obvious to me that Kanata is of special interest to you," Staff Sergeant Ripley had said dryly.

"How so?" I had asked mildly, frowning. I had thought that by being tougher on Laena—the guys agreeing with this tactic—she would want to jump ship and quit the Cadet Corps. We had already ensured that we would be on the top of the list when it came time for Laena to choose husbands, all thanks to Barclay Ardarien's hand in making it happen.

Ripley had replied in a tone just as dry as mine, "I'm not stupid. I've read her file, and I know you three discovered her out there in the boonies of the Outer Ring. I'm warning the three of you to let her be. She doesn't need you three harassing her."

"We're not harassing her," Reese protested defensively. "Have you seen her test scores? She's miles ahead of all the other recruits. Time after time, she's proven herself capable of handling anything we've thrown at her."

"Yes, and you need to back off," Ripley had warned. "I've got Councilman Ardarien breathing down my neck about her treatment." That had given me pause; Barclay Ardarien hadn't been as welcoming to Laena when he had first learned of her existence.

"Why does he care?" Rennick had fired back. We all knew how he reacted to Laena when he was brought to meet her. There was no love lost there on his part.

"All you need to know is that the Ardarien family are adopting her, registering her as part of their family," Ripley had said.

That tidbit of information had the three of us stunned. Knowing how Ardarien felt about Laena being a genetic impostor of his son, we had thought that he wouldn't want anything to do with her. Later, I had called my mother and fathers, who were all on the Elite Council and who knew the Ardariens well, and asked about this new development.

"Oh, didn't you know? Marguerite was thrilled to hear of a daughter to carry on the family name," my mother had oozed happily. "It was she who influenced Barclay to begin the adoption process, and we all know how doting he and her other husbands are on her."

When I asked why, Mom didn't hesitate to bring up how she would like grandchildren of her own and that Marguerite Ardarien had every right to want to carry on her family name through a daughter. Mom was unlucky enough to have only sons but had never held it against my brothers and me that she couldn't provide us with a sister. Only, Mom had no idea I had designs on Laena Kanata, soon to be Laena Ardarien. If the guys and I were very careful, we could be

Ardariens, too, once we married Laena. But I wasn't telling Mom or the Dads anything more until we were sure that Laena would be ours.

With drill training outside and now out of the way, I could tell that the cadets were happy it was the last thing on today's agenda. The sun had been unbearably vicious today, and I was awarded with tired smiles of relief when I announced we would be done early.

Having watched Laena all day, I noticed she made no complaint about the heat. Neither did she join in the chorus of happy whoops that sounded around the courtyard from the nineteen cadets grouped around her. Drayna, Rennick's sister, who had latched onto Laena from day one, tried to get Laena in on the suddenly relaxed atmosphere surrounding them. Drayna nudged Laena with an elbow while chatting companionably with her and eventually made Laena smile in response. It was good to see Laena loosening up a bit with people.

While they were still in formation, I had another announcement to make. "Cadets! Listen up! It's been exactly one month since you've started basic training. Now it's time to put what you've learned to good use."

Rennick and Reese stood on either side of me, while the men we had under our individual commands lined up behind and fanned out around us. "Starting today, we will be assigning each of you to patrol duty," I continued. "This is considered light duty and is required of all cadets. Each of you will be partnered up with one of us," I stated as I waved my arms out to indicate the row of men behind me.

Patrol duty was usually done by Elite Army soldiers who double-dutied as policemen. Cadets who began their training were also required to participate since we didn't have enough soldiers to work the whole city. I barked off the list of names along with who they were partnered with and what area. Since Laena was the newest recruit, she was reserved for last. "Kanata, you're with me. Inner Ring, Area 7."

"Everyone, report to Requisitions at 1900 to suit up for your assignments tonight! Dismissed!" I barked and everyone scattered in all different directions. Rennick and

Reese both gave me a look that warned *take care of our girl,* before they headed for their respective homes.

Laena, however, remained behind and by the pissed-off look on her face, I could only guess that she wasn't happy about her assignment. Since I was in charge of the assignments, I was genuinely looking forward to spending time with her tonight, even if it was for work.

"Colonel Vance, could I talk to you for a minute?" Laena asked.

"Of course." I was already smiling like a fool down at her.

"I've done everything you've asked of me, and now I'm being punished?" she said, squinting her eyes and scrunching her nose at me in disbelief.

"How do you think you're being punished, Laena?"

"By saddling me with you. Isn't it enough that I've done everything you've asked and then some in training? I've worked my butt off to prove to you and everyone that I'm not a threat."

Since her release from Medical and as her instructors, we were told to keep a close eye on her as per Barclay Ardarien's orders. Barclay had it in his head that we couldn't trust her, and that one day she would prove him right. In a way, Laena did the right thing by signing up as a cadet; if she hadn't, she would have been labeled as a spy, an assumed assassin, or worse. Then she would have been locked away for the safety of the public. And so, Laena had every reason to work doubly hard and keep her spot in the Cadet Corps. She would have been incarcerated otherwise.

"*We* know you're not a threat," I answered on behalf of Rennick and Reese, "but the rest of New Phoenix is still waiting to see what you'll do. Just be glad it's me and not Handsy McGrabsy Colton who you're paired up with. I'd hate to see what you'd do to him once he got grabby. So stop pouting."

"I'm not pouting," she said frowning. But she really looked like she wanted to kill me. And having seen her in combat training, she was a formidable and unstoppable opponent. Even when paired up with either me or another instructor, she flawlessly bested every single one of us and she looked amazing doing it. "Then, who did you pair with Captain Colton?"

I laughed at her concern. "Don't worry. I paired him with Cadet Riggs. As a strictly heterosexual male, I'm sure Riggs wouldn't let Colton's hands anywhere near his person. But on another note, why are you so opposed to being partnered with me?"

She looked slightly uncomfortable for a second before answering, "Because I don't think it's a good idea. Some of the cadets seem to think you give me special treatment."

"Are they harassing you?" I growled, my protective instincts rising to the fore.

"Well, no. But it gets brought up every now and then, and then I have to shut them up."

"And how do you shut them up?"

She blushed adorably, smiled, and said, "With a well-placed kick in a highly sensitive area."

Ah. So, it's one of the boys, then. There were only a handful of females in this cohort who had to prove themselves to be on equal footing with their male counterparts. And when they were subjected to occasional harassment from said males, we turned a blind eye to the girls' own brand of punishment served to their harassers.

"So what if you get special treatment? You know as well as I do that I put you through your paces harder than the others. Do they want that kind of treatment, too?"

She took a second to digest that, then shook her head no. "Please don't. I don't want to give them any more reason to pay attention to me."

I knew why she tried to keep a low profile. These cadets also came from well-placed families in the Elite, and they reported all they could about unknown Laena Kanata back to their families. Meaning it could get back to the Ardariens, who seemed to distress Laena whenever they came by for routine visits. I had meant to ask her why she was alarmed by their presence when she was so fearless with everyone else, but never got the chance.

I was about to ask just that, but she slapped me twice on the shoulder, turned away, and waved, "See you at nineteen-hundred. Gotta go eat. I'm starving!" Her pert ass swayed side to side as she walked away, leaving me with a hardening dick as I enjoyed the view.

I sighed, thinking that this woman successfully pulled me in all directions when she was near. One minute, I wanted to protect her from the tiniest threat, and the next minute, I was ready to drag her to the ground and have my way with her the second she graced me with a smile. And so, I kept to my constant reminder that good things come to those who wait.

But God! The things I want to do to her and with her! I had never felt this powerful urge to claim her, make her mine—make her *ours*. I couldn't help the attraction I felt the very first time I noticed her, and I haven't been able to curb the many fantasies I've had of her in my shower once again. Or the fantasies where she beckons me to join her in there, helping her lather her slippery wet curves with my brand of soap. For a solid month now, I've had to hold myself in check from showing her how much I want her; jacking off to thoughts of her just to ease the ache she makes me feel. A month in, and I've turned into one hulking frustrated horndog with blue balls the size of basketballs.

God help me.

Watching her closely during her first month of training, I could honestly say that everything she did astounded me. To the point that I would break into a sweat just watching how her petite lithe body moved like that. From the way she held a rifle and hit a moving target to grappling with a partner, she got me hot during the times I had no business thinking about her like that. I had always held myself to a standard of strict professionalism with my work, and Laena made it challenging to adhere to that standard whenever she was around.

It wasn't easy to keep my hands to myself, especially during training exercises, but there were times I'd deliberately touch her under the guise of instructing or correcting. A hand to the shoulder in affirmation of a command; a pat on the head when she did something well; or a well-timed brush of my hand against hers. I couldn't help it; this need for physical contact became something of an obsession.

Laena doesn't know how tightly she has me wound up. I promised myself that once she says the word, I'm not holding anything back. But until that day, it's hands off until the guys and I can persuade her that she's meant for us and us only.

At nineteen hundred, the senior officers on patrol duty stood off to the side as they waited for the cadets to finish gearing up for the evening shift. I spotted Laena right away as she strapped on her tactical vest, keeping an eye on those around her. I had to admire how Laena never let anyone around her get the drop on her by keeping everyone in sight.I stepped into her line of vision once she picked up her standard issue SIGPRO SP 2009, and I watched admiringly as she quickly inspected the weapon before holstering it at her hip. I smiled at the confidence she oozed while she quickly racked the slide to the rear, making sure it stayed open and locked, then pressing the mag release. Slamming the magazine back into place, she released the slide forward, and she gave a small hum of satisfaction at the smooth workings of the gun's mechanisms. Safety flicked on, she holstered the weapon and looked up at me.

"Ready to go, sir," she said in a businesslike tone. Reese and Rennick swiveled their heads our way at the sound of her voice. Those two have been just as attuned to her as I have. I nodded at them as my way of saying, *I'm taking care of our girl*, and they nodded back before heading off with their charges in tow.

"Let's go," I said as I waved her in the direction of our vehicle. Patrol duty on any other night in any other district would have been just a regular night. But we were heading to Area 7, a rougher neighborhood that required a more experienced hand in dealing with its unruly residents. We sent more patrol units to Area 7 than any other area for that reason.

Even with Laena being a new recruit, she had proved herself physically capable of dealing with the undesirables of Area 7. I had no doubt she could dish out her own brand of kickass on anyone dumb enough to mess with her. Plus, our assignment tonight involved following a lead on an illegal fighting den. One that profited on the blood spilled by poverty-stricken citizens looking to make quick cash.

As we drove past the Inner Circle's walled perimeter, I wondered if Laena's own mysterious past may have touched on something as underworld as this fighting den. It wasn't too far from where she supposedly lived in Area 5, so it wasn't too much of a stretch to speculate if it was even a thing.

I would have asked her about it if she didn't have her body angled away from me and if she didn't have ear buds jammed in her ears. This would be the first time we've been alone together since that one time in my bathroom, and I had been looking forward to this evening. Even if it was only for work. And because she had been working so hard for the past month, I thought she might appreciate me showing her that it doesn't always have to be about the job.

The guys and I thought it would be good for Laena to show her how to cut loose a little and relax her guard. At least, around one of us. Not once have I seen her with her guard down, and Drayna had confessed to Rennick that she had never seen Laena in off-duty mode. And that was when they were both off duty after hours.

And while Rennick may think that Laena's dedication is 'adorable', as he put it, I don't think this version of Laena will get us anywhere with her. Not if we want to win her as our wife. And so, without putting a rush on things or any undue pressure on Laena, I thought that tonight I could get her to open up if it was just the two of us.

Here's to hoping.

11

LAENA

Ugh. On top of the news I'd received this morning, now this.

I didn't count on spending the evening with Vance, and in fact, I would have spent it figuring out what to do about this latest development. The Ardariens wanted to adopt me? At my age? Why bother at all when I'm a full-fledged adult?

Oh, but wait. Females are treated like princesses because of breeding potential and our only rights afforded us are the ones involving which partners we would want as our mates. Dad had taught me that feminism died a quick death once humanity was in danger of extinction.

All of these thoughts spun around in my head as the music ebbed through my ear buds as background noise. The ear buds in my ears also served to keep the man who sat just a few feet away from striking up a conversation. While I didn't feel like talking, it irked me that every cell in my body was acutely conscious of him being close by. I hated to admit that his nearness was affecting my thought processes, when usually I have no problems thinking things through logically.

Apparently, logic flew out the window the moment Vance slid into the driver's seat next to me. Since then, I've been on high alert, all of my senses highly sensitized to this man who looked and smelled like my own personal brand of yummy goodness. I've never before been so tightly wound up because of a man. Or in my case, because of three of them.

At least, just for tonight, I only have one of them to deal with, and I thought that I could keep my unruly emotions in check if only one of them was in close proximity. But I hadn't counted on the actual experience of being this close to Vance to wreak so much havoc on said emotions. I had no idea that another person could cause such an unpredictable reaction in me, and I was very much opposed to it. Especially when I held myself to a pretty rigid standard, thanks to Dad's teachings.

Speaking of Dad, I was missing him so much today and couldn't stop thinking of him after I had gotten the Ardarien's adoption *notice*. It wasn't even a request to ask me if it was something I wanted. Clearly, that family had never been told no and didn't know how to ask for things nicely. Dad would want to know about this, but there was no way of knowing where he was or what he's currently doing for me to get word to him.

Plus, I hadn't gotten very far with the mission he'd given me; the one to research more into my past. Cadet training hadn't left me with a lot of free time, and what little free time I did have was spent at the training center gym. I also didn't think using the computer workstations in the cadet classrooms would be suitable for such an in-depth search.

Where would I even begin to look? The only thing that had me thrust into this world was the revelation of my weirdly identical genetics to Kane Ardarien. Maybe once the adoption was finalized, I would be closer to the very family I'd be tied to, and maybe they might let me have a laptop or tablet of my own. I could start my search once I had a better machine to work with. And maybe delving into the Ardariens' own background might help me find the answers I'm looking for.

For the moment, I really wished Dad was around to give me clues. And guidance. The past month without him was a big shock for me. I had never lived among so many people before, and it had been so awkward for me. I had no clue how to navigate social situations, and if it weren't for Drayna Rennick, I would have been totally lost.

Without her I wouldn't have known it wasn't improper to walk bare-assed throughout our barracks. She taught me how to do things in a more civil manner, like table manners. How to be courteous. How to behave around the few women who were cadet recruits like us. I had no idea that there were behavioral differences between the sexes. Because of her, I learned about sarcasm. With her around, I finally had a friend along with a few others she was also close to.

A woman like me was a true anomaly among our cadet class. One who didn't have a family background as extensive as the others. When asked where I had come from, I made up a story of having been found living in the "wilds" of the Outer Ring of New Phoenix. Like I had only been born at the moment Vance, Rennick, and Reese had found me. I didn't dare bring Dad into the conversation; if he was still in hiding, I didn't want nosy officials looking into who and where he was. As it was, no one was really interested in what I had been doing up until that point.

No one, except for Barclay Ardarien. While Marguerite Ardarien had the adoption papers drawn up, I guessed that Barclay wasn't too keen on the idea but had no choice in the matter when she was determined to have me in the family. Just the same, it didn't stop Barclay from sniffing around asking questions about me. And the handful of times he had dropped by the barracks to ask me questions of his own, I had to wonder why the man hated me so much.

Who was your father? Who did he work for? Why would he train you like a soldier?

Those were just some of the questions he had fired at me over and over, and every time I had no concrete answer to satisfy him. He gave up once he realized he wasn't getting anywhere and left in a very sour mood.

Before I could even guess why he kept coming back to interrogate me, Vance called out, "We're here."

Here was Area 7, a den of iniquity for those looking to profit from illegal activities. Dad had brought me here once or twice, usually under the cover of night, to broker some kind of deal. Why he had needed me there with him, I couldn't even begin to guess, but both times were fuzzy memories in the back of my brain.

Jumping out of the vehicle, I followed Vance down the narrow alley and out into a major street. The street itself was enlightened with neon signs everywhere and bustling with activity, both of the human and the AI kind. Holographic images hawked their virtual wares, be it gambling, kink, or some other form of hedonistic entertainment. People milled up and down the street, some either selling or in search of the next high.

The people we passed didn't react much to our presence; our uniforms clearly stating who we were and what we were there to do. Only a few hostile glances were aimed our way, the only form of aggression we were dealt so far. Vance and I walked side-by-side while he whispered, "Stay alert. They don't appreciate the presence of the Elite Army here, but we're here as peacekeepers."

I nodded, getting it. Then taking a page out of Drayna's book, I teased, "So, not everyone here would appreciate *your* being here, with you being a celebrated Elite Army hero?"

Vance looked taken aback, but he smiled warmly at me. "What would you know about that?" he asked.

"Only what the women in my barracks say about you. They say you have a following of fans everywhere you go."

He chuckled, "Not everywhere. Area 7, for instance. Do you see my fans following us now?"

"No, and I'm glad."

He perked up at that. Peering down at me closely, he asked, "Why does that make you glad?"

"Because that wouldn't be very productive to our job tonight. We can't have an unstable crowd distracting us," I said. Meanwhile, my heart pounded at the way he looked at me then. Like he was expecting more than the practical answer I had given him. And I seemed to keep forgetting that I'm still pissed at him and the other two for tasing me.

Coming to a fork in the street, I stopped mid-stride, also wanting to stop my train of thoughts involving his lips. He had gotten too close for my own comfort, and I faced straight ahead. "Where to?" I asked, masking my sudden bout of nerves with a voice that was steadier than I was actually feeling.

"We go right," he said, brushing past me to take the lead. While there were still people crowding the streets, there weren't as many brightly lit signs or hologram ads flashing here.

"Stay close and watch my back," Vance urged. "There are less cameras down this stretch. If we were to get jumped, this would be the place to do it."

I nodded in response, keeping an eye out over my shoulder. I surveyed my surroundings, looking for spots that could easily hide someone who would be stupid enough to jump either of us.

Vance led us to a dimly lit side alley, and he beckoned me to follow. "Come on!"

Without questioning what we were doing there, I quickly followed. I trusted Vance to know what he was doing, but at the same time, I wondered where such a blind trust would lead me. It wasn't like me to jump all in with trust shining in my eyes, especially after being warned all my life not to trust anyone. But Vance and the others had never given me a reason *not* to trust them, besides the tasing. They were actually a solid group of people, who lived up to their celebrated status as heroes.

Squeezing past a narrow entrance that he had jimmied open, Vance went on ahead of me, still waving me over to keep up. Clearly, this was a lesser used entrance as it was blanketed in darkness. I wouldn't have known it was there until Vance had pried it open, and I carefully made my way through the equally narrow hallway. The floor below my feet vibrated with the noise coming from somewhere deep into the building, and it sounded like a large crowd cheering as a commentator on a mic animatedly described the real-time action.

Close behind Vance, I tapped him on the shoulder. He turned just his head to look back at me with a side glance, and he mouthed, "Fight club."

Immediately, those words threw me back to a time when I was twelve, and Dad had brought me to one of these. But only to observe while deep in the shadows. Dad had dragged me there, made me watch, and then asked me to spot the weaknesses of the fighters in the ring. We argued between ourselves the best way to end the fight, and I had always sided on ending the fight quickly. Dad had liked to include some elements of style to the resolution of the fight, and I had argued against drawing it out so long.

We continued deeper into the building, and I finally took a closer look around. It was quiet back here, but we weren't alone. There were a number of people, about five or six by my count, who were locked up behind a chain-link fence and dressed in worn-out battle gear. Usually, the people who did the fighting in the ring were one of two types. They either were there for the pure enjoyment of the sport or they had been coerced into fighting as a way of trying to pull themselves out of poverty. Mostly the latter made up the majority of those in the ring, but almost none of them made it in the rounds very far. In other words, none of them survived past the first or second round.

Vance had gone further ahead of me, signaling silently to let me know he was checking things out in the overcrowded arena. And so, I found myself alone, staring back at the forlorn looking people behind the fence. I drew up short to find a boy, no older than about fourteen, hunched in the back corner. This was no place for minors, and if he was behind that fence, then it could only mean that he was meant to fight in the ring sooner or later. Rage almost overtook me at the thought; the boy was too young and probably untried in the dirty ways that lowlifes use here.

I approached the fence and waved the boy over. He didn't move, but he watched me. "What's your name?" I asked.

"Wade," he answered, the look in his eye, wary as hell.

"What are you doing here, Wade? This place isn't meant for someone like you."

His face hardened, and he spat, "You sayin' I'm too young? That I'm too young to fight?"

He shook his head in disgust, and continued, "I'm also too young to be taking care of three younger brothers who haven't had anything to eat in the past three days. Our dads all shoved off when the money ran out, and Mom can barely make enough to feed all five of us. If I win this fight, they'll give me triple what they paid me for signing up. Still think I don't need to be here?"

I pursed my lips together, mostly to keep myself from biting his head off with a quick retort. I had known what it was like to go hungry, but that had usually been because my hunting forays weren't successful. Dad had taught me that if I really wanted to eat, I had to work hard for it.

But what really got me going was that Wade felt that this was his only resort. "Listen, the fact that you're here means that the people running this show don't give a shit about you. They're making money by banking that you'll do everything wrong in the ring. Believe me, I know how those fuckers think."

"You sayin' I'm gonna lose? What if you're wrong?" The hard look in his eye was pure steel.

"I'm saying that no matter what skills you've learned, they'll be throwing in something impossible for you to beat. Your odds in that ring are slim to none."

Uncertainty clouded his hardened features. He was obviously second guessing his choice coming here. "Then what should I do? I was told that I'd be up next."

Thinking fast, I came up with a plan that would later seem ridiculous. Vance hadn't come back here to check on me, and I was glad he didn't. For this to work, I couldn't have him stop me.

Guards came through what I now know as the "backstage area", and one of them bellowed Wade's name. Without answering, I stood up at the summons from the corner I had occupied. I was lucky that Wade and I were the same height and of similar build; his battle gear fit me snugly and his helmet's visor shielded my features just enough in the dim light. I had discarded my Elite protective gear in favor of Wade's own shoddy vest, and my dark clothes matched Wade's own dirty ones. No one would tell the difference unless they looked too closely.

Before leaving backstage, I turned towards Wade who huddled in a dark corner, unnoticed, and I offered him a tiny salute. He watched me leave with wide eyes, still unsure as to how far he could trust me. I did promise him the winnings from the first round and no more than that; I didn't want him getting too greedy.

I followed the guards through a short, dark hallway until we finally emerged into the arena. Bright spotlights aimed my way, blinding me at first, but the guard behind me pushed me forward and onward when I faltered a step. The roar of the crowd almost deafened me, and it took me a while before I realized they were booing at me.

I had no idea where Vance was, but at the moment I didn't care. I had a fight to win, and I had been itching to do what I did best for a while now. Cadet training had nothing on what I had been trained to do and here was my one opportunity to save a life and kick ass while doing it.

Getting closer to the ring, I saw it was entirely encased in chain-link fencing except for the two entrances opposite of each other. I entered one entrance as the guards shoved me roughly inside and locked the gate behind me. My opponent had yet to enter so I stood alone in the ring while the crowd's cacophonous voices rang around me.

A large, hooded figure struggled drunkenly towards the opposite entrance, pushed, and prodded forward by two burly men. They held the hooded captive by two poles hooked to the figure's collar. Already I could smell the fetid stench coming from the newcomer, and I realized who I was going to be fighting.

Or rather, *what* I was going to be fighting.

I tuned out the sudden cheer that erupted from the crowd at the newcomer's entry into the ring. The hood had been ripped off and the poles removed from his collar before the guards hastily made their exit and locked the gate behind him. I was now alone with an Eidolon monster.

Thinking about poor Wade, I inwardly raged at the thought of pitting a young, inexperienced boy against a monster as big and hungry as this one. This one wasn't too advanced in its rotting state and still had most of its bulky muscle mass intact, meaning I would have to be careful not to let it grab me. Once it did, it would never let go, hell-bent on keeping me in its clutches until it ate every bit of me.

But I wasn't going to let that happen. Now that it had been discovered that I was immune to Eidolon, I wasn't ready for it to be public knowledge, and I was doubly determined to make sure Wade and his family had the money to put supper on the table tonight.

As the giant Eidolon monster let out a roar upon spotting me, I rushed forward, bent on meeting it head-on.

12

VANCE

I panicked when I couldn't find Laena backstage, but a small boy I almost didn't notice behind the fenced cage pointed in the direction I had just come from. "She's out there. In the ring."

Not believing him at first, I froze in my tracks as the meaning of his words sunk in. "What do you mean she's in the ring?"

"She took my place so I wouldn't have to fight. She promised me the winnings though."

I took off running back towards the arena, no longer caring who saw me in uniform. All I cared about was Laena and getting to her as fast as I could.

I had to fight my way ringside; those closest to the ring had gotten out of their seats to crowd what little space was left around it. Elbowing and shoving my way through, no one spared me a glance as it was the action happening inside the ring that had them all enthralled. It took some doing, but I finally got a better view by climbing onto the chain link fence and gripping a post.

Inside the ring, I watched, horrified as Laena rushed headlong into the monster. Someone had spared the expense of finding one that was freshly turned and hadn't yet lost its basic motor skills. From the looks of it, it must have once been a bruiser who was used to fighting with such muscle girth, and it reacted quickly to Laena's threatening offense.

Laena surprised us all as she darted faster than our eyes could follow, zipping past the creature's beefy arms and dodging around until she was behind it. I had only seen her move like that once before, and I remembered feeling the same amount of awe as I do now. But this time, it was diluted with fear for her; fear that the show runners might scheme against her chances of winning just to increase their profits.

I didn't breathe for a full minute as I watched her suddenly go on the offensive. As small as she was, she was still a force to be reckoned with, and she didn't even have a weapon close to hand except for what she was born with. With powerful strikes, punches, and kicks, Laena slowly reduced the rotting monster to just a bag of tenderized sinew and flesh sagging around its bones. The crowd went wild at her results and cried for more. I remained silent, half-afraid I'd jinx her if I spoke aloud.

Yet, the Eidolon creature still tried to lunge for her despite what she had done to its frame. Only now, its arms were twisted off of its sockets and his jaw kicked clean off by one of her kicks of massive force. It couldn't bite her even if it tried, but its one directive to reach out for live flesh was still driving it towards her. The ring was now coated in the creature's blood and gore, but Laena carefully maneuvered through it like she was skating on a frozen river, intent on delivering the final blow.

Everyone expected her to give them a show, and she completely delivered with her big finish. She broke into a sprint away from the creature and towards the opposite end of the ring. The creature lumbered in her direction, intent on her alone. To me, it looked as if she was deliberately trapping herself in the corner with the Eidolon creature, and my heart rate sped up with what that could mean for her.

But Laena surprised everyone by running up the chain link just as the creature was two steps behind her. The crowd roared again when she back flipped over the creature's head and used its shoulders to vault behind it. However, she maintained her grip on the creature, using the momentum to bring it down over her head. Cheers erupted all around as she used a booted foot to smash straight through its skull, earning her a win.

With the creature dead at her feet, I heavily exhaled the breath I had been holding for most of that fight. The fight might have only lasted about three minutes, but it had felt like a fucking eternity for me. Before I could get to her, the chaos around me escalated as she was declared the winner and escorted out of the ring with the prize voucher in hand.

Because she had finished under four minutes, she won a total of twelve-thousand credits, triple the amount of the original four hundred promised to the winner.

Fortunately, no one had thought to remove her helmet to further expose who she was to the world. I had guessed that Laena took it upon herself to replace the boy from backstage, all while concealing who she was. Having seen Laena's "opponent", it didn't take a genius to figure out that the boy would have been the creature's next meal if she hadn't intervened.

Still covered in gore, Laena rushed past everyone to get backstage. People gave her a wide berth probably because of the stench of the creature surrounding her, but it was probably more plausible that they did it out of respect for her and her wildly imaginative fighting skills. I quickly followed after her, mostly to shield her getaway, but she was ten steps ahead of me.

When I caught up to her backstage, I saw her hand over the prize voucher to the young boy whom I had seen earlier. She quickly gave him back the battle gear she had worn into the ring and placed it on him before shuffling back to me. The boy flashed her a grateful smile before disappearing into the crowd outside.

She looked almost sheepish as she got closer, and I could do no more than stare back at her in stunned awe. "I've never seen anyone fight the way you just did."

"That's probably because I had never let anyone see me fight until now," she said shyly.

That got me wondering the reason why that was. She clearly had skill that seemed to surpass anything I've ever seen in anyone else. And if her unknown past was any indication, then Laena's AWOL father maybe did the right thing by keeping her a secret. Everything about Laena screamed of mystery and untold depths that I was just starting to discover, and it occurred to me that maybe there was a very good reason for keeping Laena out of the limelight, so to speak.

"Do you know that what you just did, would have been impossible for anyone else?" I told her, as we left the building, heading back towards our vehicle. Our assignment was only to observe the goings-on and report what we saw. Although there were so many counts of illegal activities I had seen tonight, we couldn't bust everyone in the building with only two of us. We would have needed the entire Elite Army to back us up.

Laena shrugged and said, "Couldn't someone like you, Reese, or Rennick do something like that? You guys are supposed to be the heroes in this city."

Truth was, the three of us hated being known as New Phoenix's answer to keeping the Eidolon-cursed at bay. Sure, we've been known to take down hordes at a time, but we were hoping to pull away from that part of our careers and seriously think about settling down. Putting ourselves at risk daily was no way to keep our chosen female safe, and we thought it was time to switch out our priorities.

"But I wasn't in that ring. Neither were the guys. Our battles happened out there, outside city walls, not inside them. We fought to survive, not for sport."

Frowning at me, she asked, "Do you think I did that just to put on a show?" The way she looked at me then was warning enough for me to watch my words carefully. One wrong answer, and I was sure I'd get my head bitten off.

"No, but you put yourself at risk unnecessarily." We had stopped at an alleyway at this point, where I had dragged her to keep this conversation between us alone.

She exploded, "That boy would have lost his life for nothing if I hadn't stepped in! He was there because he had no other choice!" Her eyes blazed back at me in furious indignation, clearly believing she had no other alternative either.

"You could have talked with me first! It didn't have to be only you to decide how he survived!"

"There was no time for that!"

"And you didn't have to put yourself in that ring just to save him!"

"Then what do you suggest I should have done?"

"Radioed me and let me know what was going on! It's not your duty alone to save everyone who's in trouble!"

"It was my call to make! Even if I did call you, there wouldn't have been time for you to get backstage to help him. He would have been a monster's dinner tonight if I didn't take his place!"

Furious as I was with her impulsive behavior, I had to concede that I wouldn't have gotten there in time to help. The boy would have been rushed into that ring so fast, he wouldn't have had time to scream before he was ripped apart by the gargantuan Eidolon creature. I also couldn't move past the fact that Laena had put herself in danger willingly for a strange boy, with no thought to her own safety. That thought alone was enough to give me nightmares; she was meant to be ours to treasure and keep safe. The guys and I had promised this amongst ourselves.

Before she could scream at me one more time, I did the one thing that would stem the flow of words coming from that beautiful mouth.

Catching her quickly off guard, I swooped in to kiss the bejesus out of her. Finally, I was tasting the lips I had been aching to feel against my own, and to my surprise, I didn't get a punch to the face like I expected. Because she opened that sweet mouth beneath mine, I took that to mean I could thoroughly explore and taste her like I had been wanting to for almost a month.

The instant my lips touched hers, I felt electrified from the inside-out. She felt and tasted amazing, like she was everything I didn't know I needed. The fact that she was an eager participant in our kiss had all my blood rushing south, my mind whirling with one thought, *I want this woman bad.*

I loved that she let me push her up against the wall behind her as I continued to ravage her mouth with mine. It felt amazing to feel her smaller frame pressed into me, and suddenly I went straight from only wanting her to full-on *needing* her. With her in my arms, I've felt more alive with her than with anyone else.

Gasping as she broke away from the kiss, she panted, "Vance? What--?"

Before I could let her finish, I needed to taste her again. I was that hungry for this little slip of a woman who proved herself selfless despite her inability to think of her own safety. Once again, I mashed our lips together, our teeth crashing against each other, as I proceeded to arouse her on kisses alone. She moaned as I slid my arms around her to push her further into me using her ass as an anchor point. With handfuls of her ass in both of my hands, I shoved her groin into mine, and then it was my turn to groan at the feel of her grinding against my aching, hard dick.

The need for her overrode all thought except for the one that rode me to take her, to claim her now. I knew she was a virgin, and I knew that her own response to me was unschooled and inexperienced. But she was matching me move for move, her own arousal evident when I dipped a finger inside her pants, inside her panties to find her wet. Using the heel of my palm, I rubbed against her clit, applying enough pressure to make her throw her head back and moan.

Eyeing me head-on, she gasped, "Vance! That feels so good!" On a primal level, I was elated that the look in her eyes was fueled by the feelings of desire I inspired in her.

"Yeah? Tell me what else makes you feel good," I spurred her on.

"I-I don't know," she admitted weakly, still panting as I continued circling my palm against her. "I've never done anything like this before."

"I know, sweetheart. I'll take care of you," I promised. I knew she had never been with anyone before, but I wanted to make this good for her, memorable. An alleyway was no place to introduce her to what lovemaking was all about. If I wanted only sex, I wouldn't have cared if we were outdoors where anyone could see us.

I had been suffering from blue balls for the past month, and there was no way in hell I'd let go of her now. Not when I finally have her in my arms, enjoying my kisses and caresses. I couldn't wait to sink into her body, to feel her heat surrounding me.

But I wanted her first time, *our* first time, together to be about how good the *both* of us could be together, both physically and emotionally. Not to mention that I'd have to share her with Rennick and Reese and have her be comfortable with the idea. It was what we had always wanted, and the three of us had looked forward to the day when we would become part of a polyamorous group, protecting and loving the same woman.

For now, I was desperate to have her. Her innocent kisses were wreaking havoc on my self-control, especially since she was now licking the column of my throat. Suddenly it was imperative that we head someplace that had a bed. A dingy hotel here in Area 7 was not at all appealing. My house was a sterile, germ-free environment compared to one of those places.

"Let's go to my house," I said between kisses. "We can continue this there where we can be more comfortable." Looking down at her, I added, "And maybe you can revisit my shower. But this time, with me in there with you."

13

LAENA

"Yes," I agreed. My eyes almost crossed with lust at the thought of Vance and his ropy muscles all wet and on full display.

I had to agree that I needed to wash the gore off of myself, and I wondered how Vance could be so aroused at the sight of me all filthy and unkempt.

But my God! I had no idea I could get so lost in a few kisses and caresses! Never before have I lost my head over anything, and with a man at that! And I had completely forgotten about why I was supposed to be pissed at him in the first place!

I only knew I wanted more of what he was making me feel, and I didn't want it to end. Didn't want reality to intrude on a moment I never thought I would have the pleasure of experiencing for myself.

Over the past few weeks, I'd been exposed to more kindness and careful concern from Vance and the others, and I'd been slowly letting go of my grudge against them in the face of their care and compassion. They had pled their case the day they found me crying in the equipment shed, and they hadn't brought it up again since.

But they didn't have to.

They were worming their way slowly into my heart with their heart-stopping smiles and devastatingly hungry looks aimed my way. All it had taken was for them to show me their true selves, their capacity to love, and their willingness to wait for me. And it thrilled my cold, little lonely heart that these three were so strong in their devotion. I felt that I no longer had any defenses left against such strong evidence of their desire and attraction for me.

And I was ultimately curious about what it would mean to be ravished by these three. To completely surrender to my own desires concerning them. Tonight would be chance to find out what it would be like with at least one of them.

Leading me by the hand, Vance half-dragged me across the street to reach our utility vehicle. I sobered a little, the sight of the vehicle reminding me of the reason of our being out here in the first place. My first official assignment as a cadet, and I ended up making a spectacle of myself, both inside that fight club then later in a dingy alley with Vance.

Never mind that I completely disregarded Dad's edict to stay inconspicuous. And on top of that, men were never supposed to feature in Dad's plans for me. Or at least, Dad had never made mention of whether or not they were allowed in my future. It just wasn't a topic either of us had brought up.

But that wasn't to say I never thought about it. Living on the outskirts of society as we did, I had watched and learned. Women, young ones around my age especially, seemed to hold all the power in choosing life mates, and I had been curious about that. About what it might be like to be the focus of not just one man, but several.

Living alone with Dad, I never got the chance to find out what it was like to choose that direction in life. It just didn't seem to be in the cards for me, not when Dad kept telling me that I had a higher purpose. Still hadn't figured out what that purpose is just yet.

Just moments before, Vance had touched me in places I didn't think would make me heat from the inside out. His touch was so electric and intriguing; it was so much different than when I did it to myself. Since that dream I had of Vance, Rennick, and Reese, I had quickly learned about my body's response to certain touches in certain places. That dream had taught me all about feelings I had never encountered before, all-new sensations I was ready to explore.

Because of my newfound curiosity, I had mistakenly tried to make such discoveries in a place not suited for such an activity. Drayna had caught me in the communal showers touching myself, just like the way the guys did in my dream. She had gently set me aside to tell me that kind of thing was not meant for public display. I remembered her chuckling softly at my naivete, and I was only slightly embarrassed when she mentioned that she was all about self-love but that it was best suited for when one was alone.

Embarrassment overridden, I had learned how to touch myself just to lessen the ache every night that dream would return, alone in my bunk. I had learned which places on my body were more sensitive than others, and most of all, I had discovered that my touch alone was not enough to assuage the ache.

And therefore, I've discovered that I do in fact possess the ability to be aroused. Problem was, there were only three men on this Eidolon-ridden planet that could inspire such arousal. One of them being not more than three feet away from me at the moment.

How the hell do I reconcile all of these new feelings while keeping focus on Dad's mission? All my life, it had been drilled into me that my existence was important and yet I had to hide who I was. But I still haven't found a single clue as to who Laena Kanata even was. For now, all I knew was that I wanted to find out more about whatever this was between Vance and me.

We sat in silence as Vance sped through the streets, yet the tension inside the vehicle was charged with something ignitable. If one of us spoke one word, I was pretty sure that one or both of us would combust. Soon enough, we pulled up in front of Vance's house, and I could swear that every cell in my body vibrated in anticipation of what would happen next.

Just like he did when he had first brought me here, Vance got out first and rounded the front of the vehicle to open my door. Only this time, he forcefully pulled me out of my seat and out of the vehicle. The urgency was still there as he looked at me with an emotion that looked halfway like hunger and another emotion I couldn't name. Could it be desire that I'm seeing? Again, another emotion I've only observed from afar on the faces of men who were either pursuing an intended wife or on the men who were already happily married to their one fated female.

Once inside and the door slammed behind us, Vance grabbed me and slammed me up against a wall, not unlike what he had done to me in the alley earlier. Mashing his lips against mine, he moaned as I gave as good as I got in that singular kiss. He was about to strip me down until he looked down at me, and said, "Oh, right. Shower first. Let's go."

Grabbing me again by the hand, he led me upstairs to his bathroom, invoking the memory of my first time in there. But this time, we were going to shower *together*. A wave of giddy anticipation rose up inside me, and I almost giggled at the thought that this would be my first time seeing a man fully nude.

Both of us wasted no time stripping out of our gear and our uniforms until finally we stood in the nude, facing each other. My mouth watered at the sight of Vance, his bronzed skin encasing hard muscle all over, his body a prime example of strength and beauty wrapped in one package. And my God, the sight of his hardened dick was enough to make me a little nervous, having only discovered recently how that appendage was used in the sex act.

How the hell was that monstrous thing going to fit inside me? I didn't think that was physically possible, but since the propagation of the human race was dependent on such mechanics I had to concede that it must work somehow.

He moved to fiddle with the taps, adjusting the temperature of the spray he had just turned on. Then he turned to me to lead me inside. I could practically feel the heat of his desire with him this close, but he gently tugged me into the shower without further preamble. Once under the deliciously warm spray of water, Vance took it upon himself to lather me up with his own soap. His hands, now slippery with suds, traveled lazily around my body, scrubbing away the grime with slow strokes that heightened my arousal once again.

Turning to him, I grabbed the soap from him and reciprocated. The both of us scrubbed each other, while treating each other with the most sensual caresses. It was all so highly exciting, and I loved every bit of it. I loved the feel of a man's strong fingers gliding across my soap-slicked skin. I loved feeling the heat of his breath skating across my face as he watched where he guided his hands around me. I especially loved the feel of chasing the soap bubbles across his own work-hardened muscles.

How lucky was I to be doing this with a man I knew so many other women went stupid for? Myself, included. Only I wasn't just hot for this very wet, very naked man before me; I had to be greedy and fall for two others.

This early in the game, I didn't think it was prudent to play the type of run and chase games that women played. I had often observed many other girls playing these kinds of head games with the men they were truly interested in. So, my first foray into sex and desire would have to be more direct without any of the hemming and hawing. If I wanted this—and I believed I would die if I didn't have this man—I was going to go all in.

I was driven by pure instinct, and I thought why not test what I could do to this man that he wasn't already doing to me. His hand was already buried between my legs, and in turn I reached for his granite-hard cock.

"God, that feels good," he groused as I kept a firm grip around him, sliding my fist slowly up and down his length. Tit for tat, he stroked that little button of pleasure hidden between my folds with more pressure. I gasped at the zing of heat that his treatment caused.

"You like that?" he whispered in my ear as I let my head fall onto his shoulder. Pulling me closer, he continued the delicious way he handled me as I quickened my strokes on his dick.

I found heat enveloped me everywhere: from him, from the showerhead, and from the inside. How anyone endured this without overheating I couldn't fathom, but I guessed that the entire human race would have been obliterated a long time ago if that were the case.

And here I found myself conflicted. I wanted more of what Vance could give me, yet I also wanted relief from the rising heat that threatened to make me go up in flames. "Vance," I said his name like I was begging. But I couldn't say more than a gasp or a groan from what he was doing to me.

"Tell me what you want, Laena," he purred as a finger of his slipped past my folds to discover my body's own wetness there. "I know you're ready, but you have the power here. Tell me what you want me to do."

I shook my head in frustration. I didn't know what I wanted except for the ache between my legs to be appeased somehow. "Just make me feel good. I'll let you show me what that means. I promise I'll like it all."

"Are you sure?" he said, dead serious. "If you let me take control, it might get a little rough."

I smiled up at him. "Didn't you see me fight in that ring tonight? I think I can handle rough. Anything I don't like will be treated with a fist to your nose."

Grinning broadly enough for tiny wrinkles to appear at the outer corner of his eyes, Vance chuckled out, "Deal!" Shutting off the water, Vance hustled us both out of there fast enough to make my eyes water at the speed he got us out of there and into his bedroom.

I bounced a few times when Vance tossed me onto his bed, and the momentary loss of Vance's body heat chilled my water-slicked body. Soon enough, Vance covered my body with his own, his body heat seeping into my skin, igniting me once again from the inside.

I loved the feeling of his weight on top of me, a sensation that was brand new and incredibly delectable. He captured my mouth with his, close to devouring me whole with his mouth alone. His tongue swept inside, swirling against my own tongue. I hungrily accepted his kiss, as I clutched at his back, trying to shove more of his weight into me.

Vance kept my body pinned beneath his as he used one thigh to wedge between my thighs. I let him settle himself there, my knees bending to fan my legs further open and to align his hips where I wanted them. His cock settled heavily against my clit, the pressure there so delicious, but Vance made no move to finalize the act I had been wondering about.

While his hands wandered all around my body, his mouth still occupied with mine, Vance's hips remained unmoving against me. The arousal that his touches heightened within me incited me to urgently yell, "Vance! I need you to move!" In response, he let go of my mouth to move lower, kissing his way down to my breasts.

"Not yet. You need to come first," he crooned against one of my nipples. Then his mouth surrounded one nipple, sucking gently at it. I cried out at the heavy pull he made on it, and a large tidal wave of hot feeling crashed through me as he prolonged the sucking.

I writhed beneath him while he worked on both nipples, and I wanted something to counter the ache that grew between my legs. With the whimpers that escaped from my lips in increasing frequency, Vance slowly moved further down my body until he settled his arms beneath my bent legs to cup my bottom.

I brought my head up to see what he was doing, and I was almost unsettled by the directness of his gaze locking with mine. I could feel the heat of his breath against my groin, and that slight caress made me ache more for any kind of contact down there.

Thinking back on what he said, I had to ask, "What do you mean I come first? Doesn't this require the two of us to be participating?"

He chuckled directly against my mound, the vibration intensifying the ache against my sensitized body. "It means that I'm gonna make sure you feel really good before I take your virginity."

"Oh." And before I knew it, I was being rhythmically licked down there. Every flick of his tongue against a spot of highly sensitized nerves shot upsurges of delicious heat through my body, and I felt myself clenching against nothingness where I ached to be filled.

Vance held me down by my hips as I writhed in sync with the lapping of his tongue. I moved instinctively, trying to find a way on my own to soothe the ache he encouraged between my legs. Then, I felt something probing at my entrance, realizing belatedly that it must be one of his fingers. With a single digit, he slipped inside me, and my body momentarily clamped down at the welcome invasion.

I arched my back to better feel the pressure of his tongue against that miniscule spot above my entrance. I gasped loudly when he changed tactics and began curling his fingers inside as he pistoned them in and out of me. Aware that those curling motions increased my pleasure, I didn't know how to ask for some kind of unknown pinnacle that seemed just out of reach. I whimpered instead, and maybe even sobbed a little, but Vance seemed to understand when I met his gaze.

With renewed vigor, he picked up the pace with his tongue and fingers as I tried to lean my mound further into his face. I felt hot all over, inside, and out, and I found myself panting loudly with short, staccato breaths. In any other situation, I would have thought such noises coming from me as terribly embarrassing, but I didn't know how else to audibly respond to the mounting pleasure Vance created for me.

Suddenly, I felt this blast of heat explode from my core, right where Vance played with my body. That's when I understood that all the hard work Vance had put in was to bring me to this point. Not having anything else to compare this to, it felt a lot like being shattered into a million pieces and then exalting in this cataclysmic destruction of oneself because the pleasure has finally crested. Then wave after wave of pleasure continued to crash through me as Vance didn't let up his manipulation of my body.

I had to push him away when I became highly sensitized to the flickering of his tongue against me, and he finally pulled away when I tried to break free of his grip on my hips.

Panting hard, my heart still beating at a fast clip, I eyed him and asked, "Is it always like that?"

Before he answered, he moved up my body to settle himself again between my thighs and then nipped at my nose with a kiss. "No," he said finally. "But with me it will be."

Since his cock poked heavily at my well-pleasured core, the trepidation from earlier came back. I felt swollen after his treatment, and I wasn't sure he would fit.

"Don't be scared," he cooed into my ear as he lowered himself on top of me. "I'll make sure it's good. Hold onto me, Laena."

I did as he said, and in the next second, I felt his cock slide slowly inside. He was definitely bigger than his two fingers and I gasped at the feel of him stretching me.

"Relax," he said. "It will get better in a second." I was doubtful since the amount of pressure I was feeling down there was very uncomfortable. But I was never one to just let things happen to me, so I decided to help things along.

Arching my back, I moved my hips to glove him inside me to the hilt. I cried out at the feel of him, the pressure too great for me to relax any of my muscles.

"God! You're tighter than a fist, Laena!" he hoarsely cried out. Other than the kisses he peppered on my lips and face, he didn't move a muscle, his lower body frozen. Then, I realized he was allowing me time to adjust around him, for me to get used to the feeling of him being inside me.

Soon enough, the ache inside me began to grow again, and I was suddenly desperate for Vance to do something. But the stubborn man wasn't moving. So, I undulated my hips against his, developing a rhythm I hadn't known my body could produce. In doing this, my movements abraded my nipples against his hard chest, and just like that I was sensitive everywhere.

Every touch, every slide of his skin against mine made my arousal escalate once again. Vance watched me move beneath him, and whatever he saw in me produced a sudden change in him. He began thrusting in and out of me, and I gasped anew at the rhythmic feeling of him entering and leaving my body.

I loved the feeling of his body pressed into mine; of our bodies sliding against each other; and of how possessively he took from me. But that's not to say I rubbed myself against him, using his large, hard body to get what I needed, too. But the angle wasn't right for what I needed; I was frustrated that I couldn't get to that same place he had brought me earlier.

I was mewling now; trying to get there but didn't know how. Vance seemed to clue into my distress because he stopped his thrusting to adjust himself. Without withdrawing himself, he moved further up my body so that the base of his cock hit me right where I felt the most nerve-tingling pleasure.

And instead of deeply thrusting into me, he opted to grind himself into me, his groin also grinding gratifyingly into that spot that no longer felt bereft from his inattention. With every shallow thrust, I was brought so much closer to the inevitable end I was seeking.

"Faster, deeper," I urged up at him. He quickly complied with a small smile that shone brightly through his sweat-soaked features. Shifting to hold me tight against him, his hips sped up against me, and I held on to him like I feared I'd fall out of bed if I didn't.

Soon enough, the beginnings of another orgasm unfurled within me in a few small waves of tingling heat. I must have cried out in anticipation of it, and Vance sped up even more to get me there. Then, I clamped down around him as the first wave hit, and I screamed out my pleasure as he rode with me through it.

I had barely come back down from it when Vance switched course and began deeply thrusting into me, prolonging my pleasure. Now, he took from my body what he needed, his breath becoming more labored and unsteady. His thrusts were intense and quick, but I loved how hard and rough he was with me. Then finally, he roared, "Fuuuuck!" as he pushed himself into me as far as he could go, spilling himself into me as he groaned heavily into my ear.

After a few passing moments, Vance didn't move a muscle, but eventually I felt his cock slip out of me. I was still riding so high on the bliss of everything that had happened between us, that I didn't care if things were messy or that he was crushing me into his mattress. Finally, Vance rolled off of me, but not before pecking me lightly on the lips.

"I'll be right back," he promised as he made his way back to the bathroom. I had never felt this relaxed or blissful. Since I had no pressing reason to move, I stayed put. Vance came back with a dampened washcloth in hand.

"Open," he directed. When I didn't move, he splayed my legs wide and cleaned all traces of himself from between my legs. The warmth of the washcloth soothed my battered female parts, but Vance was gentle as he wiped away all traces of himself. I couldn't complain about the treatment I was getting; I really liked being pampered in this way.

Tossing the washcloth away into a bin, Vance plopped himself next to me and gathered me close, nose to nose. "You're amazing, you know that?" he said wonderingly.

Not knowing how to respond, I remained silent. I didn't think he required an answer, so I sighed contentedly as I snuggled further into his embrace, nodding off instantly, surrounded by his body.

14

LAENA

After that night spent with Vance, I felt like my eyes had been opened to a world I never knew existed. When I glanced Vance's way—or for that matter, in Reese's or Rennick's—I found myself heating in arousal. It was like a shot to my nervous system each time they smiled back, and suddenly I would be fighting off the urge to rip my clothes off as an invitation to either of them.

While I didn't understand my reaction to them, it didn't make it easier to work with them around. They made it very hard for me to focus either during training or whatever I was working on when they were around. My powers of concentration had never been tested to the breaking point when it came to these three virile men.

And I had to remember to focus on unraveling the mystery of me. The longer I take, the further away Dad's visit. And I so badly needed to talk to him.

Today was the day that my adoption became official. I was now styled as Cadet Laena Ardarien; Kanata had been shuffled off in my new naming. And with the adoption came a new home: I was expected to live in the Ardarien household, with Marguerite as my mother, along with her three husbands as my fathers. And of course, Barclay Ardarien was none too happy that I joined a household that he was a part of. Since my new "mother" had pushed to get me adopted this quickly, he couldn't say too much when it made her so happy to finally have a daughter.

I had met with her prior to my official day of adoption, and I found that I liked the older woman, much to my surprise. She was a spitfire who blazed her way into your life, but she tempered that with her friendly and approachable demeanor. Upon hearing of my existence, she had come to see me right away. I didn't understand her reaction when she first laid eyes on me, but she had burst into happy tears as she embraced me like I actually was her long-lost daughter.

Accepting her hug, I had never felt a mother's arms around me before, and I surprised myself again when I melted into it. How she could be so unguarded and accepting was beyond my comprehension, especially since I was practically a stranger to her. She must have been telepathic since she explained, "I had always wanted a daughter, and here she is right in front of me. From what they tell me, your DNA is what makes you mine. It doesn't matter how; it's the proof that you are here in front of me that this was meant to be."

I was flabbergasted at how trusting this woman was. Barclay was another story, but her other husbands, Maximus and Antonio couldn't be more thrilled that I was part of their fold. Yet, back at the hospital, the very first day I had met Barclay Ardarien, he had mentioned that he was there at Kane's birth. If I was supposed to be Kane's genetic twin, I wondered how exactly did I come to be. I must have been born, and yet there was no one around who could tell me the exact details of my birth.

Marguerite couldn't have given birth to me while under her husbands' watchful eyes, so how did that work? I couldn't dream up a plausible explanation for my existence without resorting to the ridiculous and impossible.

But here I was, sitting in my very own suite of rooms within the Ardarien mansion, high on a heavily guarded hill. Was this the kind of luxury and extravagance that Rennick, Reese, and Vance had grown up with? They had grown up inside the Inner Circle, the innermost walled circle of the city, and yet, Vance's house was nothing like the opulence of this neighborhood. The three of them may have come from affluent families with money, but from what I've seen, neither of them lived extravagant lives.

I couldn't fathom living in the lap of such expensive tastes, not when the worst place I'd lived in was a street gutter. I guessed that being an Ardarien in this town really meant something and that they had the money and the power to back that up. Judging by the number of beautiful things packed into my bedroom alone, I guessed I was supposed to at least look like I belonged to this family.

But I didn't care about half of what was in that closet or the jewelry the family had purchased for me. Tricking me out as an Ardarien in their own environs wasn't going to make me one of them, even if they had the power to change my last name.

If I could only have one thing that the Ardariens could give me, it was Dad. So not going to happen, but the next best thing they did give me was my own laptop, the finest their money could buy. With it, I could finally set to work and find out more about my past and get a message out to Dad somehow.

And maybe while I was digging in there, I might as well find out as much as I could about the three men who drive me to distraction whenever I think about them.

While I had given my body and virginity to Vance last night, I now found myself imagining what it would be like to be with Rennick or Reese. Or Rennick and Reese. Or all three. In a society such as ours, it was pretty rare to find a one-man woman around here, like Reese's mother and father. But it was becoming clear to me that I wanted in on just such a relationship.

Why I hadn't been exposed to this information before I had been taken, I couldn't guess, but it might have something to do with the nonsense Dad had kept spouting about my being special. It was almost like he didn't see me having a future with anyone, let alone three males. Whatever higher purpose Dad had seen me having, I was no closer to finding out what that was, and therefore I allowed myself the chance to dream about the three most attractive males in New Phoenix.

A knock at my door interrupted my thoughts and my online search. "Come in!" I called out.

Kane Ardarien popped his head in through my door. I watched as he scanned the room for me until his eyes landed on my form sitting cross-legged on my bed, the laptop open in front of me. His eyes widened, and I guessed he must be counting the similarities between our looks. Being his genetic identical twin was an odd thing to be, since as a female, I couldn't possibly be that much similar to him. But when I really looked, we were the same in stature, build, and looks. We even had the same coloring. No wonder Trey had been flabbergasted when he had seen my blood results.

"Hi," Kane said, almost uncertainly. "You must be the new sister I keep hearing about, Laena." He moved further inside my room to stand directly beside the bed. Maybe he wanted a closer look to see if the resemblance stopped anywhere else.

Remembering the manners that Drayna had drilled into me, I stuck out my hand at him. "You must be my new brother, Kane."

Taking my hand and shaking it, Kane whistled. "God, how do we look so much alike? Dad said it was uncanny, but I didn't believe him." Letting go of my hand, he stood back a step to continue studying my features.

"Barclay talked about me?"

Looking sheepish, "Yeah, and from the way he talked I was expecting a snarling bitch who coerced her way into our family somehow."

I was surprised at that. I never thought to expect what the rest of the Ardariens thought about my presence here. "And is that what you think?"

"Naw. I had always wanted a sibling growing up, someone to keep me company when everyone was at work. Just wish I got my wish when I was a lonely six-year-old, but I'll take it," he said with a smile.

"Aren't you curious about why I'm here? I know I am," I admitted.

Nodding his head, he said, "Well, sure, but who am I to question what Mom wants? She was like a bulldog, getting your adoption sped up the way she did. You should have seen her when Dad Barclay was dead set on keeping you away from her, from us. She was that determined to have you."

"Huh. I'm a stranger to you and this family, and you still welcome me here? I don't get it."

"What's to get? In a world ravaged by Eidolon, family is something that not a lot of people have to go home to at the end of the day. And with birth rates so low, it doesn't help that there are so few families left to continue the next generation."

"Yeah, I know. But what does that have to do with me? Why bring me here?"

Kane shrugged a shoulder. "I can't claim to understand Mom, but I do know that having a girl in this family gives her a lot more power in the world of the Elite."

I didn't know that. "How does that work?"

"This may be a matriarchal society now, but it's also cutthroat in its design. Mom had to earn her right to the topmost spot by virtue of her mighty army. An army that has you as a cadet in it, by the way."

I guessed I still looked confused by what he was telling me, so Kane explained, "With a daughter, her spot as New Phoenix's governor is guaranteed. As her successor, New Phoenix will also be yours to govern when she retires."

Whoa. I knew she was governor of New Phoenix, but I had no idea that it was a hereditary position. And at last, I found out her true reason for wanting me. She was in this to hold on to her power here. I knew I wasn't wanted here just because of who I was but what I represented to her and this family. I didn't feel slighted by that in the least, and instead, I was happy to know that I wasn't the only one who had something to gain from this adoption.

"Oh, and by the way, Mom has another present for you," Kane said easily. "She sent me here personally to deliver it."

Handing me a rectangular object, I took it in one hand and realized that it was a phone. "A phone?"

"Yeah, it's got all the bells and whistles. Plus she had her PA add all of the events into the calendar that you'll need to be there for."

"And let me guess, location services are active on this, too?"

"I knew you'd be smart! Yes, Mom wants to make sure her asset is easily accessible at all times."

Okay, then. "I wouldn't expect any less from her," I said, grinning back at him. I knew of ways to confuse that particular function without anyone else the wiser.

"Oh, and dinner starts in a few minutes. Can I take you downstairs to join the rest of the family?"

"Sure. Lead the way." On the way downstairs, Kane indicated which door on this same floor was his and which door was where his parents slept.

Without thinking, I blurted, "They all sleep together in the same bed?"

Laughing at my incredulous look, Kane cringed as he said, "I don't want to think about what goes on in that bed when it comes to *our* parents, but yes, that's where they all sleep." I imagined that his expression must be what I look like when I'm slightly disgusted. That was how alike we were.

Studying me again, Kane asked, "Why do I get the feeling that you're not used to the idea of multiple male partners for one woman? You seem clueless about all of this."

"If I seem to be clueless, it's because I am. I didn't grow up knowing that was possible."

"Dad Barclay did say that you were ignorant of our ways, I just didn't understand in what way he was talking about. He also said you have three males interested in you at the moment, and I believe they are our city's very own war heroes."

Blushing, I said, "And I still don't understand why they're so focused on me. Our first meeting wasn't, um, conventional, by any standards."

Understanding dawned in his eyes as I watched his smile grow wider. "I think the attraction is mutual given your reaction just now. If I were you, I'd make Vance, Rennick, and Reese work very hard at gaining your attention. They've already had a lifetime of people catering to their every wish. They don't need you fawning over them to make their heads any bigger."

I laughed. "You're right. Rest assured, the last thing I want to do is inflate their egos any further."

"Good. Those three could use a dose of humble pie now and then. I believe you would be the first woman I know who has willingly resisted their charms."

Little did Kane know how hard it was to do. Last night was a pleasant aberration with Vance, and it didn't help that I was too curious to know what it would be like in Rennick's and Reese's arms, too.

Dinner was a mixed bag. On one end of the dining table, Marguerite was happy as a clam to see me sitting directly across from her. Dad Maximus and Dad Antonio were delicately nosing into my life as a cadet up until now, using clever questions to find out what they wanted to know. Barclay—I could never call him Dad given the way he felt about me—shot wary glances my way, looking every bit as though I would jump at him. With my dinner fork to stab him with it at any given moment.

Halfway through dessert, the phone I kept in my pocket trilled. Marguerite looked at me curiously and said, "Consider this a freebie, Laena. You may answer it in private, but for next time, no phones at the table. Understand?"

I murmured an embarrassed "Yes, ma'am" and hurriedly left the table. I picked up the call and answered, "Hello?" as I navigated my way back to my room.

"Laena!" a laughing voice answered my greeting. It was Reese. "Hi, sweetheart! How are the new folks treatin' ya?"

I smiled, imagining Reese's face to be colored with his amusement and his general happy-go-luckiness. "I guess complaining about being spoiled rotten here will earn me your sympathy? How'd you get this number anyway?"

"Your new Daddy Barclay wanted your 'babysitters' to have it. Vance and Rennick have it, too."

As an aside, Reese chuckled, "Unfortunately, I can't drudge up an ounce of sarcasm when I say I'm a little sorry for you. That kind of spoiled rottenness comes at a steep price. Believe you me, sweetheart. Been there, done that."

Despite how down to earth Reese was, I tend to forget that Reese came from this same world. Rennick and Vance, too. However, all three seemed to be living lives independent of it. One of these days, I'm going to ask them why they chose the military instead of living as one of the Elite.

"Anyway," Reese continued. "You ready for us to break you out of that joint?"

Smiling, I asked, "Who is us, and what do you mean by that?"

"Rennick and me, of course. Since you've been given two weeks before you return for your training, we thought you could use some fun."

"What did you have in mind?" Knowing those two as I did over the past month, those two were willing to do anything for a good time. From the stories I heard from the girls in my barracks, Rennick and Reese knew their way around a woman, treating her body like a familiar back road, making their way skillfully around her curves. That revelation had me wondering what that would be like whenever I had spied them watching me.

"Let us come get you and you can find out," he said mischievously.

Hungry for more than just an adventure with them, I was ready to bolt out the door the moment they pulled up in the driveway. "Okay, just let me get dressed. We had just finished dinner and these clothes are much too formal for a night out." Truthfully, I left the dinner table abruptly, and I could definitely use an outfit that didn't scream money.

"Doesn't matter what you wear, sweetheart. Strictly speaking for myself when I say that you could wear your cadet uniform, muddy it up in the garden after the rain, and I'd still say you're the hottest one in the room."

"One muddy, bloody cadet uniform coming up," I said playfully, before hanging up. Reaching for the one outfit in that cavernous closet that was more my style, I finally blush at Reese's compliment. As new as flirting was for me, I found it extremely enjoyable with someone I was just attracted to as much as they were to me.

15

REESE

Reluctant as I was to hang up, I was more eager to see her than ever before. This time we were going to see each other outside of work, and I finally get to shed my commanding officer persona with her. Finally, I get my turn! After Vance told Rennick and me what he and Laena had been up to last night, there wasn't much we could do about it. After all, the three of us had agreed we would leave it up to Laena how and when she would take the three of us on. It was just too bad that we didn't discuss how it would work individually.

But these boys were my brothers, despite our belonging to other families. I wasn't jealous; just eager to have us become a foursome, becoming a family of our own creation.

We all knew she was a virgin until recently, and we had thought it best for Laena to have her first time be one-on-one. The three of us all at once would have been too much for someone as inexperienced as our Laena, considering how hungry the three of us were for her. We were in this for the long haul, and we could stand to wait when the time was right.

Obviously, Vance had thought that the right time was last night. But I don't blame him in any way; all of us had been chomping at the bit to get to Laena this past month. But we all wanted to be sure she was ready for all of us. Something must have happened for Vance's iron control to snap last night.

And now, both Rennick and I are on our way to pick up our little lady, a skilled warrior and innocent miss wrapped up in one beautiful package of a woman.

Pulling up at the end of the Ardarien mansion's driveway, I spotted Laena waiting for us. Instantly, I approved of the pencil skirt and simple button-up blouse she wore, giving off that sexy schoolteacher vibe. I would have made a suggestive comment about how good she looked, one that would make her blush, but she wasn't alone. Kane Ardarien stood next to her, and for a split second, my brain fully registered just how much the two looked alike. Kane was even wearing the same colors. It was both eerie and interesting to see how close the resemblance between them really was.

But no way, no how does that mean I'm attracted to Kane. Laena's own naiveté and innocence was what drew me to her. Her helplessness hidden behind a tough-cookie exterior. But the three of us couldn't shake the feeling that Laena herself was deliberately hiding something from not only us, but the rest of the world. Knowing how guileless and utterly clueless she was about a lot of things in our world, we couldn't imagine she was hiding anything nefarious or anything like that. She didn't seem the type.

I hopped out of my Jeep to help her into the vehicle when Kane set me aside. "Hey, just so you know, the Dads wanted to arrange protective detail for Laena. Mom said no since she knew you and Rennick would be with her." The little shit was actually being nice!

I raised a brow at Kane and said, "This little lady, needing protection?" Clearly, Laena's new brother had no idea how high up her ranking was among her fellow cadets.

Smiling a lopsided smile, Kane answered, "I know. I've heard the gossip and the reports, and I know she can take care of herself. I just wanted you to know how protective the parents are of her now that she's ours."

I almost growled at those last two words, a phrase I myself would like to utter in reference to Laena. One day, we will make it official, but for now, we had to stick to our agreement to properly woo the little lady. To us, she was special, and therefore required special handling that would leave no doubt about the future we want, with her in it.

Laena looked at the two of us questioningly through the passenger window, and called out, "We ready to bounce?"

From the backseat, I heard Rennick groan, complaining, "You've been talking to Drayna, haven't you? That's her catchphrase you're borrowing."

Chuckling, I reassured Kane, "We'll take good care of her. You can tell your parents that she's safe with us." Kane nodded and waved at Laena before he turned to re-enter the house.

Once he was out of earshot, I grinned at Laena wickedly as I slid into the driver's seat. "But of course, that entirely depends in which context the word 'safe' is used here." Waggling my brows comically at her, I explained, "The only danger you'll be encountering tonight is the two of us getting naughty on your fine ass."

She flamed tomato red but didn't say a word in response. Looking back at Rennick then at me, Laena almost looked eager to know what I meant by those words. I felt proud that our chosen woman was brave enough to not back down from what might seem like a challenge to her. Two men who sought her attention at once may be a bit overwhelming for any woman who wasn't used to it, but Laena looked like she was looking forward to it.

"Okay, but you want to tell me where you're taking me?" she asked in a steady but breathy voice. I had already veered onto the main road, but I took one hand off of the steering wheel to grab one of hers. Kissing the back of her palm, I explained, "Someplace fun, of course."

She scrunched her nose and said, "That's not very specific."

I spied Rennick rolling his eyes in the rearview mirror. Rennick explained, "We're taking you to our private club, a members-only type of place."

Intrigued, Laena asked, "And what kinds of things do you do at a private club?"

I smiled, "The kind that requires discretion and secrecy. But don't worry, Laena, the two of us will make sure you enjoy yourself immensely." Her wide-eyed look slayed me, making me hunger for her even more. Her lack of knowledge about pleasure and the ways between men and women had me eager to teach her, to train her into becoming the one woman perfect for me, for the three of us. She had no idea how much she affected me and the guys.

Nestled inside a mansion once belonging to an affluent family, our club wasn't but ten minutes driving distance. Being an exclusive, upscale kind of club, our family names allowed us automatic entry, and our status as heroes allowed us free lifetime admission. As our guest, Laena was also allowed through the doors with the instruction that she stick close to Rennick and me.

Judging by the way Laena's head kept whipping around, it wasn't the club's opulent interior that caught her attention. We knew she wouldn't be impressed by the richness of the place or the expensive furniture. It was the various public displays of all kinds of hedonism that occurred all around us that we were sure she was shocked by.

In one dimly lit corner, two men pleasured their woman to the brink of her orgasm as we walked past. Laena's eyes rounded at the sight as the woman caught her gaze just as she screamed out her ecstasy.

In one alcove, one woman was bent over a small end table, her wrists strapped to the legs of the table. One man rammed into her from behind while her mouth was filled with another man's cock.

Everywhere she looked, Laena was clearly affected by the different scenes of varying stages of pleasure. Her lips parted as her breathing grew unsteady; her color rose high in her cheeks; and her eyes glazed over with her own arousal.

"Why did you bring me here?" Laena barely squeaked out.

Rennick had one arm around her shoulders and tucked her into his side. With me on her other side, we both looked down at her as I said, "This is a taste of what we would like to do with you. Does this scare you?"

She shook her head, and then asked, "If the both of you are members here, have you done this before? With other women?"

I quickly explained, "Yes, we've done this before. But not here. This is our first day as members here because we wanted to treat you to something special."

Rennick added, "Our prior experiences didn't involve an emotional attachment if that's what you're thinking. Our last serious relationship involved a woman we thought we could marry, but in the end she didn't choose us."

I kissed her bare shoulder before saying, "Neither of us have a bed large enough for the three of us, and this place affords us one at no charge. It's an added bonus that this place also sets the right mood for what we have in mind."

Biting at her lower lip, Laena looked a little nervous. She said, "And what do you have in store for me?"

"We're trying to seduce you into becoming ours. Exclusively," I stated baldly.

"And Vance, too?" she asked, swallowing against a crack in her voice.

We both nodded. Before she could change her mind, we ushered her quickly to the room we were assigned when we called ahead earlier today. We stopped at a lone door in a wide hallway, thankfully finding the hallway itself completely devoid of anyone else. I had picked the room because it was the furthest from any others and we would be afforded as much privacy as we wanted. With a cardkey I fished from my back pocket, the door unlocked with an audible click when I waved it in front of the magnetic locking mechanism. Rennick gently pushed her through the open door as I held the door open for them to enter.

Anticipation sang through my veins, just as I'm sure it did in Rennick's. We had this planned as soon as we found out Vance had her first, and we wanted to insinuate ourselves into the mix before Laena could set up preferences. We wanted her to prefer the three of us all at once, since we came as a package deal. And what better way to get her used to the idea of polyandry than giving her a small taste?

Rennick and I stayed silent as Laena inspected the spacious room. Her eyes settled first on the king-sized poster bed outfitted with silky sheets and pillows. We had ordered a small table piled high with finger foods and wine, on which her eyes landed next. There was also another table stocked with all kinds of instruments and oils for our pleasure, and we caught her puzzled glance at the various bottles lined up there.

Candles were placed everywhere in the room, giving a soft glow to the room and lending to the air of seduction already surrounding the place.

A tapestry enshrouded one entire wall of the room, and Laena asked, "There's just the one entry point here, but we're too deep into the house to be near any windows. Why the curtains?" Smart girl to know where she was relative to the house itself.

I supplied, "It's not a window to the outside, if that's what you're asking." Then, Rennick picked up a remote from one of the end tables and clicked a button, parting the tapestry to reveal a wall to ceiling window. The window was momentarily blacked-out, but once the curtains were wide open, a spotlight on the other side of the window flicked on.

"What's supposed to happen now?" Laena asked. Somehow, her sweet innocence when it came to sex would still be ours to bask in even after we've given her a quick education about how it was going to be with us.

I didn't want to give away too much, so instead I instructed, "Just sit back, watch, and learn."

There was a long, padded bench placed a few feet away from the window, and I led her straight to it. Once I had her seated in its middle, I poured the three of us a healthy portion of the rich merlot Rennick had ordered. Rennick took a seat to her left; I handed out the wine and stood just behind her right shoulder.

Rennick clicked another button on the remote, and a door opened on the other side of the window, highlighting a woman's form. Laena watched as the woman walked into the glow of the lone spotlight, and gracefully took her seat at a bench, similar to the one she was currently sharing with Rennick. The woman's features were obscured by the Grecian mask she wore, but there was no hiding her shapely form underneath the sheer robe hanging loosely about her body.

I had planned our evening's entertainment, requesting this display for Laena's benefit. Innocent as we believe her to be, Rennick and I had discussed this and thought this the best way to introduce her to what we want. We've wanted her from day one, and we made the conscious decision then and there to have her in all the ways that mattered. We wanted to seduce her into becoming ours and only ours for as long as we could keep her. Laena was worthy of the wooing just as she was deserving of a lifetime of being loved. We wanted to be the ones to give that to her.

Most of all, I wanted to be part of a family, a family of our own design, that had love in abundance, and not forced to marry someone who our parents picked out for us. No more waiting around for my own parents to see me as more than a pawn. For my own family's sake I would be better than my parents, making sure my own children knew that they were loved.

But before I could start naming those future children, they need a mother. And Laena was it for us. She was the only one who would fit the bill. All the guys and I needed to do was to convince her that she need look no further than us.

And from the look on her face when she saw us pull up, I thought it was safe to say that she was half-convinced already. I had caught the smoldering look Rennick shot her way, and as he looked her up and down approvingly, she had blushed to the roots of her hair while her face gave nothing away. I did catch the way her nipples had poked through her thin blouse and the way her breath had hitched as I touched the small of her back to help her into the Jeep.

She wasn't immune to me, and neither was she to Rennick as I watched her unconsciously scoot closer to him as the three of us watched the show begin. Two men, both dressed down to black boxer briefs, walked into the room from opposite ends and approached the woman at the bench with a slow, predatorial gait.

I kept a close eye on Laena, more interested in her reactions than the window display before us. She held her petite frame stock still; I knew she held her breath, like she was scared that even the smallest puff of a breath would break the spell of what was happening before her eyes. Her eyes themselves held a sheen that spoke of how affected she was, understanding and awaiting what was about to happen.

As for myself, I had remained semi-erect since the moment we had entered the room. I couldn't speak for Rennick, but I was sure that he held the same measure of expectancy heating his blood that I had in mine, if the heated glances he kept sending Laena's way was any indication.

The three of us watched as both men slowly rid the woman of her robe, one caressing skin newly uncovered; the other feathering kisses along her throat once she was fully made bare. Through speakers piped into the room, we could hear every sigh, every moan, and every gasp the threesome uttered at each new touch.

Laena sucked in a breath as she watched one man bite down on one nipple, eliciting a high-pitched gasp of surprise from the woman. The gasp soon mellowed into a drawn-out sigh as the man soothed the ache he produced by laving it slowly with his tongue. The other man gently angled the woman's face towards him, and he met her lips with his own, swallowing her mewling cries in his kiss. I watched Laena with approval as she clenched her thighs together, knowing she was trying to ease the ache that grew there.

Rennick whispered something in Laena's ear and took one of her hands in his. Kissing the back of her hand, Rennick blazed a lazy path of kisses along her slender forearm, until he reached her mouth, capturing her lips with his. Leaning forward until I reached her other ear, I whispered, "Don't take your eyes off the show. We're going to match what they do."

Reaching around her front, I worked at slowly unbuttoning her blouse, removing it, and leaving her in just her bra and skirt. "Now, we're going to do our best to keep up with what's happening in the other room, but you have to keep watching. Okay?"

Rennick was now nuzzling her neck with kisses and licks, so Laena could only nod in answer. I bit down on her earlobe, making Laena cry out in surprise. Still whispering, I asked, "See how she's fully naked now? See how her partners are making her hot for them?"

"Yes," Laena gasped out, just as Rennick swooped down and engulfed her nipple with his mouth the moment I bared both of her lovely breasts.

I smiled, knowing that this was just the beginning. And I knew how hard both Rennick and I were going to work tonight to make Laena ours, now and forever.

16

LAENA

Never have I ever experienced the kind of attention that made me want to lose my mind as Rennick and Reese worked my emotions and feelings into a frenzy. I prided myself in being in control of my body and emotions, but I had never had reason to have two men driving me crazy at the same time before.

Until now.

With Rennick sucking away at one nipple, Reese nibbled away at my neck while his hands slowly roamed by body, exploring the feel of my skin under his hands. I wanted to close my eyes and luxuriate in what they were doing to me, but at the same time, I was intrigued by how much of our actions really mirrored that of the threesome next door.

With Reese pressed close behind me on his knees and Rennick playing with my breasts with his mouth and tongue, I could see that the woman behind the glass was also in the same position. We caught each other's eye, startling me a little as our gazes clashed. And I was a little taken aback by the slow but saucy wink she gave me. She knew I was watching, and it only took a second for me to realize that she was also watching me and measuring my own reactions.

With my inexperience on display for everyone to see, I imagined it was a stark contrast to the woman's own sure movements and her own seemingly natural reactions to what was being done to her. Reese must have guessed where my thoughts had led, and he assured me, "Don't worry about how we may look to outsiders. Just relax and enjoy. Those three over there are here just to help set the mood since we want you to see and experience what we alone could give you."

I let out a choked cry just as Rennick licked a scorching path between my breasts, clamping down on the other nipple. On a gasp, I asked, "What is it that you can give me that others can't?"

At that, Reese growled, "Everything you need and want, including the things you don't know you need and want." He took that moment to swiftly capture my mouth in a kiss, in which I moaned into his mouth at the same time he swooped inside mine with his tongue.

The things you don't know you need and want? How would he know? Or better yet, how would the combined mental faculties of three men exactly compute what it is I need and want? Maybe this thought of mine may be a nod to my own naiveté, but I had a tiny bit of an issue when it came to enforcing those kind of opinions on me.

However, I couldn't deny that my body, singing and stretching languourously against the two men was making me feel like a cat joyously stretching and basking in a patch of sunlight. I luxuriated in their smooth caresses done by work-roughened hands. I loved feeling their hot breath and moans vibrating against my skin. But most of all, I loved that these men were *mine*.

Mine for the night, mine for however long this thing between us was going to last. My one and only experience with things outside of my control had taught me to believe that nothing good ever really lasts. That I only had now, and that the future was never guaranteed.

Firmly in the present, I ate up everything these two virile men gave me with the knowledge that my future will be filled with looking back at this moment. I knew that I had become an obsession of sorts for them, and I couldn't deny that I was drawn in by their good looks and their openness to having me within their fold. Vance, Rennick, and Reese were so very generous with me: giving me their time, their kindness, and although they haven't said it, *their love*.

Despite my sheltered upbringing, I knew what love was and had always been curious about it. I knew Dad loved me, but I had been more curious about romantic love. I had observed from afar what Dad called *love at first sight* among some of the younger girls, and I had also witnessed what heartbreak did to both sexes. Most of all, I wondered how love sparked in a foursome and how a quadrangle made it all work in the end.

And with Vance, Rennick, and Reese now firmly entrenched in my life, I was beginning to believe that it could work. That together we could *make* it work.

As Rennick and Reese seduced my body, drawing out my innermost lustful desires involving them, I feared they were seducing my mind, too. Vance, too, had gifted me with his own vulnerability the other night, and I had been lured in by his alpha-male magnetism. All three of these men were out to seduce me into becoming part of their family, and I, with my inexperience and my own reservations, was very close to letting them.

Caught up in the moment, it felt so good and so right to watch and feel what Rennick and Reese were doing to me. I moaned when they found a new sensitive spot, discovering that they were learning my body, uncovering what I liked by the sounds I made.

In the next room, behind the glass, the masked woman was gently being pushed onto her back. The man at her feet parted her legs and grabbed her by the hips to scoot her bottom to the edge of the bench. My breath caught as I watched the man feasting on her pussy with lips and tongue. Through the speakers, I could hear that man moaning against her nether lips just as the woman's cries rose in volume in response.

Rennick grinned. "Your turn, sweetheart." Reese rose to his feet then and gently urged me backwards until I was lying prone on the bench. He told Rennick, "You take care of the top half, and I'll get the bottom."

Before I could ask what he meant, Rennick's hands slipped underneath me to unclasp my bra, then ridding me of it completely. Reese unzipped my skirt and in one smooth move, whipped off the remainder of my clothes until I lay there entirely nude. I didn't dare to move a muscle or even breathe; I was on high alert for whatever was to come next.

Reese knelt once more, this time between my dangling, splayed legs. "I have to taste how sweet you are, Laena. Will you let me?" They said they were going to mirror everything that was done in the next room, and I was eager to know if I'd like it or not. Nodding yes at him, he smiled in answer, then proceeded to move me slowly towards him. As I raised my head to watch him, my mound hid his features from the nose down. But I could feel his warm breath cascade across my most sensitive flesh, the sensation foreign but pleasant.

I was ill prepared for the tentative touch of his tongue to my clit, and I cried out in surprise. Behind me, Rennick crooned, "Easy. Just relax and feel. But most of all enjoy." Rennick leaned down to give me an upside-down kiss as if to soothe me into submission. Below, Reese traced lazy circles between my legs, covering everything down there before centering completely onto my clit.

In Rennick's mouth, I howled, feeling all sensation centered on the one place Reese was currently working. Rennick chuckled against my mouth as he continued to war his tongue with mine. My awareness narrowed only on what these two men were doing to me, and through the speakers I could faintly hear what the threesome next door were doing. By the sounds of it, I imagined we were a close mimic to what was going on in there.

Rennick released my mouth to lean further forward and take his turn to nip playfully at my breasts. Each brush of his lips or tongue against my nipple caused a further jolt of sensation zinging through my core. If anything, Reese and Rennick's combined efforts made me highly sensitized to what the other man was doing to me.

Not to mention, it was extremely hot to hear what was happening next door and to know that we were following suit. I heard the woman breathily whisper, "What about you, darling? Can I take care of you, too?"

My place on the bench still provided me a view of the threesome. The other man shucked off his boxer briefs, displaying an impressive erection in profile. Unhurriedly, the nude man straddled the woman, his knees under her arms and on either side of her chest. I watched as his cock butted almost playfully against her smiling lips as the two shared a teasing glance.

My eyes rounded as the woman allowed him entrance, permitting him to glide his cock slowly past her lips until he was fully in her mouth to the hilt. I was impressed that she took his full length, and I wondered with some trepidation if I was able to do the same. Fascinated, my eyes were glued to the back and forth motion of the man's hips thrusting gently into the woman's mouth. The woman moaned loudly around his cock, and I could see that the other man had stood up to thrust his own cock in between her legs.

The suddenness of the change in positions was dizzying; I wasn't sure if it was the sight of the threesome or if it was the treatment I was given by my partners that was responsible. Whatever the case, my own arousal was heightened to a fever pitch, and I ached terribly because of it all.

"I-I need…something," I finished lamely. I arched my back to mash my core harder into Reese's face, sending him a silent message to apply more pressure where I needed it. My breasts jutted high above me, and Rennick eyed them briefly before reaching out to massage them both, teasing my nipples with sharp tugs and flicks.

"Okay, sweetheart," Rennick crooned. "Let's take this to the next level. You ready?"

I nodded purposefully, eager to see what the next level involved. My heart skipped a little, wondering if I would soon be experiencing what the woman next door was feeling. To know what it felt like to swallow Rennick whole like the woman did to her man.

And just like I witnessed and envisioned, I watched with bright interest as Rennick stripped himself of every shred of clothing. Our eyes locked as he lazily worked at the fastenings of his shirt and pants. I was sure he could see my eyes glaze over, partly from what Reese was doing between my legs and partly from watching him tease me as Rennick slowly bared the parts of his body I was eager to see.

Now, I had always known of these men and of their valor being celebrated in the streets of the Seven Cities. I had seen their photos, their banners bearing their images, and I had always marveled at their male beauty. I knew that their bodies had been carved and hewn from endless hours of training for actual combat. That distant knowledge was nothing compared to intimately knowing what each of these men looked like beneath their uniforms.

To finally see Rennick in all of his nude glory nearly took my breath away. Or my breath might have actually been stolen by Rennick suddenly picking up speed with his tongue against my clit. Everything I was experiencing was happening so fast, and yet this feeling of urgency within me was telling me that things weren't happening fast enough.

My moans must have sounded impatient to both of their ears since Reese lifted his head long enough to say, "Easy, Laena. We have all night so there's no need to rush this. Just lie back and let us teach you what it's like to be loved by the two of us." Rennick's unwavering gaze never left mine as he slowly straddled me, seating himself just above my breasts. My mouth watered as I glanced at his cock hovering just inches away from my nose, and I could smell the clean scent of him just underlying the wet evidence of his arousal beading there.

"We'll teach you what we like for every lesson we give you in being ours," Rennick declared. Pinning me with both his body and his stare, he continued, "On my count, both Reese and I will enter you at the same time." My eyes flared in understanding, and my lips fell open as Rennick slowly counted down, "Three…two…one!"

Reese and Rennick, in one concerted motion, entered me just as they promised. Slowly, inch by inch, they invaded my body as I hummed in pleasure at the ease of their penetration. Reese plunged deeply into my core, settling there while Rennick's cock glided past my lips until I had as much of him as I could comfortably fit. "Swallow more of me, baby," Rennick urged softly. "Just breathe through your nose and take all of it."

I did as he suggested, and to my surprise I felt like I had all the power as I swallowed his entire length. Below, Reese worked himself in and out of me with slow withdrawals and quick, deep thrusts. I moaned each time he buried himself deep inside me, and the vibrations of my throat must have made Rennick groan in response.

"So good," Reese murmured just as Rennick crooned, "That's amazing, Laena."

Soon, we were a writhing mass of bodies balanced precariously on that bench, gaining our pleasure where we could. The threesome next door had already hit their crescendo of their performance, while we were just starting ours. I whimpered around Rennick's cock, eager to get to my still far-off orgasm.

Reese seemed to instinctively know what my whimper meant, so he lifted my hips off the bench, thrusting heavily into me. This new position had my clit colliding directly into his rock-hard abdomen each time he used my bottom to leverage himself into me. While Rennick thrust himself in and out of my mouth, my moans increased in frequency around him. Soon, our movements became more hurried, more frenzied; the three of us now rushing to get to the height of our pleasure and desire.

With Rennick's cock deep in my mouth, I could feel him getting close. His cock became impossibly bigger and more turgid than before, and above me, I watched as Rennick's eyes burned intently with heated desire. He had never looked more beautiful to me than in that moment; that look on his face seemed to tell me that only I was privy to such passion and vulnerability from him.

As for Reese, I could feel the same response within him as he was buried deep inside me. Both men were heaving bellowing breaths as they continued to work themselves in and out of me. Their efforts had a profound effect on my own sensitized nerve-endings until with one well-placed thrust from both of them, I shattered into little pieces with the orgasm they wrenched from me.

My own screams around Rennick's cock must have pushed Rennick over the edge as he spurted himself deep into my throat. My own pulsing walls around Reese's cock milked Reese into his own release as both men above and below me roared against the relief my body provided to them. As my own orgasm subsided, I relished the thought that it was me who brought them to such noisy, messy heights. I couldn't begrudge either of them for teaching me the dirty, almost-forbidden side of passion, not when I had experienced otherworldly bliss at their hands.

Moments after, my eyes still closed and my chest still heaving, I felt myself being gently lifted off of the bench. My eyes opened once my fever-hot skin hit cool sheets, and I looked up at Reese and Rennick's worried faces.

"What's wrong?" I asked tentatively, not liking that they weren't as blissed out as I was.

"Did we hurt you?"

"Are you okay?"

Their concern was sweet, but I assured them with a smile, "I'm fine. More than fine, really. You don't have to worry that you'd break me. Remember? I'm tougher than I look."

Relief flooded their faces and they both moved simultaneously to join me on the bed. I squealed as Reese pounced on top of me and Rennick dove between my legs. With a wicked grin, Reese warned, "Good, because now I want to feed that naughty mouth of yours with my cock."

I didn't need Rennick to tell me what else he intended since he was already lapping away at my clit.

As I opened up for Reese, he continued, "Neither of us will let you sleep until we say so."

With my arousal begun anew, I had nothing to say against their wishes, since they both skillfully worked at bringing me pleasure over and over again.

17

RENNICK
Two Weeks Later

Our one night with Laena would have to be enough to sustain us for the weeks after—duty called in the worst way. Reports of Eidolon hordes were cropping up around various areas outside the city, and numerous squadrons were sent out to keep them at bay. Casualties from each mission were on the rise, and with our dwindling manpower, we soon had to resort to utilizing our latest recruits for these scouting missions.

In other words, we were ordered to bring our Cadets into active duty, which in turn meant Laena would be brought into the mix. No matter what strings we tried to pull, we couldn't prevent our Laena from joining us on each mission; the Elite had claimed we needed every able-bodied being out there. And our girl delivered when it came to wreaking all kinds of badassery on Eidolon monsters even when it wasn't her job to do so.

She could track and hunt those things like she was born to it, and it didn't cease to amaze the three of us how quick and adept she was at it. Because of her, there were less surprises out on our missions, and things were relatively safer, if not completely without danger.

The things Laena could do with her innate fighting ability were enough to spark enough hard-ons on my part, every single time I got to witness her kick ass hard on those things. Her hands and feet delivered blows with deadly accuracy; her speed almost inhuman as she cut a wide swath through a herd of them. But the three of us couldn't stop worrying over her.

While we knew that she was deliberately placed in our cohort of Cadets, all thanks to Barclay Ardarien's doing, there were things about her that still remained a mystery. There were times she would disappear from the group, and for all intents and purposes, it looked like she was going on ahead to scout for another wayward herd. Just when it seemed like she was gone too long, she'd suddenly appear to announce she spotted a herd further on ahead.

The terrain outside the city provided too many places to hide with its abundance of tall trees and rocky outcroppings. It wasn't too far a stretch to imagine that Laena could be hiding behind one of those rocks or high up in the trees, with a pair of binoculars in hand, searching for signs of Eidolon movement. However, it had been glaringly obvious to us that Laena's own seemingly inconspicuous movements had more to them than what we were actually seeing. Questions like *why does she disappear with no word after calling point* and w*hy does she prefer to do it alone* rang through our minds and were later voiced during our debriefs just among the three of us.

And it just so happened that we never got the chance to ask because we would find ourselves suddenly waist-deep in dealing with an Eidolon herd. Or running away from one. After five missions just like this, I decided I'd find out what our Laena was up to.

Now on our latest mission, we had been ordered outside and west of the city, plodding along in our slow procession of Humvees outfitted with Gatling guns. The bulky vehicles were no good to us past the tree line, so we disembarked except for four guards who were to keep watch over our transport home. Now on foot, Vance and Reese split up the group between the three of us, and I made sure that Laena stayed with me. I had talked it over with them earlier, and they were totally onboard with my plan to see what our Laena had up her sleeve.

And like always, Laena called point while none of her fellow cadets would protest, already resigned to the fact that her tracking abilities were next level compared to theirs. With my cap's visor held low over my eyes, I surreptitiously watched her march away while pretending to be in deep conversation with the other cadets in my charge.

I had to remind myself that I was working right now; protecting New Phoenix and its citizens was our duty and I was still on the clock. But I couldn't help feeling a bit of a thrill from the chase, especially when I knew my quarry was Laena. After Reese and I had introduced her to menage those few weeks ago, I wanted nothing more than to dive headfirst into loving her again, feeling her against me, skin to skin. But out here in the wilds surrounding our city, there was something entirely primal about me hunting her down, unearthing her secrets this way, and it spoke volumes of how much this little woman could rile me up and unman me.

The three of us—Vance, Reese, and I—had seen her that first day, and we had decided that she was meant to be ours. No other woman but Laena sparked a cloying need for her deep within ourselves, and just at a time when we despaired of ever finding a wife who willingly wanted to be ours. So, while she may be everything we ever wanted, she still wasn't forthcoming about who she really was. Or why, after being hidden away for so long, would she abruptly reveal her existence the day that we first met?

I liked to think I was the more discerning and perceptive one in our tight-knit crew. While I followed after Laena through the trees, this inward battle raged within me: my desire for Laena pitted against my nagging misgivings about the woman herself. If it weren't for Vance being so love-struck at the first sight of her, all it would have taken was for me to voice my immediate distrust of her and that would have been the end of it.

But I also trusted Vance and his choice for our future wife. I was the one who had chosen Carisse, thinking that my more cautious side would help in the choosing. Obviously, I had chosen poorly, or she wouldn't have left us for another trio of fiancés more suited to her needs and high-end tastes. Laena was—something else, someone who was outside our realm of experience with her innocence and naiveté, and yet was deadly and skilled enough to kill numbers of Eidolon-resurrected with her bare hands.

I liked to think that that incongruous part of her was what drew me to her. She had no clue how awkward she looked amongst the princesses of Elite society, but she didn't give two shits about appearances. That just wasn't part of her nature. She wasn't raised to care about things like that, and I liked that she wasn't a spoiled princess who thought that she was owed the privilege of marrying us.

But then there were times, when she thought no one was looking, that I'd catch a glimpse of this look on her face, one that was different than her open, warm self. To my assessing eye, those were the times she looked the most removed and cold—robotic, even. If I were to do a micro-inspection of her in those rare moments, I was sure I wouldn't find her breathing. Those moments of utter stillness for her, I suspected, had everything to do with her past, or at the very least, they were moments where her past came rushing back to her. Reminding her of who she was and where her place was in this world.

And as I watched her double-back down a different route through the trees, I instantly knew my fears weren't easily dismissed. She had another motive for being out here, alone, where she thought no one was watching. I continued following after her a safe enough distance away so she wouldn't be aware of my presence, ducking behind mounds and wide trees when I got too close.

Her stride was sure and swift, like she knew the terrain well enough not to make a misstep. Ahead of her I could see the end of the tree line, maybe thirty or so yards away from her position. She stopped suddenly, and I scrambled to hide behind a boulder, tall and wide enough to hide someone twice my size. I froze, even slowing my breathing, so she wouldn't spot the sound of my exhalations through the quiet in the forest. Over the years, wildlife was harder to come by out in these woods with Eidolon numbers increasing, and I couldn't pretend to be a wild animal out here just to throw Laena off even if I wanted to.

Crouching low, I peeked out the side of the boulder to spy Laena standing stock still in the same position, her head cocked to her left, then to her right. She didn't say a word, but I thought that maybe she was listening for non-forest type sounds, like that of the Eidolon or human variety. Continuing to watch, she swung off her rucksack, rummaging through it to pull out a laptop, one that I was sure the Ardariens had gifted to her.

Squatting down on the forest floor with the laptop squarely in her lap and her back to me, Laena began typing furiously away on it. More questions concerning Laena arose now instead of getting any satisfactory answers for what was happening here. At first glance, it looked like she was doing some serious hacking, with the ungodly amount of code that scrolled down the screen. But to do what? My mind immediately jumped to *she's a terrorist*, and that everything about her, her first appearance, her abilities, pointed in that direction.

And the three of us blindly let her in, thinking she was nothing more than a naïve little girl, who knew nothing of our way of life. My anger simmered at a low boil, believing the worst of her, no longer trusting who she was when she was with us and no longer open to having her part of our future family. I wouldn't make the same mistake of letting the wrong person into our lives again, not when I was so careless the first time.

Springing from my hiding place, I shouted, "What are you doing here, Cadet?" My feet quickly swallowed up the distance between us, my movements and words clipping each syllable as I approached.

Laena sprang up, still clutching her laptop, as she rounded to face me. Her eyes wide, she cried, "Rennick!" I half-expected for her to say in response *what are you doing here*, but I almost forgot that she wasn't like most other people. Or was that all a ruse, too?

"I asked you a question," I sneered down at her once I was a mere foot away. "And I expect an answer."

Laena blinked up at me, her expression giving nothing away about what she might have been thinking. Stretching out a hand as though to keep me at bay, she calmly said, "I think you've seen what you wanted to see. But I'm going to explain myself anyway."

"Please do, Cadet," I said, nastily.

"Look, you don't have to believe me, nor do I expect you to, but I'm going to tell you something I should have said before." I nodded once curtly.

With a huge sigh, she admitted, "I didn't think I could trust you, Vance, or Reese. Not from the start. But then, the three of you did so much for me. You showed me that the world isn't just about survival and fighting. There's compassion and friendship, too."

"Yeah, and then we fucked, and now it looks like you're up to something. Still doesn't explain what you were doing just now."

"Okay, I'm getting to that part," she said with a blush. "At first, I couldn't picture myself with anyone in my future. And now I know different. What I'm trying to say is that I've wanted to trust you, the three of you, because I have no one else."

Unsure of where this was going, I hardened my heart. "And you think because you say you can trust us that this excuses you from why you're not following orders? I just followed you towards the city wall! Why are you even here?"

Narrowing her eyes at me, she said coldly, "For your information, I knew it was you following me. I could smell you the moment you left our last position."

"Smell me?" I made sure to shower with an unscented soap before missions; the better to mask our scent from Eidolon monsters. Now it made sense why Laena would rub dirt and shrubs all over herself before heading out to take point.

She chose to ignore that comment, and said instead, "And because I *knew* it was you, I didn't attack you for that very reason. Maybe I wanted you to follow me."

I couldn't wrap my brain around her logic. "What the fuck? Why?" My baser side was intrigued by that thought, thinking she might have wanted to lure me away and be alone with me. However, my quieter, logical side warned me that this could have been a trap.

In a manner that reminded me of Drayna, Laena rolled her eyes at me, like I should have already known the answers. "Because since we've started these missions, I thought I could get some answers. Answers about me and my past. Until today, I knew nothing. Now, I've finally found something."

"Okay, back up here. First, tell me how you got these answers," I said, trying to still process what she was trying to get at. So, she didn't know anything about her past; why couldn't she have gone straight to the Courts to request any of the archived records? Looking down at her, hugging her laptop to her chest, I realized she had a reason for not going that route.

"It doesn't matter how I found them! What matters is that I found something at all! Didn't you ever wonder where I came from? Because I do, all the time! I didn't know how much my past really mattered to me until it did," she said sadly.

So, she as good as admitted that she hacked her way into the City servers. Then I recalled an offhand question of hers to Reese about our long-ago prank with the surveillance cameras we'd done as kids. We had brought it up in casual conversation over drinks, and Laena had sounded curious about it. Perhaps we gave her the idea to do it and she somehow figured out how to do it on her own. But that would take an advanced amount of coding to be able to hack her way through so many complex layers of encryption.

"But why would you hack your way to that information? Couldn't you have just asked? It's simple, you just--"

"I-I couldn't," she interrupted me, stammering. "And this is the part where I am fully putting my trust in you, the three of you. You've placed a lot of faith in me, believing I'd be perfect for the family you want to make. But I'm far from perfect. And because of that, I don't want to keep this a secret anymore. I promise only the truth from now on, no more hiding. I need your help."

"Okay, why couldn't you have gone the more legal route? Why the secrecy and the hacking?" I wanted to hold on to my earlier anger, but she was finally going to admit to something truthful. And it seemed like this was her way of telling me that she was finally opening up to us, finally letting us in on her secrets.

"Because of this," she said, tears flooding her eyes as she turned the laptop screen towards me. My eyes dove straight to a grainy thumbnail picture of a smiling woman.

"What am I looking at?" I said, all confused. "Or who am I looking at?"

"That's just it. I don't know yet. The attachment is encrypted, and I'm guessing it'll take some time before I can take a proper look."

Still confused, I asked, "Then why are you a weepy mess right now?"

Brushing her tears away with one swipe of her sleeve, she sniffed wetly, "I'm sorry. I didn't think I'd get this worked up. All this time I was searching through archives and sealed files using just my name, Laena Kanata."

I stopped myself from rolling my eyes at another Laena habit: her habitual pauses during the wrong times, especially when she was in the middle of saying something important. "And that made you cry?"

"No! It's the file name! Read it!" she commanded with the force of an irate drill sergeant.

Looking back down at the screen, I found there were at least nine different files attached to the thumbnail picture of the smiling woman. At the moment I read the first filename, I was sure my mouth hung open dumbly in confusion. "Who is Kay-lay-nee-ah K.? Why would that make you upset?"

"No, dipstick," she said dryly, using another one of Drayna's favorite nicknames for me. "It's pronounced like say-LAY-nah, only spelled C-A-E-L-A-E-N-A like in the filename."

"And tell me again why that would make you cry."

"Because I think this, these files I just found, is a link to my past. I think Caelaena K. was my mother, who died having me," she said. "Problem was, I found these deep in the deleted files of old archived records. Someone wanted to delete all trace of her."

18

LAENA

Dad had taught me to rule my emotions, to not let them get the best of me. But this new revelation pushed me past my limits; I could no longer rein in the sudden barrage of feelings that arose from seeing that file name. Elation and sadness. Eagerness and regret. Triumph and loss. Too late, my tear ducts had a will of its own, and they poured themselves out onto Rennick's rough t-shirt as soon as he had wrapped me into a fierce hug.

"Sweetheart," he crooned above my head and into my hair. "It's ok. We'll figure this out and somehow make sense of it all." I stayed just where I was as I let him soothingly rub my back and I clutched at the back of his t-shirt. After some time, he pulled back just enough to look down into my face, and he asked, "What are you going to do about the encryption on those files? Who would we consult on something this complicated?"

"Me, you dummy. You'd consult me," I said snarkily.

"Huh?" he said, stupidly. Dawning lit in his eyes after a few heartbeats, and he said incredulously, "So, this is what you've been hiding from us, you little sneak! What else is there about you that you haven't told us?"

I cringed a little, knowing it would take more than just a few minutes out here to tell all. "Er, can we wait until we're in a more secure place? With Vance and Reese there, too?"

"Wait. How do I know you won't leave anything out?" he said darkly.

"You'll just have to trust me then, won't you?" I countered back. "Besides, didn't I just say that I was tired of hiding and that I promised the truth? Well, I meant that." In a more serious and lower tone, I added, "I can't be part of this family if I didn't come clean with you."

That's when I saw joy brighten his handsome, but dirty face, and he swooped down to crush me in a bear hug.

"You mean it? You're not going to turn around and run on us, are you?" he asked in a rush.

"If I did that, I know the three of you would just come after me."

"Hah! See how well you know us already? You're damned straight we'd come after you!"

"Well, let me go just long enough to head back. I'm on point, remember?"

Sobering slightly, Rennick said, "For the record, we have to report you wandering off to go do—"

"No!" I burst out loudly.

"But you know the rules! You know how strict our higher ups are! They'll publicly execute you if they find out!"

In a quieter tone, I pleaded, "No. Please. You can't. I'll tell you why when we're in a safer place. Just not out here. If you report me, I will run."

"But you just said—"

"I know what I said. Reporting me will only leave you with no answers and me out of here."

Sighing, Rennick said, "Fine. But you have to explain everything. No leaving anything out."

I simply nodded and brushed past him to do my job: to take point and scout for herds of Eidolon-infected. I had already spotted a slow-moving herd southwest from where Rennick had "cornered" me, and it wouldn't be long until we eventually came across them.

However, the roar of a motorcycle engine approached from my nine o'clock, and instinctual habit had me ducking behind a tree until I could determine if it was friend or foe. Rennick did the same behind me, but not quickly enough to remain unspotted.

"Adrian!" a feminine voice rang out. "What are you doing over there?!"

Rennick sprang out and jogged ahead to meet Drayna, who brought the bike to a stop in front of him. "What's going on? Why aren't you with Vance?"

Panting and frantic, Drayna choked out, "We got separated! A small herd snuck up on us, and we couldn't rally in time to fight them off."

Vance! My heart in my throat, I asked in a small, voice, "Vance? Where did he and the others go?"

Shrugging helplessly, Drayna moaned, "I don't know. It all happened so fast; I was lucky to have even started up this old clunker. A lot of the others were on foot."

Without a word, Rennick raced ahead, running at top speed. The man was fast, and he was already out of sight. Eager to follow after him, but I couldn't let Drayna go back there. "Drayna, go back to the city! I'll go find out where the others are."

"I'm coming with you, Laena. We can get to the others and outrun Eidolon-infected on this," she said, meaning the bike. "Hop on," she said in a commanding voice, not unlike her older brother's.

I complied, but only because I needed to see that Vance and Reese were all right. All I could think about was getting to them, and it was very telling how much these men consumed my thoughts and how much space they took up in my heart. Dad would be disappointed that I was letting others become a distraction for me, I was sure, but at the moment, I didn't care.

These men were important to me, and I was ready to do anything, even give up my mission for these men, if need be. But while I wasn't ready to give up on either at the moment, I was hell-bent on reaching them in time. I now believed that I needed them more than they needed me; without them, I didn't think I'd have found the kind of strength that they alone could give me to do what needed to be done.

As we sped through the trees, all I knew was that they needed me, and I needed them. And I wasn't going to let any of them face danger of the Eidolon variety without me to protect them. With this on-fire desire to protect my men, I felt like I could easily take on a large horde of Eidolon-infected just to keep them safe. There was no way I'd let them leave me willingly or no; I was going to be there to save them.

On the bike, Drayna had caught up to Rennick and sped past him without stopping. He didn't break stride and kept running in the direction where we had last broken off into groups. Drayna braked hard, but we skidded to a stop while making a semi-circle in the dirt.

"Why are you stopping?" I yelled, incredulous that she stopped when we hadn't caught up to Vance or Reese yet.

Drayna said nothing. Her pointed stare straight ahead told me all I needed to know. A few of our fellow cadets were on the ground being slowly devoured by a pack of Eidolon monsters, the life from their bodies leaching out with each bite the monsters tore into them with. At my careless shout, a few of them swiveled their heads our way, and I felt Drayna flinch the moment she noticed they had spotted us.

It took me a few seconds to scan how many there were, and after I confirmed that there were nineteen of them, I smiled at my odds. Drayna drew her gun on them and opened fire on the ones that were approaching, but the sound of her gunfire roused the ones who had been on the ground feasting to follow after their hungry comrades.

I knew her Glock had twelve rounds left while I still had a full clip in my Sig. At this close proximity, I scrambled off the bike to gain a better stance for accuracy. Drayna had downed a few with headshots while the rest of her shots went wide and didn't manage to slow a few of them down. Keeping my breath steady, I blasted off headshots left and right until I came up empty. Between us two, we didn't think we'd encounter this many in one place, and neither did we think we needed the extra mags.

Rennick was still thirty yards away, but he wouldn't reach us in time, not when we were both out of ammo and the remaining Eidolon-cursed circling in around us. With resolve, I unsheathed my hidden blades out from each sleeve, and warned Drayna, "Go get Rennick. There's only six left."

She made a cry of dismay, but I rushed headlong into the closest monster. With the one blade, I slashed its throat while embedding my other blade into its skull. Dislodging that blade, I swiped it in a wide circle as I spun to implant it straight into the eye of another. Jumping high into the air, I spun mid-air to kick away one that got too close, while I landed on top of the chest of another to dig both blades into its skull.

I counted three more to go as I performed my "dance of death" as Dad liked to call what I did. Whether it was six or twenty of them, Dad had said that I was magnificent to watch when I dealt with any Eidolon threat. He had said it was like a switch would turn on inside me, and I knew immediately the best and shortest path for eradicating them.

The three remaining weren't clustered together like the others were; these were the ones who lagged behind the others because they were busy chowing down on our fallen friends on the ground. The sounds of our gunshots were enough to distract them from their dinner to search us out in hopes of a more substantial meal. Greedy SOBs.

Again I took a mental snapshot of where each of them were, and I sprang into action. Sprinting towards the closest one on my left, I leapt in the air once I was feet away from it, with both of my bloody blades raised high above my head. With gravity to aid me, I swooped both blades downwards into the top of its skull.

Drayna yelled, "Behind you!" Rennick had caught up to her, and had his gun, ready to take the shot once I got clear. But the growl of creature number two signaled its closeness, and I remained crouched, spinning around to face it with my blades held ready and crossed in front of me. Low as I was, I uncrossed both blades, swinging them outward as I slashed both ankles of the approaching creature. Its balance lost, it toppled to the ground, its hands still trying to reach for me. Dismembering both of its hands so it couldn't grab me, I underestimated the speed with which the other one had to suddenly appear behind me. The third creature had already snuck up and grabbed at my shoulders, ready to take a big bite out of my shoulder.

Drayna yelled at Rennick, "Shoot now! Help her!"

I heard him yell back, "She's too close. I'll hit her if I do!"

While I was distracted with their yelling, the two creatures took that moment to bite me almost at the same time. Their bites didn't sink in too far; I had plunged my knife into the eye of the one behind me the moment I felt its teeth get past the skin. Rennick shot the other one in the head as it tried to bite through my booted ankle.

With the carnage of our kills surrounding us, there was nothing left moving that could still be a threat. I panted lightly, partly from the burn of the bite on my shoulder, as I turned to face Drayna and Rennick.

Drayna was white as a sheet and shaking. With a trembling finger, she pointed, "Your shoulder, Laena. You're bit."

To Rennick, she sobbed, "Adrian, you've got to do something! One of those things got her, and she's got God knows how much time left!"

Rennick ignored her, his eyes squarely on me. "Baby girl, are you all right?"

With a bright smile, I answered assuringly, "Of course! It's nothing but a scratch. In fact, I've had worse than this."

Drayna looked at me like I had grown two heads. "Are you fucking kidding me? Why are you acting so cool about this?" My poor friend looked crazed, her body and hands trembling so hard, she looked like she was either going to vomit or faint.

Rennick turned to her and clamped both hands on the tops of her shoulders. "Look at me, Drayna!"

But she kept turning her gaze towards me, with hysteria written all over her face. "Look at her! You can't tell me she'll come out of this all right! No one survives a bite! No one!"

Shaking her by the shoulders, Rennick raised his voice loud enough to be heard over Drayna's mad rambling, "Drayna! Laena will be all right! She won't turn into one of those things, I promise!"

"How can you promise that? She was bit right in front of us, and the wound is still gaping open! That wasn't just pretend, Adrian!" Her eyes were wild, and now that my shoulder was stinging something fierce, I couldn't do anything to reassure her.

"Of course, it wasn't. But we know she'll be fine because she's immune!" Rennick yelled. I watched the tension slowly leave Drayna's body once she finally let Rennick's words sink in. Rennick let go of her shoulders so he could step around her and reach me.

"Are you all right?" he asked me, his eyes going straight to the wound on my shoulder. I was bleeding through my shirt, the bite mark made even more obvious with the blood seeping through the holes made by Eidolon teeth.

The bite really hurt, but I was worried more about a staph infection if we didn't disinfect it soon. Rennick had already produced a bandana from one of his pockets, one that he folded into a dressing, stuffed it inside my shirt, and held it against the oozing wound.

"Hold that there," he instructed me, firmly. "Drayna, help her off with her shirt. We need to get her wrapped up." He pulled out a roll of gauze from his mini emergency medkit and unrolled a good length of it.

Drayna shook herself out of her shock and moved to help me carefully out of my shirt. As she gingerly helped me pull off my dirty t-shirt, she asked, "What did he mean when he said that you're immune?"

Once I was free of my shirt, I told her, "Exactly what he said. I can't get infected. When Rennick and the others found me, the tests on me only confirmed what Dad has told me all along. And I've had a few bites here and there over the years, whenever I got careless." Rennick shot me a deep frown at that.

Drayna looked at me hesitantly. "How is that even possible?" she asked. "Our scientists have been searching for a cure for, well, forever, and we still don't have one."

I shrugged my good shoulder, as Rennick wrapped up the other in gauze. "I can't explain it either. Only that I'm still searching for answers while at the same time trying to keep it all under wraps from everyone else."

"Except for us," Rennick piped up. I knew that by 'us', he meant himself, Vance, and Reese. "Drayna, it's important that you tell no one about Laena. The Ardariens know, but even they're not telling anyone about it."

"Why? Why is it so secret?"

"Because it would mean my life," I said boldly. Or at least, that was the reason Dad had given me over and over. "If it was ever found out that I alone kept the secret to Eidolon immunity, I'd be locked up in a lab somewhere all cut up just to find out what makes me immune."

Rennick snorted. "It's more than that, I'm sure. But while we're out here chatting, we still have to find the others. Let's go."

I dressed in a fresh black t-shirt that I kept in my small pack for moments like these. With just a bit of gauze peeking out from my shirt, I could easily explain it away with something less scary than an Eidolon bite. Remaining inconspicuous as possible was still one of my main directives, and an Eidolon bite would destroy that if anyone were to find out.

"Promise me you won't tell, Drayna," I said fiercely. "I promise I'll explain everything when we get to a safer place. But we have to find the others first."

She only swallowed and nodded before saying, "I promise. But you owe me the whole story. If Adrian knows more than I do, I will make you pay."

I smirked. Her version of revenge would be either spiders or stinging nettles in my bed. "Of course," I assured her.

19

VANCE

Laena was nowhere to be found. To say that I was panicked was an understatement. After the horde had scattered our troop in all directions, my one thought was that of getting to our girl. Reese was with me, leading the other half of our reduced numbers back to where we left the Humvees. We lost a good number of our Cadets during the skirmish with the Eidolon horde, and it gave me hope that I didn't see either Laena or Rennick among the fallen.

Scanning every which way for any sign of either of them, I could tell Reese was doing the same. If it weren't for the charges under my responsibility, I would have crashed through the underbrush myself, searching for the both of them. Underneath an ice-thin veneer of calm, fear for Laena raged within me, but I forged ahead, leading our group back to safety.

We soon reached the clearing where we left our transport. With the Gatling guns on the Humvees, we could lay an entire horde out flat, if they managed to follow us. But we couldn't risk giving away our position to more hordes out there, and we couldn't leave without making sure Laena and Rennick were okay.

We made sure everyone left was loaded onto the vehicles before Reese and I each manned a Gatling gun, with the third taken over by Colton. It didn't take long before we heard footsteps crashing against the forest floor, and I tensed, ready to shoot if necessary.

Rennick popped into view, followed by his sister and Laena—thank God—and I blew out a breath I didn't know I was holding once I saw that they were safe.

I heard Reese call out, "Rennick, what took your fat ass so long?" Rennick and Drayna helped Laena into one vehicle, and right away, I knew something had happened.

"My fat ass was making sure these ladies were safe," Rennick retorted. Looking to me, he gave me a familiar sign that didn't mean anything to an outsider but us three. It meant that he needed until we reached a safe place to tell us something very important. I only nodded, then I let out a loud whistle.

"Roll out, everyone. We're heading home early," I called out to the drivers.

Whatever Rennick had to tell us, I was sure Laena was involved, and I was doubly sure that we were in for a doozy.

With the loss of more Cadets than we could afford, we sent everyone home with heavier hearts than when we had left. Sure, I sympathized with the families who lost a son or daughter today; we all took it personal when we lost anyone under our command. But this world was too damned fucked up for us to sit and wallow in our sorrows over someone else.

Sometimes I wondered why even tying ourselves down to one woman was worth all the shit we go through on a daily basis. But the thought of Laena alone was all it took for the feelings and reasons to resurge within me with a vengeance. She made me worry endlessly, and then...this.

Looking at her across my kitchen table, I kept my cool while listening to her spill her secrets. Secrets she explained she couldn't tell us until she was sure we could be trusted. And while I get her reasoning, I still couldn't get over her mistrust of us from day one when we had been nothing but open and honest with her.

I practically seethed at the thought of the skills Daddy dearest had taught her, and I half-wondered if the motives behind such an education would help her breach Elite secrets. As sons of high caliber Elite families, Rennick, Reese, and I stood as unofficial representatives of the Elite, but we didn't give a flying fuck about what secrets the Elite could be hoarding.

Laena, on the other hand, had been hard at work behind the scenes to dig up the biggest secret of all: who she was. But no one could know she was doing it, not until now, until she had just confessed what she was up to. The three of us, including Drayna, sat there at my kitchen table, stunned after hearing it all.

"I'm sorry; I wanted to tell you all, but I couldn't risk it," she ended lamely. Drayna gave her a lopsided smile while I held onto the same stony-faced expression I wore during the whole confession.

"But you haven't told us why," I said coldly. I loved this woman, and yes, I could forgive her for keeping secrets, knowing she had never trusted anyone before. But I was angry at myself for not figuring it out sooner. For not realizing she had something up her sleeve that could potentially harm her and by association, the three of us.

Rennick answered for her, "Come on, man. Even she doesn't know why. She's only following what her old man told her to do. A man she had relied on solely until us. Weren't you listening?"

Laena's widened eyes met mine, and I could see wariness there along with something else, fear maybe? She said, "I know it doesn't look good, but I have no intention of hurting anyone. I never did."

"I only know that a father who's left his own daughter on her own to figure this out is a selfish bastard, looking out only for his own interests. What kind of father does that?" I burst out.

"One who wanted to see me safe and hidden," Laena retorted smartly. "You know what they say about hiding in plain sight? Well, this is Dad's version of it. He knew I wouldn't be okay by myself once I was found. Somehow he knew that the three of you would help me. Is that not still true?"

Rennick held out a hand to take one of hers. "Of course, it is!"

Reese blew out a long breath, then said, "How did he know to trust us? How did he even know that we would cross paths?"

Laena shrugged, "I don't know. Dad just seemed to know things, but he didn't tell me everything. Just things I needed to know."

"Great," I said, heavily with sarcasm. "Blind trust as your motivation for all the secrecy? That still tells me nothing about why he would do such a thing."

Laena growled in frustration. "Vance, if I could tell you why, I would. But maybe if I unencrypt these files, we'd find out." She had already explained to us what she had found buried in the archives of the Elite.

Shoving her open laptop in my direction, I looked down at its display. A series of folders with the name 'Caelaena K.' written on each of them sat in the form of thumbnails with a woman's picture attached to them on the screen. I looked up at her, ready to form questions with my lips and tongue.

Before I could, she explained, "I'll crack these open, but it will take some time before we discover what's in them. I think these have something to do with my past."

"Where did you go searching for these?" Reese asked. After what Laena had just revealed to us, he knew as well as I did that these weren't found in any public registry.

"In the R&D section of old archival records. I'm not sure what ties this woman had to any kind of research, but I think it might have something to do with my origins. The name alone is so close to my own," she explained.

Drayna asked, "How will you find out what's in them?"

Rennick smiled, "Laena claims she can do it herself. And I'm willing to watch her try."

Laena raised one brow at him. "Try? Just you wait. I'll show you that I can do more than just try."

Then her fingers rapped out strings of code in rapid fire succession. The four of us watched as she silently worked her hacker magic, stunning us into silence with her hacking knowledge until Drayna brought up a question.

"How do we know that your little online searches won't be traced back to this laptop of yours?" Drayna asked.

Laena smiled reassuringly as she typed on, "Don't worry, I have my ways. All and any searches I've done will only be traced back to what I call burner IP addresses that blink in and out of existence. They're almost untraceable unless one knows how to really look."

"Huh," I grunted, fascinated by the flood of code coursing over the screen of Laena's laptop.

Laena continued, "It's also one of the reasons I did my searches outside the city limits. So that it would look like an outsider trying to take a sneak peek inside a few servers without actually taking anything."

I couldn't help being fascinated all over again with her, impressed beyond belief that this tiny woman could hold so much knowledge. Knowledge no other woman in New Phoenix had any business knowing. It was almost like she was someone from another world, not quite fitting the mold of what we knew women to be here in this world.

Drayna yawned and announced, "If this is all you'll be doing tonight, then I'm going to go home and get some sleep."

Rennick stopped her before she could rise from her seat. "But first, do we have your word that you won't tell anyone about what you found out about Laena today?"

"Naturally, I won't tell a soul. Do you think I'd enjoy having our family name dragged into the mud if word gets out? Think of what Mom and Dads would say!" Drayna said with dramatic flair before flashing a wink at Laena.

Rennick walked his sister to the door, where she had parked her Jeep just outside. When he returned to the kitchen, Laena finished typing and looked up. "That should do it," she declared. "Now we wait until we get what we need from those files."

"Good. Maybe we can finally talk about why you chose now to finally trust us," I said, still smarting from the idea that she had never fully trusted us from the beginning. I had no idea how deep my feelings were for this woman until it felt like she had almost trampled them with her secrets.

Shoving the laptop aside, she sat up a little straighter to look me dead in the eye. "The secret was getting to be too much to handle alone. Being alone for too long made me think that I could have done this on my own, but I got so damned tired of it."

"Tired of what? Keeping secrets?" I asked.

"Yes. No. All of it. Being alone. Keeping huge secrets. Not being open with the people who care about me," she admitted in a small voice.

Reese understood me best; he always had without my having to say anything. So he said for me, "Honey, Vance has some big trust issues, especially when it comes to people he cares about, sorry, *we* care about. Keeping secrets was always one of his biggest triggers."

She looked down at her folded hands, and said, "I understand. I wouldn't trust me either if I were in your position."

"But you're not, sweetheart," Rennick crooned. "In our position, I mean. We've been burned by a woman before, and since meeting you, we thought you'd be the key to our future. The one person we could trust."

I continued, "Your little secret-keeping could have big consequences if these files have to do with Elite secrets. You know what the penalty is for digging your nose where it doesn't belong?"

Without waiting for her to answer, I stated, "At the least, a dime in a max security prison. At the worst, exile from the city with all surrounding cities notified not to harbor you."

"And you're the ones who wanted to tag me with a traceable barcode," she retorted. "I would have been fine if you hadn't found me that day. But you did, and that's when the plan changed. Dad changed it on the fly to suit the situation."

That caught my attention. "Wait. Did your Dad actually pay you a visit? When did that happen?"

Laena didn't answer for a few seconds, and it riled me up all over again. "WHEN, LAENA?" I burst out, making her jump in her seat.

In a calm voice, she answered, "Area 5. Where Dad said we owned an apartment, and Dad found me there."

"How? We had that apartment under watch," I said, but I realized the answer the moment I uttered the last word.

"Ah, never mind. If you could hack your way easily into city servers, then it makes sense your dad would know how to evade surveillance cameras."

Laena only nodded, but her expression looked pained. "I know you can't trust me now that everything Dad wanted is going as planned. But I didn't count on you. I didn't know how the three of you would fit in to my plans."

I had to admit to myself that despite the secrets, I still needed this woman. Day in and day out, I woke up wanting her, and when I went to sleep I prayed that she would finally see how much she needed us. Needed me. Never in my wildest dreams did I ever picture this scenario. That she would acknowledge her need for us when she was tired of dealing with her own insecurities, when she couldn't deal.

"Are you messing with me right now?" I asked. "Because I'm very confused by all these mixed signals you keep sending me. And not just me, but to us."

Rennick laid a hand on my shoulder, like a warning. "Whoa, there, buddy. You can't speak for all of us in this. A few weeks ago, we bared more than our souls to each other. You know this."

Laena looked up at Rennick over my shoulder, and I could see the remembered desire there in her eyes as she gazed back at him. On that one night I had her to myself, I remembered the way she had looked at me the same way. So, she wasn't impervious to the idea of us.

"What I'm trying to say, Vance," Laena continued in a small voice, "is that I think I've fallen for all of you. And it scares me shitless that I don't know what I'm signing up for when I want to be yours. To be yours to all three of you."

I froze, not expecting to hear her confess that colossal admission in such a tiny voice. She went on, "I might not know a lot about relationships, but I thought it might help to trust you with all of my secrets. And I've opened up to you about every single one. If that's not enough for you to trust me, then I understand. I can leave if you want."

Well, hell. I couldn't have her leave looking like I just kicked her puppy. She was laying herself bare, and I was still hanging onto my petty angst. For what? So I could lose the love of my life?

And I could honestly say that when I thought I had been hurt before it hadn't felt anything like this. Laena was doing what she could to repair things, to make things right, and I couldn't do more than wallow in hurt feelings? What the hell was I doing?

"Okay," I said finally, more to myself than to anyone else in the room.

Laena looked puzzled. "Okay? You want me to leave?" And she got up to head straight for my front door, but I stopped her.

"No, I don't want you to leave, Laena. I just—I don't know—I needed to fully understand. What this would mean for all of us."

She looked up at me, biting her lower lip in a way that made my eyes flare and my dick hard. The things she was doing to that lip, I wanted to do with my own tongue and teeth. "I couldn't move forward with you and the guys until I became fully transparent about what I'm doing here. I'm not here to hurt anyone. I just want to find out who I am and why I'm supposed to be a big secret."

Reese got up from his seat at the table to face Laena. He told her, "And I'm glad you've finally been up front with us, darlin'. It can't have been easy to finally come out and tell us the truth." I looked at him, and I could see from the look on his face that that bit lip of hers had him all hot and bothered, too.

I traded gazes first with Rennick, then with Reese, and both gave me a nod. It was a lot sooner than we thought, but we all knew how much we wanted this woman. Today, we wordlessly decided, would be the day we introduce her to the delights of having all three of us at once. And we wanted the first time we came together as a foursome to be something special, for all of us. But in this time and space, the air was rife with our mutual arousal for this one woman, the only woman we all wanted to make ours.

With the three of us surrounding her already, we closed in further on her, until each of us could feel her body heat through our clothes. We still wore our field uniforms, grungy and dirty as they were, but it didn't look like any of us cared about that. I knew without asking that Rennick and Reese were as ready as I was for this to happen.

The sudden flaring of her eyes and nostrils gave away how affected she was by our close proximity. I noticed her breathing hitch once my chest bumped with hers, and I couldn't fail to notice the hard points of her nipples abrading against my t-shirt. I was sure I could also speak for the guys when I say I was drawn in by the magnetic pull of her, urging us on to claim her finally as *ours*.

We can make it official the first chance we could and drag her with us to the Courts. But for now, it was more important that she learn what being family with us means.

Looking down first at her mouth, where she still worked that bottom lip with her teeth, I slid my gaze to hers. "Baby, you already know how much we want and need you. Are you sure you're ready for us? For all three of us at once?"

She nodded firmly. "Yes. With everything in me, I want you. All three of you."

20

LAENA

After a whole life of choices made for me, this was the one choice that I've made myself that I firmly believed in. I trusted these beautiful men with everything in me. It made me high just thinking of all three of them on me, in me, all over me. They showed me that they have always been mine; I just had to let go of my own trust issues and finally let them in. And I knew that finally revealing my forays into New Phoenix restricted files and my reasons for doing them would also mean that I have nothing left to hide from them.

Vance stood before me, my chest brushing just under his own pectorals. Both Reese and Rennick also stood so close. Reese's nose brushed against my right ear, and Rennick's front was flush against my back.

"Yes," I continued, "it's time."

"Sweetheart, you sure?" Rennick whispered.

I nodded once again. "Mmhmm," I hummed. Vance was now kneading both of my breasts, with his thumbs strumming against my hardened nipples. Reese was stringing kisses and licks along my other ear and down the side of my neck.

I gasped when Vance pinched both nipples, and he said, "Good. Because we've been needing to do this for a long time. Even longer than before we had even met you."

Rennick explained further, "We need to show you and my brothers here that we're a family now. And to do that, we want to make love to you, all of us at once."

My head spun at the thought of all three of them driving me crazy with three-fold pleasure, and I was eager to learn what it would take to fully pleasure all three of them. It also made me a little nervous about my ability to fulfill their needs as the sole woman in this foursome. I didn't know how this was going to work, but I was all for finding all the ways that would make my men fulfilled and happy.

I nodded again, as a wave of heat rushed upwards from my feminine core, flooding my body with more heat as

Vance bent his head and nibbled at one nipple through my shirt. I cried out and all three of them converged on me at once with their hands lingering and stroking the places on my body that produced the most pleasure.

I loved every bit of attention their hands and mouths paid to my sex-starved body. It was hard to believe that not so long ago, I had gone from an asexual existence to this. If it weren't for these three men, I wouldn't have experienced any kind of sensual pleasure at all. And now I had the love of these three men, men who were eager and determined to please me here and now.

I was dizzy with the headiness of their sensual treatment. I swayed a little, falling back against Rennick, who caught me to him. Vance popped his head up and said, "Whoa, there." Then looking at the other two behind me, he asked them, "How about we get cleaned up first? My shower's big enough for all of us."

I was too high on my own bliss to answer coherently, but Vance scooped me up before the other two could protest and headed towards the stairs. Vance said over his free shoulder, "Last one in comes last!"

Groans followed us as Reese and Rennick scrambled over each other to reach the stairs first. I laughed, but that gave me a great idea. Vance hadn't made it to the stairs just yet, but he was going at a fast clip to get there. His grip on my hips was loose so I slid my body further down his back, gripping his own hips to swing my legs backwards and over his shoulder. Vance was so startled that he let go of me, and I was able to do my little backflip, landing on my feet and down into a crouch. With a burst of speed and a devilish smile, I bolted across the room.

I heard Reese laugh loudly. "I get it! Laena wants to be the one who comes last!" Pulling Rennick with him up the stairs and past Vance, he announced, "Then, let's make it happen!"

Vance shot me a lopsided smile; his one foot poised on the first stair. "Okay, baby girl. Your wish, our command.

See you up there." And he jogged up the stairs towards his bathroom.

I followed some distance behind, drawing out the anticipation even further. With each step, my heart pounded harder with the thought of the three men waiting for me. Before I even stepped through the bathroom door, I was grabbed impatiently inside only to be caught flush against a naked Reese.

"Took you long enough," he complained good-naturedly. I giggled, but the sound was cut short when he caught my lips in a kiss that set me ablaze. The naked feel of him against my still-clothed body had me shuddering, knowing that I would soon be as naked as him.

Then I was pulled away from him to be caught up against a very nude Rennick. His mouth descended on mine, and while I was thus occupied, Rennick unbuttoned and unzipped my pants as Reese reached around me to slide them down my legs. Without breaking our kiss, Rennick lifted me up and against him to better aid Reese in releasing my bunched-up pants from my ankles.

From behind Rennick, I heard Vance bark, "The faster we get her and us clean, the faster we can get into the bed." Rennick released my mouth to grin unabashedly down at me, but in my kiss-induced haze I couldn't even protest when he whipped my shirt up and off in one smooth move.

Vance was already in the shower stall, adjusting the temperature of the shower, and my mouth watered at the rear view he afforded me. Vance had an amazing ass to go with all the rippling muscles in that gorgeous back of his. I still had my bra and panties to contend with, so without any further help, I managed to dispense with those last two barriers of fabric.

But I hadn't counted on the uneasy silence that descended suddenly. Then Vance and Reese burst out over each other:

"What the fuck happened to you out there?!"

"How did you get that wound?"

Looking down at my shoulder, I saw fresh blood seeping through Rennick's hasty first aid. I hadn't even noticed it until they all stared at it. Vance and Reese stared angrily at it, while Rennick stared at it uncomfortably.

"I got bit. What's the big deal?" I said, shrugging. "I'm immune, remember? I'll heal."

I swore I could see steam coming out of Vance's ears. He exploded, "WHAT?!"

Rennick moved closer to inspect the wound under his makeshift bandage, and said placatingly, "In this world, we can't even begin to understand how that is normal. But it looks like it's reopened."

Reese blew out a frustrated breath, and complained, "You're a woman, one who's supposed to be protected from harm. How can you have been raised by a crazy man allowing you to be put into harm's way is just—fucking crazy!"

Vance looked like he was struggling to remain calm, but he too blew out a breath, much like Reese's. Finally, he said, "You shouldn't have taken point on your own. One of us should have been with you."

After my confession earlier, I knew they knew that I had Rennick tailing me. So, technically, Rennick was with me, but we didn't know that we would be caught by surprise by a horde that attacked and scattered our group.

"The fact is, I still had someone with me, and I'm here alive and okay. Can I get cleaned up now?" I asked, shivering a little from being entirely nude in front of them. But I shivered mostly because I had all three of them staring pointedly at me.

Vance beckoned me into the shower with him, and the other two followed me in. It was a large shower stall, but with three large men and a tinier me, it was still a tight fit.

The sensual haze we had all been under from earlier was replaced with something else. Rennick helped me with washing the wound properly, and he said he would properly bandage it with antiseptic. What amazed and amused me the most was the sight of three big men trying to wash themselves while bumping arms and elbows. But there wasn't much room for me to move, squashed as I was in between the three of them.

That problem was soon fixed once Vance tackled my hair with his shampoo, Reese soaped up my front, and Rennick washed my back. Their gentle scrubbing turned lazy once the lather built on my body, and their touches turned slow and sensual once again. I groaned at the magical feel of their fingers playing against my scalp and my skin; it was a treatment I didn't know I missed all this time.

"Like that, do you?" Vance asked as he applied pressure against my skull with his fingertips, and I groaned once more. It was divine; I had no idea that pleasure could be found just by having one's scalp massaged.

Every little touch and each slide of their hands against my soap-slicked skin produced groans and sighs in quick succession. With all of their attention focused on me, I was sure I was drunk on it and on the bliss of their touch. On the occasions I blinked open my eyes, I was struck by the look on their faces. And by their cocks jutting out and standing at attention. They each wore the same expression of languor and desire meant for me.

Vance rinsed off quickly and announced he'd straighten up the room and the bed we would soon all be using. Alone with Reese and Rennick in the shower stall, they shared the task of rinsing the suds off of me. But they did it teasingly.

"Reese!" I squeaked at a high pitch when he slid a hand up between my thighs and pressed the heel of his palm there. He stroked me there, and I shuddered.

Rennick chuckled beside me. His hands slid towards my ass, stroking my buttocks, until he reached the cleft. I jolted at his touch when he reached my anus, rimming the opening with a finger. "I can't wait to make this mine," he said. "I want to be the first to breach you here."

The dizzy feeling came back at his words, and I wasn't quite sure how that would work. I already had him inside my pussy once before; I couldn't imagine his length and girth finding its way inside a much smaller hole.

Reese reassured me, "Don't worry, Laena. We'll go slow, and we'll make it good for you. I promise."

I merely nodded, and I let the two of them usher me out of the stall. They took turns drying me then wrapped me in a large fluffy towel so they could dry themselves off, too. The job done, they led me to Vance's bedroom, where Vance stood waiting at the foot of the bed, now stripped of its duvet.

Reaching out a hand toward me, Vance took up one of my hands while he used his other hand to slide the towel off of my body. Rennick produced a first aid kit and Vance led me to sit at the edge of the bed. With antiseptic applied to the fresh wound, Rennick wordlessly dressed it with a fresh bandage.

"There," Rennick pronounced. "All clean and covered up." Then, he and the other two turned to me, anticipation and desire written on their faces. Before I could utter a word, all three helped me scoot further up the bed and onto my back. Rennick and Vance took up either side of me on the bed, while Reese took the spot between my legs.

From between my legs, Reese looked up at me across the expanse of my naked torso, and said, "And this is where we prepare you for us and our cocks. All you have to do is lie back and let us do the work. Let's forget about you coming last. We need you ready for us."

I raised a brow, a little apprehensive about what he meant by work, but I knew that because it was these three, that I would thoroughly enjoy it.

Rennick and Vance each claimed a breast, torturing me with licks and nibbles on my sensitized nipples. But neither man used the same technique, each choosing to draw out my pleasure with their favorite method of teasing me. Vance nibbled at my nipple with soft nips and using his teeth gently. Rennick liked to swirl his tongue around my areola, making each circle tighter until he grazed the nipple with either the flat or tip of his tongue. Either way, the actions of both men made for thrilling torment.

Reese was between my legs, stroking his cock as I watched him watching us. He let go of his cock so he could bend forward and touch his mouth to my clit. He pressed a light kiss there, then pulled back to blow a breath across my heated flesh down there. I moaned at the sensation of his breath, but I craved to have his mouth and tongue covering my sex.

He smiled at me naughtily when I raised my head to shoot him a look in frustration, and said, "Relax. Just enjoy." Then, he got to work, eating me down below like I was his favorite snack and he was starving. Reese licked me, tasting me like he couldn't get enough of my flavor. With his probing tongue, he slid its tip inside me to learn my inner heat, and he moaned audibly against me, the vibrations of his moans warming me further down there.

Both Rennick and Vance redoubled their efforts on my breasts, both alternating capturing my lips with theirs. At the same time, Reese licked his way further down my slit, his wet tongue now meeting my anal entrance. It felt unusual to have him lick me there, but it was also sensitive to his tongue's probing in a pleasurable way. I gasped as soon as I felt a finger skimming across my tight ring, but Reese tempered the sensation by also sucking and licking my clit at the same time.

Rennick warned, "I called dibs on her ass, Reese," as he popped his head up to inspect what Reese was doing.

Reese soothed, "Don't worry, I'm getting her ready for you." As soon as Reese returned to sucking my clit, I gasped loudly then moaned quickly after at the hot feel of Reese's finger probing inside my ass.

"Relax," he urged against my pussy. Rennick and Vance distracted me away from the foreign feeling by clamping down on my nipple and rolling it gently between their teeth. The distraction was enough for Reese to plunge his finger in, a finger made wet with the combination of my own wetness and Reese's saliva. I tightened against his finger, not used to the invasion, and I couldn't do more than tremble as all three men had me pinned down.

Against my ear, Vance crooned, "Push against his finger, baby girl." His coaxing voice and his hot breath on the shell of my ear soothed me enough to do as he said. When I did, the pressure inside lessened a bit, and I relaxed further to let Reese add in another finger. Again, I concentrated on pushing against both of his fingers, but soon lost my concentration once Reese ate me out with earnest gusto.

I found myself thrusting my own hips against Reese's mouth, and soon realized that my thrusting was also matching the rhythm Reese had set with his fingers in and out of my ass. I obviously enjoyed each and every sensation my three men doled out for me, and I let go, letting my body's needs and desire to take over.

Opening my eyes, I lost Rennick at one breast as he shuffled to join Reese. Now, Rennick traded Reese's fingers for his as he discovered for himself my backdoor heat and tightness. Reese took up Rennick's old spot on the bed beside me, and he pulled me close for an open-mouthed kiss where I could taste my own flavor on Reese's tongue.

Until now, Vance had been working one breast, but once the other two traded places, he was no longer content where he was. Without a word, he pulled me away from Reese's kiss, planted a ferociously soul-stealing kiss on me, then rolled me on top of him. Meanwhile, Rennick had kept his fingers thrusting inside my ass, still working me into a frenzy from the sensations he produced there.

As I straddled Vance, he reached between our bodies to poise his cock at my entrance. Reese, not eager to be left behind, instructed me, "Suck me. You remember how." And he stood up on the bed, so I was eye-level with his straining cock.

I opened my mouth so Reese could gain entrance past my lips, while at the same time Vance thrust upwards to impale me fully. I groaned around Reese's cock at the feeling of fullness in my aching, drenched pussy, and Reese answered with a groan of his own.

"God, that felt good, Laena," Reese breathed out. "Keep making humming noises like that."

That wouldn't be too hard now that Vance was thrusting wildly up into me. Rennick dislodged his fingers only to move in closer so that the wide head of his cock now lined up with my anus. "I'm lubed up so it should make things easier," Rennick assured me. "Just relax and let me in, baby. I promise it will feel amazing."

With sucking Reese's cock and Vance ruthlessly bouncing me up and down his cock, I still tensed despite Rennick's urging. Something passed between the three of them that I couldn't see, and suddenly both Vance and Reese didn't move a muscle. We all paused, and I had stopped breathing once Rennick eased his way through that tight ring of muscle. I let go of Reese's cock to cry out at the sensation, feeling even more stretched than when Vance first took my virginity.

Rennick's voice sounded strained. "Just ease up a little, I'm almost all the way in. Breathe, baby, breathe."

I tried to do as he said, but all my thoughts centered on the feeling of being stretched as far as I could possibly go. Then, Vance and Reese sprang into action all at once. Reese filled my mouth once more, and Vance thrust hard up into me. That's when Rennick pumped his hips fully forward and seated himself fully into my ass.

I screamed from the fullness of it all, my throat vibrating around the rod in my mouth. I was shaking now, not from pain, but from being impaled by three cocks at once. It was more than I knew what to do with, and I quivered helplessly along with their thrusts. I felt buffeted by their treatments, helpless to do no more than take what they gave.

Rennick must have sensed me pulling away from them all mentally, and he protested, "Oh, no, baby. You're staying right here with us. Let us see and feel you come." And he wrapped an arm around my waist, dipping one hand between my legs. With fervor, he stroked at my clit, bringing me back to full pleasure once more, making me wail and moan around Reese who was still pumping my mouth.

Both Vance and Rennick took turns alternating in and out of me, sheathing themselves deep inside me. Everything happening inside of me and around me both shocked and delighted me. I wasn't even worrying about how I could return the pleasure they each were giving me; I was so far gone. Soon, a tidal wave of an orgasm crashed through me at Rennick's ministrations, and I screamed around Reese as the two men in my pussy and ass thrust into me even harder to draw out the pleasure even longer.

"Shit! Do you feel her squeezing you as hard as she is me?" I heard Vance ask Rennick.

Rennick didn't answer his question, only to grunt, "Ah, fuck." One second later, he spurted hotly inside my ass, breathing hard through his own orgasm. When he was replete, I was just coming down from my own orgasm high, and Rennick withdrew from my ass, making me regret the loss of his hardness and heat there.

Reese pulled out of my mouth with a wet pop, and it didn't take him long to position himself in Rennick's old place. Rennick didn't leave; instead he kept me propped up, twining our tongues together in a lust-crazed kiss. While both Reese and Vance got to work thrusting into me simultaneously, I felt the familiar curl of another orgasm building within me, being filled with two large cocks at once.

It wasn't long before I screamed through another orgasm, the bliss hitting me just as hard as the first time. "Oh, yeah," Vance encouraged me. "Milk my cock, baby girl, so I can come, too." Seconds later, he made good on that promise and filled my pussy..

"Me, too, sweetheart," Reese said just a second later behind Vance. And I gasped as his cock grew larger right before he spurted deep within my ass.

We were a sweaty, sticky bunch, but we were also satisfyingly sated from the all the delights we had just shared. Surrounded by my men, I was happier than I had ever been, knowing that these three were the family I had always wanted and never knew I needed.

21

VANCE

Funny how a small slip of a woman could turn your whole world on its axis and suddenly change everything you knew about the world. The four of us lasted as long as round three when Laena threatened to twist off our balls if we dared come near her for a fourth round. As tired as she was, she was insatiable until that point, just as the three of us were. I didn't know we even had it in us to go longer until she cried for mercy.

As I slipped out of bed, leaving Laena sandwiched between Rennick and Reese, I went downstairs to check on the progress of those files. I still had some trouble wrapping my head around what Laena was trying to imply: that the Elite had something to hide and that somehow Laena was tied up in all of that.

The kitchen clock read 3:10, and Laena had said it would take all night to get those files unencrypted. Waking up the laptop's screen, I found to my surprise that the nine status bars for all the files were lit up green, indicating their completed status. I double-clicked on the first file at the top and was surprised to have video footage pop up on screen.

On the lower left-hand corner, a time and date stamp read *January 6, Year 100 AEc.* Twenty-five years ago. The camera was focused on two people in the tiny room, sitting on chairs with a table between them. A man in a white lab coat and dark hair was shuffling papers in front of him on the table as the woman across from him sat silently. She was pretty, slender, but fair-haired with clear brown eyes, and she wore a simple hospital gown and paper booties on her feet. However, she looked anything but happy, if the look of pained impatience was anything to go by.

Finding the right sheet, the man spoke, "Ah, here it is. Let's begin. What is your name?"

The woman said in a clear, strong voice, "Caelaena Kanata." The man made a check mark on his paper.

A series of questions that asked her date of birth, birthplace, parents, etc. ensued—boring—until Caelaena interrupted, "Dr. Lightbourne, when can we begin the program again?"

The man, apparently Dr. Lightbourne, sighed, then chucked his pen across the table and swiped off his glasses. He leaned in to gently say, "You know the rules. We have to do the preliminaries first before we can properly assess your fitness for the program. And you know they're watching us." He pointed at the camera.

Caelaena seemed agitated by his patronizing tone and seemed to go to some effort to speak calmly. "I know," she drew out slowly. "Since I lost my baby boy, I want to try again. I *need* to *try* again." Each word was staccato-like, spat out between clenched teeth.

"I understand that. The Elite understands that," the doctor said. "But we have to make sure that you, our patient, are healthy enough for the procedure. These things take time as you already know."

The woman sighed, deflating like a balloon against the back of the chair. Tears streamed down her face as she said, "I know. But why can't my body do what it's supposed to? I know you can help me, Doc. Please help me." She sobbed into her hands, great, shuddering sobs that shook her small frame as she wept noisily.

Caelaena Kanata had similar features to our Laena, and we already knew that Laena's DNA was an almost exact match with that of Kane Ardarien. Laena's Asian looks were comparable to the woman I watched on the screen, and I still had yet to discover why a video like this one was kept hidden away for twenty-five years.

I kept watching, but the sobbing continued, and no amount of the doctor's placating her was getting through to her. The video stopped, meaning that I had viewed the full file. Since there were eight more to look through, and I wasn't ready to join the others back up in my bedroom, I settled myself into a chair to watch the rest.

The other video files were pretty much the same as the first, except for the dates. And each file seemed to be a testament of the poor woman's deterioration as she underwent disappointment after disappointment monthly, it seemed. Each video witnessed Caelaena Kanata's unholy obsession with carrying another child, but nothing ever came out of each treatment.

Until the last file, the ninth file, dated October 10, Year 101 AEc.

This time, Caelaena appeared in the video, happier than the last eight videos, and Dr. Lightbourne seemed to be just as happy as she was.

"Congratulations, Caelaena," Dr. Lightbourne said with a wide smile. "It looks like you are pregnant."

The much thinner Caelaena beamed, "Thank you, Doctor. And please, I'd rather not know what I'm having. All I'm concerned with is that this baby is carried to term and healthy." I frowned, seeing that Caelaena had somehow shrunk in the months since the first video. Her once healthy skin and hair now had a dull sheen to them, and her new condition didn't give me much confidence that she could carry this baby to term.

"Of course. And we'll keep close watch on you and the baby to make sure of it."

Getting up from his chair, Dr. Lightbourne walked to a cabinet full of medicines, from which he retrieved two syringes and a few vials of different clear liquids. He assured her, "I want to give you a shot of vitamins as well as a steroid to make sure that this baby stays where it is."

She nodded, and said, "Of course. Whatever the baby needs."

I watched as the doctor administered the two drugs, and then he stepped away to dispose of the used syringes. Caelaena chattered on throughout the procedure and continued on while he stepped away. But as I watched, her words garbled then slowed completely as she slumped in her seat. Passed out completely, her small frame slid to the floor as the doctor calmly turned to observe her.

"Ah, there we go," he said lightheartedly. Then two men entered the room through a door off-camera, pushing a gurney between them. Dr. Lightbourne instructed the two men, "Put this one in room six. I'll meet you there when I finish up here." The orderlies, judging by their nondescript white uniforms, lifted poor Caelaena from off the floor and onto the gurney, strapping her in, before leaving the room to wherever room six was.

Dr. Lightbourne faced the camera and spoke as if to an audience, "As you can see, after the ninth attempt, we were successful. With my re-worked formula, we will see how the serum works through the progression of Caelaena's pregnancy."

The video cut off for a few seconds and then cut back in to a much later date. It was Caelaena back in the same position but with her swollen body showcasing the advanced stages of her pregnancy. She was restrained, her hair in knotted disarray around her head, but this time she was anything but calm.

"YOU BASTARDS! HOW DARE YOU KEEP ME HERE! DO YOU KNOW WHO MY BROTHER IS? HE WILL KILL YOU ALL IF HE FINDS OUT WHAT YOU'RE DOING HERE!" Caelaena screamed. The restraints around her wrists and ankles kept her rooted to the wheelchair, but still she struggled.

Dr. Lightbourne, appeared on screen, now wearing a surgical gown, mask, and gloves. Calmly, he told her, "Now, now, Caelaena. You had signed the several dotted lines necessary that got you here. You wanted this baby, and you are about to deliver him or her any minute now."

She spat angrily, spittle flying, "You lied to me! I didn't sign up for this! You took advantage of me and my inability to carry a child to term, and now you're making me carry a monster! I've seen the other women! I've seen their bodies!"

In his annoyingly calm voice, Dr. Lightbourne explained, "I never lied to you. You knew you would be under our care for the duration of your pregnancy."

"Yes, but—"

"And you knew that you risked another miscarriage if we hadn't given you the care you know was needed these past nine months."

Caelaena, riled up once more, yelled, "You are a LIAR! You've kept me prisoner here; drugged me without my knowledge; and you've injected me with things to create this-- this MONSTER inside me! How do you dare to do this when I am the sister of an Elite official!"

I froze when Dr. Lightbourne casually claimed, "Barclay knows about this. He consented to it himself, signing in the stead of your dead husband."

Caelaena Kanata was Barclay Ardarien's sister?

Caelaena stopped struggling and in a cracked whisper, she asked, "He knew about this?"

Dr. Lightbourne snatched a form from off the table and pointed to the page to show it to her. "Right here," he indicated. "That's his signature, is it not?"

Caelaena seemed to shrink as she said in a defeated voice, "Yes." Then with a wail, she cried out, "But why? Why would he do this to me?"

Lightbourne shrugged and simply said, "You wanted this baby, remember? You said to do whatever it takes. And we did! Now let's get you ready to meet Caelaena Junior, shall we?" He moved to wheel Caelaena out of the room and off screen.

Another few seconds of video static, then a bloodied Lightbourne holding a small squirmy bundle appeared on screen. He held up the bundle to the camera while exclaiming excitedly, "We were successful in a way we never imagined! We didn't find a cure; we've created a perfect being! One that's immune to the effects of the Eidolon virus! We still have yet to see her abilities as she grows, but for now, Test Subject 8-007 is already showing extraordinary motor skills unseen in normal newborns."

More video static seconds followed, then Lightbourne appeared again, this time wearing dark clothing and looking grave. The background had since changed to that of a larger room, with more shadows in it than there was light. As I moved in to better inspect the screen, Lightbourne wasn't just wearing dark clothes; he was outfitted in battle gear, complete with gun in hand aimed at two other personnel in white lab coats.

He shot at both people, shooting both in the head. As Lab Coat One and Lab Coat Two fell away, the operating table they stood over revealed a bald little child strapped onto it, still conscious. The child cried out at the shots, but Lightbourne soothed, "Sh, sh. It's okay. You're safe now. I'm going to take you somewhere far from here, okay?" Lightbourne moved to undo the bindings and swooped the child up in his arms. The child looked no older than a toddler, maybe two or three years old, and I couldn't tell if the child was a boy or a girl.

"Okay," the child said trustingly, holding him round his neck. Lightbourne swung around, and with his gun held high, he looked about the room until he spotted what he was looking for. He now looked directly into the camera, and with one shot, he blew out the screen. Then more static, and then the video stopped.

Before I could blow out the breath I held during the last few seconds of the footage, I heard a feminine cry of distress sound behind me. I whirled to find Laena wrapped in one of my shirts, holding her hands to her mouth as she stood there, shell-shocked.

I went to her, not liking that she looked so pale. "Baby girl, how long were you standing there? What is it?"

I could already guess that the video affected Laena somehow, and she had said that she believed these videos may be a link to her past somehow. Her hands felt icy as I took them in my own, and I sank back down into the chair, clutching her close as I sat her on my lap. She said nothing as I wrapped my arms around her, trying to infuse as much of my own body heat into her much smaller frame.

Bare feet padding through the kitchen sounded behind us, and I turned to meet the bewildered gazes of Rennick and Reese.

"We woke up to find the both of you gone, then we heard Laena cry out. What's happened?" Rennick asked.

Laena didn't volunteer an answer, so I explained, "The files were ready for viewing, and I sat here watching them all. It's this last one that reveals a lot more than the others. Laena seems to be shocked by what she'd seen so far." With a thumb, I pointed toward the laptop. "Take a look for yourself."

Both Rennick and Reese played back the footage from the beginning, and I caught Laena poking her head up to watch along with them. She must have caught just the last thirty seconds and didn't see the beginning. I watched her watching the video, stroking her back gently as she did so, and I waited to see any telltale signs that could give away what she thought. Unfortunately, she didn't give up even a penny's worth, but I noticed that she peered even closer to the screen as Lightbourne appeared in battle gear, her eyes drinking in every detail.

"What's the matter? Do you know who Lightbourne is? Or who the little kid could be?" I asked carefully.

She nodded and tried to speak, but her voice cracked. Her throat must have been dry, so Reese produced a glass from the cupboard, filled it in the sink, and handed it to her. "Here you go, sweetheart."

She accepted it and drank it down before shocking us all by saying, "Dr. Lightbourne? No, that man is my father. The man who has loved and protected me all these years."

I did a double-take, and my hand froze in mid-stroke against her back. Reese and Rennick moved each to a kitchen stool, and sat heavily into them, obviously shocked as hard as I was.

"What do you mean? That man had kept an Elite woman against her will! And Barclay Ardarien helped put her there! How could that be your father?" Reese asked, not fully understanding.

I reached out to tap on the first video file I had watched and pressed play. "Watch this one. It explains what Caelaena thought she was doing there." I waited as the three of them silently watched through the footage. When it was done, we all looked to Laena.

She still looked pale, but her voice was clear and strong. "That child was me, and that woman was my mother. I can sort of remember that day he took me from that lab. I was three, I think. Lightbourne, or Atsushi Kanata as he later called himself, was never my biological father. My DNA proves that. But he was the man who raised me, and I still call him Dad."

"But how could he do that to my mother?" she asked angrily, more to herself than to us. "How could he play her like that when she was hurting so bad and for his own ambition?"

"We don't know, sweetheart," Reese leaned in, peering into her tear-filled eyes. "We only know what we saw on the videos."

"He was so different from what I know of him," she protested. "How do I reconcile the man who raised me with this man who clearly lied and used my mother?" Laena looked ready to crumble into pieces in my arms, and she shook with the effort to keep it together.

This strong woman who could face ugly odds with Eidolon monsters seemed so tiny and helpless, and I wanted to fight this internal battle for her. But I didn't know how.

"Baby girl, let's look at it this way," Rennick stated gently. "Those files had been hidden for a reason we don't know yet. Your dad wanted you to uncover the truth about you. And he wanted the best for you. If the man who raised you is the same man in those videos, I think he must have had a sudden change of heart to get you out of there."

Rennick was always the better diplomat than I ever was, knowing the right things to say to pacify or settle an argument.

Reese joined in. "Right. The videos are showing us something true. What you know about your father is also true.

Somewhere in the middle is an event that caused a change in your father to be the man you know and love."

Laena moaned, "I don't know that I can trust my own memories now."

Then, I got it. I was overcome with what I wanted to say.

"Laena," I called her name softly, and angled her chin to face me fully. "You know we love you, right?"

She took a quivering breath, and smiled, saying lightly, "Do I?"

"In case you don't know, I love you. Just as I know my brothers sitting here feel the same way about you," I said, following up with a small kiss on her nose. "Does my saying it make you doubt our sincerity?"

"No," she said. "Where is this headed, by the way?"

"Just bear with me," I pleaded. "Now answer me this: what makes you sure of what we say when we say we love you?"

Taking a few seconds to think it over, she finally answered, "Because of what you do. Your actions back up those words. You've cared for me and looked after me from day one. You showed me with your bodies how much you love me. Just as I love all of you; I gave up my secret to you, for you."

Smiling down at her for her admission that she loved us, I touched my forehead to hers as I said, "Right. And wouldn't you say your father's actions over the years that he raised you says a lot of how he felt about you? How did he act towards you?"

"Like a father. He loved me. He taught me to survive, and he protected me," she said, with a wan smile. "Dad may have been weird about our hiding, but now I kind of know why because of those videos."

Reese snorted, "While I think you could have done without the education he gave you, he did good by you, by doing the best he could with what little he had."

Rennick added, "And he made sure you were the badass Eidolon monster killer that the three of us fell in love with. You know I fell in love with that roundhouse kick of yours before I even knew you were a woman."

Laena laughed. "Is that all you love me for, Rennick?"

Rennick stood to lift her from my arms and into his own. Holding her against him, he nuzzled her cheek against his as he said, "You know we love the entire package. You're everything we wanted and then some."

Pulling back from Rennick's embrace, Laena shyly admitted, "Well, you're about to love me some more, when I tell you of another development."

I braced myself for another secret she failed to share with us, but I knew I had to be patient, knowing she would tell us everything on her own time. "What does that mean?" I ask, trying hard to keep the suspicion from creeping in my voice.

"Did I also mention that once I found out what Dad wanted me to know about my past, he'd come find me?"

"WHAT?" I burst out. "Why did you leave that out of our earlier conversation till now?"

"Because I think he's here," she said simply.

Slow, deliberate footsteps sounded above our heads, coming from the floor above us.

22

LAENA

Oh my God. Dad showing up was the last thing I expected, and I should have known better. As soon as I heard the creak of a window sash being shoved upwards, coming from upstairs, I knew it was Dad. He had promised after all.

And I didn't expect to be half-dressed in front of him as he showed up in the kitchen. Of course, the guys didn't know him, whether he be friend or foe, so I was a little surprised to see them all pointing a gun at Dad when he walked on in. And the surprise was more from the realization that there were weapons hiding in weird places in the kitchen. *And that they all knew their locations in Vance's house and were able to whip them out without my noticing.*

Looking at Dad now, he looked the same with his unkempt goatee, salt and pepper hair, and wiry frame. Only his eyes looked tired, and now that I looked closely, he lost a few pounds that he didn't need to lose.

"I'm unarmed," Dad said his hands up and empty. "I wouldn't bring anything here that could hurt Laena." The guys all visibly relaxed from their intense postures and lowered their guns, but all three raised them again when Dad moved to retrieve something from behind.

"Relax," he said smoothly. "It's a small thank you for looking after Laena. I knew you boys couldn't help yourselves." And he presented a tiny, rectangular object from a back pocket and deposited it onto the kitchen table, next to the laptop.

Huh, an SD card. "It has the evidence for everything I'm going to brief all of you," Dad explained.

Then, I gasped, thinking Dad must have watched me closer than I thought. Did Dad know about us?

Dad must have understood what I was thinking because he shot the others a disgusted look, and then at me before he said, "These guys are known for their heroic acts on and off the field. Of course, they couldn't resist a damsel in distress type."

I almost sagged with relief, but he continued in a chastising tone, "And don't think I don't know what you've been up to upstairs, young lady. I saw that bed." Shit, he must have entered through Vance's bedroom, then. "While I'm grateful you found these men to be your protectors, I didn't realize that you'd be paying them with your body!"

"No, Dad! You got it all wrong! That's not how—"

Placing an arm around me protectively, Vance interrupted, "Laena will be our wife, once we get our marriage registered in the Courts. She will be legally ours to protect."

"Huh," was all Dad said after a few beats of silence. Then, with a shake of his head, he looked down at the floor, letting out a small chuckle. "Well, you've managed to surprise me. Marriage wasn't an option I thought any of you would consider."

"Dad, it didn't occur to me either in the beginning, but these men showed me a different way of living. A way of life you've kept from me!" I shouted, finally venting how I secretly felt about the way Dad had raised me.

"No, Laena. I had no choice but to keep you out of society," Dad said forlornly, slumping into an empty kitchen chair. Sighing, he said to me, "Now that you've uncovered those video files, I owe you what I promised." I looked at him dubiously, not believing that those video files were what he wanted me to find. "Well, I promised you what I know, didn't I? Now's the time to hear it all. For all of you to hear it all."

Nobody moved a muscle, and Dad waved us all to take a seat. "Come on, might as well get comfortable. This could take a while."

I wanted to hear this, so I moved to the seat recently vacated by Vance, and the guys all settled into whatever chair was closest to them. So, Dad began:

"The files you watched just now? I had them set to notify me the moment they were viewed. They once belonged to Elite R&D, but even the Elite have secrets they'd rather keep hidden. They deleted these files originally and made me a wanted man.

"And as you've found out, my name isn't Atsushi Kanata. It's Montgomery Lightbourne, formerly senior scientist of the military division of the Elite Army. I was the reason Caelaena was in those videos from the start, and she was the reason I got out and took you with me, Laena. In fact, I named you after her to honor her memory. She was just a poor, lonely woman who the Elite had selected for the program I had designed."

"Program?" I asked.

"We had been searching for a vaccine against the Eidolon virus, but it mutated faster than we could keep up with it. Anything we tried *in vitro* all ended up in failures, and I had the bright idea to use pure, unadulterated fetuses for our research."

I blanched at the idea of using defenseless, unborn babies in the name of science. "Why unborn babies?"

"Because they hadn't been exposed to the filth of this world yet. Something about the environment is allowing the Eidolon virus to flourish, and we still haven't pinpointed what factors allow for its proliferative state. The fetus, from an immunological perspective, is a parasite to its own mother, yet it is protected quite safely from the mother's own immune response to it. My research heavily involved curating ideal candidates for vaccine development, only there were so few volunteers.

"And so, the Elite resorted to looking to our infertility clinics to look for proper incubators. Poor unsuspecting women who, once they conceived, were snatched away to my secret laboratory. The Elite covered up their disappearances, telling their families that they had been killed during an Eidolon attack."

Vance, Rennick, and Reese were up in arms at this bit of information, as they were our government's most celebrated champions.

"How could that shit be even true?"

"There's no way my mother would stand for such unethical treatment!"

"You've gotta be shittin' me!"

Dad went on, "And I was obsessed with my work, not caring who got hurt in the process. I only cared about seeking a cure. Until Caelaena."

I had a hard time believing that the Dad I knew as a child was the same man who made my mother along with untold numbers of others suffer. I remembered the day he unstrapped me from that table, but since then I had known him only as 'Dad', who was kind and sought only to protect me. He had taught me how to protect myself, to fight, to hack—skills to survive in this world.

"What can you tell me about her, about Caelaena?" I asked, still trying to reconcile who Dad was in light of what he was telling us. "How did she end up in your program?"

"Caelaena, like so many other women out there in the world, had problems carrying her babies to full term. It's part of this Eidolon-cursed world. Our infertility clinics could only do so much, and only the richest could afford the best treatments. Caelaena may have been the sister to one of our Council, but the Kanatas didn't have the same wealth or prestige as the Ardariens have.

"Her husbands died during a routine patrol, and they had been overcome by an Eidolon horde. Her last treatment at the clinic was from a reserve of her husbands' banked sperm, resulting in a pregnancy that only lasted a few months.

"Then I stepped in, under the guise that my renown could help her with her fertility issues."

"But you used her for your research instead," I said, the accusation burning in my eyes.

"Yes," Dad said, remorse on his tongue. "She was my eighth candidate. It wasn't until my newest formulation after the seventh trial produced an unprecedented result. You." But I still haven't heard why.

"But why stop there? We know Laena is immune. Something about her blood attacks the Eidolon virus, neutralizing it," Rennick stated, asking in my stead, the question I wanted the answer to.

"Because after Caelaena, I learned that I wasn't the first to make such a unique discovery. The Elite had been successful in finding a cure years before me, but they liked their position too much to make people aware of it."

That was baffling to me. "What the hell does that mean?"

Vance seemed to understand much more than I did. Nodding he mumbled, "It means that without the Eidolon virus, they wouldn't have the power that they have now. Elite society exists only because the Eidolon virus created them in the first place, to protect the rest of humanity."

I had lived most of my life outside of society in general, not knowing what I was missing. And so, I partially understood what Dad had done to raise me outside of it after Vance had cleared that up for me.

"Yes," Dad said. "Without Eidolon causing people to live in fear, the Elite will have lost their power. Because of Caelaena's death and your arrival, Laena, I discovered that the Elite would sooner have you destroyed than to let you and my research continue on. Two years of testing proved that you were completely impervious to the virus; two years of pain that you seem to have forgotten I inflicted on you before I took you away.

I still had trouble wrapping my head around everything he was saying. Instead, I asked, "What made you save me? What changed that made you change your mind about keeping me alive?"

Dad looked at me sadly and replied, "It was your mother who changed my mind. Just before she died giving birth to you, she begged me to let her only legacy live on, to raise you like any normal child. She made me promise as you ripped your way out of her, your birth being so similar to that of the seven other candidates before her.

"But in the two years after her death, I-I began to care for you, and you had looked at me like I was your whole world. Then the Elite canceled the program and ordered your termination. And I couldn't let you go. After that last bit of footage you'd seen, I had faked our deaths, making it look like we both had been overcome by an Eidolon horde in our escape. There had been no reason for anyone to continue looking for us."

That was the first I've heard about his previous research. "What happened to the other seven women in the program?" I asked, not sure I was ready to hear the answer.

"They didn't survive. Those test subjects ripped their mothers apart during delivery, only to be born as mindless Eidolon creatures. They were eliminated shortly after birth."

Horrified, I could only stare at him. The man who I had thought was my father for twenty-three years wasn't my biological father. And the years I spent believing that he was, he hid a horrible past from me that showed how monstrous he had been. Was he still?

"I'm not that man anymore, Laena," he strongly stated, seeming to have read my mind. "You have to believe I changed the moment I took you from that lab. You and your mother inspired that change. But I know I have much to atone for, and I tried to do the right thing raising you. Please believe me when I say that everything I have done since then has been for your sake."

Reese asked, "Then, why is Laena so special? What did you do differently with her?"

Dad smiled lopsidedly and confessed, "Caelaena's husbands' banked sperm had been completely used up by the time I came into the picture. At the time, I had also been given charge of prenatal care for Elite women. It was a simple thing to take an amniotic sample from Marguerite Ardarien, and clone Laena from that."

I was sure that my men and I all gave Lightbourne stupefied looks. "You did WHAT?" I screeched. "Is that why I'm a genotypic twin to Kane Ardarien? I'm his clone?"

"Yes," he said simply. "Like I said, volunteers were hard to come by, much less any pure, unadulterated genetic material. For a fetus, its DNA remains untouched by environmental factors that would cause any spontaneous mutations. I needed a human genome that remained mutation-free to work with."

"And as his clone, you would be immediately recognized as a member of the Ardarien family. That's why I've told you to stay away from the Ardariens, but I hear you've already been adopted into their fold. It was the Ardariens who ordered your termination!"

"No, thanks to you! You should have told me!" I cried, even more horrified. "If you had done a better job explaining why, then maybe I would have tried harder to stay away from them. They already know I'm Kane's twin, and I'm sure they now know what my existence means with the work you've done."

"Laena, haven't you listened to what I've been saying?" he barked. "The Elite have hidden any evidence of my work, and before I had faked our deaths, they've made sure that if I were to reappear in society that I'd be executed without a trial." Letting out an impatient breath, he explained, "You are already registered into society. I know you've been barcoded and tattooed. It's far easier for the Ardariens to acknowledge you as an adopted daughter than to do away with you as unwanted evidence of my research. But the Elite are devious and are too dangerous to deal with. They would rather play it cool until one of us slips up and gives them reason to do away with either of us."

Reese joined in, "Right. Remember how upset Barclay was when we first found you, Laena? Something about you made him nervous. His agitation that day seemed excessive, even for his normal self."

Rennick agreed, "Yeah, he cared more about how unexplainable and how inconvenient your existence was. That dick always cared more about appearances than anything else."

While I agreed with those two, I was still a part of the Ardarien family, regardless of my origins. And Barclay Ardarien had made it known from the first day that I wasn't a welcome addition. He made me feel like I was someone he just had to suffer through in order to keep his very powerful wife happy. I had always thought that their reasons for adopting me was about keeping appearances, and after what Dad/Lightbourne had revealed, I was inclined to stick to that theory.

"Okay, then what am I supposed to do now?" I asked, disgruntled.

"What we had asked you on that first day," Vance cut in. "Marry us. That gets you out of the Ardariens' clutches, so to speak."

Dad's eyes bore into mine. "He's right, Laena-love." He hadn't called me that since I was small. Hearing him say my old nickname jolted me a little, but his use of it meant that he was serious and that he really needed me to listen. "You in the hands of the Elite would be very dangerous. Having these boys marry you would keep you safe."

Huh? How? I must have asked those questions out loud because Vance said, "Laena marrying us would mean that she also marries into our equally as powerful families. They would back us in protecting her as well as supporting our own vested interest in her."

"And since she had already agreed to be ours, the quicker we get her married to us, the better," Reese said happily. "And while I wish for her sake that this wasn't so rushed, I for one, couldn't be happier that this situation puts a rush on things."

Dad seemed to reluctantly agree. "While I didn't count on you suddenly discovering hormones and sex, I'm only agreeing to your marriage because it means you will be safe."

"Wait a minute," I halted, not yet understanding everything. "Explain to me first why the Elite is so dangerous to my health. What would happen if they discover who I am in light of your research?"

Dad wryly smiled, "Laena-love, it's not who you are that would have them running scared. It's *what* you are that threatens their very existence."

God, he could be so damned irritating, not to mention confusing. "What are you talking about?" I asked, irritated that he wasn't telling me straight out.

Sighing a heavy sigh, he admitted, "Laena, you are an entirely new subspecies that has emerged through my work and through the work of others before me. You are *Homo sapiens eidolon*, born with abilities far superior to that of us mere *Homo sapiens sapiens*."

Huh. That admission seemed the least likely to be believable out of all the things he could have told me. I mean, I had envisioned him telling me who my real father was. Or admitting that I was kept a secret because he was crazy and didn't want to share me with anybody. I didn't think that anything so grandiose and out there would be the reason for him hiding me away for twenty-three years. And I was so shocked, I had no words.

Reese complained, "Great going, Lightbourne. You broke her. She can't even talk."

Vance peered closer at my face, and asked, "You okay, baby girl?"

Rennick clapped a heavy hand on Dad's shoulder. "Gotta tell ya, I didn't see that one coming, and neither did she. But you didn't tell us what would happen if our government finds out what she really is."

Dad said sadly, "Digging into old research files, ones they thought they destroyed, I found that they had come across more of you before. Not just in the lab, but out there, in other cities. And they've destroyed every one of them before the rest of the world could discover that you have evolved to adapt to this world."

"Wait, you mentioned abilities earlier. What abilities does Laena have?" Vance asked curiously.

Dad looked at me with a slightly amused look. Then he looked at each one of my men. "Think about it, geniuses. What have you seen her do so far?"

Well, they've all seen me fight off Eidolon, even when the odds didn't look so good for me. I had always thought that Dad was a great teacher and I was an exemplary student. And I thought that was why I retained all of his training through the years. But the guys simply looked at each other and grinned.

"Right," Dad continued, "she's got keener senses and heightened reflexes, among other things, compared to even a highly trained soldier. All the better to survive an Eidolon attack. So, she's got quite a bit in common with several different arachnid species in terms of survival instincts."

I was half-afraid Dad would say I had more in common with the lowly cockroach, but he added nothing more. To me, he said, "Laena, I'm sorry I've kept this from you all these years, but you were too young to understand then. I left you alone in the Outer Ring that day because I knew you were ready to fend for yourself. It was a test."

"You were testing my ability to survive?" I asked, incredulously.

"No. It was a test for me to see if I could actually stay away. I loved you from the day you were born, and I love you still," he confessed softly. "I knew I couldn't be there forever to keep you safe, and I knew these boys would continue the job for me if they were so inclined."

He knew? Did he plan for them to find me that day?

"No, I can tell what you're thinking. It was a spur of the moment thing. I saw them that day and took the chance that they'd be drawn to you. And I was right, wasn't I?"

He was, but I wasn't going to admit that out loud. We all knew the answer to that question.

"Laena-love, I don't expect you to feel the same about me or to forgive me after what I've just told you, but I—"

I stopped his vocal train of thought right there and flew into him, gripping him tight. "I love you, too, Dad. I'm glad you kept me." He hugged me tightly into himself, slightly shaking as he did so. I wouldn't have known that he was weeping until I felt his hot tears soaking through my borrowed t-shirt.

23

LAENA

Suffice it to say that things were kicked up a notch once Dad revealed all. I had thought that once Dad showed up, he'd stick around, but instead, he had warned, "No one knows I'm even alive, so let's keep it that way."

Well, he was still a wanted man, after all, and no one would mistake the once clean-cut military-trained scientist for this scraggly, unkempt homeless man in ragged clothing. When he left the same way he came through, he had melted away into the shadows of early morning before the day broke with a hint of sunrise.

But before his unconventional exit, he had embraced me tightly, and I melted in those thin, yet still strong arms. "Don't worry about me, Laena-love. I feel better that I'm leaving you with the overgrown Boy Scouts downstairs and that they'll keep you safe. I'll check in every now and then to make sure they're doing their job."

I had sniffle-laugh-cried at that. I loved that I had three men willing to catch a grenade for me, but I also wanted to have the first important man in my life still around. But before I had the chance to reply, he pulled away abruptly and launched himself through the open window. When I had rushed to the windowsill to see which direction he had taken, there wasn't a trace of him to be found.

When I rejoined those overgrown Boy Scouts downstairs, they were sitting around the kitchen table, each with a steaming cup of coffee in their hands. It was still early, but I guessed with everyone now up, there was no chance of going back to sleep, not after the news we just had.

Reese got up and offered, "Want some coffee? I'm just about to start making breakfast."

"Sure," I answered and made my way to a seat at the table. But Rennick caught me about the waist and pulled me into his lap. With the intimacies we had shared this evening, my body still felt languid and a bit sore, so I comfortably relaxed against him. Reese and Vance, both looking happy, watched the two of us, and I positively glowed. The atmosphere in Vance's kitchen felt more intimate to me than anything we could have dreamed up for creative bed play.

With a mug of hot coffee placed by Reese in front of me and the men I loved surrounding me, I was suddenly overwhelmed by a foreign feeling, a good and warm one. Coming from a life where I had next to nothing except for Dad, this moment could be encapsulated by a phrase I had never said out loud before: I was home.

With his voice vibrating through his chest and into my back, I heard Rennick say, "Once we finish breakfast, we'll have to take you home." That snapped me out of my happy musing, and now it felt a lot like a wet blanket had been slapped in my face. But he was right, as an unmarried woman, I still 'belonged' to my adopted family, and I 'belonged' at home until I married. Ugh.

"Do we have to leave right after breakfast?" I asked, careful not to sound whiny.

Vance observed me over the rim of his coffee mug, then took a sip before saying, "You don't want to go home?"

From behind me, I could hear the grin in Rennick's voice. "Why, baby girl? You up for another round with us?" His eyes danced as he looked me up and down suggestively, then he said reluctantly, "But as much as I'd love to repeat the experience, we have to get you home."

I turned my head and frowned back at him, "Is there a reason to rush me back into the Ardarien household? The very people who wanted me dead in the first place?" Now that I thought about it, my adoption didn't make sense at all.

While busy slicing fruit, Reese joined in to answer, "While you were seeing Lightbourne off, we had been discussing what to do next. And we decided that the sooner we get you home, the sooner we can make our intentions known."

"Huh? What intentions? Why can't you explain it to me in simpler terms?"

Vance sighed. "I forget sometimes that you didn't grow up knowing how our society works. If we want to marry the woman of our choice and she has already consented, we have to bring the matter formally to her family."

"Oh, is that all?"

"Yes, but they also have to consent to changing their family registry to include our names. We will take on your last name once our marriage is registered with the Courts."

"So, does that mean your last names will change to Ardarien?"

All three men nodded. "Yes, and that means we will belong to you, Laena," Vance continued. "So, when we bring you home, we will formally propose marriage to you in front of your adopted family."

"But I already said yes, didn't I? Why all the fuss?" I really didn't like all this formality, nor did I enjoy the pretentiousness of it all. I had always thought marriage was so simple a thing, until now.

"The fuss, sweet baby girl, is all because you've been adopted by an Elite family. They will want all the pomp and circumstance to show off who can throw the biggest wedding or the most lavish engagement party," Reese said, while rolling his eyes. I smiled, knowing he wasn't as impressed as I was about all this unnecessary tradition.

"Yeah, if you don't, you'll have Marguerite shitting bricks if you cheat her out of a party for her daughter," Rennick said, wide-eyed. "She'd want to lord it over her frenemies that she has a daughter and they don't. Reese! Your toast is burning!"

Vance jumped up to save the toast as Rennick teased Reese about not paying attention to the food.

I sat silent, mulling over everything that was said, while the guys continued their chatter around me. I knew that daughters were few in number among the Elite, and that only a handful of them were still unmarried. Drayna was one of them, but only because she chose to join the Cadet Corps. So, it made me nervous to think what Marguerite would say if I refused all the parties that went with a wedding. Knowing how strong-willed she was, I was sure my protests would fall on deaf ears.

More like, she would eat me alive if I didn't let her throw me at least a big wedding.

Once the toast was redone and done right, and the eggs cooked the way I liked them, the four of us sat down to a nice, simple breakfast. If it weren't for our losses yesterday, we wouldn't be sitting around Vance's kitchen table talking about a short engagement before heading to the Ardarien mansion.

The few days off would keep us inside the city and inside the Inner Circle, giving us a bit of freedom from Eidolon hunting to announce the guys' honorable intentions to my adopted family. But right then, I wasn't sure if I was any safer inside the city; not when the truth about me and my origins could possibly be leaked to the Ardariens or to anyone in the Elite Council.

In retrospect, I think the scarier scenario would be where they already do know about me and are just biding their time until an opportunity presents itself. An opportunity to follow through with their original intention when I was just two years old. Elimination.

Suddenly, Eidolon hunting seemed a whole lot more appealing than going back to the Ardarien mansion.

...

When we arrived at the Ardarien home—I never really thought of it as mine—the four of us were ushered into the breakfast room right away. I had almost forgotten we had an earlier start to the day than most people did, and Marguerite was only up at this time because it was still in the middle of the work week. She would be expected in her Council chambers later.

Upon entering, Barclay, who sat facing us, eyed me suspiciously. Nothing new there. I only nodded to him in greeting, and he returned to his food without acknowledging our arrival.

Antonio and Maximus were both busy reading from their tablets, probably reacquainting themselves with their agendas for the day. Marguerite was the first to look up from her breakfast to greet us with a wide grin. Getting up from her seat, she rounded the table to take me into her firm embrace.

Pulling back from the embrace, she asked, "Why haven't you returned my calls, hm?" Her voice was all syrupy-sweet, but I sensed a bit of an edge to her tone. "But seeing your escort here, I think I know why you haven't," she added slyly, giving me a conspiratorial wink. "I remember what it was like to be young once."

"Ugh, Mother. Please, not another reminder of what it was like to be young and horny all the time," Kane said, suddenly appearing from behind us. But he moved around us, greeted me with an exaggerated gesture of pretending to vomit, then sat down at the table. As he did so, he watched the three men standing silently behind me with interest.

I grinned at him, also not wanting images in my head of my adopted mother with her three husbands frolicking in the sheets.

"Kane, you wouldn't be here if it weren't for that," she chided him. In turn, Kane groaned in answer, looking down at the floor like he wanted it to open up and swallow him whole. Seemingly, satisfied at her son's discomfort, she then turned to face the four of us.

She asked, "To what do we owe the pleasure of having our city's heroes here in our home? Colonel Vance, Captain Reese, and Captain Rennick, welcome to our home." Before I could answer, she moved towards Rennick, who was closest to her, and she said, "Thank you for bringing our daughter home safely. I had heard that your Corps had run into some trouble just outside the city yesterday."

The woman switched gears so quickly, it was hard for me to keep up with her. But Rennick took it all in stride and answered, "It was no trouble. It was late when we got back into the city, and Laena had been already been asleep by the time we finished our supper at Vance's house. So, we let her sleep there." He lied so effortlessly, but I was thankful he didn't spill the truth of what we were really up to last night.

"Then, why don't all of you join us for breakfast. It's the least I can offer after bringing Laena home safely," she said graciously.

"No, thank you. We've already eaten," Vance had said. "But we would like to make an announcement, if we may."

With a slight incline of her head, she allowed, "You may."

Clearing his throat, then glancing at me as if to bolster his confidence, he declared, "Captains Reese and Rennick and I would like to offer our hands in marriage to your daughter, Madam Governor."

"Oh my," she said breathlessly. "That was unexpected. And so soon after we had just finalized her adoption."

"Yes, we would like your permission to register our names in your family registry. Today if possible. We know this isn't the usual way of doing this, but Laena is special and this requires special circumstances," Vance added.

Maximus said with a smile, "In days past, a father would have been outraged to hear such a hasty proposal, implying that one's daughter had gotten knocked up, as they used to say."

Antonio joined in with a good-natured laugh, "But these days, we need the numbers and we would welcome babies in this household. So, Laena, are you pregnant? Is this why these boys are offering themselves as your husbands?"

I was mortified. Me, pregnant? Why would they assume that?

Barclay said nothing, and he looked stupefied, his eyes rounded and focused on me.

"I'm not pregnant!" I shouted, cutting off the chuckles emitted around the room. "I love Vance, Rennick, and Reese, and they love me. Isn't that enough reason to marry?" You wouldn't think it to look at me, because I was damned sure I was glowering at everyone as I said it.

"Of course, it is," Marguerite soothed, touching a hand to my cheek in a tender way. "But I'm just not sure that's enough to convince us to say yes to changing the family registry."

Reese burst out, "From the start, we knew Laena was it for us. But we finally wore her down, she said yes, and now you're telling us we're not enough?" I laid a hand on Reese's arm, trying to pull him away as he stood threateningly over Marguerite.

Vance laid a hand on Reese's shoulder to bring him back at ease and calmly said, "Excuse Captain Reese. We do have much to offer Laena, and the three of us are wealthy in our own right. Laena will never want for anything as long as she is with us."

Rennick added, "With our families combined, we could offer you the support you would need in the Elite Council."

"Hm, those are all interesting points," Marguerite mused thoughtfully, pacing the length of the room as she talked. Stopping in front of me, where I protectively stood before Reese, she sighed, then smiled. "But truthfully, I was already going to give my permission from the start. I just wanted to hear what everyone had to say about their reasons for marrying Laena."

Barclay, Antonio, and Maximus all looked upon their wife with mild exasperation touched with a bit of fondness, an expression born of knowing her and her mischievous ways all too well.

Reese inclined his head formally and apologized, "Please forgive my outburst. I humbly thank you for granting us your permission." I was a little stunned to see my mischievous, playful Reese look and sound like someone too rigid for my taste. All of this formality wasn't something I was used to seeing in him.

Vance and Rennick beamed happily and turned to shake hands with my adopted fathers and Kane, who all seemed just as happy with this new event. Reese even went so far as to wrap Marguerite into a hug, lifting her clear off her feet. "Oh, my goodness!" she exclaimed when he lifted her too high.

"Put my wife down," Barclay ordered, springing from his seat to retrieve her from Reese's grasp. Once Reese did as he was ordered, Barclay scolded, "I will not have my wife be manhandled by big brutes like you. As she will soon be your mother-in-law, please see that she is afforded the respect she deserves."

I hid a smile behind a hand, but not before Barclay could miss it. Facing me fully, he reprimanded, "And you, Miss Ardarien, should be the shining example for your husbands to follow. While I can't say I'm entirely pleased by this turn of events, I can say that these men of yours would be a welcome addition to any household." And on his final word, he brushed past me to leave the room.

"What was that?" Kane asked, puzzled. "Dad Barclay not into you four getting married?"

Marguerite only sighed in answer. Maximus assured us, "Don't mind him. He's had a lot on his mind lately and hasn't been himself." As if that explained Barclay's attitude towards me since the day we first met.

"Then, by all means, let us begin planning the engagement party!" Marguerite exclaimed, chattering excitedly about details I had no interest in.

So, I excused myself from the room, citing that I needed to use the toilet. My men were already bombarded with questions about dates and the like, and I didn't think I was really needed at the moment.

But instead of heading towards the nearest washroom, I went in search of Barclay. I was determined to know why my marriage would cause him displeasure and why he'd been a dick to me for as long as I've known him.

So, it was an astonishing surprise to find him in his office, drinking heavily from a bottle containing an amber liquid. Damn, day drinking this early? His office door had been open just a crack, but I could see his profile clearly and hear everything he was saying.

Or rather, *hear* what he was doing; he was in fact weeping. Once he put the bottle down, I watched his shoulders shake as he sobbed, his face scrunched up with tears spilling down his cheeks. In his other hand, he held a photograph, but I couldn't see it from this far a distance.

He sobbed harder, until I heard him say through his shuddering sobs, "Oh, Cee-cee, why aren't you here? Where did you go? How could you leave us, the family that loved you?" Then he slugged back another a long swallow from the bottle he held.

When he finally came up for air, he sounded less like the regal version of him I was used to. "Why am I being punished?"

Barclay's behavior, while interesting, was the strangest I had ever seen from him. And who was Cee-cee to him? And why would he be crying about this so shortly after our engagement announcement?

To make things even stranger, I heard him continue, "She looks so much like you. Why is she leaving me, too?"

Okaaayyy. Not going to lie, it sounded like he was talking about me right there. But I sure as hell wasn't going to waltz right in and ask if that was the case. He believed himself to be in private, with no one observing him. It didn't seem right for me to barge in on his moment of crisis.

God knows, Dad never gave me that courtesy while I was growing up. He had always had to be in my face about everything, and it pissed me off to no end that I couldn't keep much hidden from him. Now, I understood why I wasn't allowed to keep any secrets back then, even while he could keep the biggest one from me.

Because secrets could kill. If my secret were ever to be let out, *I* could be killed.

And so, I crept quietly away from the door and headed back to the breakfast room. I had no idea what happened to set Barclay off into a tailspin of woe, but I had a feeling that I may have had something to do with it. But what?

24

RENNICK
One Week Later

Who's to say that things wouldn't all turn out for the best, after everything we had learned about Laena? The Ardariens seemed elated with our plans to marry Laena, and the voice of caution that I heavily relied on to get me out of sticky situations didn't even make a peep around them. Marrying Laena eased my mind a little more concerning her safety, and between Vance, Reese, and me, the three of us would gladly fight down to the bone to guard her secret. There was no way any of us would put her in danger by giving away the truth about her.

With the wedding plans already underway, Marguerite Ardarien made it known to all of us that only she was capable of seeing to every detail of the wedding. And since Laena hadn't a clue of the inner workings of Elite weddings, she was more than happy to let Marguerite have her way.

At least without the chore of wedding planning, the four of us could focus on returning to duty, staving off hordes from storming our city walls. Returning to our normal routine gave us a reason to keep Laena under our watch, and the continuation of her training kept her busy and out of trouble. No more running off for Laena to do her covert missions for Lightbourne.

However, my usual instincts for trouble must have been faulty lately since the three of us have been consumed by our lust and need for Laena nightly since the first day of our engagement. Even during a full workday of training and patrolling, we always had her on our minds, just waiting until the four of us were off duty to drag her back to one of our homes and make love to her. If we were too rough on her because we were too eager to get her beneath us, she made no complaints. In fact, she continually begged us for more just when we thought we had her sweaty and satiated.

Dylan approached me the night before our engagement party, not long after I had dismissed our cadets for the day. Judging by the somber look on his face, I could already tell that he wasn't going to discuss what he was going to wear to the party.

"Dylan, what brings you here?" I asked genially, as he gestured for me to follow him into an empty office. "Everything okay with Trey?"

Once he shut the office door, enclosing us in a tiny room, he brushed off my first question and only answered the second. "Trey's fine. Although he's been asking how Laena's been holding up."

"Laena's fine. Better than fine now that we're marrying her," I replied with a happy grin.

Dylan offered a wry smile, and I knew that the small talk was over. "The reason Trey's been asking about Laena is what concerns me. Her records have been recently hacked into."

My blood froze in my veins. "What records?"

"Her medical files straight from Trey's server. Strange that they didn't look into anything else. Just Laena's file. Couldn't say what exactly they were looking for. Trey said there wasn't much in there that would interest anyone. You know he keeps his files locked up tight."

Shit! What can I say without giving away too much?

Dylan gave me a hard look. "Look, I don't know what's going on, but I've always looked at Reese and you boys as my younger brothers. Whatever it is, you can tell me."

I sighed, knowing he was someone the three of us could trust. He was a gruff but fair man, but he was also a loyal Elite soldier, one who directly served the interests of the Elite Council as one of their generals. It made me uneasy to think that I couldn't trust him with Laena's secret, but I also didn't want to play loose with Laena's life at stake.

"C'mon, Rennick. This is me. Just from your reaction I can see you know something else about this."

"All right! Fuck!" I exclaimed, running a hand through my hair, trying to gain back a semblance of calm. Just the thought of anyone threatening our woman had me ready to do bloody battle on some asses.

Blowing out another breath, I started, "The one thing I can think of that makes Laena's medical files valuable is her DNA profile."

Dylan's brows slammed down together in puzzlement. "I don't understand. Does someone want to know how Laena's immunity works? Is that it?"

I had forgotten Dylan was there when they registered her in the Cadet Corps, so he would be privy to that information. Other than him and Barclay, there was no one else outside of Vance, Reese, and me who knew about Laena's Eidolon immunity.

So, I answered, "Maybe? I can't say for sure, but what I'm about to tell you is strictly confidential. Can you promise me that this won't go beyond us?" He nodded without further hesitation.

Dylan listened without saying a word as I related to him what Lightbourne had revealed to us about Laena's true origins and the secret of her DNA, but I carefully left out Lightbourne's connection to her. His brows raised in startlement when I first made mention of Lightbourne. That one little action made me nervous, and I hesitated to go on with the rest of the story.

Dylan must have noticed my reluctance to continue, and he explained, "Lightbourne was a renowned scientist the world over until he defected and stole entire data sets of research from a lab in New Capital. He disappeared shortly after, and it was reported that he and the child that he had stolen from the lab had been overcome by an Eidolon horde. Their corpses were so mangled that there was no hope of them even returning as Eidolon creatures."

"What if that child didn't die? What if she was found alive and well?" I asked, suddenly wanting to know what the Elite would do if they found Laena.

Taken aback by the vehemence in my voice, Dylan answered simply, "Well, that child would be grown by now.

Wait. You said she. I never said what sex the child was." Looking at me suspiciously, I stared him down and watched as he made the connections there behind those intense eyes of his.

With wide eyes, he shouted, "Oh, my God! Don't tell me—Laena? Laena is that child?"

Without waiting for me to confirm or deny, he asked incredulously, "How do you know that? They said that Lightbourne and the child died!"

Without giving away that Lightbourne was in fact alive and well, I said, "Their deaths were faked and that was what we found out from Laena." Laena, of course, was the common denominator between Lightbourne and us, and if it weren't for her, we would never have met Lightbourne at all. So, technically Laena *was* our source for any information concerning her father. At least, that was going to be the case from now on when it came to being cautious about telling others about her father and their shared past.

"Okay, but how did she survive all that time till now? What happened to Lightbourne?" Dylan's sharp mind just had to go there, the nosy bastard.

Brushing that question aside, I deflected smoothly, "That's not as important as how she would survive if someone finds out the truth of what lies in her DNA. The Elite wanted her dead when she was two just because she was perceived as a threat to their superiority! What's to prevent them from going after her if they find out she survived?" My voice rose in pitch at the horrifying thought of Laena's fate in Elite hands if they ever discovered what she was. *I couldn't let that happen!*

"Okay, okay, relax, Rennick! Just breathe, buddy!" I felt on the verge of a panic attack, my thoughts already too focused on what could happen to Laena if she was discovered to be the next step of evolution for humanity.

"With me, Rennick. Look at me. In. Out. In. Out." I looked him in the eyes and followed his instructions as he led me in slow, elongated breaths. After a few more slow breaths, I slowly felt my heartbeat slowing down to a more normal pace. When I could think more clearly, I apologized, "Sorry, man. Laena ties me up in knots so tight when it comes to her safety. I can't afford to lose her, you know?"

"I know," Dylan said softly. "I feel the same about Trey. He's my everything."

"Okay, if you understand, then please don't tell the Council or the Courts about Laena. I mean, you can tell Trey. I'm sure he's dying to know why his 'secure' server got hacked into. But that's it," I warned.

Dylan contemplated me for a moment before saying, "Under normal circumstances, I would be reporting the server breach. As a doctor, it would compromise Trey's integrity and his doctor-patient confidentiality agreement if it was made public."

I growled, waiting for Dylan to issue a threat or ultimatum of some sort. But he surprised me by saying, "But Reese is my brother. I wouldn't be a good brother-in-law if I got in the way of his happiness and well-being. So, for his sake, the Council and the Courts won't hear about Laena from me."

I relaxed, slumping a little, and gratefully said, "Thanks, Dylan. And thank you for helping me down from my panic high. I didn't know you were such a calming influence, you being a big, strong general and all."

He chuckled, "I have my moments. Being the big and strong type can only get me so far in certain situations. But like I said, you are like a brother to me, too. What concerns you also affects me. You and your brothers by choice are not alone in this. Trey and I will always be here to lend a hand when you need it. And that includes Laena, too."

I nodded in thanks and acknowledgement. "Thanks again. But now the question remains: who would want the genomic information on Laena? It's almost as if someone knew what they were looking for when they were digging into her medical file."

Dylan shook his head. "Neither Trey nor I would know. But you, Vance, and Reese might have a better idea, given how close you are to Laena. Maybe, just to be safe, take a closer look at those around her now. You and I both know how the Elite can be disarmingly charming but deviously calculating when it comes to their desires and ambitions. How far can you trust any of them? The Ardariens or anyone else in any of your families."

"Hm, that's a lot of food for thought right there. If Trey's security on his server is compromised again, let us know. We do have a hacker who's soon to be our wife who could probably search for the culprit."

"Laena? Shit, she's just full of suprises, isn't she? You guys sure that she's not too much for the three of you to take on as your wife?"

I chuckled. "We're sure she's the one. Besides, have you seen her sweep kick? It's perfection!"

"Leave it to you to fall in love with a woman for the way she fights. Well, I'm just grateful I have only Trey to contend with. When it comes to him, I found I'm not willing to share."

"Yeah, lucky for us, we were taught since preschool that sharing is caring. Reese and Vance, at least, were also taught the same and that's why we get along so well. Where did you go wrong?" I teased.

"Okay, you little shit. I think you should go home and make sure your bride-to-be is well rested for her party tomorrow. Make sure Marguerite has my favorite beer available for me," Dylan concluded.

"Hah! With Marguerite in charge, I'm sure she'll only have wine to serve," I said as Dylan gave me a long-suffering look. "But don't worry, the guys and I can sneak in the contraband. What brand do you like again?"

"Nah, that's okay. Don't want her husbands gunning for me if I offend Marguerite in any way. I'll see you tomorrow."

Turning to exit the office, I waved, "Yeah, see you tomorrow. And thanks again for the heads up."

"No problem."

25

LAENA
Night of the Engagement Party

I wished we could skip tonight and just fast forward to the wedding already. I didn't see the need to show off to one hundred plus guests that I, a newly-adopted Ardarien, was soon to be married. Couldn't we be just celebrating the wedding itself today instead?

But instead, Marguerite had ordered me straight to my room the moment I stepped into the Ardarien mansion, still dirty from a day of training and patrolling. To my horror, I found a team of people waiting for me to, as Marguerite put it, beautify myself for the evening. She had said that as an Ardarien, I had to look the part. Whatever that meant.

So, in the past two hours, I had been scrubbed, exfoliated, and polished. I had been tweezed, trimmed, and lasered in weird places. I was sure that Kane, whose room was closest to mine, could hear my screeches and yelps at every pinch and yank I was subjected to. Believe it or not, I was exhausted from all of the 'pampering' that Marguerite had ordered for me.

Once I was tucked into a fluffy robe and seated in front of my vanity, a hairstylist tackled my shiny, clean hair with a vigor I had only seen in Cadets who were on latrine cleaning duty. The young pretty stylist was quick but efficient and had only yanked at my hair hard enough to make me wince once or twice. She apologized each time I made a small squeak of pain, but she followed it up with, "Resisting will only make it worse." So, I let her be. Besides, I've been accustomed to worse than what could be felt in the occasional hair pull.

Then, another stylist applied cosmetics to my face, surprising me with her skills. She made my face look dewy and fresh, and she lined my eyes with liner and shadows to make my eyes look even more exotic. In other words, I looked like a very glamorous edition of myself when she was done.

Finally, another stylist brought me to my armoire, where she had selected a gown that had not been in there until just now. She explained, "Madam Ardarien had it ordered last week. It was lucky that it arrived in time for the party tonight just this morning." The gown was a simple sheath, made with a shimmery midnight blue fabric that was unlike anything I had ever felt against my own skin. Once the stylist helped me into it—I had no idea how to put the thing on with its complicated straps and strings—the dress skimmed against my curves, accentuating everything I had.

"God, if they didn't already, your men are going to love you in that dress," the stylist gushed.

I stole a look in the mirror, and I nearly lost my breath. I didn't recognize the woman in the reflection and didn't believe that I could ever look that pretty. Pretty was for women who cared about looking like this, and I knew I clearly didn't. But God, the stylists definitely knew their stuff!

A knock on my door sounded. "Can I come in?" It was Drayna.

"Yes, come on in." I was still busy admiring my reflection, with my hair in a style I wasn't used to but loved and my body encased in the most gorgeous dress.

"What are you doing? Everyone's wai—Oh my god!" Drayna had interrupted her own train of speech.

"What? Is something wrong?" I asked, looking down at myself to see if anything was out of place.

"No! No, that's not it. I'm just blown away by you," she said, awe in her voice. "You're fucking gorgeous."

The stylists who were still present gasped, probably unused to hearing Elite women cursing. "Oh, come on! You all know she is!" Drayna protested. "Anyway, Reese sent me up to see what was taking you so long. He and Vance are threatening to drag you down the stairs if you weren't ready by now. Adrian looks like he wants to kill Dylan any second, so I think you better come on down."

"Okay, I'm ready to go. Lead on."

"Copy that. The guys are going to have kittens when they see you."

"Kittens? They're going to get me kittens?"

"No, Laena. Sorry, it's just an expression that means that they'll be blown away by how beautiful you look. Now, hurry up!"

The two of us made our way downstairs to the formal dining hall. It had been cleared earlier today to make room for one-hundred people with small standing tables set up for drinks and trays of hors d'oeuvres littered artfully around the room. And in heels I wasn't used to, I managed not to stumble too badly on the trek there. Luckily, I had Drayna propping me up, our arms linked as we hurried down the wide hallways of the mansion.

As we approached closer to the sounds of people conversing and laughing amidst glasses tinkling, my heart sped up when I caught sight of my fiancés. Vance, Rennick, and Reese were standing just outside the dining hall and were resplendent in simple but elegant semi-formal wear, a sight my poor female heart was helpless against. Dressed in black and white, my men were killer gorgeous, and my breath caught when their gazes suddenly laser-focused on me.

The three of them seemed to freeze at the same time, their bodies held stock-still as their eyes ate me up and their faces froze with shocked expressions. Suddenly feeling like too much of me was on display, I held silent as I slowly advanced on them.

Drayna broke the silence, "Aaaaaand I'll leave you to yourselves. Don't be too long, you have guests waiting. I'll be at the bar if you need me." And with that, Drayna flounced off into the dining hall.

With nerves I didn't know were capable of being wracked, I tentatively asked, "I don't look funny, do I? C'mon, say something. This stunned silence isn't reassuring me one bit."

Then, Rennick growled and reached for me, clasping me tightly against him. "God, anyone who sees you right now will want you for themselves. You're just too beautiful." Then, he pulled away to take a closer look at my dress, and he remarked, "That dress is almost indecent."

"It is?" I asked. "I've never worn anything like this before so I wouldn't really know."

"You look stunning, baby girl. Don't mind him," Vance said, as he stepped closer and walked a tight circle around me. I watched him as he carefully inspected me and my attire until he came to a stop behind me. I felt him press close against my back as he nuzzled my one bare shoulder then the shell of my ear as he said in a low voice, "But you in this dress is making me think we should skip the party and start one of our own upstairs." Then he nibbled on my ear, sending warm tingles down my spine. Those tingles got stronger as Vance pressed himself between my buttocks, his hardness unmistakable.

I moaned but was stifled the moment Reese pressed his mouth to mine, ruthlessly wreaking even more havoc on my hormones as his plundering kiss had me enthralled. Rennick was quick to press closer to my side, snatching up my hand to cup his erection straining against the fly of his pants. I rubbed him through the fabric and was rewarded with a strangled groan from him, delighted I could drive him crazy just as the three of them were doing to me.

The loud and deliberate clearing of a feminine throat sounded from the doorway of the dining hall, and the four of us guiltily jumped apart. Marguerite stood there, and even with her smaller stature, she managed to look down at us like the naughty children we were being. "Goodness, save it for the wedding night, all of you," she chastised. Looking down at the obvious tenting of each of my men's crotches, she tsked, "You are already late to your own party, so I urge you boys to either calm yourselves immediately or I will tie those things down myself."

Around me, I heard the three of them say in unison, "Yes, ma'am." If I wasn't already in awe of Marguerite and her commanding ways, I was right then and there in a big way. With her no-nonsense demeanor, she did have the command of the entire Elite army, after all. "All right then, the four of you follow me into your own party." And she led the way, regal as a queen, into the room.

Vance, Reese, and Rennick followed close behind me, and I imagined that they were still sporting some major wood. But they negated that thought when Rennick whispered just loud enough for all three of us to hear, "That woman is too scary for words. Just the thought of her hands anywhere near my dick was enough to shrivel it back into my body."

I giggled, finding it amusing that my three big, alpha-male fiancés were brought to heel by a petite woman who treated them like disobedient puppies.

Vance, who walked directly behind me, whispered in my other ear, "You think that's funny? Just wait until we get you alone. We'll make you pay for laughing at us." His voice sounded threatening, but I knew what he had in mind when he caressed my butt. They'd make me pay in ways that I knew would make me crave for more, and I couldn't be more eager or delighted at the thought.

I couldn't help feeling shy underneath the stares of everyone as we walked further into the room. Next to me, I felt my men close ranks even closer around me. I think one of them even growled while another whispered, "I'll kill the next man who undresses her with their eyes."

Thankfully, we came to a stop behind Marguerite when she stopped in the middle of the room to join Maximus, Antonio, and Barclay. Everyone stopped mid-chatter and turned their faces towards us as she held up her hands for silence, indicating she was about to break into a speech. I had never been the center of attention before, and I wasn't sure I felt comfortable underneath so many unfamiliar gazes.

At least, I spotted Drayna and Kane nearby, standing next to Dylan and Trey. And the people I assumed to be the parents of my fiances stood close by, smiling at us with genuine happy smiles. The one couple whose smiles didn't reach their eyes stood further away, and I assumed them to be Reese's and Trey's mother and father. While they looked at home here among the elegance of the party in their elegant attire, their stiff demeanor told me that they were here just for the sake of appearances and nothing more.

I barely listened as Marguerite introduced the four of us and had begun a toast to celebrate us with a flowery, stylish speech meant to wow the crowd. I hadn't prepared a speech nor was I willing to volunteer one, so I let Vance, Rennick, and Reese each say a few short words in my stead to thank everyone for their presence here.

Once all the words that needed to be said were dispensed with, my adopted parents along with Kane and my future in-laws came up to bestow hugs and kisses on the four of us. I guessed all of this embracing was supposed to be a formal show of them giving us their blessings for the marriage. Accepting a lukewarm embrace from Reese's parents furthered the illusion for the crowd that they were happy about our union, but I could have done without the pretension. Reese had shot me an apologetic look the moment I was released from his mother's perfunctory hug, and my heart went out to him.

Reese reached for me to peck me softly on the lips and whispered, "Sorry. My parents were never the affectionate type."

"Don't be," I reassured him. "You and the guys have more than enough love for me. I don't mind that they're not jumping for joy that I'll soon be their daughter-in-law."

As Marguerite glided out of the room, the party resumed its cacophony of conversation and laughter around us. Vance rushed me from behind, wrapping his arms about my waist. With his chin resting on my newly healed shoulder, he conspiratorially whisper-yelled to Rennick and Reese, "Quick! Let's get outta here."

Turning my head around to face him, "And go where?"

"Any place private. Preferably with a bed in it," Vance said, his tone too eager.

Glimpsing the twin expressions on Reese and Rennick's faces, I presumed they were on board with Vance's idea, too. "Lead the way, sweetheart," Reese urged. "Find us someplace we can be alone."

I sighed, and asked, "Now? Do you know how long it took for me to get ready for this party? With all the effort it took, this dress deserves more than a twenty-minute showing."

Rennick snorted, "With the way you look in it, I think it deserves its proper place on a bedroom floor." I frowned at him, disliking the idea of ruining such a beautiful dress.

In front of me, Reese tried to sweeten the deal by sweetly kissing me and saying, "C'mon, Laena, we can step out for a little while, and then we'll bring you back for the rest of the party before guests start to leave."

Vance agreed, "Yeah, these parties usually last all night. Problem is, I don't think we can last that long. We have to have you *now*."

Looking at each of their faces, I could see that they were dead serious. Already, they were herding me towards the exit, and it didn't take me long for my own eagerness for them to resurface once we stepped out into the hall.

"Where to?" Vance asked, his hand on my elbow.

"My room," I said, sounding breathy. "This way." I hurried my steps toward the main stairs that led up to the second floor. Unfortunately, my dress prevented me from making my usual long strides, and I nearly tripped.

"Whoa, there," Reese said, catching me deftly from falling on my face. Vance snatched me then from Reese's grip, hefted me over his shoulder, making me yelp. Without further preamble or even waiting for the other two, Vance rushed up the stairs with me bent and bouncing helplessly in his awkward hold.

"Better tell him where your room is, sweetheart," Reese called after us. "Otherwise, any room will do." Since it was all bedroom suites up here, I was disinclined to get down and dirty with my men in a room that didn't belong to me. God forbid we end up in my adopted parents' suite! So, I angled myself to properly see which direction Vance faced, and I mumbled a few short directions to my room to which Vance practically raced. Reese and Rennick weren't too far behind.

My room was dark and thankfully empty of the stylists who had assisted me earlier, and Vance flicked on the switch to bathe the room in light. However, Vance refused to put me back on my feet until we reached my bed. I was grateful that the Ardariens spared no expense in purchasing a king bed for me, a bed big enough for the four of us to swim in its sheets.

Vance and Rennick carefully helped me out of my dress, mindful of keeping it free of wrinkling before draping it on a nearby chair. Reese closed my bedroom door and locked it before joining us. Standing almost entirely nude before them except for thigh-high stockings, I couldn't help but feel the weight of three very intense stares.

Vance choked out, "No underwear at all?" His voice sounded like he was strangling on something.

"The stylist said she didn't want lines to show through too delicate a dress," I explained. Plus, I had no idea what she meant by that.

Two more choked groans sounded and then all three men exploded into action, stripping off clothing left and right. I squealed as they bore me onto the bed, their rough treatment exciting me to a whole other level. In their impatience, they left off finesse for their demanding quest for gratification, and I thrilled at being the sole focus of their combined lust.

Hungry, all-consuming kisses ensued, and my body was so attuned to my own arousal that I couldn't keep track of whose lips were whose. All I cared about right then was the feel of them surrounding me, touching me in all the right places, and loving me the way only they knew how.

With tongues and hands, they brought me to bliss two times before claiming I was ready for them. Almost mindless with my hunger for them, I begged them to fill me the way only they could and tried to reach for their cocks with questing hands. But being literally brought to my knees, I couldn't do more than use one hand, and the three of them swerved to avoid my touch.

"Look how bad she wants it," Vance said, more to me than to the other two in my bed. "Think she deserves having us fill her the way she wants?"

In my lust-filled haze, it slowly dawned on me that they would choose now to exact payback for earlier. "No," I pleaded, knowing that if I pretended to deny myself, they might do the opposite of what I asked. "I'm sorry I laughed. I won't do it again. I promise!" My pussy ached to be filled, and I squirmed uncomfortably on my knees wanting one of them to enter me from behind.

"Hah!" Rennick interjected. "Sorry doesn't get you out of your punishment."

My eyes widened. I didn't think they'd follow through on their threat of punishment.

As my eyes pleaded with them, Reese added, "And I think I know the perfect way to do it." Rounding me so that he knelt on the bed before me, my eyes on the same level as his erect cock, he commanded me, "Wrap your lips around my cock, sweetheart." To the others, he said, "No one touches her ass or pussy until we get off."

I moaned, and I swore I could feel my pussy drench further at the sight of Reese's thick, hard cock. "C'mon, baby girl," Vance urged. "Open up those sweet lips and suck him dry." I did as I was told, and I knew just the right way to suck to get him to blow his load sooner. But not before Rennick and Vance each led one of my hands to their own cocks, directing me to pump them both within a tight, clenched fist.

With my mouth and hands busy, my men were no less busy with their hands roaming my breasts, my inner thighs, and my various other erogenous zones. Eager to get through my punishment so I can finally have them fill me where I ached longingly for their cocks, I worked them as hard and as fast as I could manage. I moaned around Reese's cock, giving him throaty vibrations all along his length. I squeezed Rennick and Vance up and down their hard rods at a steadily faster pace than before.

It didn't take long until I felt one spurt in one hand, groaning out their release. Only for the other one to do the same, until Reese finished last, spurting down my throat and forcing me to swallow unless I choke on his cum.

All of them were breathing as hard as bellows and I asked saucily, "Have I been punished enough?"

"Not quite," Vance said, still out of breath. Reaching for his discarded tie from off the floor, he bound my wrists together, and Rennick reached for his, too, only to use it on me as a blindfold.

Bound and blinded, the three of them proceeded to take my pussy without allowing me the courtesy of knowing who filled me full of whose cock. All I knew was that their filling me was what I wanted and needed, and all that mattered was knowing that it was my three men who were with me here and now. Pleasuring me just to the point of shattering me, then stopping right before I tipped over the edge. And then they'd start the cycle all over again.

"Pleeeaassse," I begged, "make me come." My body was so highly sensitized to every brush of their skin against mine, and I was almost there, just on the brink. I don't know how long they took turns plunging into my body, and I was aware of nothing else outside the perimeter of my bed and the men in it with me.

"Come, baby girl, and I'll be right there with you." That was Vance. The thrusting became more frenzied, his pubic bone scraping against my already engorged clit, and it was only a few more seconds before I completely shattered and shuddered around him. Vance gave a shout, coming hard and deep inside me until he was spent and rolled off me. Not long afterwards, grunts could be heard on either side of me, and the next I knew, I was inundated with splashes of hot semen from both directions.

Once my breathing returned to normal, I was untied, and the makeshift blindfold ripped away. Exhausted smiles from all three of my men were gifted to me, and I glowed underneath the love they held in their gazes, meant just for me. They each took turns to kiss me with a sweet, loving kiss, and I happily sighed, only to have them remind me we were due back at the party.

"How was that for punishment?" Vance asked me with a playful smirk as he bent to retrieve his shirt.

"Hm," I mused, not willing to give away what I really thought of it and turned to catapult myself off of the bed. I knew they knew that I thoroughly enjoyed everything they dished out for me. So, when I happened to glance at their faces, the three of them said nothing, but they did a horrible job of trying to hide their satisfied grins.

26

LAENA

It took some doing to hastily make myself look presentable once again. My hair miraculously stayed in its complex updo, probably due to the amount of lacquer in it, but I needed a speedy shower to rinse off traces of cum from my skin. They helped me back into my dress, but I had to do something about the smeared mascara and lipstick. Vance, Rennick, and Reese tucked themselves back into their clothes, and I envied their ability to look just as gorgeous as they did before we carnally rough-housed in my bed.

They left the room, making me promise to join them back at the party once I was finished messing around with a mascara wand and a lip brush. When I was satisfied that I did my best at repairing my makeup, I hurriedly headed back downstairs, eager to rejoin my men.

On my way through a couple of wide hallways, I stopped when I heard Marguerite's voice, sounding both disgruntled and irate from inside one of the many rooms on the main floor. Creeping closer towards the sound of her voice, I found her gesturing wildly, in deep conversation with someone I couldn't see. With the door only slightly ajar, I was only afforded with a view that had her in my sights.

She had never raised her voice in my hearing; she was always the epitome of gentility and calm. To hear her talk, it sounded like she had a huge bone to pick with the other person on the receiving end of her ire.

"We know he's out there," I heard her say. "It was a simple task I gave you, and you couldn't even do that!" The other person in the room who dressed all in black with a hood covering his or her face said nothing in answer.

"Find him, like I asked you to do, and only then will you get the money I promised. And not a moment before." Marguerite continued in a calmer voice, "We know that Laena would not have survived this long if it weren't for Lightbourne. I know he had her hidden away, making us believe that the two of them were dead all these years."

I was stunned to hear her use Dad's real name along with my own in the same sentence. So she knew who I was! Why hadn't she said or done something to indicate that she knew? Why adopt me if the Ardariens were the ones who ordered me dead all those years ago? The questions continued to flood through me, sending me almost into a tailspin of what-ifs and what-nows.

"Now go do as you were told, and only come back once you locate that infernal man!" Marguerite barked at the black figure. Without a word, only a whisper of the figure's movement could be heard as they made their way out of the room. Just in time, I ducked out of sight before either Marguerite or the unknown person could spot me in the dimly lit hallway.

Hiding in a recessed wall, out of the line of vision from the opened doorway, I waited to see if Marguerite would also follow after and rejoin the party. Moments passed until I heard her sigh loudly from inside the room. And then, she barked, "You might as well come in here, Laena. I know you're out there."

How she knew, I wasn't about to ask, but she managed to surprise me. All of my senses were now on high alert, wondering what I could now expect from her. Mostly out of curiosity, I entered the room, suddenly wondering too late if this was a bad idea.

"Ah, there you are," I heard her say upon my entry. I almost missed seeing her, sitting as she was in the shadows on a plush chair, away from the lamp closest to her. Once my eyes quickly adjusted to the room's dimness, I could clearly see that her expression was hard, no longer the open and friendly one of earlier when she formally announced my engagement.

"Have a seat, girl," she ordered, gesturing to one of the many chairs available. I took the one directly across from her, mechanically plopping myself down, and waited for her to continue.

"You must have heard me mention you and your erstwhile guardian, Lightbourne. Curiosity reeled you in, did it?" I didn't answer, and she only gave me a hard, piercing look. She continued, "And now, here we sit, and you're likely wondering how much I know about you."

"Do you want to know how much I know, Laena?" she asked, her tone biting.

I only nodded in answer, and she replied in a harsh whisper, "Everything! I know everything about you." I schooled my features to blandness, and she kept giving me more information than I think she meant to. "I knew about your conception and the program Lightbourne had you in. I even know about his stealing you away from your own scheduled termination. A termination I ordered!"

I might have flinched a little then. Dad was right in telling me not to trust the Ardariens, and I felt dread pool in the bottom of my stomach at the thought of being caught by the worst one of the bunch.

"Then why adopt me? Why not get rid of me the moment I was found?"

"Because it was too late once you've been added to the registry with your medical profile and with your uncanny resemblance to my Kane! No one with two eyes could deny how much the two of you looked alike. If I acted then, a full investigation would have gone into your death, not when unmarried females today are a hot commodity. And then my family's good name would be dragged into the messy aftermath."

"Okay, but tell me why you adopted me! You could have left me on my own as a state ward. I was already an active recruit in the Cadet Corps."

"Because with your DNA on public record in the Court registry, you would expose everything! My adopting you had the strong appearance of a mother wanting to bring a daughter into the fold, and then any searches into your background could only be halted by someone powerful like myself. That's the only reason for your adoption. In addition, I had someone search Dr. Trey Reese's sealed files the other day to confirm what I feared."

Not sure I wanted to know, but I asked anyway, "And what's that?" Her reason for adopting me sounded both sane and puzzling at the same time, and I wanted to know more.

"Your secret is also my Kane's secret! The both of you are the key to humanity's continuation and survival in this world. With further scrutiny into either yours or Kane's genomic DNA, they would find what I've been trying to hide from the world!"

She didn't need to say anymore; I knew she meant my place in the Animal Kingdom, that I was *Homo sapiens eidolon*. But to discover only today that Kane was just like me? Why try to terminate me and keep him?

She went on, "I bore Kane and loved him the moment he was born and the doctors placed him close to my chest. I didn't discover his 'uniqueness' until we had him registered. And because I headed Lightbourne's own program with funding, I knew what the DNA profile of Eidolon-immune species looked like. And Kane's DNA profile had all the same markers. But I kept it quiet, using my influence and power to do so. Kane would be raised like any other son of an Elite family.

"But then you were born the same day as my Kane. The moment I saw Lightbourne's files, I looked at your photos and I knew that Caelaena was your mother. I was the one who put her in that program, pretending to help her with conceiving her husbands' child. And because you looked just like my Kane, questions I wasn't willing to answer would soon arise. So I ordered the end of the program and your termination."

Anger on behalf of the little defenseless child I had been then rose up within me. "And so you thought to kill me just to keep your son safe? You do know then that I'm his clone? Born from his own DNA and implanted in my mother's womb?"

She sighed. "That I didn't know until recently. With Kane's features also similar to Caelaena's, it made sense since she was his aunt. But Lightbourne had destroyed all of his notes along with his research before the Elite could get their hands on them. One of our scientists under my payroll drew up that conclusion having studied your DNA profile alongside Kane's."

"Then why destroy all others of my species? Dad told me that there were others before me, and none of them were given the chance to live."

"Ah, you think me responsible for that. Well, if it weren't for Kane, I might have been, once upon a time. But no, two generations ago, that might have been true of the Elite Council then. What I want now is to make sure that no one knows about Kane, Lightbourne, or you."

"I heard you earlier," I admitted. "I know you want to find Dad. But why?"

Sounding tired, she sighed and said, "Yes, I hired someone to locate him, but when he doesn't want to be found, he has become very skilled at hiding."

"Why not leave him be? What he knows and has done in the past aren't enough to threaten the Elite or their power."

She tsked, "And that's where you are wrong, Laena. Because of his past work and with you alive and well, your very existence is enough to have any of the Elite running scared. I need Lightbourne to tell me if he made any more of your species out there in the world and how many. Do you think that you are the first of your species to have survived in this world?"

My blood ran cold at the patronizing tone in her voice. She knew so many things that I didn't know, and I knew she was going to lord it over me. She informed me, "We have had evidence that there are more of your species littered around the Seven Cities, but all hidden away. The Elite fear that if there are enough of you, it wouldn't take much for your numbers to overthrow our government. And because of your individual and unique abilities, the masses would view you as their saviors from the Eidolon-cursed. They would look to you to keep them safe and not the Elite. That's why your kind is a threat to the Elite way of life, and that is why they have tried to eliminate you altogether."

"But Kane? You do want to protect him from being found out, don't you?"

"Of course I do. And now that you're here, he is the only reason I'm not going to get rid of you. Having you marry is the next best thing, and I can continue to guard the secret you both hold in your DNA."

"Does Kane know?"

"No, he doesn't," she said quietly. "And I'd like to keep it that way."

"Well, I think it's only right for him to know the truth about himself." With a myriad of thoughts zipping through my head, one stood out clearly, and I had to ask, "If I was a result of experimentation, then how has Kane come by—"

She cut me off, "He came by it naturally. Lightbourne thinks that his seventh formulation is what caused your immunity, but I know better. I know he had stolen Kane's own DNA—from my womb no less--to form you. As Kane's clone, you are also a natural result, the next step in our evolution. So, nothing Lightbourne did altered your genetic makeup in any way; you were already meant to be what you are now."

I took in all of that information in silence, pondering what this could mean for Dad, myself, and my soon-to-be husbands, who were probably wondering why I haven't yet shown up. Marguerite took it upon herself to reveal her true colors to me, but to what end? Why tell me all of this now?

Finally, I thought to ask her what I was thinking, "Is there a reason why you're telling me all of this now?"

She smiled, a glint of something I couldn't name sparkled in her eyes. "Why, yes. I wouldn't have told you everything without there being a point, right? Well, since you asked, and because of what you are, I would dearly love to have someone like you working on my side. As a favor, of course."

Tentatively, I replied, "Well, since I am your adopted daughter, that doesn't sound so strange." But I couldn't fail to notice that she used the word 'what' in place of 'who'.

"Of course, but that's not what I meant. Your training and special abilities make you a valuable asset, an asset I intend to use."

Not liking the sound of this, I asked, "Use how?" She made me sound like a high-tech gardening tool to be brought out for use on only special tasks. Instead of a favor, it sounded like she was voluntelling me what to do for some unknown date.

"I will decide that when you are needed," she said cryptically. "For now, just enjoy your party and look forward to your upcoming wedding in a few weeks. I will summon you then."

"Wait. My abilities as you put it—"

Again, she cut me off for the second time. "Ah-ah. You know and I know what you are capable of. Let's just leave what that is unsaid for now. Go on now, your fiancés are waiting for you," she said, dismissing me from her mind completely.

I complied and bit my tongue, but I knew she was talking about my military and fight training. How was that going to help her?

So, I got up from my seat, ready to leave the room when another thought occurred to me. One I had to voice. "What if I refuse what you ask whatever it is you want me to do?"

Once again, I saw her face harden before she said, "Then, I would think very hard about the safety of your husbands. Also, telling them about any of this will do you no good. All it would take is a simple order that could see them overwhelmed by a well-placed Eidolon horde. I am not above doing what is necessary to get what I want, my dear. Surely, you understand."

Yeah, I definitely understood what she was getting at. The woman was a bitch, but a terrifying one at that, and it was obvious that she believed that a subtle, veiled threat would be enough to keep me under her thumb. So, I left the room, eager to return to Vance, Rennick, and Reese and eager to rid myself of the bitter taste my conversation with her had left in my mouth.

The threat she made on my men, no matter how subtle it was or how gently delivered, was still a threat I had to take seriously. But since I saw no other alternative, there was no other way for me than to do whatever it is Marguerite wanted at the time she needed. God, if there was ever a time I wished that I wasn't found that one day, now was the time.

27

LAENA
Two Weeks Later

After our conversation the night of the engagement party, Marguerite had left me to my own devices, and I guessed that the reason for it was that her days had been consumed with planning my wedding. I knew nothing about what went into such planning, so I was happy to let her be since I was in no way knowledgeable or equipped to assist her. Her busy schedule had also provided me with the relief that there was no way she would make good on calling in that 'favor'.

With my wedding day having finally arrived, the ceremony, the signing, and the reception all seemed to blend into a kaleidoscopic blur of events that signified how fast everything breezed by me. Now, I had an altered tattoo on my ring finger to signify my change in marital status, just as my three men had new tattoos newly inked onto their ring fingers. All of Marguerite's planning had made for a perfect, seamless occasion, where nothing was out of place and where everything in it positively screamed luxurious elegance. My wedding dress was one such example of her work and own design.

While Marguerite had seemed to care much more about making sure everything was perfect and worthy of the Ardarien name, I couldn't have cared less about the trappings of my wedding day. I was more eager to bind Vance, Rennick, and Reese to me legally; I didn't need the lavish backdrop, or the obscene amount of food served at our reception. Yes, it may have been all expected of an Elite wedding, but none of it mattered as much as staking my claim to my three men before everyone.

However, I couldn't have been more grateful for the generosity of their families in gifting us with a home of our own. A place that was solely ours was just what we needed to establish the beginning of our life together. No Ardariens and no in-laws to interrupt our stay-at-home honeymoon was just what I needed to resume a peaceful existence with my men.

Thankfully, the wedding reception was cut off early, due to my men's one sole request, the one concession Marguerite agreed to. As soon as our wedding duties were done, all I had to do was give my three husbands a look, and the three of them wasted no time in ushering me out the door.

Racing through the streets in Reese's Range Rover, our now legally bound foursome steadily drew closer to the home that would soon be christened by our presence. The ride there was silent but no less highly charged with anticipation, especially since the last two weeks had seen us too busy for any kind of premarital visits. The wedding was just a hoop for us to jump through before we could finally be together as a family of our own making.

Reese sped past all of the urban neighborhoods where most Elite families made their homes. However, Elite Council members were the only ones who owned mansions like the Ardariens, and I was grateful that my in-laws chose the place that would fit us best. Rennick and Drayna assured me that our home would only be outfitted with the best security and privacy that money could buy. I hadn't stepped foot in it yet, nor have I seen what it looked like, but I trusted that my men knew what we needed.

It wasn't long before Reese slowed down in an unfamiliar neighborhood and steered the vehicle towards a building and stopped at its closed gate. Looking out the Rover's window, I noticed that the area mostly had tall buildings, with eight to ten floors tops. Nothing about the area looked like any of the homes I've seen that belonged to most Elite families, and there was nothing around to show that people actually lived here.

Grinning at me, Reese announced, "Welcome home, sweetheart," and he entered a code into his phone, which activated the gate to open before us, and he drove right on in and down underground. The interior was dark except for spotlights that dotted and marked the pavement before us. I was confused by our surroundings, and I said as much.

"Where the hell are we?" Turning on Reese, I gave him my best frown. He was too busy parking the vehicle deep into the cavern of this too-dark building, so he didn't see.

"Our home," he said proudly, bringing the Rover to a stop.

"Well, I don't see anything that looks like one," I retorted.

Vance jumped out first and came around to help me out of the front seat. Unfortunately, my billowy wedding dress was too big for me to safely jump out on my own, so Vance deftly extracted me out of the passenger seat without marring the dress.

In the dim light, I could see Vance grin down at me, and he said, "This is just the garage, baby girl. The house has several entrances, but this is our own private entrance, accessible only to us. Guests can come in through street level and even then they still have to use the elevator."

Baffled, I stated, "This house is nothing like I've ever seen before."

"You haven't even seen the house yet, and you're judging it already based on what the garage looks like?" Reese said, sounding both disappointed and incredulous.

Rennick took me by the hand, and good-naturedly said, "Well, wait until you see the house proper before any more judgments are made, deal?"

Feeding off of his easy-going mood, I exclaimed, "Deal!" And then I was yanked by my arm further into the garage, with the other two flagging behind.

A light flicked on, one on automatic sensors, and revealed an elevator which opened at our approach. The four of us climbed in, and we all just barely fit, considering my dress took enough space that could have been reserved for another person. Reese pressed the button for the tenth floor, the topmost floor, and I guessed, "We live on the top floor?"

"That's where the best view is," Reese replied.

"Then what are on the other floors?"

"Guest rooms are on each floor, complete with their own kitchens and bathrooms. We have an entire gym and training facility on the eighth floor, a shooting range on the second. And another floor has comms and all the tech you'd need to make a hacker like you happy," Rennick answered.

That was only four floors he had mentioned; what about the other six? So, I asked, "Why so much space? Are we really going to be needing it all?"

Vance grinned. "If you hadn't already noticed the security features we used to enter, this 'house' is really more of a stronghold than a house. Everything in it was chosen and designed to protect you."

"And it's up to you what you want to do with the other floors. They're still empty," Reese added.

Amazed that my husbands chose this place with my safety in mind, I melted just a little. This place was a far cry from all of the places that Dad and I had lived in, so I was all the more appreciative of what my new family was giving me. They've given me a real family, a sense of belonging, and so much love—more love than I believed I deserve.

Arriving at the top floor, the elevator doors slid open to reveal an open floor plan of our entire living space. With floor to ceiling windows all around, the city lights glowed like tealights all around us. But before I could step further in to admire the place, I was surrounded on all sides by my very big, and very horny men. They closed in on me, crowding me as their eyes greedily drank in the sight of me.

With all three of them towering over me, they made me feel petite and delicate, words I never attributed to myself before meeting them. "Can we have you now, wife?" That was Reese, breathing the question directly into my ear before nibbling on my lobe.

Already sucked into a sensual haze that had begun as soon as I stepped onto our floor, I replied, "Not until I can see you. I mean, the three of you. Clothes off!"

We were standing in the middle of the room with lamps lending soft lighting to the space. With the lights down low, Vance, Rennick, and Reese took my breath away as they slowly stripped. Jackets shucked off broad shoulders. Dress shirts recklessly unbuttoned and tugged off. Pants dropped to the floor.

Stepping back to admire the sight of them with nothing on, I was heady with the realization that these gorgeous men were truly mine. The stiff skirt of my wedding dress was the only thing keeping me upright since the sight of my husbands looking so sexy weakened my knees. They were my own personal visual and sexual buffet, and I was going to gorge myself on them.

But I wanted to take my time indulging myself and them, of course. It was our wedding night, and we had all night as well as the rest of our natural lives to indulge ourselves.

Looking at my three warriors, I surveyed the differences between them: their skin tone, their build, and their coloring. Their male beauty may be vastly different from each other, but it in no way detracted from how devastating they each were in the looks department. And with the looks of love and lust combined and aimed at me, my poor heart thumped faster in anticipation of what those looks would mean for me later.

So, I walked closer, trailing a hand, a finger across a pectoral. Across a set of abs. Across a well-muscled back. They stood still, not moving a muscle as I circled about them, touching, and caressing them at my own whim. "You are all so beautiful," I whispered, suddenly willing to admit long-held secret longings. "I had always thought so."

From Reese, "Always?"

"Did you know who we were even before we met?" Vance asked curiously.

Rennick said nothing. Instead, he shot me a saucy, knowing grin.

"Yes," I answered simply. I didn't need them to grow bigger heads if I admitted I had admired them since before I had met them and known of their exploits. So, I thought it was best to stick to the one-word answer ploy. And God knew I wasn't going to tell them about my obsession over them after our first meeting.

"Huh. I think I like knowing that our wife was into us before we laid eyes on each other," Vance grinned at me with a touch of arrogance in his tone.

I said nothing in response, except to continue my leisurely touching, only I used my short fingernails to scrape against skin as I continued circling them. I applied slightly more pressure in strategic places, and it was satisfying to hear the groans or slight yelps that I've elicited with my rougher touch. I was careful to use a lighter touch against a nipple here or a more firm scrape of my nails down an exposed or abdomen.

After one full revolution around them, I came to a stop before them and smiled. By this time, the shit-eating grins on their faces had been soon replaced with lust-heavy looks intended just for me. I knew they had once decided on a woman who wasn't me before they had even met me, but I loved the fact that they had chosen me to be their forever woman. And I would forever be the woman those heavy-lidded looks would narrow their focus on.

Satisfied that I'd teased them long enough with just the touch of my hands, I decided it was time for a bolder move. Once I moved in closer to Vance, the other two closed in on me further so we were standing in a tight circle, with Reese coming up from behind and Rennick to my right. This move was so telling of how instinctual my men acted around me when their arousal was at an all-time high; they moved perfectly in sync.

I knew they wouldn't expect this, so I cupped Vance's scrotum, massaging, and rolling his testicles gently in my one hand. He couldn't help the automatic sucking in of a breath before relaxing into it. I smiled back at him as he gazed at me blissfully. At the same time that I had Vance gently by his balls, I reached behind me with the other hand to pull Reese in closer by his engorged dick. He, too, gave a small yelp that segued into a groan as I stroked him up and down.

But just because both of my hands were occupied didn't mean that Rennick was completely left out of the fun.

He was already nuzzling my neck by the time I had my hands full, and it wasn't long before he began nipping up my neck with little bites until he reached my mouth. There, he plundered past my lips with tongue and teeth, as he expertly wrenched muffled groans that reverberated past my throat and into his own mouth.

Vance and Reese's hands didn't remain idle for long; their own hands were eager for the feel of me skin-to-skin. As eager as I had known my men to be on past occasions, this time they seemed to be taking their time exploring what skin my wedding dress did expose. It was like they were savoring every moment, with every reverent touch on my skin like they were worshipping me with their hands alone.

But I was growing impatient; they weren't touching me where I wanted them to, and I was doing my best to keep all three moaning at my touch in pleasure. It hadn't completely registered in my brain that my own feet were doing a two-step, dancing from foot to foot in my own attempt to assuage the ache between my own legs. "Easy," Reese crooned, and he settled both of his hands firmly on my hips to keep me still.

With the pressure of his hands on my hips, I stayed as still as possible. I was rewarded when Reese grabbed hold of my dress' zipper and deftly unzipped me, careful not to snag the lacy fabric in the zipper's teeth. The dress parted in the back, and my ribcage and lungs were more than happy to be free from its confining grip.

Rennick pulled away from his bruisingly forceful kiss to help me out of the voluminous skirts, and I gasped the moment he released my mouth with a loud smacking sound. He grinned down at me before dropping to his knees to ease my stiff skirts down my legs and then helping me to step out of them. I was left with my bustier and lacy panties still on my body, but they were quickly removed by three pairs of quick, enthusiastic hands.

Still, I maintained my grip on both Reese and Vance, who were now taking turns at my mouth, plying me with soul-sucking kisses. Our kisses were growing frenzied, and our touches becoming more exploratory and exuberant. Rennick remained on his knees, and I didn't know why until he braced my knees apart slightly and dove into my feminine core with his tongue.

It was more than I could stand to even stay upright, but both Vance and Reese were holding me up as Rennick vigorously lapped away at my clit. I moaned in rhythmic sync with the waves of heat and arousal growing stronger in frequency the more Rennick continued eating away at my pussy.

Vance's kisses were drugging, interrupted every so often by a gasp of my own as Rennick brought me closer and closer to the height of my pleasure. Reese was playing with my breasts, teasing, and plucking at the hardened tips of my nipples, and I tightened my own grip on both his cock and Vance's.

I became a wriggling mass of heat and pooling desire, waiting for the inevitable climax that Rennick was rushing me towards along with Reese's and Vance's help. Once the waves of pleasure melded closer and closer together, my breathing hurried, and my heart pounding, I came with a vengeance, my three husbands keeping me upright and coming hard. The scream that emerged from the depths of my throat rang loudly in the cavernous entryway, helping me along with this tremendous release of pressure from all of this pleasure.

It was so hard not to collapse with the force of my orgasm, but Rennick had me balanced at his shoulders while both Reese and Vance each had a strong arm wrapped around me. Was I strange for reveling in so much pleasure without even having stepped inside our bedroom? Aren't married people supposed to be doing this kind of thing in a bed?

Either way, I sagged in happy relief when Vance whispered, "Let's find the bedroom and continue." My body may have been replete from its recent burst of pleasure, but I was in no way yet satisfied. To give my men as much pleasure as they had given me was as much a need to be gratified for myself as it was for them.

With the revelation of love revealed between us four came the happy realization that when love was present, there was more giving happening from all corners. My men and I were equidistant points in our quadrangle, and there was no inequality when it came to how much of ourselves we gave each other. This dynamic was so obvious and clear-cut for all of us, and it made me happier knowing that we were all in this together. And I loved that Vance, Rennick, and Reese had loved each other as family first before meeting me, even though there wasn't a drop of blood between them. And having them loving me like they did was nothing like I'd ever dreamed I could ever hope to have.

Everything I had, everything I never thought I needed or wanted was right here with me in this moment: my men surrounding me with their love and affection. Racing with me bouncing between them towards the bedroom, my men couldn't stop themselves from stealing alluring kisses from my swollen lips, but we eventually made it into our bedroom.

A quick glance around the expansive room held me in awe momentarily before my husbands bore me down to our bed. If I had been given the time, I was sure I would have leisurely viewed the room in admiration for all of the details in it, details that my men had spared no expense. Our bedroom boasted of deep, rich tones in the accents, large windows framed by diaphanous drapes, and simple, elegant feminine touches that I was sure they thought I'd appreciate.

Our bed was wide as it was long, and it was the perfect size for the four of us to playfully romp in without the danger of us falling out of it. Next to our bed, my men had thoughtfully placed a small table whose top was filled with bottles and other items I wasn't sure about. Their placement and the contents of some of those bottles reminded me of that night I had spent with Rennick and Reese in the private club where I had seen something similar.

Before I could ask about it, Rennick had grabbed a full bottle, uncapped it, and dispensed a healthy amount of the liquid onto his cock. I licked my lips as he rubbed the liquid up and down his cock, coating his entire length and I could smell the sweetness of whatever that liquid was. Grinning wickedly, Rennick told me, "Your turn, sweetheart. Onto your stomach."

I obeyed, anticipation building in me once again, and Vance helped me roll over and then propped me up on all fours. My pussy and ass jutted up and towards them in this position, and I wriggled a little as Rennick applied the same liquid to my ass and pussy, rubbing it in. "Oo, that's cold!" I exclaimed at the first drop, but I relaxed again as he massaged it into my labia and backdoor entrance. "What is that stuff?" I asked. "It smells like candy."

"Salted caramel lube, baby girl. It will make sucking my cock like you were sucking on a lollipop," Reese commented.

"What's a lollipop?" I asked, having no idea what he was trying to convey.

"Open up, and you'll see," he volleyed back. Then, Reese moved to lube himself up from the same bottle and circled round to face me, his cock bobbing in front of my eyes. Looking him in the eye, I grinned at him, and playfully licked at his tip.

Mm, that liquid lube was delicious! And I was eager to get the full effect of the flavor combined with Reese's own unique flavor, so I opened up and took him to the hilt inside my mouth. The lube made for a different but enjoyable experience; the salted caramel flavor still lingering in my mouth as I continued lapping and sucking away at him.

Meanwhile, Rennick spread my ass cheeks wide and used a hand to position his cock between the lips of my pussy. Shuffling forward on his knees, he plunged deep inside with a drawn-out groan. I stiffened at his abrupt entrance, but my drenched pussy was more than ready for him and I melted around him. With my pussy and mouth occupied, I wasn't in a position to wriggle around and locate Vance.

As Rennick thrust heavily into me and as I devoured Reese's cock, Vance assured from somewhere behind me, "Don't worry about me, sweetheart. Right now, I'm enjoying how beautiful you look being dominated. I'll get my turn in soon."

It wasn't long before Rennick declared, "I want her tight ass. Vance, you want her pussy?"

Without a further word, Rennick pulled out of me and pulled me up and off of Reese's cock. With both of their help, they lifted me onto Vance who lay on his back, arranging my legs on either side of his hips. Vance gripped me by the hips and pressed downward on them, directing me to impale myself on his cock. My already abused pussy gratifyingly swallowed Vance's rigid length, and my nerves sang once again the moment my clit came into contact with his hard pubic bone.

Straddling my legs and Vance's, Rennick came in close behind, parting my ass cheeks once again and adding more lube onto my ass. I shivered as Rennick pushed me forward so that my front was flush with Vance's, smashing my breasts fully into Vance's solid chest. Next I knew, I was being slowly entered from behind, mind-numbingly deep into my ass and my breathing seized.

"Easy, Laena," Rennick crooned, as he rhythmically sawed into me, one inch at a time. When he was deeply seated within, he and Vance took turns to rock and thrust inside both of my holes. I gasped, feeling impossibly full just as Reese took advantage of my parted lips and slipped himself back inside my mouth. It almost blew my mind that all that separated Rennick's cock from Vance's was a thin wall of muscle and tissue. And from their groans, I was sure they could feel each other's movements within me.

The four of us worked ourselves into a frenzy, a writhing mass of bodies, slippery with sweat. Guttural groans intermixed with my own gasps and keening moans, as my husbands rode me slow and long. I was so ready to come, almost sobbing with wanting it so badly, almost mindless in the ecstasy they brought me.

Then, it happened. The three of them drove me straight to the edge and drove me almost out of my mind with pleasure that finally crested into a mind-shattering orgasm. I screamed from the force of it, not caring if I busted anyone's eardrums, the pleasure was that great.

As if my orgasm was the cue for theirs, warmth suddenly flooded me in my pussy, my ass, and my mouth.

Their own groans filled my ears, competing with my own heaving gasps as I rode out my own pleasure. When it was over, as one, we all collapsed in a heap, our breath still heaving inside our chests. I smiled sleepily at each of them before they carefully tucked me in under the covers.

I was the happiest I had ever been, with my men surrounding me in this enormous bed. Before I fully nodded off, I regretfully thought of the one person who could have made this day complete. Dad should have been there at the wedding. But knowing how wily the man was, he had probably found a way to witness the proceedings without being discovered. With that consoling thought, I fell into a deep slumber, my mind and body both utterly exhausted.

28

LAENA

It wasn't long into our first week of wedded bliss that I was called to see Marguerite. I shouldn't have been as surprised as I was when I received her call, but I had dreaded the moment she would finally decide what it was she needed me for. There went my hopes for an extended honeymoon.

Surprisingly, she didn't call me to her Council office chambers, but instead had instructed me to meet with her at home. She was usually found in the Council building during this time, so it already didn't bode well that we were in more private surroundings.

Seated behind her ornate desk, as I entered her home office, she instructed, "Close the door, please, Laena." Watching her closely for any clues to what she might be thinking, I concluded that she would have been perfect for a game of poker with my husbands. She definitely gave good poker face.

I took up a seat at the sofa instead of one of the chairs closest to her desk. Because of the further distance, it made Marguerite get up from her desk and move to a plush seat opposite from me. I waited for her to say something, but she didn't volunteer anything. Instead, she stared at me, almost as if she was assessing my abilities just from a glance.

"You called me here, Mother," I said, breaking the silence. She only allowed me to call her by that title in public and insisted I call her Marguerite when we weren't. Using the title now was the only concession I had to show her how disgruntled I was by her summons. "Maybe you can tell me why."

She frowned at me. "You know why. It's not too hard to guess you are now needed to do something for me like we had previously discussed."

I frowned back mightily. "You want me to off someone, don't you?" I had never taken the life of a fellow human being before, and it sickened me to think that that was what Marguerite had in mind.

Marguerite huffed and stuck her nose regally into the air. "You make it sound so distasteful. If anything, you would be doing the Council a favor by helping us get rid of Councilman Fang. He has been nothing but a nuisance to our plans for redevelopment of the city."

I knew who Fang was and knew that he was trying to win Reese's parents' support for his ideas for city planning. His ideas were progressive, and I was all for repurposing an older section of the Outer Ring for new homes for the disadvantaged and homeless like he proposed.

"Why would you want to get rid of Fang?" I asked.

"That's not for you to know, girl," she stated coldly. "All we need you to do is get rid of him. We don't care how."

"We?"

She stared daggers at me rather than answer. I shrugged and sighed, "And remind me again what would happen if I don't do as I'm told?" It was all I could do not to growl at her. Fang was innocent and didn't deserve to have his life cut short just because someone didn't agree with his ideas.

"What do you think? I have ways of destroying the lives of those close to your husbands if you refuse. For instance, Ansel Reese? I could crush his parents flat for daring to defy the will of the Council."

I knew that there was no love lost between Reese and his parents, but I didn't think he'd ever want to see them dead prematurely. Besides, I was also charged with the care of my husbands and I would see to it that they were also protected from Marguerite and her insane amount of power.

"And let's not forget your husbands. Defy me, and all it will take are some well-placed calls. The threat of an Eidolon horde outside the city could be easily staged to draw them into a trap."

Anger surged hotly within me. Threaten my men, will she? It took great effort to calm myself since I knew that she would make good on her threats, and I feared that she would at the tiniest disobedience from me. She had everything at her disposal to work for her own desires, including me.

"Fine," I bit out between gritted teeth. "When?"

"ASAP," she said mildly, unaware of how I was seething. "I don't care to know how. Only that it is done by tomorrow. The Council convenes tomorrow afternoon, and we can't have Fang oppose the general consensus of opinion."

Soon enough, after further minor instructions, she dismissed me with, "You will be monitored to make sure the job is done right. Anything that traces your actions back to me will count as a failure and I will have no choice but to punish you then. See that you don't fail, and you will have no reason to see what that punishment will entail."

Curling my lip, I left the Ardarien mansion, making my way home on foot. By the time I arrived at our compound, it was full dark. Vance, Reese, and Rennick weren't due back home for another hour, so I had the house to myself to work out all this tension stiffening my body. Making use of our training floor, I put my body through a punishing workout to clear my mind and give myself a much-needed distraction.

When I was through, I finally had a clear-cut plan of action in place. First, I would need to find out as much as I could about Fang and his daily movements. It would take some time, but I was going to find out everything available about the man that could be an advantage. Public records and sealed records with his name on it would be the next thing to sift through while on the war room floor. It didn't take long before I discovered everything I could about Fang, right down to the very minute of his predictable, patterned life.

The sounds of the elevator rushing up to our living floor broke me out of my musing, and I rushed up the stairwell to meet them. With a bright smile for each of them, I greeted them, always happy to see them. If my smile wasn't as bright as usual, I had Marguerite's summons and plans to thank for that, but luckily neither of my men noticed. We had no plans for the evening to leave the house, so we opted to stay in, sharing in food prep duties while Reese manned the stove.

Food and wine filling our bellies, we soon made our way to our bedroom. Since we married, my men took it upon themselves to enact their lustful desires upon my very capable body, and tonight would be no exception. They managed to sate me so well that I was in danger of ruining my own plans well after they fell asleep.

I was grateful that it didn't take too long for snoring to ensue from three sets of mouths, and I surreptitiously snuck out of our bed. Instead of using the elevator down, I took the stairs, making sure to pick up the backpack I had placed in the stairwell earlier. I had packed a simple outfit into which I changed into, leaving my nightgown behind on the stairwell landing as I made my way down towards our garage.

Dressed all in black and my hair slicked back into a simple, low knot, I stole out of our compound in Reese's Rover. Hopefully, my men wouldn't notice I was gone until late; by then, I would most likely be back at home without any of them the wiser. But that was being optimistic.

Making my way past the Inner Circle gates, I drove the route I had memorized earlier, keeping close to lesser traversed side streets. Finding a narrow alley to park the Rover, I made the rest of the trip on foot, not wanting Reese or the others to be implicated in any way with what I was about to do. The closer I got to my destination, the more that dread pooled heavier in my belly.

As I had discovered earlier for this time of night, Fang could be found caring for his daughter's children, a boy and a girl. The daughter, a single, widowed mother, scrounged what she could by working at an all-night diner. From security camera feeds that I had hacked into, I found that he would walk to his daughter's meager home at 10:55 and arrive there at 11:00. The daughter would come home at 5:00 in the morning to relieve him, and he would venture home shortly after.

More and more, I detested Marguerite for stealing away my choice to be free, only to be a pawn to be used for her own devices. I hated her for tying me to her; for making my choices difficult for me. With her threat to harm my husbands, the same men she had declared as her sons-in-law, I hated myself for being weak against her, for not knowing what else I could do. It sucked big-ass donkey balls, as Drayna would say, but I still couldn't come up with a plan to counter Marguerite's plans.

Finding nothing that could mar Councilman Fang's reputation, I couldn't figure out why Marguerite would want him dead. The only thing I could see within the realm of possibility was that it was something personal. I already had a taste of Marguerite's motivations stemming from her protective instincts when it came to Kane; she adopted me because of it. I didn't want to be the weapon Marguerite used to do the deed, but I saw no choice. It tore at my soul as I asked myself: how could I be so willing to sacrifice this innocent man just to keep my husbands safe?

That was it. I couldn't go through with this. It was a morally repugnant mission, and I chose right then and there to refuse to do Marguerite's bidding. Once I talked to Vance and the others, maybe we could figure something out before Marguerite could retaliate as she had threatened to do. Ending the life of an innocent man was not what I was about, and I wasn't going to start now.

I stopped. I wasn't more than a house block away from Fang's daughter's house, but I needed to gather my bearings. Since I had left the Rover, I had been aware that I was being followed. I couldn't see who, but my heightened hearing could hear the doubled sound of footsteps in sync with my own. A disturbance in the air around me, the smallest whisper of sound apprised me of the fact that there was someone slowly knifing through the space behind me at a distance.

All of my senses fully tuned in to my surroundings, and I guessed that whoever was following me wasn't on street level. Looking up at the tall houses around me, I cursed, finding that there were numerous balconies and low overhangs where a person could hide. I turned my head to the right, and in my peripheral vision, I spotted a dark figure crouching on top of a railed balcony.

"Tch, you found me," the figure dressed in a similar fashion to me announced resignedly. I was surprised to hear a feminine voice coming from within the deep hood that hid most of her face. Standing up to her full height, she flipped forward from the ten-foot drop and landed easily into a crouch before me. We were now face-to-face, the hood having fallen from her head, and again I was surprised to see someone who was around my age grinning back at me.

"Marguerite sent you?" I asked, narrowing my eyes at her. Marguerite did promise that she would have me monitored, but I didn't count on or even recognize this girl with a pixie cut and large, over bright eyes.

"Who else?" she remarked, her eyes squinting into slits as she smiled even bigger. "I've been instructed to make sure you get the job done, and so, here I am!" She spread her arms out wide to emphasize her announcement, and I was somewhat relieved to see she had no weapons in either hand. But I knew better than to let my guard down around her; for all I knew, she was probably hiding flat, hiltless blades beneath her form fitting clothes.

With eyes that glittered like black ice, she asked, "I assume that you will get the job done, right?"

When I didn't answer, she continued in a sing-song voice, "Don't mess with me!" Then, in a hard, steely voice, she claimed, "If you don't get rid of Fang, my orders were to get rid of you first and then the councilman. Then I report all to Madam Ardarien, and trust me, you will not like what she will do to your men."

Anger bubbled within me with the proposed threat to my husbands, but I knew better than to let this subordinate goad me into action. In a truly calm voice, I stated, "Don't worry. I'm going to do what I set out to do. No hesitation about it, the consequences be damned!"

I managed to surprise her with a sudden burst of activity, throwing punches and kicks at her. I got in one good hit to her solar plexus, knocking her back a few steps, but she got back her bearings and threw herself fully into brawler mode.

We attacked each other; me, with the intent to subdue; she, with the express intent to kill. She cursed when my fist grazed her cheek, a result of her sidestepping just in time to avoid the full impact of my punch. In hand-to-hand combat, we were evenly matched, and neither of us showed signs of stopping until one of us was laid out flat.

She ducked one of my kicks and crouched forward into a roll, ending up behind me. In that moment, I got slammed from behind with a kick delivered between my shoulder blades. I went flying, but I used the momentum forward to tuck and roll, only to pop back up, facing her once again.

I don't know how long we fought, but with the lunging back and forth with no quarter, I was tiring. But I wasn't ready to concede the fight. Quickly, I unsheathed two blades, which had been hidden up my makeshift vambraces. She did the same, and we flew at each other, blades sparking and clanging with metallic echoes throughout the narrow street. I was surprised no one in their homes and in their beds weren't awakened by the noise that was echoing around us in the street.

The fight itself was more than just a chess game of dance, deflection, and offensive strikes. It had gotten messy with stabbing and slicing each other in less vital spots, and I had no doubt that one of us would find a lucky opportunity to deal the final blow. She was as strong as me and just as fast, and with us equally matched, it took great effort not to give up the fight, leaving us panting.

Then, a hand grabbed at my wrist, keeping me from dealing her a blow with my elbow to knock her off balance. The sound of a suppressed gunshot whistled past, then I heard her yelp as she was knocked flat on her ass. I swung to face the owner of the hand gripping my wrist and was shocked to find Vance gripping me. Looking back towards my yet unnamed assailant, I found Reese and Rennick standing over top her, kicking her knives further away, and their guns aimed down at her.

"You bastard! You shot me!" I heard her yell. They must have used a silencer; otherwise we would have had the whole neighborhood alerted to our presence out here.

Rennick growled, "You're lucky we haven't done worse. Now, shut the hell up." With one foot on her chest to keep her down and the gun aimed at her, she wasn't inclined to make any further moves or say anything more. Reese bent down to examine the bullet's entry into her right shoulder.

While Rennick and Reese tended to her, I turned to Vance and asked, "How did you find me?"

"Sweetheart, the Rover has a geotracker. The moment it left the house, we knew you had taken it. But why?" The look of consternation on his face was enough to make me feel guilty. I knew how he and the others felt about my safety. But I was equally as determined to see to theirs.

And I didn't know what to tell them or even how to begin. So, I settled for giving them an apology. "I'm sorry. I should have told you what I was doing, but I couldn't. It would mean all of your lives if I did."

Vance was clearly taken aback by that, and he shot the other two a look. Unfortunately, the moment they took their eyes off of my attacker, she used that to her advantage. With a speed neither of us expected from her, she dashed away, melting into the shadows. The guys tried to make a move in her direction, but I stopped them by saying sadly, "Let her go. Even if we detained her, Marguerite would still win."

Questions formed in three sets of eyes, but before they could voice them, I said, "It's a long story, but if you don't mind, I'd like to be home and cleaned up before I tell it."

"You're bleeding," Reese said finally as we made our way back to the Rover. Vance's Jeep was parked next to it.

"Not deep. They're just shallow cuts," I assured him. "Please. I want to go home."

My men said nothing as they packed me into the Rover with Reese driving, while Vance and Rennick followed after us in the Jeep. The way home was just as silent, the seconds ticking by increasing the despair I felt at failing the people I loved. I dreaded what I would have to tell them eventually, and I was afraid of what they would say about my keeping this from them. They had been angry about my keeping secrets before, and who was to say that they would react the same this time around?

Whatever the outcome, I needed to tell them why I'd done it. They needed to know I wanted them safe and alive no matter the cost to me.

29

VANCE

The moment the alarm sounded, the three of us woke up in a panic to find Laena gone and a blaring notification that the Range Rover had left the premises. We froze at first, wondering if she had finally decided to leave us, to find her fortune lay elsewhere other than us. At first, I blamed myself for falling so lax in my vigilance, questioning if my quest for our happiness had blinded me to Laena's own secret motives.

Truthfully, the three of us knew something was up. Since the night of our engagement party, we noticed that Laena had seemed a little more subdued than usual. It wasn't anything we could pin our fingers on, but we knew that she was hiding something, and we feared that it may have been another big secret she refused to tell us. Reese had reasoned, "She committed to us; maybe she'll tell us on her own time."

Still, I had reservations about leaving our girl all on her own, and I hated that she thought she had to go it alone without us being any wiser. I promised myself that I wouldn't be kept in the dark when it came to anything involving Laena, and neither would I let her keep me there. I didn't care what that said about me just as long as my end goal was to keep her safe and hidden from Elite officials who would view her as a threat to their way of life.

Personally, I couldn't see how the evolution of our species into something adaptable and able to survive this Eidolon-riddled world was a threat. But I didn't think like the high-powered Elite man, and maybe that was where the scope of my vision was limited. I tried to envision a world where a population of people like Laena thrived and flourished, and all I could foresee was a species that would see humanity continue on.

"How can we get a hold of Lightbourne again? Maybe he might know what she's up to," Rennick mused as we walked up into my Jeep.

I groused, "We don't because he didn't give us even a mailing address." I climbed into the driver's seat and waited for the other two to climb in.

Reese reminded us, "I wouldn't be surprised if he knew something about what's going on with Laena. He even knew the moment you opened up those files just weeks ago and then showed up like he had promised Laena." Still, I waited for Reese to get his ass into the front passenger seat, but he remained just outside the vehicle, staring at a spot over the hood of the Jeep.

"Yeah, I'd bet he's been spying on us all this time," Rennick continued, then yelled loudly, "Hey, Lightbourne! We could really use your help here!"

A wiry figure dressed in dark clothes dropped in front of the vehicle, startling me. "What the fuck?" Recognizing Lightbourne's slight build and stature, I yelled out the driver's side, "Were you hanging from the ceiling this whole time?" To Rennick, in a quieter voice, I asked, "Did you know he was there?"

The other two were just as startled, frozen in shock at Lightbourne's sudden appearance, but they recovered quickly. Rennick comically commented to me, "Told ya. I knew he'd be lurking close by somewhere." In a quieter voice to me, he answered, "But the real answer is no. I didn't know he'd show. I was just trying to pinpoint what Reese was looking at."

Incredulous, Reese said to Lightbourne, "I thought that might have been you, scaling the wall. How the hell did you get in here?" The garage was sealed, and the alarm was still on.

Lightbourne straightened from his crouched position and moved to the driver's side rear passenger seat. "Never mind all that. What's more important is that Laena's in danger. Use the geotracker on the Rover to find out where she is!"

Reese grumbled, "I was just going to do that, old man. Now, get in."

The four of us sped out of the garage, not caring that I had left a heavy cloud of exhaust behind in our hurry to get to Laena. Reese barked out directions as he narrowed down where Laena was. She was in the Inner Ring, in a residential area meant for middle-income families. While it was an area not known for its luxury, it did have a bit of an undesirable element that only came out after dark. What children that did live in the area knew not to be outside once the sun set. What business could Laena have there?

It didn't take us long to find Reese's Rover hidden in a narrow alley, but no Laena.

Lightbourne stopped us before we could jump out of the Jeep. Looking around the neighborhood outside the Jeep, he said, "Given the area, I think I know why Laena is here. She was sent here."

So, the old man knew something. "Okay, let's have it. Tell us what you know," I said gruffly.

"This was what I was trying to prevent: Laena in the hands of the Ardariens. Now, I know Laena is not acting on her own; she's being controlled by them somehow."

I shot him a puzzled look. "Controlled? Is that why she left our bed in the middle of the night?"

In return, Lightbourne shot me a look of mild disgust. "Nothing fancier than blackmail though I'm afraid. And I take it that whoever has threatened Laena also knew the three of you to be her weakness."

"How do you know this shit? Is this for real?" Reese shot at him.

"The things I know about this city and the Elite would be enough to give you nightmares, boy," Lightbourne said, a cold glint in his eye. "The lengths they've gone to in order to guard their secrets were nothing to sneeze at. And I'm proof positive that they would do anything to make sure their secrets stay buried. Why do you think I have no family other than Laena and that there's a fat price on my head? They wiped out my entire family the moment I defected. Laena is all I have."

We stayed silent, digesting what he told us and trying to understand what that meant. "So, then tell us. Is Laena in danger, right at this moment?" I asked.

"Yes, in danger of losing herself to them. The moment she assassinates Councilman Fang, she will belong to them. A weapon to be used whenever it suits them. We have to stop her."

The three of us wasted no time in scrambling out of the Jeep, leaving Lightbourne behind. Laena belonged to us, and we weren't going to let her be the Elite's puppet. Whether or not she knew it, she needed us to save her from a fate at someone else's hands. Better that she live a life with us to protect her and keep her safe than to leave her fate in someone else's unworthy hands.

"Cut us some slack here," I heard Rennick mumble as we searched through the streets. "Whatever happened to my dream of living in peace and quiet once we got married, huh?"

"Sorry, bud," I answered, but I couldn't show any real sympathy for him. Not when Laena made us so damned happy. "We're in this for better or for worse, right?"

Reese, the optimist of our group, remarked, "Never a dull moment, that's for damned sure. Laena needs us to rein her in every once in a while, and this is one of those times."

I agreed, "Gotta hand it to her. I never saw us three having a stay-at-home wife anyway."

Finally, we spotted her down a narrow residential street made up of mostly brick townhouses, but she wasn't alone. Her petite figure was in a frenzy of motion with her combat knives, attacking and dodging with another figure of similar build. A woman. Their movements were slowing, but neither of them were willing to give up the fight.

"Come on, we have to stop them," I urged the other two. Following my lead, we got up close enough for me to grab Laena's wrist, keeping her from striking the other female. Rennick had already pulled out his 9mm, silencer attached, and took a shot at the female, with intent to bring her down, not kill.

The female went down, knocked on her ass, as she shouted, "You bastard! You shot me!" Rennick and Reese closed in on her, guns still trained down at her as they kicked her knives further out of reach.

Still holding onto Laena, I could hear Rennick answer the female in an angry retort, but the words didn't register. Instead, I looked over Laena for any injuries she might have sustained and saw only a few shallow cuts here and there. Even while I was upset by her abrupt disappearance, I still managed to get swept up by her avenging-angel beauty, remaining pure of heart while ready to do battle at any given moment. She wouldn't be out here if she didn't have a good, legitimate reason to be. Even after all this time, she remained pure of heart with no malicious intentions towards anybody.

But before I could ask her if she was all right, Laena asked, "How did you find me?"

"Sweetheart, the Rover's geotracker. The moment it left the house, we knew you had taken it. But why?" More than wanting to hear her reason, I really wanted to hear who had commissioned her to take out Fang.

"I'm sorry. I should have told you what I was doing, but I couldn't. It would mean all of your lives if I did." That wasn't what I expected to come out of her mouth, but she looked so defeated and tired, I wanted to take her home and tuck her into bed with me beside her.

I glanced back at Rennick and Reese, who both heard what she said with shock revealed on their faces. When we signed up to be her husbands, we never envisioned having a wife who was willing to give up herself to save our sorry asses. And now that we're faced with exactly that situation, we were all floored to have it happen.

Unfortunately, Laena's attacker took advantage of our stunned silence to make good her escape. I made a move to follow after her just as Rennick and Reese raised their guns in her fleeting direction. But Laena stopped us by saying, "Let her go. Even if we detained her, Marguerite would still win."

My suspicions were confirmed once Laena uttered her adopted mother's name. Rennick and Reese looked confused, so she continued in a tired voice, "It's a long story, but if you don't mind, I'd like to be home and cleaned up before I tell it."

Eager to get Laena home safe and her minor cuts sealed up, we made our way back to the Rover and Jeep. With no sign of Lightbourne to be found once we approached the vehicles, I guessed he made himself scarce once Laena was found and Fang's assassination prevented. I was sure he'd turn up again when he needed, or when we needed him. The man was downright weird, but he proved useful when we lacked information. Plus, he was the one person who loved Laena as much as we did. We could be sure to see him only when he wanted to be seen.

When we got home, Reese pointed out that Laena was quiet the whole ride home, and even when he prodded, she gave one-word answers only. Wordlessly, the three of us cleaned her wounds, patched her up, and dressed her in a white sleeveless top and dark grey sweats. We prepared a very early breakfast for her, toast and fruit with a healthy mug of steaming hot coffee.

As much as I wanted to fire questions at her, I knew she'd clam up the moment I went on the offensive. She'd taught us as much the last time we tried to get answers from her, and it only served to give me a headache from my rising temper. Laena must have learned the skill early on, being cool under forceful interrogative pressure.

She ate and drank like everything was normal, while we watched and waited. There was no way I was going to eat while the worry I had for her still tightened my throat.

After her last swallow, she finally spoke. "If you haven't already guessed, I was under orders from Marguerite."

She stopped to take in our reactions. Whatever she saw there encouraged her to go on. "She knows about me, about my Eidolon DNA."

"Is that why she's controlling you? To keep your secret hidden?" Reese asked.

"No, that's not why. It's much more than that. She said if I didn't get rid of Fang for her, she was going to do something terrible to the three of you." Her voice faltered there at the end; her face hidden as she bent her head low.

"Sweetheart, she doesn't have that kind of power," Rennick assured her gently. "Marguerite Ardarien's seat on the Council carries her only so far, and as governor, she's still subject to our laws."

Reese added, "She'd have our families breathing down her neck if she tried."

I growled under my breath, my blood already boiling at any perceived threat to anyone in my family. I wasn't the type to let anyone get away with trying to harm those I loved. And despite the three of us growing up Elite and having careers that served both the Elite and the people's interests, we also had tricks up our sleeves to see everyone we loved safe.

Rennick had hold of her one hand, and when he turned to give me a look. I nodded back in answer, understanding what that look meant. The three of us had made a promise to this woman, and we would go to unfathomable lengths to see her protected and safe. He told her, "Trust us when we say that we won't let anything happen to you or to our families."

She wailed, "Yes, but I don't see how you can do that when Marguerite has done so many terrible things in the name of the Elite. What can we do that could stop her from ordering your termination or mine?"

I swooped her up in my arms, holding her tight as I hissed, "That's not going to happen, Laena! C'mon, have a little faith in what the three of us can do."

Reese made light of the situation by saying, "Yeah, you may have married us for our good looks, but we're more than just pretty faces. We're very capable of protecting this family."

Clapping his hands together and rubbing them palm to palm, Rennick joined in, "Okay, family, then it looks like we've got work to do." Knowing him so well, I grinned at him, understanding exactly what he was doing when he said that.

Laena looked up from my shoulder and asked, "Work?"

With a wolfish grin, Rennick replied, "Yeah, sweetheart. The three of us have to convince you properly that we are more than capable of handling any threat aimed our way." He moved in closer to place a reassuring hand on her back, rubbing circles slowly into it. Softly, he pecked her on the nose with a sweet kiss before diving in to seize her lips with a hot one.

Already, I could feel Laena melting in my arms at his kiss, and I loosened my grip on her to allow her to fully turn into Rennick. With me at her back, I caressed her ass while dotting soft, slow kisses on her bared shoulders and neck.

Reese mock-protested, "Aw, c'mon! I thought you meant we were gonna talk about this!" But his pout soon morphed into a salacious grin, and he announced, "Move over, you two! It's my turn."

Shoving Rennick and I aside, Reese engulfed a dizzy Laena in his arms, lifting her above him to wrap her legs around his waist, and slammed her up against the nearest wall. Smothering her with his kiss, the two could be heard moaning against each other, their hands roaming wherever they could reach.

It didn't take long to convince her to come back to bed with us, but I knew we hadn't completely swayed her thinking. With our combined skillsets and with the connections we each garnered over the years, we were equipped with an unusual arsenal to combat any threat.

What Laena didn't know was that despite our being born Elite, we were more rebels at heart than people really knew. Our jobs as Elite military gave us the look of being New Phoenix society's trained dogs, but we were so much more. Having seen what we've seen around the Seven Cities, the three of us have seen how precarious the peace actually was. And how oppressive and restrictive some of the other city governments actually were.

The three of us already had put into motion a plan that would afford us permanent protection from the likes of Marguerite Ardarien. All while keeping Laena's secret intact.

But even then, did we really want that secret to stay a secret, knowing what we knew?

There were more Eidolon-immune out there, all with different, special abilities. Only, the ones we've encountered were subdivided into two completely different factions. The first, being a small community of wanting to convince the Elite that they could help combat the Eidolon hordes. The second claiming themselves to be 'Freedom Fighters', wanting to overthrow Elite rule in all of the Seven Cities.

It was just our luck to have found Laena, to have fallen in love with her and married her.

Now, it was up to us to balance the craziness that were our lives, while protecting our Eidolon-immune wife. God help any man, woman, or Eidolon-cursed who dared try to harm her.

30

LAENA
One Week Later

Marguerite had taken much longer than I anticipated to finally retaliate for my insubordination. After I had failed to take Fang's life, it was later revealed that he was responsible for implementing a new clause that would amend an old bill of rights that Marguerite herself had introduced.

Basically, this bill's aim was to protect the rights of people like his daughter. As a widowed mother who refused to marry again out of loyalty to her dead husbands, she was under pressure to marry again in the eyes of the law. After all, it was her supposed duty as a registered, unmarried female to help repopulate the much-diminished human race.

Fang didn't see things the way the Council did and had fought hard to see that the law be amended to allow for widowed mothers to remain so, to better be able to care for any children resulting from the union. Apparently, Marguerite had issue with his proposed clause and thought it prudent to get rid of him by using me as the tool to do so.

Scary woman, my adopted mother. While she appeared the picture of motherly gentility towards me in the past week, I knew that she was plotting some way to get back at me. I said as much to my husbands, but they were silent on the issue, choosing to wave off my protests to watch out for anything that smacked of Marguerite's handiwork.

After a week of regular patrolling outside the city walls, General Dylan Thompson had sent orders directly and in person to our house one evening. Bewildered was the best description I could give for Dylan's face, when he read it out to the four of us. Because of its hand-delivered nature, the orders were deemed an emergency and had my husbands packing up as much gear as possible.

"I don't understand," I protested. "Why would the three of you be called on a rescue mission? This late at night?" Typically, a rescue mission outside the city would warrant more than just three men to be wandering blindly in the dark.

And a runaway from an Elite family sounded less likely when I knew it was Marguerite's modus operandi to send people unsuspectingly into a trap. Much like a spider and her prey.

Dylan explained, "While it smells fishy to me, too, Laena, the orders came from on high. The Executive Elite Council. They specifically asked for these boneheads to go and rescue a spoiled brat who ran away because he couldn't get Daddy's money to pay for his new toy."

My husbands had known I was worried that something like this might happen, and we were now facing that moment. Turning to Vance, I pleaded, "Don't go. This might seem legit to all of you, but I know better. This could be a trap."

"And this could really be legit," Vance said gently. "We can't take chances when someone really could be needing our help."

Rennick drew nearer and reached out to caress my cheek with an open palm. "Sweetheart, we know what you're thinking and why you're so worried. Just trust us. We can handle anything that comes our way."

Reese assured me, "Yeah, we got this. Trap or no trap, we go where we are called."

"No," I shook my head fiercely. "This should be the one time you don't answer when you are called." Dylan looked at me funny, but I ignored him. Obeying orders was paramount in our line of work, and this was the first time Dylan witnessed my contesting them.

"Baby girl, you've got to calm down. We will come back to you, I promise," Vance said.

"Even Dylan doesn't trust what's going on here!" I went on. "Let me come with you, and we can work together to find out—"

"No, Laena!" Dylan barked out. "While they may be your husbands, they are still called to do their duty to the Council. And it is their duty to carry out those orders."

Desperation had me yelling, "And I'm about protecting the men I love from a threat they won't be able to see unless I'm there with them!"

Dylan cocked his head at that. "What do you mean? You'd be able to sense a trap?"

I nodded, admitting, "It's not something I do well, but I can still do it."

Just as something suddenly dawned on him, Vance mused, "So, that's what he meant."

"What? What did who mean?" Dylan asked, his brows scrunching together. I had almost forgotten that Dylan knew as much about me as my own husbands did, with the exception of Dad.

Vance smoothly lied, "The files Lightbourne had squirreled away. In them, he mentioned that Laena's Eidolon abilities were similar to that of spiders. She must be able to sense danger like a spider can."

"That's fascinating and all," Dylan broke in, dryly, "but your orders state specifically that you three go alone. We can't risk a large group go out this time of night."

Frustrated, I blew out a breath and argued, "But you're okay with risking my husbands?"

Reese cut in, "Okay, that's enough from both of you." He moved to get in between Dylan and me, keeping me behind him as he faced off with Dylan. "We'll be outside in a few. Can you give us a moment alone with Laena?" I looked around to find that Vance and Rennick already had their duffels in hand. With the three ready to leave at a moment's notice, I felt defeated and powerless that they were going without me to protect them.

Dylan raised a dubious brow, and I guessed he knew that I was going to try to sway my husbands from going. But Reese reassured him by saying, "We won't be long. Just gotta talk to Laena and then we'll head out."

All three of my men turned to me, their faces giving away their determined resignation. "Laena, I promise we will come back to you," Vance assured me. "We won't do anything stupid or unnecessary."

"We just have to find the kid, bring him back home safe, and we'll come home. Simple," Rennick said.

Reese wrapped me in his arms, and whispered into my hair, "We're trained soldiers who also have a few surprises for anyone who dares to fuck with us."

I giggled, amused by the thought of anyone daring to try. But I was also curious. "What do you mean by surprises?"

"Wouldn't you like to know," Reese teased as he pulled back and touched the tip of my nose with a single digit. Instead of elaborating, he released me and said, "See you later."

The other two mumbled the same and left me to catch up with Dylan. Dylan would be there to see them go only to leave once they headed out of the city.

Sighing, I made my way over to the living room, resigned to sit and wait for them to come home. Who knew how long it would take for them to complete the job, but I was determined to be facing the elevator doors once they all came home. Even if it took the next three days, I was going to stay firm and stay put in my oversized easy chair until they were home safe.

With our home so quiet without my men and the room awash with the dark, I must have dozed off not long after their departure. Sometime later, I jolted awake at the moment the hair on my arms and back of my neck suddenly raised in alarm. Danger was near, and I shuffled off the grogginess in record time to reach out further with my senses, staying still and quiet in my chair.

My pupils enlarged even more to see better in the dark, looking for anything amiss in the shadows of the room. With the hairs on my skin alert to any disturbances in the air, I scanned the room with my eyes, until I felt it.

There in the corner, where a shadow seemed much deeper than it should be. I pinned it with a stare, unmoving, daring it to back down. Seconds ticked by as I continued to stare it down, until a voice called out, "How do you do that? You found me again!"

It was the same girl from the alley. *How the fuck did she get into my house?*

Another voice called out from the kitchen, "I know what you're thinking. And the answer is, I let her in." Marguerite's voice. She stepped into the living room and stopped to face me. She towered above me as I sat still in my chair. Everything in me bristled at her presence, knowing she was responsible for sending my husbands out into an Eidolon trap just like she must have done to my mother's husbands in the past.

Before I could utter a response, she cut in, "Let's not waste time, shall we?" I couldn't see where the girl was, but I could sense her general direction, and my internal alarms of heightened danger rang loudly.

Then, I felt pressure and a pricking of my skin in my upper arm. Looking down at its source, I was stunned to find a tranq dart sticking out of my arm. The girl stepped out from the shadowed corner, a dart gun in one hand, while the other arm was encased in a sling.

Dizziness and blurred vision suddenly overtook me, and I slurred, "Whatcher gon' doo?"

"That didn't take long at all, did it?" Marguerite asked the girl. "I didn't believe it when you said the effect would be instantaneous. But I have to hand it to you, Mariana. You are proving yourself trustworthy once again."

To me, Marguerite said, "As for you, I have no use for a pet that won't obey its master."

It was so hard to keep my eyes open and focused on her. "Huh? Whut 'bout my hubbands?" On any other day, I might have laughed at my own dumb-sounding speech, but I struggled to keep my wits about me despite the tranquilizer running through my veins.

"Your boy toys are wandering aimlessly outside of the city, looking for someone who isn't even out there," the girl called Mariana cackled.

A heavy wave of sleepiness threatened to suck me under. "Whut. Yoo doo-in' heah?"

"Screw it, Madam Ardarien. Let me do her in now," she insisted.

"Not until I tell her that her screw-up cost me my son!" Marguerite hissed angrily. "Fang knew about Kane and his Eidolon DNA somehow. He had the audacity to threaten me with the knowledge if I didn't let his clause pass at Council! I did what I had to! To protect my boy, just as Fang was doing with his daughter and his proposed clause!"

I knew it had to be something big for Marguerite to use me as an assassin. But if Fang knew and remained alive, what was he going to do with the knowledge? But my mind was turning fuzzy, and it was getting harder to focus or recall certain things. But Marguerite kept up her bitching as I worked to understand what she was saying.

"Kane has left for Newport this morning after we argued. He just couldn't see that I was doing my best to secure his place in this world." Ugh. She sounded like a petulant child, unhappy not to get her own way. All I understood from that was that she was grossly obsessed with her only son. But I hadn't a clue how much was too much since I never knew my mother.

How did it make sense again that she adopted me? I couldn't remember why. The drug coursing through my veins had me completely subdued and unable to summon any strength to defend myself. In other words, I was at the mercy of Marguerite and this Mariana girl, and I was pretty sure that Mariana was there to deliver whatever final blow that were forthcoming.

Unable to form speech, I stared groggily at them both, helplessly awaiting the next move. Then, Marguerite ordered, "We will deal with her now, but not here. We don't want my sons-in-law to find the body here."

Fear gripped me hard. This may have been the first time I've allowed fear to fill my heart, cloud my mind, and color my outlook. Before, I had just been surviving; I'd never questioned the many times I've risked my life, fighting off Eidolon. Surviving was just something I did.

Until now. Now, I had three men who loved me, anticipating my greeting them when they returned home. And

I had Dad and Drayna. Maybe even Kane, wherever he was. And now my current situation was going to endanger their happiness and maybe even spur them all on into a vengeance that could get them all killed. I was sure the Elite would see to that.

I closed my eyes, willing my heart to slow its too-fast rhythm. With my eyes closed, at least, I didn't have to look at Marguerite or Mariana. I didn't want to have their smug faces be the last thing I saw. I would rather have the names of my husbands on my lips and the memories of their smiles in mind before Mariana's death blow took me out for good.

"Quickly, now," I heard Marguerite urging impatiently. Clearly, she was too cowardly to do the job herself to have Mariana do all the dirty work for her. Or she could just be the cleverest woman to have someone else dirty their hands, while leaving hers free of being bloodied.

"Ree.Spons.Uh-ble. You," I garbled, my mouth feeling like it was full of peanut butter. "All. You. Fault." With my senses terribly dulled, I couldn't do more than drowsily accuse Marguerite when what I really wanted to do was rip her head from her body. Adopted mother or no, she had some serious sociopathic issues, and I would say I'd be forgiven of anything I did in self-defense at this point.

Looking disgruntled at Marguerite, Mariana groused, "And I can only go as fast as my one-armed status will allow." I chuckled, remembering that Rennick shot her in the shoulder last week. Or was it Reese? Anyway, I knew she wasn't going to get much help from Marguerite to lug my ass out the door one-handed. I would have laughed in her face if my mouth would only cooperate, but all that came out were tiny snorts of amusement out my nostrils.

"You two deserve each other," Marguerite huffed. I guessed she didn't like that I found any of this funny. "You're both cheap, defective versions of the real deal, and I won't have your incompetence ruin things now."

What the fuck did that mean? I was in no condition to coherently ask what she meant by the both of us being cheap and defective, but I didn't have to. Mariana unwittingly came to our defense; well, hers more than mine.

"You bitch! If that's how you really feel, then screw this. You can take her out the door yourself. I don't care how much you're paying me." I did a double take, not expecting Mariana to defect so quickly. In fact, the girl couldn't get out of my house fast enough.

As a farewell, Mariana called to me, "Sorry, none of this was personal. I hope you don't come after me when this is all done." Then, she jumped out of a window that had been left open that must have been her entry point. Strange that the security system didn't kick in earlier. Even stranger that she jumped out of a four-story window with no balcony or anything else below it to catch her fall. Since I didn't hear the crunch of a body splatting on the pavement below, I guessed she must have survived somehow. Or flew.

God, this drug was really taking me for a loopy ride.

Then, I heard Marguerite fume, splitting the air with her cursing and little sounds of rage and frustration. "Fine!" she seethed. "I'll just have to do this myself!" I watched as she produced a blade from her pocket, aiming for my heart as she charged at me. My legs, my entire body failed me, and I could do nothing to save myself from her wrath.

What else was there to do but wait for her blade to pierce my heart and kill me dead? So, I shut my eyes and willed my body to relax, waiting for her inevitable strike.

But instead of feeling the kiss of Marguerite's blade, I heard a steady rapport of gunshots and a pained cry instead. Three shots, to be exact, and in quick succession.

I opened my eyes to find Marguerite slumped on the floor, her hand bloodied and each of her kneecaps taken out. Behind her, Vance, Rennick, and Reese lowered their still smoking guns as they surveyed Marguerite and me.

31

LAENA

Thankfully, my boys left Marguerite alive but moaning from the pain, ensuring that their shots weren't fatal. Immediately, Reese rushed to me, checking me over for injuries, while Rennick called for a medic to be brought along with Elite Guardsmen. Vance promptly shackled Marguerite in cuffs and bound up her wounds, but I doubt she would have rushed off in her injured state. She had nowhere to go but prison after tonight's stunt. Attempted murder of a daughter was deemed a major crime these days, and Marguerite would be charged and tried mostly for that reason.

To add to the numerous surprises that the night held in store, Barclay showed up, knocking at our guest entrance. Once Rennick allowed him access, Barclay rushed in, ready to descend on me, I supposed, but he caught sight of his errant wife on the floor, bandaged and trussed up in cuffs.

He blanched, then imperiously demanded, "What has happened here?" To her, he asked, "Are you all right, love?" And of course, he dared to look at the rest of us accusingly, then swiveled his gaze towards his wife. The looks my husbands returned to him were stone cold and unrelenting. "Marguerite, what have you done?"

Her voice, strained because of the pain she was in, still came out steady as she said, "Only what had to be done. For Kane's sake."

Reese shot out, "You tried to have Laena killed, you murderous bitch! We had everything you've said and done recorded as evidence!"

Barclay's face lost its color for a second before mottling with rage before he said, "Do you know what your foolishness has cost us? I can only begin to imagine what you've been up to these past months. First, Fang, then Laena. And now, Kane! Our son is gone because of your meddling ways!"

Her voice rose in anger, "You fool! It's her fault he's gone!" Pointing her chin towards me, she continued in vehemence, "If it weren't for her existence, Kane would be safe with us. And no one else the wiser for what he is and what he can do. The four of us had worked hard over the years to keep his talents secret, but since she arrived, it's spoiled everything!"

Fortunately for me, another one of my talents is that I metabolize drugs and poisons at an alarming rate. The tranquilizer was now loosening its grip on my brain and senses, and I was readily able to respond. While Reese held me in his lap, keeping me warm with his body, I said steadily, "I'm sure you think that your reasons give you the means to back up your actions. But the optics of everything you've done do not put you in a good light."

All three of my men frowned and nodded in agreement. Vance spoke up, "We knew you'd try something after Laena didn't follow through on your orders. So, we had cooked up a plan to bait you into giving yourself away. Why do you think you entered our house so easily?"

A-ha! So, our house security system was disabled on purpose! No wonder I wasn't alerted to Mariana and Marguerite's presence sooner!

Rennick joined in, "We also knew you'd try to get to Laena somehow. So we also had the camera feeds around the house sent to our phones. We knew the second you entered the house, but through different entry points. So where's the other one?"

He meant Mariana. I waved her off by saying, "I don't think we need to worry about her. She was just after the money that this job would bring but backed out at the last second."

Barclay stood there, looking at his wife, aghast. "I knew you were up to something the day Laena entered our radar," he said. "I, too, was suspicious of her turning up so suddenly. But she looked so much like Caelaena, I was just so happy to have her back in whatever form that was."

Really? The man had never shot anything that resembled a smile at me since we met!

To me, he said, "Laena, the truth is that having you with us, even for a short while, was like having my sister back." Holy shit! He was finally admitting that my mother was his late sister! He must have known all along who I was to him!

He pressed on, "Since she went missing after her husbands died, I never found out what happened to her." Looking at his wife, he said contemptuously, "But I suspect Marguerite had something to do about that. And it's come to my attention that she has done things in my name that I was never made aware of."

Then, this silent exchange occurred between Barclay and Vance, and there was something about it that clicked for me. "Do you mean that you've seen the recordings and the other files?" Marguerite squeaked at the mention of them but said nothing more.

Barclay nodded. "I now know everything. Vance and the others had sent them to me last week with a warning to not say anything until something like this happened." He waved a hand, indicating Marguerite and the mess she'd made of attempting to murder me. "I now know she had forged my signature on the documents that sealed Caelaena's fate as well as on the documents that would have seen to your termination as a baby. I did some digging of my own and found a messy trail that would have led to me if any of this were found out."

Still muddled in the brain, I asked, "So, you don't hate me? I thought you wanted nothing to do with me." I thought of all the times we've interacted, and none of my memories painted Barclay as caring or benevolent towards me. Other than that one day I had found him weeping.

"Oh, God, no!" Barclay protested. "Dear girl, you are my niece, my sister's daughter! I only wanted to protect you, making sure that Marguerite didn't do anything to harm you! At first, I didn't want you anywhere near Marguerite. I had half suspected she had something to do with Caelaena's disappearance but didn't have anything concrete. I couldn't chance having the same happen to you."

I just didn't get it. Was Barclay really sincere? Did he really believe what he was saying?

He explained further, "Because of our position, we've had impostors claiming to be Caelaena's long-lost daughter, trying to extort money from us. Up until recently, I wasn't fully aware of what Marguerite was doing behind the scenes to get further ahead politically, and she has used the same methods to deal with you. And I'm sorry to say I willingly turned a blind eye to all of that for love of her.

"But that's not to say I've been completely blind to what she has tried to do to you! I've watched over you carefully, questioned you harder, trying to find a weak point that she might exploit!"

Even while shackled, Marguerite maintained her air of importance as she seethed, "You don't know how people like her could upset the balance of our world as we know it! The lot of you know nothing of what it takes to make this world run."

Vance interrupted her, "And while I'm sure you're willing to tell us all about it, I'd rather not hear it." And he produced a roll of tape, cut off a good portion, and slapped it over her mouth. She glared at him and the rest of us while I felt Reese's chest rumble with laughter beneath me. I couldn't quite contain the smirk that reached my lips, but I was sure that no one had ever dared to stand up to her or even treat her the way that Vance just did.

Barclay approached his wife who still sat on the floor where she first dropped, and said, "My love, I can forgive you for so much, but this is the first time I cannot forgive or forget what you've done here tonight. I've only ever wanted a family with you, and you've destroyed that with your secrets and lies!"

She teared up then, looking at him with anguished eyes, but she couldn't respond through the duct tape the way she wanted. Barclay guessed, "You want to say you're sorry now? When it's already too late? And after you've tried to kill our daughter, who is in fact my blood niece?" Shaking his head sorrowfully, "I've had many regrets over the years, not standing up to you when I should have. But this time, I'm not protecting you anymore."

Looking up at the Guardsmen who had just arrived, he ordered, "On my authority as a member of the Executive Council of the Elite, you may arrest this woman." One of them nodded, while the medic checked over Vance's first aid. Once she was cleared by the medic, two Guardsmen left with Marguerite in tow.

Nothing more was said between us until Marguerite was escorted out of our house and a report was given. Barclay stayed behind a little longer, intent on telling me something. "I need to share something with you," he told me, reaching for my hand.

I gave it willingly while I was still held protectively in Reese's lap. Barclay placed something small between our palms, and I pulled away to take a good look at it. It was a small picture of my mother, happy and smiling, framed within a small golden locket. "You can have it. It was the only thing of hers that I kept with me to remember her by."

"Thank you," I whispered. "But now you don't have anything of hers."

"I have you, don't I?" Barclay asked. The question seemed more expansive than its simple utterance, but I understood what he was trying to convey.

I let a few beats of silence pass before I nodded. "Yes, you do. I am your adopted daughter, aren't I?" My family by blood seemed to be getting bigger by the minute the more things were revealed.

Instead of replying, Barclay only smiled in relief and patted my hand fondly.

Rennick broke through our moment to ask, "Sir Ardarien, what do we do now? I suspect you know the full truth about Laena, but what do you plan to do about it?"

"Nothing for the time being," he assured all of us. "Unlike my wife, I have no desire to discriminate against those who don't share the same DNA profile as fifty percent of our remaining population."

Fifty? How was it possible that Eidolon species and the rest of humanity were equal in number? And God knows how many of Eidolon-cursed were actually out there roaming outside our cities!

He smiled wryly at my dubious look and continued, "Yes, I know more than Marguerite thought I knew. I was aware of how she used our money, and she didn't do a very good job of hiding the project that Lightbourne headed. I know about him, too, and have been tracking him for some time."

My breath hitched, but Barclay added, "But he's still so damned evasive."

"Why do you want to find Dad?" I asked. What I was really after in the asking was whether or not I could completely trust my legally adopted father.

"I need his help. If we had his knowledge and notes, we could prove to the rest of the world that we need not fear this next stage of evolution of the human race. But first, I aim to prove to our own Council that those who are natural-born Eidolon aren't a threat to us. It will take hard work and time even with his help, but I believe that we can dispel their fears over the emergence of a new species."

I had my doubts, given my past, but I could see he earnestly believed what he was saying. And for his sake, I hoped that one day, people like me wouldn't have to live in fear of being hunted.

So, I said mildly, "Dad can be found only when he wants to be found. I think that's a noble goal and all, but I think he might need more convincing."

Barclay shrugged and said, "I'll take what I can get, but we could really use him full time. I have a plan put in place alongside my brothers Maximus and Antonio, and we'll need Lightbourne's findings to back up our statements in the Courts."

Rennick claimed loudly, "And you have us, Sir Ardarien. The three of us will back you along with our families to protect Laena and others like her." Reese and Vance nodded in unison and in support of Rennick's declaration.

"Thank you," Barclay acknowledged, but he addressed all of us as he said, "And please, call me Barclay. We're family, after all." Looking at me last, I understood that the gesture meant that he wasn't about trying to assume Dad's place in my life. But I was grateful just the same that he was extending a branch of familiarity to not just me, but to my husbands, too.

He continued, "While I am happy that my sister can live on through you, Laena, I am just as happy that my sister got her wish. To have you. It was all she talked and dreamed about before she lost her husbands. By then, I had already married Marguerite, but I didn't keep my promise to protect Caelaena. I now know that she needed me, locked up in that lab as she was, and I didn't know about any of it! No thanks to my own wife." Tears unshed welled up on his lower lashes as he anguished over past wrongs.

Rising from Reese's lap, I went to Barclay and took both of his hands. "I misjudged your attitudes towards me at first, and now I think I understand you a little more."

Smiling sadly, Barclay replied, "Thank you, Laena. When the time comes, I'll be sure to call on you. But for now, you must continue to keep your secret until our Council can change things for your kind."

Turning to my three husbands, he said, "The three of you, guard her constantly. As for me, I have to make sure Kane is safe in my wife's stead. Only this time, I will make sure to use my authority for the good of all involved."

Nodding in agreement, Vance, Rennick, and Reese all shook hands with Barclay, one after the other. Barclay left unescorted, using the elevator entrance and to the main level below.

Now, fully alert, with none of the tranquilizer's effects, I turned to each of my husbands and pointedly asked, "What did you three do and how did you know it would come to this?"

Rennick shrugged and answered cryptically for all of them, "We have our ways, too. You're not the only one with skills."

"Yeah, I get that. But why did you let me think that you were walking into a trap knowingly?" I had been worried sick that Marguerite would try to attack them unawares.

"We've planted bugs in strategic places and did some surveillance since last week. Some of it was with your Dad's help, too," Rennick said smoothly.

My brows raised. "Really? Dad showed up and helped you guys out?"

"Yeah, he seemed to know you were in more danger than the rest of us. He was the one who rigged our security feed into our phones, using a motion sensor to trigger the recording. That's how we knew two different intruders broke in," Vance explained.

Glad that they had the foresight to counterattack Marguerite's own plan, I decided then that I couldn't have fallen in with a more intelligent or sexier group of men. And they were all mine. Suddenly feeling exhausted from all of the explanations tonight, I sighed wearily and asked, "Can I ask a favor?"

I got three nods. "Can we all go to bed now?"

"To bed? Or to sleep?" Reese asked cautiously.

I smiled a sultry smile. "What do you think?"

I'd never been rushed so fast to the bedroom before, nor did I care that they ripped my clothes to shreds to get to me. Grateful for their loving and their need to protect me, I decided then and there that the four of us together were going to create a better world for us and for everyone. Their love gave me the strength and confidence I was going to need for the future ahead.

EPILOGUE

MONTGOMERY LIGHTBOURNE

While Laena had found her happiness with men who fiercely love her, I am content to have her so. Even in the shadows, I will continue to watch over her, and love her, while working to atone for my past sins. If a baby girl at the age of two could inspire love in a soiled man like me, then maybe there is hope for me yet.

If it weren't for her, I'd most likely be living in a palatial mansion, smackdab in the middle of the Inner Circle of New Phoenix. But instead, I'm presently holed up in a makeshift shelter in a city southeast of here: New Springs. And if it weren't for Laena, I would not have made the discovery of a lifetime: that humanity had leveled up in its evolution.

And it was the truth of my findings that I was obsessed with. I believed that this groundbreaking news just had to be shared with the rest of the world.

Only, others before me had died of mysterious causes shortly after making the same discovery I did. And there were evil people behind those circumstances that were willing to do whatever it took to keep the next stage of evolution from happening. Thus, Laena and I were forced into hiding, moving from place to place, from city to city, always living on the furthest outskirts to avoid detection.

If it hadn't been for that one wayward measles strain, our planet wouldn't be cursed with flesh-seeking Eidolon creatures. But out of that one disaster, humanity was gifted a budding miracle: people like Laena who could survive an Eidolon bite without turning. Now, if only there weren't an entire subset of people who wanted to cleanse the planet of Eidolon-gifted, that miracle might actually have a chance to grow and thrive.

I had been lucky to find old colleagues, who also went into hiding, and who were also guardians of the children we rescued from the Ardarien-funded lab that night. I had thought that most of us had scattered throughout the Seven Cities, never staying in one place, just as Laena and me did.

Growing up, Laena had never questioned where I went during the times I'd left her to herself over the years. But if she had asked, I would have told her the where and why.

But having listened in through the bugs I planted in the Ardarien mansion, I was surprised to learn about Kane Ardarien. That was the one surprise I didn't expect, nor did I expect that there were more who were naturally born Eidolon-gifted. My scientist's mind and hands practically itched to get more tests done on him, but that wasn't on the top of my priority list.

Now was the time for Laena to meet the others. The others and I have agreed that it was time.

They are ready.

Made in the USA
Middletown, DE
29 June 2021

43227345R00159